SKΔC

D0929052

The Island Villa

Also by Sarah Morgan

Snowed In for Christmas
Beach House Summer
The Christmas Escape
The Summer Seekers
One More for Christmas
Family for Beginners
A Wedding in December
One Summer in Paris
The Christmas Sisters
How to Keep a Secret

For additional books by Sarah Morgan,
visit her website, www.sarahmorgan.com.

SARAH MORGAN

The Island Villa

CANARY STREET PRESS

CANARY
STREET
PRESS™

Recycling programs
for this product may
not exist in your area.

ISBN-13: 978-1-335-00633-2

The Island Villa

Canary Street Press
22 Adelaide St. West, 41st Floor
Toronto, Ontario M5H 4E3, Canada
CanaryStPress.com

Printed in U.S.A.

To my family, for all the happy memories of holidays in Corfu,
and to the locals who welcomed us.

The Island Villa

Prologue

For the first time in her life she was planning to kill someone.

She never would have thought herself capable of such a
thing—she was a romance novelist! Romance novelists didn't
kill people, but she was now forced to consider the unsettling possibility that perhaps she didn't know herself as well
as she'd thought. Perhaps she wasn't, after all, a person with
a kind and gentle disposition. She'd always thought of herself that way, and yet here she was typing a variety of decid-
edly ungentle questions into her browser and feeling a thrill
of interest. Her fingers shook on the keyboard.

How to kill someone and leave no trace.

Best way to kill someone.

Murders that remain unsolved.

It had to look like an accident, she'd decided. People would be sad, and probably shocked because death is always shocking even when it is expected. The one thing they wouldn't be was suspicious, because she was going to be clever. It would be called an "accidental death." No one would know the truth.

But was the truth really so bad? Was it truly wrong, when she was delivering justice?

The man deserved it, after all.

In fact, if she were truly giving him what he deserved, her search would read *how to kill someone in the most painful way possible.*

She stared through the window at the smooth calm of the Mediterranean Sea, so many shades of blue and dazzling in the sunshine. She'd decided long ago that the island of Corfu was her paradise. Sun-baked olive groves, soft sand, ocean waves, leisurely days, slow delicious dreams—those, surely, were the ingredients for a perfect life. It was a place where problems were suspended; a place for happiness, for relaxation, for nothing but good things. But expecting nothing but good was a fantasy. She knew that now, just as she knew that light and dark could coexist. The dark often lay hidden, simmering undetected beneath the surface, ready to take a bite out of the unwary, the trusting, those who believed in happy endings. She'd been that person. She'd made so many mistakes.

Lost in the view and her own thoughts, she didn't hear him enter. She wasn't aware of his presence until she felt his hand on her shoulder and the sound of his voice.

"Catherine?"

She jumped and slammed the lid of her laptop shut. Her heart hammered like a fist against a punching bag.

How much had he seen? She was annoyed with herself for not having had the foresight to lock the door. She'd been so absorbed by her thoughts that she hadn't heard him enter the room.

Careless.

She needed to up her game if she was actually going to do this. She needed to think like an assassin. She needed to be inscrutable and reveal nothing.

She turned with a smile (did assassins ever smile? She had no idea). "I didn't know you were awake. It's early."

"I didn't mean to surprise you. I know you hate being disturbed when you're working, but I woke up and missed you. I came to offer you strong coffee." He brushed his fingers across her jaw. "You look tense. Is something wrong?"

So much for being inscrutable.

She wasn't built for a life of crime, but fortunately she wasn't considering a whole life, just this one teeny tiny murder. That was it. She had no expectations of enjoying it and didn't intend it to become habitual.

"Nothing's wrong." She couldn't even lie without feeling guilty, which didn't bode well.

They shared everything—well, almost everything—but there was no way she was sharing this. Not yet. One day, maybe, if she actually went ahead with it. If it all went as planned, then of course he'd find out, but until then she had to keep silent. This was something she had to do by herself.

What would he say if he knew what was really going on in her head?

Would he try to talk her out of it? Tell her that her plan was foolish and dangerous? Or would he preach acceptance and tell her that she just had to let it go. That this wasn't the answer. He'd probably tell her to move on.

And that was what she was doing, of course.

This was her way of moving on. And not before time.

He bent to kiss her. "I love you, Catherine Swift."

She felt the brush of his lips and the answering warmth that rushed through her body.

It felt jarring to go from death to love but that was life, wasn't it? Brutal in its extremes. And assassins were people too. They were allowed a love life.

For the first time in weeks, she felt optimistic and hopeful. She'd been smothered in a dark cloud of gloom, fueled by bitter resentment. She'd felt like a failure for letting it reach this point. She hadn't been able to see a way forward, but now she could.

The future was clear to her. All she needed was courage.

It was time to make a fresh start. Time to put the past behind her and reinvent herself.

It was just a shame that someone had to die.

Part One

———

1

Adeline

Adeline Swift was on a call with the features editor of *Woman Now* when the letter was pushed through the door of her apartment.

"The thing is," Erin was saying, "your advice column has the highest readership of any section of the magazine. People really seem to connect with it. With *you*. The market research we did recently suggests that seventy percent of people would rather ask you for advice than their best friend. Can you believe that?"

Yes, she could believe that. Few people reached adulthood without suffering some degree of emotional hangover from the past. Hurt. Resentment. Shame. Disappointment. Grief. Regret. Life left scars and you had to find a way to live with those scars. Some people chose denial as a strategy. *Ignore it. Leave it in the past. Move on.* Others confronted those emotions and spent hours in therapy trying to understand how the past affected the present, in the hope of reaching a point of acceptance. Most just struggled along by themselves, striding and occasionally stumbling, handling the ups and downs of life as best they could. After a few too many drinks they might confide in a friend, but more often than not they'd stay silent because revealing those deep secrets and fears, those most personal parts of yourself, was a risk. It said *this is who I really am*, instead of *this is who I'm pretending to be.*

It was those people, alone with their fears, who often wrote to Adeline.

Dear Dr. Swift…

They poured out their problems in the hope that in a few well-chosen words she would help them resolve their crisis, or at least feel better about their situation.

Adeline delivered calm analysis, sympathy, and the occasional pep talk. She employed a mix of empathy, experience, and plain speaking when crafting her answers. It was a combination that worked for people. She fulfilled the role of a sympathetic stranger, someone who would listen without judgment and respect anonymity. But that role meant she existed in a world of problems. In her working day, she was buffeted by the challenges of life, drenched in the pain of others, required to ponder at length on everything from infidelity to unemployment. When people asked how she coped with it, she pointed out that it was easy to cope with a drama that wasn't your own.

When the drama was hers? That was different.

She stared at the envelope.

It rested innocently on the floor, dazzling white against wide oak planks. Even without picking it up, she could see that the paper was high quality, and embossed. Her name and address were written out in a bold script that was instantly recognizable.

Her heart beat a little faster. Emotions rushed her, buffeting her like a gust of wind. She placed her hand on her diaphragm and forced herself to breathe slowly. She was an adult with her own life, a good life, and yet this small inanimate object had ruined the calm of her day.

And she hadn't even opened it yet.

Her first impulse was to tear it up without opening it, but that would be immature, and she tried very hard not to be immature and to always exercise self-control.

She tried to be the person she pretended to be in her advice column.

"Adeline?" Erin's voice wafted into her conscious. "Are you still there?"

"Yes. Still here. I'm listening." But her focus wasn't on Erin.

She should open the envelope right now. Or she could simply drop it into the recycling without opening it. She imagined what "Dr. Swift" would have to say about that approach.

Avoidance.

With a sigh, she picked it up. She could put it to one side and open it later, but then she'd be thinking about it all afternoon. If she was advising someone in this situation, she'd say that no good ever came from delaying the inevitable and that the anticipation was often worse than the reality. That no matter what lay inside the envelope, she had the tools and mental fortitude to handle it.

Did she though?

Still holding the envelope, she walked across her apartment, opened the French doors and stepped onto her small balcony. The tension in her neck and shoulders drained away. She breathed in the rich scent of honeysuckle, the sweetness of jasmine. Bees hummed around slender spikes of purple lavender. The space was small, but she'd chosen the plants carefully and the end result was an explosion of bloom and color that felt like an oasis of calm in the busy, noisy city she'd made her home. She loved London, but she appreciated being able to retreat from the blare of car horns, the crush of people and the frenetic pace. Sometimes it felt to her as if everyone was living their lives on fast forward.

In creating her balcony garden, she'd followed the advice she'd given to a reader who had moved to the city from a rural area and was struggling with anxiety as a result.

Adeline had interviewed a horticulturist and compiled her answer accordingly.

Dear Sad in the City, you may not live in the country, but you can still welcome nature into your life. A few well-chosen houseplants can add calm to the smallest living space, and a pot of fragrant herbs grown on a sunny windowsill will bring a touch of the Mediterranean into your home and into your cooking.

After she'd finished researching her answer, she'd gone out and purchased plants for herself, acting on the advice she'd just given her reader. She'd also written two features for other publications on the same topic. It was how she made her living.

She'd trained as a clinical psychologist and had been in practice for six months when a chance meeting with a journalist had resulted in a request to give an interview on a morning chat show on managing stress in the workplace. That interview had led to more requests, which in turn had led to a writing career that she enjoyed more than practicing as a psychologist. Writing enabled her to maintain a level of detachment that had been missing when she'd seen clients face-to-face.

Adeline preferred to be detached.

She put the envelope down on the small table and forced herself to concentrate on the conversation.

"I'm glad the advice column is working out, Erin."

She *was* glad, and not only because the column kept her profile high and led to more work than she could handle. The popularity of the column pleased her. It was gratifying to know that people were finding it useful.

She knew how it felt to be lost and confused. She knew how it felt to struggle with emotions that were too ugly and uncomfortable for public display. She knew how it felt to be alone, to be drowning with no lifeboat in sight, to be falling with no cushion to soften the landing.

If the skills she'd learned to help herself could be used to help another person, then she was satisfied. When she was writing her column, she thought of herself not as a psychologist, but as a trusted best friend. Someone who would tell you the truth.

The one truth she never shared was that there were some hurts that no therapist in the world could heal. That knowledge she kept to herself. People assumed she had her own life sorted, and she had no intention of destroying that image. It would hardly fill people with confidence if they knew she was wrestling with problems of her own.

"Good? It's better than good." Erin was buoyant, euphoric, proud, because she was the one who had originally had the idea for the "Dr. Swift Says" column. "You're a hit, Adeline. The suits want to give you more space."

Adeline deadheaded a geranium and removed a couple of dead leaves. "More space?"

"Yes. Instead of answering one question in depth, we were thinking four."

Adeline frowned. "It's important to give a full answer. If someone is desperate, then they need empathy and a full response. They don't need to be brushed aside with a few lines of platitudes."

"You wouldn't be capable of producing an answer that wasn't empathetic. It's your gift. You write so beautifully—I suppose in that way you're like your mother."

Adeline clenched her hand around the leaves. "I'm nothing like my mother."

"No, of course you're not. What you write is totally different. But Adeline, this is huge. I don't need to tell you what's happening to freelance journalists right now. Everyone is scrabbling for a slice of a shrinking pie, and here you are being offered a big fat slice of your own. They'll pay you, obviously."

She was nothing like her mother. Nothing. Her mother's life was one big romantic fantasy, whereas hers was firmly rooted in reality.

And more work was definitely reality.

Did she want to do it? Money was important up to a point, but so was work–life balance. Even though she mostly worked from home, she set clear boundaries. The first half of the week, she focused on her advice column. Thursdays were set aside for her freelance work. Friday mornings were spent catching up on admin, and then at two o'clock precisely she switched off her work laptop and went swimming. She swam exactly a hundred lengths, loosening up her muscles and washing away the tension of the week. After that, she walked to the local market and picked up fresh fruit and veg for the weekend.

Saturday and Sunday were entirely her own. She intended to keep it that way.

And maybe her life wasn't exciting, exactly, but it was steady and predictable and that was the way she liked it.

Did she have time to expand the column? Yes. Did she *want* to expand the column? Maybe.

"I'd want full editorial control." She bent down and tested the moisture of the soil in one of the planters. "I don't want my answers edited."

"As long as you keep the page within the word count, that won't be a problem."

"I choose the letters I answer."

"Goes without saying."

"I'll think about it. Thank you. Have a good weekend, Erin."

She ended the call and finally faced the only letter that mattered to her right now.

She picked it up and opened the envelope carefully. In these days of emails and messaging, only her mother still wrote to her. Adeline pictured her seated at her glass-top desk in the villa, reaching for her favorite pen. The ink had to be exactly the right shade of blue.

She pulled out the pages and smoothed them.

Dearest Adeline—

She winced. Everything about her mother was overblown, flowery, exaggerated. The endearment held as much meaning as one of those ridiculous air kisses that people gave each other.

I'm writing because I have some exciting news that I wanted to share with you. I'm getting married again.

Adeline read the words, and then read them again. Married? *Married?* Her mother was getting married for a fourth time?

Why? If you failed at something repeatedly, why would you do it again? This wasn't how relationships were supposed to work. Her mother treated marriage like a game show, or a lottery. She seemed to believe that if she did something enough times, maybe one of those times would work out.

She wanted to scream, a feeling she only ever experienced in relation to her mother. Fortunately for her neighbors, she'd trained herself to keep her frustration inside.

She tipped her head back, closed her eyes and breathed slowly. In, out. In, out.

How could anyone ever think she was even *remotely* like her mother?

The world would see it as romantic, of course. Catherine Swift, writer of romantic fiction and global bestseller, was once again taking a chance on love.

Give me a break.

Who was she marrying this time?

Adeline opened her eyes and carried on reading the letter. Her mother wanted Adeline to join her on the island of Corfu for two weeks in July (total heart-sink. Adeline couldn't think of anything worse). All travel would be arranged for her, no expense spared (of course, because her mother lacked many things, but money wasn't one of them).

She went on to talk about the garden, and how beautiful the villa was right now and how good it would be for Adeline to spend some time relaxing because she worked so hard. She mentioned that Maria, who managed the villa for her, was well. Maria's cooking was as spectacular as ever, and she'd already planned a delicious menu for the wedding. Her son Stefanos was back on the island running the family boat business and maybe Adeline would enjoy catching up with him as they were once such good friends.

Seriously?

It was a remark typical of her mother, who managed to spin romantic scenarios in the most unlikely of places.

Adeline remembered exactly when she'd last seen Stefanos. She'd been ten years old. He was a couple of years older. For a while, he'd been her best friend, and she'd been his.

It had been two decades since they'd seen each other. What exactly were they going to catch up on? Their whole lives?

The information Adeline really wanted—who her mother was marrying—seemed to be missing.

There was no mention of a man anywhere in the letter. Adeline checked and then checked again. Flicked through the pages. Nothing. No clue.

She'd actually forgotten to mention the name of the man she was marrying. Unbelievable.

She gave a hysterical laugh. Had her mother remembered to invite him to the wedding?

Maybe there wasn't a groom. Maybe her mother was marrying herself. She was, after all, her own biggest supporter.

My books are my babies, she'd once purred into the camera during an interview on prime-time TV. *I love them as I love my own children.*

Probably more, Adeline thought savagely as she dropped the letter back onto the table. In fact, definitely more. She'd been ten years old when she'd discovered that painful truth.

You're going to live with your father, Adeline.

The ache in her chest grew. Old wounds tore open. But this wasn't only about her. She wasn't the only one with wounds.

What would this do to her father?

Did he know yet? Had her mother told him?

Hands shaking, dread heavy in her stomach, she reached for her phone and dialed his number. It was just after six in the morning on Cape Cod, but she knew her father would already be awake. He rose early and was often to be found on the beach at dawn, taking photographs or sketching, eager to make the most of the morning light and the solitude. Once other people started to appear, he'd return to his little clapboard beach house tucked behind the dunes, brew some of the strongest coffee known to man and head to his studio to paint. Or maybe today was one of those days when he made the trip into town to teach aspiring artists.

Her father had changed his life after the divorce. He'd given up his job in the city and spent his days focused on Adeline and his hobby, painting. He turned one of the bedrooms into a studio and spent all day splashing paint onto canvases while she was at school. Adeline didn't know much about art, but those paintings had seemed angry to her. Part of her envied the fact that her father had an outlet for his misery. It had been an awful time.

Originally from Boston, her father had stayed in London for the duration of Adeline's childhood, but the moment she'd left for college, he'd sold the family home and with the proceeds bought a small apartment so that they had a base in London, and a beach house on Cape Cod. He'd made that his home.

It had been a strange, unsettled childhood, but through all of it she'd never doubted her father's love. It had been her father who had helped her with homework; her father who had cheered her on at the school sports day and tried to make her a costume for a Halloween party. Her father was the one constant in her life and even though they were no longer living in the same house, or even the same country, she always felt close to him.

Unlike her mother, he'd never married again, and that made her sad. She desperately wanted him to find someone special, someone who deserved him. But he'd stayed resolutely single, and she couldn't blame him.

Being married to Catherine Swift was surely enough to put a man off marriage for life.

Still, she hated the idea that he'd never recovered from his relationship with her mother.

That was the reason she didn't want to make this call. However she phrased it, this news was going to upset him. She was about to rip a hole in the life he'd carefully stitched together again.

She waited, holding her breath, and was almost relieved when he didn't answer because she had no idea what she was going to say.

How was she going to tell him that her mother was getting married yet again?

How could she break the news in a way that wouldn't cause him pain?

He'd been divorced from Catherine for more than two decades, but Adeline knew he still felt the hurt keenly. He still talked about her mother. Whenever he saw one of her books in a bookshop, he'd pause, pick it up and read the back.

"You can't switch love on and off, Addy," he'd said to her once when she'd asked him how he could possibly still have feelings for a woman who had treated him so badly.

Adeline hadn't pointed out that Catherine seemed to have no problem switching it off.

And here was more evidence to support that. Another wedding. Another victim.

She ended the call without leaving a message. On impulse, she grabbed the letter from the table, stepped back into her apartment and dropped it into the trash on top of a pile of potato peelings and yesterday's empty yogurt container.

One of the advantages of being an adult was that you could make your own decisions. And she'd made hers.

She wouldn't be going to the wedding.

There was no way, *no way*, she was spending two precious weeks of her summer watching her mother make another huge mistake. It would be too difficult. It would unravel everything she kept tightly wound inside her. And the one thing she didn't need in her life was another stepfather.

She'd send a regretful note, and her good wishes to the bride and groom, even though she didn't even know his name.

His identity didn't matter.

Whoever Catherine Swift was marrying this time, she felt sorry for him.

2

Cassie

"Two cappuccinos, one Americano and an Italian hot chocolate." Cassie delivered the order to the noisy group who had bagged the table in the window.

She couldn't stop smiling, and that was entirely due to the envelope tucked into the back pocket of her jeans. Her mother was getting married again, and how exciting was that? She was truly an inspiration. Cassie kept pulling the letter out of her pocket to read it.

Dearest Cassie, I'm writing because I have some exciting news that I wanted to share with you. I'm getting married again.

The fact that there was no mention of who her mother was marrying made it all the more romantic and mysterious. Why hadn't she said something? They talked about everything, so why hadn't her mother told her she was seeing someone?

Maybe it had been a glorious whirlwind. Either way, Cassie was happy for her and couldn't wait to hear the details.

Go, Mum, Cassie thought to herself as she moved a guidebook aside to place one of the cappuccinos in front of the group.

The moment they'd walked in, she'd thought *tourists*, and judging from the way they were studying maps on their phones, she was right. On the table next to them was a guide that offered advice on how to make the most of Oxford in twenty-four hours.

You can't, Cassie would have said if one of them had asked her opinion on the matter, but they didn't so she simply delivered their drinks and the two slices of lemon-drizzle cake (four forks, which meant they were either watching calories or cash) and returned to the counter where her fellow barista Felicia was entertaining herself by creating the perfect foam heart on the top of a cappuccino. Felicia was from Rome, and she'd been studying at Oxford for two years. She and Cassie had become friends the previous summer when they'd worked in the café together.

"You're getting good at that." Cassie stowed the tray and served a waiting customer a single slice of chocolate brownie.

The Tasty Bite café was tucked away in a cobbled side street in the middle of Oxford, not far from the Bodleian Library. Their clientele consisted of an interesting mix of locals, tourists and students. Tourists were the most popular because they were drawn inside by the quaint Englishness of the place and tended to over order. Students were the least popular, because they bought one coffee and made it last all day.

Cassie was sympathetic. After all, she'd been that student. She'd completed her degree in Classics, spending four years reading, translating and analyzing texts. When she wasn't in tutorials or studying in the library, she'd spent hours sitting at that same table in the window currently occupied by the tourists, scribbling in her notebook and watching the world go by. She'd spent so long at the café that Rhonda, the owner, had offered her a job, and Cassie had gladly taken it. Not only because she welcomed the money, but because it gave her endless opportunity to people watch and there was nothing in the world that Cassie enjoyed more than studying people.

Take the couple seated side by side in the alcove near the stairs. Their legs were entwined under the table and their shoulders brushed as they leaned over a flyer advertising an outdoor performance of *A Midsummer Night's Dream* in one of the college gardens. Cassie had already booked tickets.

"What do you think? Married?" Felicia glanced toward the couple as she added two cream-topped hot chocolates to the tray already loaded with a basket of croissants fresh from the oven.

Cassie sneaked a glance at the couple. "Yes," she said, "but not to each other." It was a game they often played, inventing whole histories for people.

She waited while Felicia delivered the order and returned with the empty tray.

"They didn't even notice me."

"She's been married to the same guy for a decade, and she has never done anything like this before. Last night was the first night they spent together."

Felicia raised an eyebrow. "And your evidence for that is…?"

"They can't stop touching, and they just ordered a ton of carbs. They need calorie replenishment. They're both starving because they've been having sex all night."

Felicia snorted with laughter. "Your imagination is a lethal weapon. By the way, can you cover my shift on Saturday? Matteo has planned a surprise for our six-month anniversary."

"That's romantic!" Cassie felt a twinge of envy. If there was such a thing as a perfect couple, it was Felicia and Matteo. "Yes, of course I'll cover Saturday. The weather is going to be glorious."

"You don't have plans?"

"Nothing special." She'd planned to lie on the riverbank in the soft grass and read her battered copy of *The Odyssey* for the umpteenth time.

"Thanks. I thought maybe you'd be doing job applications. Have you decided what you're going to do yet?"

"Do?"

"With your life. Your future. You've finished your degree. Now what?"

"I'm still not sure." It was her least favorite question, because answering honestly would mean revealing her deepest secret and she wasn't ready to do that. She'd been a star student, and most people had assumed she'd stay at Oxford and pursue a career in academia, analyzing ancient texts and stimulating the brains of young enthusiastic students. But that wasn't what Cassie wanted.

What would Felicia say if she told her the truth?

I want to be a writer.

Not just a writer, but a *published* writer. That, she knew, was the hard part. The impossible dream, and one shared by many. Everyone she talked to wanted to write a book *one day*. Cassie didn't share that she'd already written one and had started another.

She was afraid that if she told people it would tempt fate, and that would be the end of her dream. They'd probably laugh or, worse still, tell her it was a fantasy and go on to list reasons to support that theory, thereby puncturing both her dreams and her confidence. They'd tell her to get a proper job, whatever that looked like. Cassie needed something that didn't suck up too much time, or emotional energy. Something predictable, without stress, that left her time to focus on her real passion. Which was why, for now at least, she was working extra hours in The Tasty Bite.

Every day she cycled from the little Victorian house that she shared with her friend Oliver. The journey lasted eight minutes, and took her past The Lamb and Flag, which had been serving ale to literary folk for four hundred and fifty years, along narrow lanes and past honey-colored stone buildings, and the whole place was sun-dappled and beautiful and so steeped in history she thought to herself, *Perhaps I'll stay here forever.*

Would that really be so bad?

She loved Oxford, with its winding river and famous colleges. She loved working in the café, which provided her with endless inspiration but placed no demands on her private time. She didn't take work home with her. Her brain wasn't crowded with things she needed to do tomorrow. She could think. She could dream, and no one cared.

"Earth to Cassie." Rhonda emerged from the small kitchen at the back of the café and snapped her fingers. "Stop dreaming. Ted could use some help back here."

She gave a guilty smile. Maybe people did occasionally care when they found her staring into space or scribbling in her notebook, but generally it was a job that fitted her circumstances perfectly. And it allowed her to eavesdrop on conversations and observe human behavior, which she found endlessly fascinating.

Cassie headed into the kitchen where Ted was busy prepping salads.

Ted was an archaeology student. Originally from San Francisco, he'd recently taken a job in the café to help fund the dig he was joining in August.

Cassie washed her hands. "What do you need me to do?"

"It's going to be another baking hot day, so I'm betting there will be a run on salads rather than the toasted paninis. And you can forget soup." He rubbed his arm across his forehead. "It's hot in here. Or maybe I've been spending too long in a climate-controlled library."

"Don't look at Cassie for sympathy." Rhonda came back into the room carrying a basket of salad items she'd picked up from the market. "She loves the heat. She spent most of her childhood in Greece."

Ted looked interested. "You did?"

"My mother has a home on the island of Corfu." Cassie reached for a tomato and lifted it to her nose. The scent told her that it was freshly picked and packed with flavor. "It's my favorite place on earth." She gathered up the tomatoes and rinsed them.

"Wait. That's why you're Cassie? Cassandra, right? Trojan princess."

"My mother loves Greek myths."

He grinned. "So you're destined never to be believed. I guess she could have called you Helen—the face that launched a thousand ships."

She was happy with the way she looked, but she doubted her face would have launched a tugboat or a kayak, let alone a thousand ships. "I got lucky."

"So why are you stuck here instead of spending your summer in Greece? That's where I'd be given the opportunity." Ted started on the cucumber, slicing it into rough chunks.

"I'm going next month, actually. My mother is getting married." Smiling to herself, Cassie removed feta cheese from the fridge. "I'm going to her wedding. Do you want me to make the Greek salad? *Horiatiki.* It's my specialty."

"Sure. That would be great. Your mom's wedding? No kidding." Ted slid a tray of salmon fillets into the oven. "That isn't awkward? What does your dad say about it?"

"My dad is dead." Cassie saw his face turn red and felt sorry for him and annoyed with herself for blurting it out without thought. "Don't feel bad. I was three. I don't have any real memories of him." Just the ones she'd spun in her head from the many stories her mother had shared with her. *Let me tell you about the night I met your father…*

She'd memorized every detail, until they were so clear they'd become real, until she could perfectly picture the moment when her father had stepped into that bar and first seen her mother. *I went into that bar for a drink, and left with the love of my life.*

Her mother had told her that story so many times, but Cassie never tired of hearing it. She repeated the story to people who told her that love didn't exist. That romance was a fantasy.

Cassie knew it wasn't a fantasy. The fact that she was standing here was proof of that.

One day, she promised herself, she was going to find a love and grand passion like the one her parents had shared. It was tragic that her father had died so young, but at least he and her mother had known true love even if only for a short time. In that sense, they'd been lucky. Cassie wouldn't settle for anything less. On every date, she asked herself, *Would I want to follow this man to the ends of the earth*? The answer was always no. Mostly she didn't want to follow them as far as the Bodleian Library, which was depressing because it was a very short distance. The only man who was a constant in her life was Oliver, but that didn't count. Oliver was her best friend, and if she followed him anywhere, they were guaranteed to be lost because Oliver had a terrible sense of direction, which was why she was always in charge of navigation whenever they went out together. They'd met on the first day of term, during the obligatory college photo. There had been much shuffling around to fit everyone in and Cassie, being on the petite side, had been placed right at the front. Oliver had been standing behind her and he'd leaned forward and whispered a joke in her ear just as they took the photograph. He'd made her laugh, and four years later he was still making her laugh. She was conscious that she didn't date as much as she probably should, because dating was hard work and a little stressful, and it was easier and more fun just to hang out with Oliver.

Thinking of him reminded her that he'd been on a date with Suzy again the night before and she hadn't heard from him since.

She felt something shift inside her. If Oliver fell in love, would that change things? It was bound to. Even if the girl of his dreams was sufficiently evolved to accept that he had a female best friend, he wouldn't have as much time to spend with her. No more mooching around museums together. No more picnics on the riverbank, no more swapping of books and long brunches. No more conversations that started with *you'll never guess what happened to me yesterday.*

Ted shredded lettuce. "Man, that's tough about your dad."

"Tougher on my mother." Cassie dragged her mind away from what her life might look like when Oliver fell in love. "Theirs was a true love story. A romance to end all romances."

Ted watched as Cassie reached for the olive oil. "She's been a widow all this time?"

"No, she married again, but she and Gordon—" she didn't even consider Gordon Pelling her stepfather "—were divorced a couple of years ago. It didn't work out."

But at least she'd tried, and she was about to try again. Her mother's courage in matters of the heart was inspirational and Cassie was happy for her. She couldn't wait to celebrate in person.

"Wow. So this is her…" Ted paused, working it out, "third marriage?"

"It's actually her fourth. She was married before she met my dad." Cassie thought about her half sister Adeline and felt a twinge of guilt, as she always did.

Felicia walked in at that moment carrying a tray of dirty cups and plates. She caught the end of the conversation. "You obviously don't know who Cassie's mother is."

Ted glanced from her back to Cassie. "Why would I know Cassie's mother? What am I missing?"

Felicia loaded the cups into the dishwasher. Her skin was evenly tanned, her hair cropped close to her head. "I assume you've heard of Catherine Swift?"

"No." Ted frowned. "Wait—you mean the romance writer? The one who churns out all those trashy beach novels? She's your mom?"

Cassie thought about the hours her mother spent at her desk, hair up in a messy bun, totally focused as she perfected her craft, writing and rewriting until she was exhausted. The implication that she threw out any old rubbish as fast as possible as some sort of commercial exploitation of the poor unsuspecting public made her want to break something.

Ted seemed to realize he was on dangerous ground because he lifted his hands by way of apology.

"No offense, Cassie."

"Saying *no offense*, doesn't cancel out the offense, Ted." Felicia snapped out the words before Cassie could open her mouth. "And those *trashy beach novels* sell by the hundreds of millions for a reason. She tackles issues that are important to women. She's the reason I dumped my last boyfriend. He was messing me around and I woke up one morning and thought, *a Catherine Swift heroine wouldn't allow herself to be treated this way,* and that was it. He was history."

Ted gulped and took a step backward. "Wow. Well that's… kind of unsettling actually. I mean, I don't read a crime book and then murder someone. But we all like different things."

"True. But have you ever read a Catherine Swift book?"

"No." The sweat on Ted's brow wasn't entirely due to the heat in the kitchen. "Not my kind of thing."

"But if you haven't read one," Felicia said sweetly, "how would you know they're not your kind of thing? You are an academic. You're supposed to seek evidence to support your opinions, no?"

"Yeah, you're right." He rubbed his hand over the back of his neck and sent her a mortified look. "I'm sorry, Cassie. That was crass and insensitive."

"Yes, it was," Cassie said, but the truth was that she was used to it. She'd trained herself not to mind. And most of the time she didn't. At least, not for herself. She minded a great deal for her mother who was clever and incredibly hardworking and had built a life for herself from nothing. In Cassie's opinion, that deserved respect. She was inordinately proud of her mother.

She probably wouldn't have even entertained the idea of making a living by writing novels had she not grown up with a mother who did precisely that. Catherine Swift's job was to sit in front of a laptop, or sometimes a notebook, and make things up. *How cool was that!*

Cassie wanted to do the same, but she knew it was probably an unrealistic goal. The chances of earning a good living from writing fiction were miniscule. Success like her mother's was a rare thing.

Cassie found that success inspiring, but also daunting and

confidence-crushing, which was why she hadn't told anyone except Oliver that what she really wanted was to be a writer exactly like her mother. Well not *exactly* like her. Cassie didn't anticipate a fraction of her mother's success. Right now, all she wanted was for someone to think her work was good enough to be published. That would be enough. That would be the dream.

She hadn't mentioned her dream to her mother, even though they talked about everything else. Cassie just couldn't talk about *this*. What if her mother wanted to read something Cassie had written? What if she hated it? That would be so awkward. And in the unlikely event that her mother liked what she'd written, she might have suggested showing it to Daphne, her agent, and Cassie couldn't think of anything more embarrassing. People would think she was trying to capitalize on her mother's name as a way into publishing, which was why Cassie had sent her manuscript to a different agent and made no mention of her mother.

She'd decided that she needed to do this on her own terms or she'd never believe in herself.

That had been two months ago and so far she'd heard nothing, which wasn't a good sign.

At the beginning, she'd refreshed her email every ten minutes, heart pounding, fairy-tale scenarios flashing through her head. She was going to get an email, maybe even a call. Hers was going to be the manuscript they'd been waiting for.

When nothing had happened, she'd forced herself to restrict refreshing her email to once an hour. Now she'd given up. The agent's website had said that they aimed to respond within eight weeks and they were past that which meant, in Cassie's mind, they hated what she'd sent. It was so very bad they couldn't even be bothered to reject her.

But she'd keep going, of course, even though her confidence was drooping like a plant in a heat wave.

Ted gave an awkward smile. "Yes, well, sorry again, and I really ought to talk to Rhonda about plans for the weekend." He washed his hands and left the kitchen so fast he knocked into the counter.

Felicia stared after him and then shook her head. "I'm not sure about him."

"He's not saying anything that hasn't been said before," Cassie said. "You get used to it."

"Ignore him. Your mother is a legend." Felicia stole a piece of feta cheese. "She taught me everything I know about love and healthy relationships. Also, resilience. Her characters always find a way through, no matter how tough life is."

Cassie's insides warmed. "Thanks, Felicia."

"Hey, it's all true. If you want to get me a signed copy of her latest, I won't say no. Italian or English—I'm not fussy." Felicia popped the cheese into her mouth and smiled. "Must be cool, having a famous mother."

"Mostly I don't tell people. I only told you that time because I saw you reading one of her books the first summer we worked here together."

Felicia leaned against the fridge. "So, another wedding. Will your half sister be there?"

Cassie's stomach rolled. "I…don't know." She hadn't allowed herself to think about that part. It was the one black cloud hovering over an otherwise sunny summer. "I'm hoping not to be honest. Does that make me an awful person?"

"Why would it?" Felicia shrugged. "It's not as if the two of you are exactly close."

Close? Cassie suppressed a hysterical laugh. The days when she'd secretly dreamed of being close to her "big sister" were long gone. That, she thought, was a bigger fantasy than being a published writer. She was more likely to hit *The Sunday Times* bestseller list than win a smile or a few warm words from Adeline. And she had no expectations of ever hitting *The Sunday Times* bestseller list.

Gloom descended, along with a certain level of trepidation, the sort one might feel before a visit to the dentist. Her sister's presence wouldn't exactly ruin the wedding, but it would be enough to put a significant dent in Cassie's enjoyment and celebration. And, worse still, it would upset their mother and if there was one day when a person should absolutely *not* be upset, it was surely on their wedding day.

Maybe Adeline wouldn't show up. At their mother's last wedding, Adeline had refused point-blank to be a bridesmaid, so it had been left to Cassie to fulfil that role alone. She'd fussed over her mother and thrown flowers and tried to make her smile big enough for two people to compensate for Adeline's stony expression. It was clear that Adeline had hated every minute so perhaps, if Cassie got really lucky, she'd decide not to put herself through that again.

It wasn't as if she was romantic. In fact, Cassie had never seen her sister display a single emotion. Adeline was so cool and composed it was unsettling. She was the exact opposite of Cassie, who spread her emotions around freely. The truth was she found her sister intimidating and a little cold. At what point did one give up trying?

All through her teens, when Adeline had spent those agonizing summer weeks on Corfu, Cassie had been friendly. Partly because it was her nature, but also because she'd badly wanted to be close to her sister. All the books she'd devoured suggested that having a sister was a gift. A definite benefit in life. An older sister was an even greater benefit, offering as it did access to superior wisdom and a level of protectiveness alongside a guarantee of lifelong friendship unshaken by the tremors that so often caused cracks in lesser relationships.

Keen to nurture and exploit this special relationship, Cassie had worked hard to build a connection with Adeline. It made her cringe to remember how hard she'd worked to make her half sister like her, but it had been a lost cause. She'd been like a comedian trying desperately to get a laugh from an unreceptive audience. A puppy trying to win the affection of someone who disliked dogs. If anything, her efforts to bring them closer had driven them further apart. The more she'd stepped forward, the more Adeline had withdrawn. Hurt, pride and confidence dented, Cassie eventually backed off too and forced herself to accept that she was never going to have a relationship with her sister. She was never going to call her when she was stressed about a boy, or worried about her exams. She was never going to be able to share any of her worries or fears because Adeline wasn't interested, which was hurtful given that Adeline seemed to have devoted her life to helping other people navigate uncomfortable feelings. She liked helping people, but not Cassie. She gave strangers access to her wisdom, but not Cassie.

Her lack of interest was personal. It was as if Adeline couldn't bear to be near her, which was upsetting because Cassie thought her half sister was pretty cool.

Adeline was a genuine adult, whereas Cassie felt most of the time that, although she was trying hard to be an adult, she was failing dismally. She was a dreamer, whereas her sister was ruthlessly focused and practical. Adeline was a clinical psychologist, and you didn't get more adult than that. *Dr. Swift.* She dispensed advice and sympathy to people like Cassie who couldn't quite get their lives sorted out by themselves.

Adeline was poised and dignified at all times, and also self-reliant and independent. Cassie needed people in her life.

She didn't know where she'd be without her mother and her friends. Adeline, it seemed, needed no one.

Adeline was sure of herself and her choices, whereas Cassie wasn't sure about *anything*. She definitely wasn't sure about the future. How many times would she allow her writing to be rejected before accepting that she wouldn't be able to make a living that way? When should she give up and get a "proper job"?

She wondered for a moment what Adeline would say if she knew about Cassie's dream to be a writer. She was pretty sure Adeline would think her dream was ill-advised to say the least.

"I used to wish we were closer, but I've given up on that," she told Felicia. "Adeline is eight years older than me, so there's quite an age gap. After the divorce she chose to live with her dad. I think it almost destroyed my mother. So we didn't see much of each other growing up." She saw no reason to edit the truth and she wasn't great at keeping secrets. In Cassie's opinion, secrets were great in fiction, necessary even, but in real life they made things complicated.

Perhaps Adeline would turn down her mother's invitation. *Please, please let her turn it down!*

It was a wedding after all, and it was clear from the advice she dished out in her column that Adeline didn't have a romantic bone in her body. Of course she didn't. To be romantic, you had to *feel* something, and Cassie sometimes wondered whether her sister felt anything at all.

Adeline seemed to dismiss the notion of romantic love as transient and an unreliable basis for a long-term relationship.

And Cassie had tried hard to be sympathetic and see the situation from Adeline's point of view. Their mother had fallen in love with Cassie's father. They'd had an affair, and Cassie had been the result. Adeline had been eight years old when her parents divorced, and that must have been *so* hard. Her family had been shattered. Adeline had blamed their mother.

From her own point of view, Cassie was able to see things a little more objectively. Would the affair have happened if Catherine had been happy in her first marriage? No. Some relationships worked, and some didn't. Some were happy for a while, and then ended. And that was sad, but it was also life. People changed. Relationships changed. Cassie regretted the hurt their mother had caused to Adeline and her first husband but, in her opinion, she'd showed emotional honesty and done the brave thing. Catherine had no longer been in love with Adeline's father. It was over. What was she supposed to do? Stay miserable for the rest of her life? How was that good for anyone? If something was wrong, then it was wrong. It was just one of those things.

Cassie believed Catherine had been right to follow her passion (and if she hadn't, Cassie wouldn't exist, so she had to admit she was biased), but Adeline clearly disagreed.

Cassie had spent long hours studying Adeline's advice columns, trying to understand her sister.

She poured over every word, analyzing every detail, feeling as if each answer gave her an insight into Adeline's soul. She'd occasionally thought about writing in herself.

My half sister hates me, and although some people might think she has reason, it really wasn't my fault. How can I help her put aside her anger and bitterness so that we might stand a chance of forging a relationship?

Felicia handed her the jar of oregano. "It doesn't worry you that your mother is marrying again?"

Cassie smiled, grateful to be nudged away from thoughts of Adeline. "Not at all."

Why would it? She would never begrudge her mother happiness. And she trusted her mother's judgment. She'd written more than sixty romance novels and sold hundreds of millions of copies. That was all the evidence anyone needed to prove that Catherine Swift knew everything there was to know about love.

You didn't marry for a fourth time because you were a failure; you did it because you were an optimist. Not because you regretted the past, but because you had hope for the future.

Cassie didn't know who her mother was marrying, and the idea that it was a secret thrilled her. She didn't need to know yet. No doubt she'd find out once she arrived on the island for the celebrations.

Her mother obviously wanted it to be a big surprise, and you couldn't get much more romantic than that.

Cassie sighed as she plated up Greek salads and slid them into the fridge.

With luck, Adeline would decide not to go to the wedding.

Please, please let her decide not to go.

3

Catherine

Catherine Swift had been born with a gift.

There was no one particular moment when she'd become aware of its existence. It was as much a part of her as her unruly blond hair and her lack of coordination. It had grown along with her until it had taken on a life of its own. She couldn't remember a time when she hadn't had stories and characters racing around in her head. But she remembered clearly the first time she'd written those stories down.

She'd been twelve years old and her mother had delivered her to Clifton House, a boarding school deep in the heart of the English countryside. Her parents were in the middle of an acrimonious divorce and her mother had unilaterally decided it would be less traumatizing for Catherine to be ejected from the family home and live among strangers than to witness the messy decline of a marriage. That was the official line. Unofficially, after a bottle of sauvignon blanc that her mother had claimed was for medicinal purposes, she'd confessed to Catherine that for the sake of her lifestyle she needed to find another husband and she couldn't do that with a daughter in the mix. It would make things far too complicated. Finding a husband was like applying for a job. You had to focus and give it your full attention.

You'll like it here, she'd said as she hauled Catherine's single suitcase along soulless corridors. *You'll make lots of friends. It will feel like home.*

Catherine hadn't liked it, she hadn't made any friends and it had felt nothing like home. Not that home was a nurturing place. Far from it. It wouldn't have taken much for school to have been the better option, and it said a great deal about the quality of the establishment her mother had chosen that it wasn't.

As far as Catherine could see, she'd simply swapped one type of trauma for another.

The school was a large brown brick building with windows that seemed to face everywhere except the places where the bullies congregated. There were no witnesses when three girls decided to push her head down the toilet, and no one to intervene when it was discovered that her long hair made a useful rope with which to drag her along a corridor.

There were, however, rules. More rules than Catherine could count, and they made no sense. Why did she have to walk on the left side of the corridor? Was it such a crime to veer over to the right? Why did lights have to be switched off at nine o'clock precisely, even if you hadn't finished the chapter of the book you were reading? Why couldn't she hack off her hair if she decided that short hair was a safer option?

"Home" was a hard narrow bed in a room with ten other girls, none of whom welcomed the arrival of an outsider.

Catherine wasn't "cool," she had no hand-eye coordination and wasn't going to be a valuable addition to any sports team. To the other girls, cruel in their assessment of others, she was a target. Sadly, it wasn't a new experience. Her father, a keen sportsman, had despaired of her. No matter how hard she'd tried, he still shouted at her. He told her regularly she was worthless, and she had no reason not to believe him given that so many seemed to be in agreement.

Fortunately, the school had a library and Catherine had taken refuge there whenever she could, tucking herself away between tall shelves and dusty books, imagining herself as Jane Eyre, alone, rejected, badly treated. She immersed herself in stories, but nobody's words provided the escape that her own did.

At home, she'd survived by detaching herself, by living life inside her head, removed from the reality of the present. There were no happy endings in her life, so she'd invented them. Her imagination spun stories of relationships that didn't end the way her parents' had, conversations that hadn't ended in broken china, broken limbs or broken hearts. She was happy to inhabit any world, as long as it wasn't her own.

At school, she'd done the same. It frustrated her that she, who loved words, could never find the right ones when confronted by a bully. She'd decided that it was probably because deep down she agreed with them. She was all those things they were calling her, so how could she defend herself?

Nevertheless, she'd spend hours at night replaying the scenario in her head and devising the perfect put down with herself as victor.

Characters lived in her brain, distracting her during lessons. They kept her company when she was lonely and stood by her side when the bullying became almost unbearable. The only subject she truly enjoyed was English, and the first time the class had been asked to write a short story was the happiest day of Catherine's life. Finally, she was going to be able to give those characters life. Finally, she was confident that she could excel at something.

She wrote easily, fluently, the words flowing from her brain to her pen and onto the page.

When she'd finished, she wrote her name boldly at the top of the page and handed the work in with pride and barely contained excitement. She'd hardly slept that night, imagining the moment when the teacher would return her work. Miss Barrett was tall, with thin lips, a thin nose and an equally thin sense of humor. She was hard to please and had expended some considerable effort into making English Literature the least popular subject in school. They read *Anna Karenina* and *Wuthering Heights*, *Madame Bovary* and *Romeo and Juliet*, and Catherine had found herself wondering if there was a subtext to those classes, if Miss Barrett was simultaneously teaching them about literature, while warning them about the follies of uncontrolled passion. They studied tragedy after tragedy, love stories soaked in unhappiness. *We're all going to die single*, Catherine thought, which to her seemed a happier outcome than dying for love.

Why did love have to end tragically?

But she'd fixed that. For her assignment, she'd written a story that had uncontrolled passion, but no tragedy.

She couldn't wait for Miss Barrett to read it and was already imagining the response.

Catherine, I had no idea you had such talent.

She imagined the other girls staring, their faces showing envy rather than contempt as they changed their view of her, wishing that they too possessed her gift. Maybe her ball skills were lacking, and her hand-eye coordination less than impressive, but she could *write*. She'd be, if not popular, then at least tolerated. Maybe they'd ask her to help with their home-work. *Catherine, you're so brilliant at English...*

As so often happened in life, things didn't go the way she'd imagined they would.

Miss Barrett handed back the papers to each girl without comment, rationing praise as if it came with serious health consequences.

Catherine waited, poised for her turn. She could see the grade of the girl next to her, scribbled in red ink at the top of the page. *B+ Good!*

She was last. Was that significant?

"Catherine." Miss Barrett returned to her desk as the bell went for break time. "Stay behind."

Heads turned. Everyone looked at her, curious, scenting the possibility of trouble.

But Catherine knew she wasn't in trouble. Far from it. She was being singled out for a different reason.

She felt herself turn pink with anticipatory pleasure. One day, when she'd had her first book published, she'd look back on this moment. She might even credit her English teacher for inspiring her to write uplifting fiction. Books that didn't make you want to fall under a train or swallow arsenic along with the heroine.

Perhaps she'd dedicate her first book to her teacher. *To Miss Barrett, who started it all.*

The teacher waited until the door closed and then thrust Catherine her paper.

Catherine stared at the words scrawled at the top of the page.

D. Fail. See me!

Fail? How could it possibly be a fail? She'd written from her heart, poured her feelings all over the page. This was the first time she'd written a story down, and the first time she'd ever shown her work to anyone. She'd loved it. Writing it had given her a high she'd never felt before. *Fail?*

Pleasure turned to pain. Every part of her burned with humiliation. It was like being dipped in acid. Her hands shook on the paper.

"I don't understand."

Miss Barrett was red in the face. "What made you write a story like this?"

How was she supposed to answer that? "Like what?"

She'd written a romance. The topic had been *together*, and her story had felt appropriate. The girl sitting next to her had written about a cat and a mouse, but Catherine couldn't see any way that would make an interesting story.

"It's..." Miss Barrett cleared her throat and crossed her legs. "I want to know why you wrote this particular story. Have you girls been watching something? Reading something you shouldn't?"

"No." Catherine, who liked to anticipate the direction of trouble so that she could avoid it, had no idea where this conversation was going.

"Then where did the idea come from?"

"My brain."

"But what, or who, put such a thing into your brain?"

Was she asking where stories and characters came from? Catherine had no idea. They appeared, fully formed, and lived their lives vividly inside her head. She'd assumed it was the same for everyone but judging from the way Miss Barrett was looking at her, evidently not.

"I like to make up stories."

Miss Barrett's mouth flattened into a thin line. "You have no talent for it, Catherine. This—" she waved a hand at Catherine's offending story "—is trash. Worthless. Whatever you're imagining, it is better off remaining inside your head. You will never be a writer. Give up, now."

Worthless. So many people used that word around her it had to be true.

Her confidence had died that day. She'd stumbled through the rest of the afternoon and later, devastated and humiliated, she'd slunk back to the dormitory only to find all the girls sitting on her bed, waiting for her. One of them, Jane, always the ringleader, was holding Catherine's essay.

Miss Barrett's words were still ringing in her head. *This is trash. You'll never be a writer.*

Catherine knew she'd never forget those words, but she'd consoled herself with the knowledge that no one but her and the teacher would ever know.

She'd been as wrong about that as she'd been about everything else.

Somehow the other girls had got hold of her story and read it, which proved that even though you thought you'd hit rock bottom, you could always sink lower. When they'd teased her for always missing the ball, she'd told herself it didn't matter. When she'd come last in a race or sang out of tune, she'd told herself that didn't matter either.

But writing? Stories? They mattered. They were everything. The world inside her head was everything, and now it was exposed to the full mockery of others.

No doubt they'd find a new way to torture her. And it would be worse than hair pulling, or the time they'd dropped her books into the toilet, because it was personal. Her writing was personal. She should never have shared it.

Jane, the ringleader, had appointed herself spokesperson. "Catherine Swift, whoever would have thought it?"

Too miserable to respond, Catherine had stood still and waited for them to have their fun and took comfort from the knowledge that they couldn't hurt her more than she was already hurting. She felt small, and wounded, and insignificant.

Jane flicked through the pages. "So who is he?"

"Who is who?"

"The boy. The boy you haven't told us about."

Boy? It took her a moment to understand that they were talking about the character in her story. They thought it was real?

"The idea came from my head." She said the same thing that she'd said to Miss Barrett.

Jane narrowed her eyes. "You're saying you made the whole thing up?"

"Yes. It's a story." She wondered why they couldn't understand that. They had imaginations, didn't they?

There was silence and then Jane gave a slow smile. "Cool. So if you really made it up, then you can give us another chapter."

"Another chapter?"

"We want to know what the hot guy does next. What do they do after they both sneak out of the house?" Jane stood up and dropped the pages onto Catherine's narrow bunk. "Tell us a bedtime story, Catherine."

It was an order, not a request, but for once Catherine didn't mind.

She did exactly as they asked. Every night after lights out, she'd lie in the dark and tell another of the stories in her head. At first just a few girls listened, and then all of them. And still Catherine told the stories, ending each evening on a cliffhanger, keeping her audience enthralled. She was like Scheherazade, spinning tales that made her listeners want more.

The bullying stopped, and Catherine allowed her hair to grow. And then the bullies became friends, and those same friends urged her to write her stories down and submit them.

Someone's mother worked in a publishing house. Catherine's book was submitted, and rejected. But not with the harsh words that Miss Barrett had used. No one said it was trash. No one said she couldn't write. The word *worthless* never entered the conversation. No one said *give up now*. On the contrary, the editor complimented her on her *compelling narrative* and *believable characters*. The word *commercial* was dropped in there somewhere, although Catherine didn't understand what that meant. What she did understand was that the editor was telling her to persevere.

It was all the encouragement Catherine needed.

She rewrote that story three times, then decided the whole thing was a mess and ditched it and started again with something new. This time she stuck with it. She abandoned the idea that if the story stopped flowing, then it meant it wasn't right. She wrote from her heart, and edited with her brain. If she hit a problem, she learned to retrace her steps and analyze where the story had gone wrong. She wrote and then rewrote, and then rewrote again. She didn't write for the editor, she wrote for herself and for the girls in her dormitory who always wanted another chapter. She figured that if the book made her heart beat faster, made her smile, made her *care*, then it would have that effect on others.

Finally, she'd sent it back to the same editor and after a long wait—a very long wait—she got the call. *We want to buy your book.*

That call still ranked right up there as one of the best moments of her life. She'd been giddy, breathless, euphoric. Sometimes she looked back on it and wished she could capture that heady moment of hope. She was a writer! No matter what Miss Barrett said, she was an actual writer. Right then she'd been at the beginning of something, with everything to gain.

Now she had everything to lose.

Catherine sat in the shade on her terrace. Her feet were bare and she could feel the warmth of the tiles heating her skin. Ignoring the notepad and pen on the table in front of her, she gazed across the lush garden, through olive groves and orange trees thick with fruit, to the glistening water. Her two cats, Ajax and Achilles, were stretched out close to her, basking sleepily in a patch of sunlight. They'd been abandoned as kittens and she'd found them, days old and close to death. She'd brought them home and nursed them until they'd gone from scrawny to strong. Remembering their awful condition when she'd rescued them, it pleased her to see them looking so content.

Success had bought her a villa on Corfu, and there wasn't a day when she didn't appreciate her good fortune. People marveled that her books were still selling, authors envied her career and wanted to know her secret.

Catherine knew that the secret, if it could be called that, were her readers. The critics abhorred her, but readers adored her. Scathing reviews, or no reviews at all, had no impact on her sales because her readers didn't care about such things. They read her not because they'd been advised to do so, not because she'd won literary awards (she hadn't), but because they loved her books and had loved them for a long time. They loved her because she gave them a good story. Because she gave them good, honest emotion. She understood their lives and the problems they faced. Reading her books, they felt *seen*. They loved the fact that a book by Catherine Swift guaranteed them a few hours of escape when they were enduring the brutality of chemo, relationship traumas or the loneliness of bereavement, and she understood that because her characters had always provided an escape for her too. Her readers loved her for many reasons, but mostly they loved her because ultimately, no matter how bumpy the ride, she gave them a happy ending. And she took that responsibility seriously. There were people who had followed her with unwavering loyalty since the publication of her very first book. Readers who had discovered her "late" in her career, immediately gobbled up her backlist.

While other books fizzled and died, a new Catherine Swift had always been a guaranteed number one bestseller.

Until now.

She stood up and looked across the bay. A short path led steeply down from her villa to the beach below. The small crescent of sand was perfect for swimming, and a narrow jetty stretched into the sea.

Andrew had taken the boat out earlier and as yet hadn't returned. He'd invited her, but she'd refused. She wanted to be alone when the call came. She needed to give herself time to digest the news. To compose herself. To decide what she was going to do. She had a plan, but she wasn't sure she wanted to put it into action.

She was braced for bad news, which was why when her phone rang, she didn't immediately reach for it as if by not answering, she could change the outcome.

The call display said *Daphne*.

Daphne Elliot, superagent and literary wizard. She'd been Catherine's agent for the entirety of her career, a partnership that had proved fruitful for both of them.

Catherine pictured Daphne at her desk in Manhattan, surrounded by stacks of books taller than she was. She had a corner office that overlooked the buzz of Fifth Avenue and would probably have spent her morning racing from one meeting to another, with a break for lunch in a smart restaurant. How many glasses of champagne had they raised together over the years? How many celebratory lunches had they consumed?

But no matter how many highs and celebrations there had been, for Catherine they were eclipsed by the lows.

And today was going to be a low.

With a sigh, she answered the call.

"Hi, Daphne. How are things?" She asked the question, even though she already knew the answer. Things weren't good, and she knew that Daphne would have been steeling herself to make this call.

"Catherine! Good to hear your voice." There was a pause. "So—I have news."

Not amazing news, or incredible news. Just news.

Catherine sat down hard on the chair. How was it possible to feel this bad after such a long and successful career? But she did feel bad. She felt terrible. Her heart was racing. She felt sick, even though she hadn't heard the words yet. And when the words came, she only heard a few of them— *difficult market... supply chain issues... factors outside our control... unlucky that the latest Miranda Patterson had been released at the exact same time. She's hot right now and she hit that coveted number one slot on the list.*

Catherine thought, *I hate Miranda,* and then felt terrible because she'd met Miranda a few times at various literary events and liked her as a person (not her books. She hated her books because the heroines always died tragically). Even if she hadn't liked her, she would have still felt terrible because Miranda was on her second round of treatment for breast cancer and everyone knew that when one part of your life was screwed, you deserved the rest of it to go well. Miranda *deserved* that number one slot. That was the law of the universe. If Catherine needed evidence to support that theory, then all she had to do was look at herself.

After years of upheaval and trauma in her personal life, things were finally perfect. She was in love with a man who loved her back and understood her. In a matter of weeks, she'd be getting married right here, in the place she loved most. Her beloved Cassie would be joining them, and so would Adeline. And although she knew that wouldn't be an easy encounter, Catherine desperately wanted her older daughter to come. Finally, she would fix their relationship and free herself of the terrible guilt that came with knowing that while she'd been a good mother to Cassie, she'd been an awful mother to Adeline.

She sometimes wondered if it might have been easier to cope with her guilt had she been an awful mother generally. She could have told herself that some women just weren't meant to be mothers, and although that wouldn't have made her deficiencies any more acceptable, at least her failings would have been consistent. Instead, she had to live with the uncomfortable nagging knowledge that she was a good mother to one child while being the very worst to the other. It was something that for years she'd been unable to rectify but finally she was confident that she could, if only Adeline would come to her wedding.

It was ironic that now, when her personal life was finally near-perfect, her career was falling apart. Once again, the universe had proved its ability to take the edge off any celebration so that it was impossible to become complacent or too self-congratulatory. Life had a way of diluting good news, with bad news. *Everything going well for five minutes? Let's ruin that for you…*

Some of Catherine's lowest points in her relationships had coincided with the high points of her career.

Daphne was soothing. Yes, Catherine's sales for this book had been lower than expected—but *disappointing* wasn't the word she'd use. (Catherine was using many words, all of which would have been flagged by a copy editor: *consider not using language that offends your reader.*) Daphne assured her it was one of those things. A reflection of a difficult market.

Catherine was trying to get her head around the idea of being number two—*second*—when Daphne broke the news that a male thriller writer had bagged the number two slot.

For the first time in decades, Catherine Swift was number three.

Three! Maybe she could have coped with being number two (she knew she wouldn't have coped with being number two), but *three*? Three wasn't disappointing. Three wasn't "one of those things." Three was failure. Three was disaster. Three was the beginning of the end.

She felt her confidence wither and shrink.

Her insecurities, kept at bay for years by the sturdy barrier of success, started to reemerge.

Three was *personal*—couldn't Daphne see that? It was no good telling herself that she'd written the best book she could and the rest of it was outside her control. The truth was that the book-buying public had chosen a love story that ended in tragedy, and a crime story that began with tragedy (dead women, so many dead women) over an uplifting Catherine Swift. They'd chosen the unhappy ending and in doing so had delivered an unhappy ending to Catherine.

Her readers had spoken.

She considered throwing her phone into the pool, as if by submerging it she could drown bad news.

Here, finally, was the evidence that she was past her peak. Her career was on the slide.

She was standing in paradise, but she felt nothing but pain and panic.

Below her, she could see Andrew securing the boat to the jetty. In a few minutes, he'd come bounding up that path, full of energy and eager to celebrate another Catherine Swift number one. He'd hear the news and immediately brace himself to be positive. He'd try to persuade her that there was still plenty to celebrate, that their wedding was just a few weeks away. She'd pretend that it was all that mattered. That it was enough.

She snatched a quick breath and paced across the terrace and back. She gave herself a sharp talking to. She was lucky. She had all the things that mattered. She still had a career, even though it had taken a sharp nosedive. She had two healthy daughters, even if one of them did loathe her. Most important of all she had Andrew. Andrew who understood her. Andrew who *knew*. It should be enough.

It wasn't enough.

She hated herself for feeling this way. What was wrong with her? It wasn't as if she needed the money, although her insecure childhood had left her with a determination to be financially independent.

It wasn't as if she needed the adulation of strangers. She was loved. Truly loved by a good man, and that was something she hadn't expected at her age. Not after everything that had happened.

Three marriages, and each time she'd been sure. What did that say about her? She could be generous and tell herself it said she was an optimist with a huge capacity for love. That she was a person who never gave up, even when life punched her to the floor. Or she could be harsh and admit that she was a bad judge of character. That her creative brain didn't clock off when she stopped writing and somehow shaped her vision so that she saw what she wanted to see and not what was really there. That she'd fallen in love with her *idea* of who someone was rather than who they really were.

But her real failing, if it really was a failing, was her desire to be loved. Maybe that was a result of the lack of emotional security in her childhood, or maybe it was something inside her (nature or nurture? It was a question she constantly asked herself when she was creating her characters). But whatever the cause, it was a fact. She wanted to be loved. Truly loved, for herself. And not only romantic love, but the love of friends. And not because she was well known, and not because she was wealthy, but because of who she was as a person.

And it was harder now, of course, because you never knew whether someone's sudden desire to spend time with you came from the fact that you were sparkling company, or the fact that a friendship with Catherine Swift came with the same perks you'd expect from a five-star hotel.

More and more, she'd found herself envying her characters who were loved unconditionally, although admittedly after navigating challenges so significant and occasionally harrowing that Catherine often felt guilty for making their lives so difficult.

Catherine had endured the harrowing and the difficult, but she hadn't ended up with the unconditional love. Until now.

She had so much to be grateful for.

She breathed in the scent of orange blossom and fixed her gaze on the dusky pink bougainvillea spilling over terracotta.

Lucky, lucky.

She kept saying it, in the hope that she would start to feel it.

But what she thought about as she was standing there, wasn't her personal life, but her career. And not the successes, but the failures. She wasn't thinking about the hundreds of times she'd been in that number one slot; she was thinking of this one time when she was number three. She wasn't thinking of all her happy readers; she was thinking about the people who hated her books. All those people who mocked her writing, who marveled at the fact that she'd sold one copy let alone many hundreds of millions. She was thinking that if she could no longer live in the world she'd created in her head, where would she live?

She was thinking about Miss Barrett. *You have no talent.*

Why was it that now, after a writing career that had surpassed her wildest dreams, she was thinking about Miss Barrett? She couldn't remember what she did last week, but she could still remember the words that Miss Barrett had flung at her. She'd never consider having a brow lift, or a tummy tuck, or liposuction, but if a surgeon could have removed those words from her brain, she would have handed over her credit card and laid down on his operating table without question.

It made no sense that it bothered her so much but emotions, as Catherine knew, didn't always make sense.

Her imagination, both her gift and her curse, spun a future for her that looked bleak and dark. No more glitter and champagne. No more celebrations. No more adoring readers. No more blanket of love. Just a career fading, until one day someone would ask, *Catherine who?*

This was what she did. This was who she was. She was a storyteller, but what happened to the storyteller when people no longer wanted to hear her stories?

In her writing, she'd always preferred beginnings to endings, and she felt the same way in real life.

If someone had said to her that this was a case of "one door closes and another one opens," Catherine would have slammed that open door in their face.

But perhaps there was an element of truth there.

She frowned as she thought about the secret she was keeping.

After each of her marriages had ended, she'd started fresh. She'd refused to let difficulties and failures in the past prevent her from forging a good future. Why couldn't she do the same with her career?

As Andrew approached, she made a decision.

It was time. Time to take the plunge and share the secret she'd been keeping. Time to tell Andrew the truth.

4

Adeline

"So you *are* going to the wedding?" Mia sat at the little table on Adeline's tiny balcony, watching the bees hover by the lavender. "What made you change your mind?"

"My father wants me to go." And that request had put her in an impossible position. If she put her own needs first and refused to go to the wedding, she'd hurt him. She would never intentionally hurt her father, and not simply because he was no doubt already hurting at the thought of another Catherine Swift wedding. Adeline adored him. He was the one person in her life who had never let her down. He'd always been there for her which was why, after she'd calmed down, she'd retrieved the letter from under the potato peelings and placed it on the kitchen countertop. It had sat there ever since, its presence filling her with resentment and dread whenever she boiled the kettle or went to remove something from the fridge.

The letter was responsible for the uncomfortable churning inside her, and for the fact she wasn't sleeping well. She kept a rigid routine. No caffeine after midday, no alcohol on a weekday, exercise five times a week. She didn't eat salty or spicy food late at night. She practiced yoga and meditation and still she was awake at two in the morning, staring at the ceiling while dark thoughts used her brain as a racetrack. And there was no doubting the source of this unwelcome nocturnal attack.

Her mother.

The whole idea of the wedding was filling her with dread, but in this instance, her father's feelings took precedence. If he wanted her to go, then she'd go, no matter the effect on her stress levels and sleep pattern.

"You're going to need something to wear." Mia tried to be positive. "If you have to do something you don't want to do, the least you can do is look good and feel good while you do it."

"Whatever I wear, I'm not going to feel good." Adeline didn't want to waste any more time thinking about the wedding. It was the weekend. This was the time she allocated for relaxation. She wanted to enjoy her Saturday and her friend's company.

"Maybe it won't be so bad, although I admit I'm biased because I *love* weddings." Mia picked up her glass and ice clinked against the sides. "Weddings are about beginnings, aren't they? They're hopeful."

"Given that this is my mother's fourth attempt, I think we can safely say that we left *hopeful* behind a long time ago. We've reached *desperate*. And she has had as many endings as she has had beginnings. She just doesn't know how to be on her own." She'd heard from plenty of people exactly like her mother, people who flitted from one relationship to another, seeking something that was missing inside themselves.

"You have mixed feelings. And that's understandable." Mia leaned forward. "But this is your mother."

Mia didn't know every uncomfortable detail of their relationship, of course, because Adeline hadn't shared it. She hadn't shared it with anyone, and not only because there was a particular type of humiliation involved when your own mother didn't like you very much.

"I was at her last two weddings. I feel as if I've paid my dues." Adeline sighed, accepting the inevitable. If she didn't go, she'd feel bad. If she went, she'd feel bad. She was destined to feel bad either way. She might as well go. At least that would keep her father happy. "I'll wear what I wore to her last wedding."

"Where's the fun in that?" Mia worked for a fashion magazine, and clothes were her job and her obsession.

"There is nothing fun about my mother getting married again." Adeline reached for her sunglasses. A heat wave was spreading across Europe. Corfu would be scorching in July. She'd fry, and keeping her hair smooth would be impossible. "Maybe you're right. I do need clothes. I don't have anything suitable for lounging around on a beach. I need a large sun hat to hide humidity hair, and I need swimsuits. Sleek swimsuits, so that if I decide to drown myself, at least I'll look good." The prospect of shopping for a trip she didn't want to take filled her with nothing but gloom.

"Adeline, you can't go when you feel this way." Mia put her glass of wine down. "Can't you just explain to your dad?"

"No, because then I come across as mean-spirited. I like to pretend I'm better than that, even though I'm not. And you know what my father is like. Forgive and forget. The past is the past. Don't bear grudges." She laughed at the irony. "I'm the psychologist, but it turns out he's the most emotionally evolved of the two of us."

Mia tilted her face to the sun. "You'd think your dad would be bitter and twisted, given the way your mother treated him. Although I suppose it was twenty years ago. Water under the bridge?"

"Maybe, although even when it happened, he wasn't bitter. Just hurt. He loved her deeply." And that moment when she'd walked into the room and found her father on his knees sobbing had stayed with her. "Anyway, I'm probably bitter and twisted enough for both of us." She was honest enough to admit that the hurt, angry little girl she'd been back then still lived inside her, along with the words her mother had spoken on that perfect summer morning when her whole life had changed.

You're going to have a new father, Adeline, and a baby sister.

"You're so hard on yourself," Mia said. "You were eight years old. It must have been a horrible time."

Horrible didn't begin to describe it.

"I've had plenty of time to get over it. I should have moved on. I thought I *had* moved on, and then that letter arrived in my apartment and wham, I'm back there again." It was more than she would usually admit to anyone, but she was frustrated that she wasn't handling it better. She dished out so much advice, trying to help others, but it seemed she was incapable of helping herself.

Mia gave her a sympathetic look. "I don't know how you're supposed to move on from the fact that your mother sent you away when she had her new family. How old were you? Nine?"

"Ten when that happened." Adeline felt uncomfortable. She couldn't quite believe she'd told Mia that. It was unlike her. "And living with my dad was definitely the best thing for me, so I don't know why it bothers me."

She knew why it bothered her.

Her mother had given her away without a fight. She'd wanted to focus on Cassie.

"Give yourself a break, Adeline. You're a human being with feelings. And you've made a really good life for yourself." Mia gestured to the sunny balcony and Adeline's small but delightful apartment. "You live in the best city in the world. You have your own place, a great job, a circle of brilliant friends. I am the most brilliant of course."

That made Adeline smile. "Of course."

"I could come with you for moral support. I could be your plus-one. I wouldn't object to two weeks in Greece. I could be a shield between you and your selfish mother." Mia sat forward, her short dress sliding over bare tanned legs. She wore bold jewelery and red lipstick and was the type of person who never entered a room unnoticed.

They'd met five years earlier when Mia had commissioned Adeline to write a feature on dressing for confidence and been close friends ever since. At least, as "close" as Adeline ever allowed herself to get to anyone. She told Mia enough to form a bond of friendship (she knew how these things worked), but not too much. There were things in her past that she knew she'd never reveal to anyone.

Dr. Swift encouraged people to "tell all," but there was no rule that said she had to do the same herself.

"I wish I could take you. Unfortunately, she only invited me. No mention of a plus-one." And she was relieved about that. She was a master at hiding her feelings. She'd describe it as her superpower, but that power was challenged in the presence of her mother and she didn't want the additional stress of having people she knew around her.

"What about Mark?" Mia topped up her wine. "Your mother hasn't invited him?"

"She doesn't know about Mark. I haven't seen her since we went for lunch a year ago when she was over here on a book tour." Her mother's assistant had scheduled the meeting as she always did. Lunch at her favorite hotel in Mayfair. 1:00 p.m. to 2:30 p.m. and on no account could the meeting overrun. That didn't bother Adeline, who usually couldn't wait for the lunch to end. It wasn't as if their conversation was deep and meaningful. Her mother preferred fictional worlds to the real thing. It frustrated Adeline that her way of dealing with life was to escape it. Adeline took the opposite approach. She faced reality and dealt with it. As a result, there was no emotional connection between them and there hadn't been for years. There was no way to cross that chasm that had been created in childhood.

She knew plenty of people had dysfunctional family relationships, but that didn't change the fact that the whole thing felt unnatural. Perhaps it would have been easier to accept were it not for those early memories nestled deep in her brain. Memories of curling up next to her mother while she read to her, of picking flowers from the garden together so that they could enjoy a painting session, of being sick and feeling her mother's cool hand on her forehead. Security. She could remember when her life had felt secure, safe and certain.

But then Cassie had arrived, and everything changed.

Adeline felt something tug in her chest as she thought about her baby sister.

She pushed them away.

Some memories were best forgotten. But the one memory she'd never been able to forget was the day she'd been sent to live with her father.

Adeline's shattered life had shattered still further. It was the ultimate rejection.

Her mother no longer wanted her around. She had a new husband and a new baby. Adeline was an inconvenience. A scratch on the smooth surface of her shiny new life. A permanent reminder of a marriage that hadn't worked.

It was the moment she'd discovered that love wasn't permanent. That it could end without warning. Snatched away. Withdrawn.

She'd learned the hard way how important it was to be independent emotionally. To always hold a little of yourself back.

Adeline adored her father, but in those early years, she'd had no confidence that his love would be any more reliable and enduring than her mother's. It seemed to her, as she watched her father shrink before her eyes, that love was a game of winners and losers that no one remotely sensible would choose to play.

And then her mother's new husband, Rob Dunn, had died in an accident. The press had called it a tragedy. The love story of the decade, cut short. Little Cassie had been just three years old.

By then Adeline's father was taking art seriously, and he'd booked himself on an art retreat in the summer for two weeks. Adeline couldn't be left alone, so it was decided that she would spend a few weeks with her mother and half sister on the island of Corfu, where Catherine now lived permanently.

Adeline had protested. She'd *begged*, but in the end had been given no choice. Her father, normally so easygoing and reasonable, wouldn't flex. He'd insisted that this was a perfect time for her to get to know her little half sister, and mend fences with her mother.

But Adeline no longer trusted her mother and she'd arrived on the Greek island sullen and wary.

Her sense of isolation and rejection had deepened with each passing moment. Cassie's sunny nature appealed to everyone and won hearts wherever she went. She was a content, good-natured child who seemed untouched by the scandal and tragedy that had cast a shadow over her life. It helped that she was too young to remember, but also she had Catherine who was a loving and protective mother, a fact that made Adeline feel worse. It might have been easier to handle had she been able to concede that some women just weren't meant to be mothers, but Catherine was an excellent mother to Cassie. Which made the whole thing personal.

After that, she'd spent a few weeks every summer on Corfu with her mother and half sister, and by the time her eighteenth birthday came around, her mother was married for the third time and Adeline was old enough to decide for herself where she wanted to spend the summer. And that wasn't with her mother and Cassie. She'd spent the summers touring Europe with her college friends, or staying in her father's house on Cape Cod.

It had been years since she'd been back to Corfu, and she was dreading it.

"I can't believe she won't let you bring someone," Mia said. "What if you'd suddenly decided to get married?"

"She knows there is no chance of that. Having her as a mother put me off marriage. It's a huge decision, and one I'm not intending to make."

Mia lifted an eyebrow. "Does robot Mark know you feel that way?"

"Don't call him that."

"Sorry, but I swear I've never seen him show an emotion.

It's unnerving. Do you guys actually talk about real stuff? How well do you really know him?"

"We've been together for a year." She chose to ignore the comment about emotions. "Mark knows how I feel about marriage. He doesn't care. He's not romantic either. It's the reason we're good together. We're both rational human beings. We approach our relationship with logic and reasoning."

Mia rolled her eyes. "Be still my beating heart."

"Stop it." Adeline smiled. "What is *romance*, anyway? Some dreamy delusion that's all in the mind. Expecting another person to fulfil unspoken wishes is absurd."

"Is it?" Mia brushed a leaf from her skirt. "Isn't that what intimacy is? Knowing someone? What you're describing sounds more like a business deal than love."

"A good relationship *is* like a business deal. You should share similar beliefs, support each other's goals, encourage each other to grow. Our relationship works perfectly for us, probably because we both have realistic expectations. We both understand that emotion and impulse provide an unreliable foundation for a long-term partnership." It was the one thing she was sure of. Although she sympathized with her father's distress, it had been obvious to her for years that he and her mother were fundamentally incompatible. "This is where so many people go wrong. They expect romance and grand gestures, and when that all ends, as it inevitably does, they can't handle the everyday reality of a relationship. Mark and I know exactly what we want."

"To be bored rigid by each other?" Mia raised her hands. "Sorry, but I hate to see you settling for a relationship that's so, so…"

"So?"

"I don't know. Dull. Dry."

"I haven't settled. I've made a choice."

"You've made a choice to keep yourself safe. You've picked a man you can't possibly fall in love with. What's wrong with romance? What's wrong with grand gestures? Flowers? Chocolates? Theatre tickets?"

"If I want flowers, I'll buy them myself. If I want a spa day, I'll treat myself." It was ridiculous to suggest she'd chosen a man she couldn't fall in love with. She'd chosen Mark because he was right for her. She changed the subject. "Talking of theatre, I have tickets to see *Much Ado About Nothing* at the Globe next month if you're interested."

"Am I interested? Too right I'm interested." Mia sat upright, momentarily distracted. "Those tickets are impossible to get."

"I interviewed one of the cast for a feature. They sent me tickets."

"And you don't you want to take Mark?"

Adeline wondered why Mia kept bringing the subject back to Mark.

"He doesn't like Shakespeare, and I respect that, just as he respects the fact I find tennis boring. He doesn't expect me to join him on the courts, or in the stands as a spectator. He has his own group of friends for that."

Mia tilted her head. "As a matter of interest, what *do* you do together?"

"Plenty of things. Just yesterday he booked a sourdough baking class for us both."

"A sourdough baking class." Mia repeated the words slowly, as if she couldn't quite make sense of them. "You're making bread together. That's the saddest thing I've ever heard."

"I'm looking forward to it."

"That's the second saddest thing I've ever heard," Mia said. "Why isn't he taking you salsa dancing, or whisking you away for a spontaneous weekend in Paris or Rome?"

"We're busy people so spontaneous doesn't work for either of us. And I don't dance."

"But you *should* dance, that's my point!" Mia leaned forward. "When did you last let yourself go?"

"I don't understand the question."

Mia waved her hand. "When did you last do something rash and impulsive? Something you haven't planned six weeks in advance? When did you last lose control, sleep with a man you've just met, go to work wearing the same dress you wore to party until dawn?"

Adeline frowned. "Both those suggestions sound awful. Although if you're speaking from experience, then I'm more than happy to hear details."

Mia sighed. "Your sensibilities would explode. Do you honestly love him, Adeline?"

"What do you mean?"

"Do you love Mark? You know—counting down the hours until you see him next, heart racing when he walks through the door, don't ever want to be with anyone else because being with him makes you feel great, that kind of thing."

This, Adeline thought, *was why so many relationships didn't work.*

How could they, when people were making a life choice based on transient feelings?

"It's not his job to make me feel great. It's not his job to meet my emotional needs. I don't expect someone else to make me happy. I'm responsible for my feelings."

"You're sounding like a textbook." Mia tried again. "Is he your soulmate? Is he *the one*?"

The conversation was starting to make her uncomfortable. "I don't believe in *soulmates*. And I don't believe there's only one person for each of us. How can there be? Statistically, it would be impossible to meet *one* person destined for you. How? Where? What if the *one* person for me lives in Peru and I'm in London? And how are we supposed to identify each other? The idea of it is ridiculous. There are many people we could each be happy with."

Mia gave her a long look. "And yet you hate the fact that your mother is now on her fourth marriage."

"Just because there are many people out there you'll be compatible with, doesn't mean you always make the right choice. My mother follows impulse. She has these wild romantic notions, and thinks with her heart, not her head."

"A trait that has made her extremely successful," Mia said dryly. "I'm still not understanding what you get from Mark. Is it sex? Or do you do that yourself, too?"

Adeline felt her cheeks heat. "Our sex life is fine, thank you."

"*Fine?* Will you listen to yourself?" Mia thumped her glass down on the table. "Whatever happened to passion? What about the heart-racing-eyes-across-a-crowded-room feeling? I'm talking about the type of chemistry, and the type of sex, that isn't scheduled in on Tuesdays and Thursdays, or whenever it is that you and Mark spend time together."

"Tuesdays and Fridays," Adeline said flatly. "I have my yoga class on a Thursday and Mark has—"

"Okay enough. Stop. You're killing me." Mia tipped her head back and then sighed. "If that's a good relationship you're describing, I'm not interested. Sourdough baking? I'll stick with walking home in the early hours wearing the dress I danced in the night before."

Adeline wasn't offended. She knew that most of the population dreamed of romantic love. It was the reason the divorce rate was so high. She found it exasperating.

"Let's change the subject. We'll never agree on this one."

"Maybe. But that doesn't mean I'm not right." Mia studied

her thoughtfully. "You know what's going to happen? One day you are going to meet someone, and you are going to have to rethink everything you believe about relationships. And when that happens, you will call me and tell me about it, and I promise that I won't say *I told you so*."

"That's good to know, because the last thing I want is a smug friend." Adeline found it easy to laugh because she knew that was never going to happen. She also knew when to let a subject go. She could respect the fact that they had differing views.

But Mia didn't seem in a hurry to change the subject. "I understand that you're scared, but—"

"Scared? I'm not scared. If I was buying an apartment, I'd have a list of things that are important to me. Good light, high ceilings, a balcony because I appreciate outdoor space. A relationship is no different. The point I'm making is that it's essential to identify fundamental elements that are important to you and not deviate. If you rely on gut instinct or emotion, you guarantee a future of regret."

"You're basically saying it's better to choose safe and boring over excitement?"

It is fascinating, Adeline thought, *how human beings can look at the same facts and interpret them so differently.* "I look at my mother's romantic history and I don't see excitement. I see carnage."

"We're not talking about your mother. We're not talking about her multiple weddings, or any of those things. We're talking about *you*. You're thirty, Adeline. You should be dancing until your feet hurt, and staggering home from a bar with a sexy and deeply unsuitable man."

"That sounds like no fun at all. Also very unsafe."

Mia leaned forward. "Promise me one thing."

Adeline frowned. "That would be rash. I need to know what I'm promising."

"Let me choose your clothes for Greece. My gift to you."

"No, but thank you."

"Are you questioning my taste?"

"No." Adeline shook her head. "Your taste is flawless. I'm questioning your motives. You'll send me naked, sexy, unsuitable clothes that just aren't me, and I'll feel too self-conscious to wear them."

"I wouldn't do that. I will send you clothes that make you look your absolute best. It's what I do. I know you hate shopping."

It was true, she did hate shopping and shopping for a wedding she didn't want to attend wasn't an experience she was relishing.

"All right. I'll let you choose. Thank you. Send me the bill."

"Between samples and my discount, there won't be much of a bill. It will be my gift to you. So—" Mia lowered her sunglasses and studied Adeline "—we need swimwear, beachwear, a few floaty dresses for hot evenings, and something for a wedding. Aren't you looking forward to it at all? I'd do anything to spend a couple of weeks on a Greek Island."

"It's not the Greek Island that's the problem. It's all the emotional stuff. And I can't stop worrying about Dad. I'm used to him being uncommunicative when he's painting, but he's worse than usual. He never answers his phone."

"He's a man." Mia stretched out her legs and lifted her face to the sun. "He prefers the real world to technology. Your dad is the last person on the planet not to own a smartphone. He spends his time gazing at scenery rather than a screen. And good for him. He's an inspiration to all of us."

"I would have liked to have an actual conversation with him."

"He's probably burying himself in his art, and his teaching, so that he doesn't have to think about your mother."

"That's true." The ache in her chest was back. "He's keeping himself busy." He'd done the same thing after her mother had left. In his own way, he was as bad as her mother, preferring to escape from reality instead of accepting it.

Mia moved her chair into the shade. "What about your half sister? Is she going? Have you been in touch?"

"Not recently. And I'm sure she will be going. Cassie is the original romantic."

Guilt stabbed at her, as it always did when she thought of Cassie.

Her half sister had lost her father tragically, but her loss was so interwoven with Adeline's loss that it was impossible to unravel the strands. Her own emotions when it came to her half sister were too complicated and painful to process, so she locked them away. It wasn't as if they saw each other so it wasn't something she thought about day to day, but occasionally the memory of it all popped into her mind and darkened her day.

Mia sat up and topped up her wine. "I know you don't particularly like your sister—"

That wasn't it.

Adeline's heart started to race and her mouth was dry.

She was surprised by the strength of her emotional response, given how much time had elapsed.

"It's not that I don't like her. I don't really know her. I haven't seen her in years." And that was her fault. The truth was that she found it hard being around Cassie. "None of it was Cassie's fault."

"It wasn't your fault either." Mia gently brushed a bee away from her leg. "What's she doing now?"

"She's just finished at Oxford. I have no idea what she's doing next. We haven't been in touch." Guilt flushed through her again, sharper this time. That was her fault too.

"Maybe the two of you will finally bond."

That wasn't going to happen.

"I don't suppose she is looking forward to seeing me any more than I'm looking forward to seeing her."

Her mother and Cassie.

It was going to be a wedding to remember, for all the wrong reasons.

5

Cassie

"How about this one? Too daring for a wedding? It's slit up to the thigh, but unless there's a strong breeze, it's only going to show when I walk. I thought maybe, as it's Greece, I could get away with showing a little flesh." Cassie emerged from the changing room and gave a twirl, almost losing her balance in the process. It always surprised her just how much of an effect clothes could have on mood. Clothes changed the way a person felt about themselves, an observation she was careful to use in her writing. The character she was writing currently dressed to blend into the background. She would never have worn the dress Cassie was modeling. "I think this could be the one. It says *feminine. Carefree. Summer.*"

It didn't seem to be saying anything at all to Oliver, who was staring at his phone.

The drama of the moment lost, she snapped her fingers. "Hello? Earth to Oliver?"

He looked up, a vague expression on his face that showed his mind was elsewhere. "What?"

"Focus! You came here to help me find the perfect dress."

"That was three hours ago, Cassie. My concentration checked out a while ago."

She looked closer and realized he looked tired. Was that because Suzy was keeping him up at night? Something else?

"It's true that this has taken a little longer than I originally planned, but it's important to find exactly the right dress for this occasion, which is why I needed you here. Clothes can say so much about you as a person."

"Thirty-two dresses in three hours tells me you're indecisive. Buy it, and then we can go home and start researching antiaging techniques to erase the damage of the past few hours."

It was a relief to hear him sounding more like himself. He'd been behaving oddly since she met up with him for a late breakfast.

"Unless you take this seriously, I will be advertising for a new best friend." She removed his phone from his hand. "I need your opinion and I need it immediately, preferably before they decide I've been wearing this dress for so long I'm now its legal owner."

He sighed, studied her with exaggerated patience and then gave a slow shrug. "It looks great, but so did the thirty-one dresses you tried on before this one. A dress is a dress."

That patently wasn't true, but he was her best friend and he was here with her despite his limited interest in fashion and a dose of sleep deprivation, so she was filled with goodwill. And she had to admit it wasn't the easiest thing for him to comment on. If he'd said she looked awful, he would have hurt her feelings. She should ask a more specific question. "What was your first thought when you looked at me?"

He raised an eyebrow. "*Please let her choose this one so we can go home before the turn of the next century?* I'm hoping it's a case of thirty-second dress lucky."

"You're very unsupportive."

"How am I unsupportive? I have given you an opinion on each and every one of the thirty-two dresses you have tried on."

"Not true. You always say the same thing! You always say *you look great.*"

He spread his hands. "You do look great."

"Ha. I did not look great in that yellow abomination with the weird bow on the hip."

"I disagree. You look good in everything. But if you didn't like it, then it should be on the reject pile. You don't need my opinion, Cassie. You don't usually doubt yourself when it comes to clothes, so what's going on here?"

If he thought she looked good in everything, then maybe she didn't need his opinion, because he clearly wasn't giving this task sufficient thought.

"I don't think you're understanding the significance of this outfit. It's possible the single most important piece of clothing I've bought since I met you on that first day in Oxford when I was trying to make a good impression. I need it to be exactly right."

"I know." He removed his phone from her hand. "I know the wedding is important, Cassie. You've talked about nothing else since her letter arrived."

"The wedding is important, but that's not the reason I'm struggling to pick the right dress. I'm not worried about the wedding, exactly. I'm worried about seeing Adeline." She turned sideways and studied herself in the mirror. If you really wanted to create a good impression, then it was important to look at an outfit from all angles.

"I thought she wasn't going?"

It seemed that finally she had his full attention.

"I said I *hoped* she wasn't going, but sadly there's a gap between hope and reality and I just fell into it. I spoke to my mother last night, when you were out with Suzy. She told me Adeline will be there." She felt sick at the thought of it. "I don't know why. It's obvious that she hates weddings. Or maybe she just hates our mother's weddings. I have no understanding."

"So this—" he waved his hand at the stack of outfits she'd rejected "—this is all about your half sister?"

"My sister. I think of her as my sister. I'm not the sort of person who does things by halves." She turned again and twisted her head as far as it would go, trying to see the back. "I haven't seen her for ages. What I wear matters."

"Why?" He leaned against the wall, his phone momentarily forgotten. "You're trying to impress her. You want her to like you, even though you said you were done with all that."

"I know what I said. I'm not trying to impress her. It's more that I'm giving myself confidence." She adjusted one of the straps of the dress. "I'm walking into a stressful situation and I need to look exactly right. I want to appear calm and in control, which basically means I can't be me because we both know I lean toward the emotional in my response to things."

"*Lean toward?*" Oliver grinned. "You face-plant into emotional, Cass. You are a one-woman drama."

"Exactly. So I'll be playing a part, and it will help me play that part if I look right. I don't expect you to understand. Can you take a photograph of me from the back? I want to check I'm not bulging anywhere." She was sure that Adeline wouldn't bulge anywhere. From what Cassie knew about her, her sister was a woman who showed rigid control in all things and that included eating and exercise.

She regularly checked Adeline's social media posts, although she did so carefully so that Adeline wouldn't be aware of it. She didn't want her sister thinking she was a stalker.

Oliver took the photograph and handed her his phone. "I don't understand why you're so stressed about this and I want to understand. Talk to me."

And *that*, she thought, was why he was her best friend.

He didn't say, *You're being ridiculous*. Or, *Get a grip, Cassandra*.

He said, *I want to understand*.

"Adeline is an impressive person. Scarily impressive. I don't want to feel inferior." She checked the photograph and reassured herself that the dress looked good from all angles.

"Why would you feel inferior? You're brilliant, Cassie. Smart, funny, warm—" He stopped. "What? Why are you looking at me like that?"

Because they didn't say that kind of thing to each other. Their conversation usually consisted of banter, insults and the occasional emotional confession (on her part, at least). They were rarely polite to each other, or complimentary.

His gaze locked on hers for a moment and she felt strange and awkward for the first time in their friendship.

"You're just saying that because you know your best friend status is under review." She chose to be flippant and he hesitated and then did the same.

"That's right. Also, I hadn't finished. I was going to add that you're also late for everything, pathologically untidy, permanently hungry, can't walk through a door without banging into it and have an irritating habit of interrupting a conversation so that you can write down a line of dialogue or an idea that just came to you for your book. Sometimes I think all I am to you is a source of inspiration."

She relaxed. This felt so much more familiar and comfortable.

"Dialogue and ideas are precious," she said. "And if I don't write them down immediately, I forget them."

"Like I said—irritating. I don't understand why it matters to you so much what Adeline thinks. She's virtually a stranger."

"Maybe, but she's still my sister. And I care what she thinks because I care what everyone thinks. It's my biggest failing, although you missed that off your list."

Did he really think she was smart, warm and funny?

"Caring too much what people think will ruin your day."

"I know. I've tried not caring, but I have no idea how to do that. And something about Adeline intimidates me. She's just so *together*. Do you think I need a jacket or a wrap or something? Not that I'm worried about the weather, but maybe I need to dress this up a bit. Look a little more formal."

"A Greek island wedding doesn't say formal to me."

"No, but best to be prepared for everything and anything. Can you pass me that little pink jacket please?"

Oliver located the jacket, checked the size and handed it over. "Why does she intimidate you?"

"I don't know. Because she's competent. A bona fide adult, whereas I'm still faking it. Also she is cool, and calm, and responsible, and everything I'm not." Cassie slipped her arms into the jacket and then paused, admitting something that she never would have admitted to anyone other than Oliver. "And because deep down I feel guilty that it was my parents' love affair that broke up her parents' marriage. If that makes any sense at all."

"It doesn't." His gaze softened. "How can you possibly feel guilty about something that wasn't your fault?"

"Welcome to my world. Heels or flats?" She lifted the hem of her dress to mid-calf and then let the fabric fall and answered her own question. "Neither. Trainers."

"Trainers? You want to be able to run away from her?"

He made her smile even when she was stressed.

"No. I need to be able to concentrate, and I can't concentrate if my feet are hurting. Okay, I'm having the jacket and the dress. Decision made." She shrugged off the jacket and he took it from her, suppressing a yawn in the process.

"Why do you think she decided to go to the wedding?"

"I don't know. Probably to punish me. She wants to ruin my life the way she thinks I ruined hers. Just kidding. I suspect she tries not to think about me at all. When we spent those tortuous few weeks together every summer, she mostly ignored me. I was a mosquito, to be brushed away. An annoying wasp, without the sting."

"You're giving me drama again, Cass. Also that was over ten years ago. Your sister was a teenager."

"I know." She glanced at him. "You look wrecked. Did you and Suzy get any sleep at all last night? I'm glad it's going well."

"It's not going well. We're not seeing each other again."

"What?" An emotion shimmered through her, so fleeting that she couldn't immediately identify it. "Are you serious?"

"Yes."

"Oh, Oliver! Why didn't you say something before now?" Contrite, she forgot about the dress she was wearing and gave him a hug. "I'm sorry. Here I am going on about dresses when your heart is broken. Is your heart broken? You've been with her for two months. That's a long time for you. I'm going to keep hugging you until you tell me to let go." She kept her arms locked around him and felt the firm pressure of his body against hers. He was broad-shouldered and solid, and she breathed in the familiar scent of him. Oliver. Her best friend. She tightened her hold on him. "I can't bear it. I can't bear the thought of you being unhappy."

"I'm fine." His voice sounded scratchy. "My heart is fine. And I didn't say anything because I don't want to talk about it. It's—complicated. You can let go now." He eased away, avoiding her gaze.

She knew he was hurting. She knew *him*. Whenever Oliver was processing something big, he withdrew a little, even from her. Her way of dealing with problems was to talk about them, but he preferred to work things through internally. But he always told her eventually. When his parents had announced they were divorcing after thirty years of marriage, Oliver had knocked on her door at three in the morning. When his sister had been rushed to hospital with suspected appendicitis, they'd spent all night drinking tea together in a cold hospital corridor.

He had that same look on his face now. And she hadn't noticed because she'd been babbling on about stupid dresses.

"Well, all I can say is that Suzy can't be as smart as everyone says she is if she broke up with you." Feeling fiercely protective, Cassie resisted the temptation to grab his phone and immediately message her unfiltered thoughts to Suzy. "If you unzip me, I'll buy it and we can get out of here and go and drown our sorrows in coffee. We can binge on carbs. Buy two of those cakes from that bakery on Broad Street that are covered in sugar, stuffed with cream and bigger than your head." She turned her back and lifted her hair.

There was a brief pause and then she felt his hands on the zip, drawing it down.

She felt the fabric of the dress loosen around her and

grabbed it. "Great. Thanks. I'll get changed. Talk to me through the door. Why did she break up with you? What excuse did she use?"

"She didn't break up with me," he said. "I broke up with her."

"Oh." That, she hadn't expected. She slid out of the dress, put it back on the hanger and quickly pulled on her jeans and shirt. "Why? You need to give me feedback since I was the one who picked her out on that dating app. I thought she had potential, not that you can tell much from a photograph. But she had good teeth. You can tell a lot about a person from their teeth. That's assuming those were actually her teeth in the photo. Were they?" She grabbed the dress and opened the door.

Oliver was looking tense. "You think she was wearing someone else's teeth?"

"Don't be gross. I'm talking about Photoshop."

"They were her teeth. But I'm still not seeing her again."

"Why not?" She handed him the dress and the jacket while she bent to tie her laces. "Was it because she didn't make you laugh? That could be because you have a strange sense of humor. I've said it a million times." She straightened and smiled, expecting him to be smiling too. He wasn't.

"There was nothing wrong with her." His voice sounded strange. Strained.

"But she wasn't *the one*. I get it. If you need ages to think it over, then it isn't right." She picked up her bag and draped the clothes over her arm. "How many couples do you know who date for ten years and then *wham*, one of them meets someone else and gets married in a month."

"I don't know anyone like that." He grabbed the jacket from her before it could slide to the floor.

"Neither do I, but I've heard plenty of stories." She pulled out her credit card. "And it proves the very obvious point, that if you've known someone for years and still haven't got it together, then it isn't right. Something is missing."

"Maybe. Or maybe there are other reasons. Maybe it takes a while for some people to figure out how they really feel about each other."

"Excuses. For my parents, it was instantaneous. They took one look at each other and just knew."

Oliver's gaze was steady. "How?"

"I don't know. Not everything can be easily explained. Love is a feeling that defies logic." Which was probably why Adeline wasn't a fan of weddings and was still resolutely single. From the little she knew, her sister wasn't big on feelings and emotions. "Come on. I'll max out my credit card with these clothes, and then we'll overdose on sugar." She was going to focus on cheering up Oliver and that would stop her thinking about her sister.

But Oliver was staring at his phone again.

She waited. "Now what? Has she messaged you? Don't reply. Be strong. Delete her from your contacts so that you don't drunk text her by accident."

"She hasn't messaged me." He glanced up. "Did you write to your sister?"

"No. Why would I write to my sister? Oh—" She stopped, horrified. "You mean did I write to Dr. Swift?" She felt her face heat. "Maybe. I mean, yes. I did it that evening when you were at the movies with Suzy. Why?"

"Because she's answered your letter."

"Please tell me you're kidding." Cassie snatched his phone. "No, no, no! That isn't possible."

"Why isn't it possible?"

"Because I read somewhere that she gets hundreds, or maybe it was even thousands of letters and emails," Cassie moaned, "and mine should have gone unnoticed." Why was she so impulsive? Why had she pressed Send? She should have written the email and filed it in drafts. That was what a normal person would have done.

"If you wanted to go unnoticed, why did you send it?"

"Because it was the Saturday night my mother rang to say my sister was coming to the wedding and the whole thing made me stressed and anxious. Also, I may have had one or two very large glasses of that Pinot Noir we'd opened together the night before."

Oliver raised an eyebrow. "You told me you knocked the bottle over."

"I lied. I didn't want you to judge me. Anyway, it lowered my natural inhibitions."

"You have inhibitions? Since when?"

"Stop. This is terrible. What if she guesses it's me? Oh, this is mortifying. I can't possibly risk going to the wedding now and I've just spent hours choosing a dress."

"Whoa, slow down. You're doing that writer thing of seeing drama and catastrophe in every situation." Oliver was calm. "If she receives hundreds and thousands of letters, she's hardly going to guess it's from you, is she?"

"*You* guessed."

"Yes, but I know you. She doesn't. And it's not as if you put your real name on it. The letter you sent was anonymous."

"Yes." Cassie scanned the phone. There it was. The question she'd sent in. What had possessed her?

She read it aloud.

Dear Dr. Swift, my sister and I are estranged and lately I'm finding that harder and harder to cope with. When I was young, I tried on many occasions to bridge the gap but she made it clear she wants to live her life without me in it. Perhaps I should let her do that, but somehow I can't let it go. It feels wrong. I don't think I'm a bad person and I don't understand why she is behaving this way. Our mother is getting married again this summer and we will be meeting up at the wedding. Should I try once again to heal the rift between us, or should I give up and accept that family ties can indeed be broken?

Yours truly,
Rejected.

Cassie felt her whole body flush with panic. Sending it had been an impulsive, reckless thing to do, but at the time she'd been sad and frustrated and hadn't thought for a moment that Adeline would actually choose to answer her letter. Oliver was right. She received hundreds of letters, but for some reason she'd chosen Cassie's. Why?

Had she somehow guessed it was from Cassie? Or was it a subject close to her sister's own heart?

No, that was definitely over thinking things.

"What does she say? Read her answer," Oliver said. "I want to hear it."

She was almost too afraid to look. Nervous, she read Adeline's response aloud.

Dear Rejected, being estranged from a sibling is a particularly painful loss. Not only do you miss the individual, but the reality often jars with our vision of what a blood relationship should be. You have two choices. Accept things the way they are, or work to change them.

Cassie glanced up. "That's obvious. What I want to know is *how* to change it."

"Keep reading."

Cassie sighed.

Your sister may be hurting too. She may have her own reasons for keeping her distance. All relationships change over time, but it can be helpful to try to analyze when it went wrong. What happened?

"I know what happened," Cassie said. "I was born. Enough said."

Oliver rolled his eyes. "Read her answer!"

"I'm reading. 'Have you ever addressed the problem directly with your sibling?'" Cassie glanced up again. "What am I supposed to say? I'm sorry my dad fell in love with your mum and she loved him back? I'm sorry that you are so unforgiving and resentful. And, by the way, it was two decades ago so could you get over it already? Also, I don't think she's hurting." She handed the phone back to him. "I'm going to stop reading her column. That's it."

"Good plan. And are you sure that's the dress you want? It's going to make you feel okay?"

"Yes." She handed it to the assistant, along with the jacket and her credit card.

It wasn't exactly true. Her sister was going to the wedding, and no dress in the world was going to make her feel okay about that.

6

Catherine

Andrew joined her on the terrace where she'd been sipping strong Greek coffee and trying to keep herself calm. Her heart pounded as she looked at his face. "Well?"

He sat down opposite her and gave her a look she couldn't interpret. "All those late nights and early mornings in your office. Those times you refused to discuss your book, even though you always talk about your book. This is what you've been keeping from me?"

"Yes." She felt raw and vulnerable. People didn't understand how terrifying it was offering up creative work for another person's judgment. Even now, after so many successes, having proved herself, she was still terrified when she sent her latest book to her editor. Sometimes she had to stare at the books she'd already written, lined up neatly on her shelves, to remind herself that she'd done it before and could do it again. "Did you hate it?"

"Hate it? No. It's brilliant. I couldn't stop reading."

The air left her lungs in a whoosh.

"Really?"

"Yes." He put the pages down on the table. "This is scary stuff, Catherine. Where the hell did it come from?"

"I don't know. My brain." She felt her mood lift and soar, like a bird catching a thermal. "You were scared when you read it?"

"Terrified. I had no idea you had this inside you. That scene at the beginning where he's locked in that room, and he hears her outside, the tap, tap of her stilettos on the stairs to the cellar. The fact that he knows she's coming... I felt his fear..."

"I was tired of the woman always being the victim."

Andrew wiped his brow. "I got that message."

"It's always a frightened woman trapped in the basement, never a man, so I thought..."

"I read what you thought. That part where he starts screaming and she..." He shuddered, let out a breath and stared out to sea. "I need sunlight and real life for five minutes to bring me back to reality. Talk about something boring and normal, I beg you. What we're eating for dinner. The weather."

She was delighted by his reaction. "The book unsettled you."

"Unsettled?" He gave a hollow laugh. "It creeped me out, Catherine. I'm afraid to ever be alone in a room with you again."

She felt a rush of triumph, but her creative mind immediately smacked that down. Flattering though it was that he'd enjoyed it, his opinion wasn't the one that mattered. And would he tell her the truth anyway? Men said things they didn't mean all the time. And women, *women like her*, believed them. Andrew was about to marry her. He wouldn't want to hurt her feelings. "You would never tell me if you hated it."

His gaze met hers. He knew what she was thinking. "I would tell you. Honesty, remember? That's what we agreed. And it's brilliant. Brutal, but brilliant." He reached for the coffee she'd poured him and then hesitated. "But it's not a Catherine Swift."

"I know."

Catherine Swift was about uplifting fiction and happy endings. Maybe Catherine Swift the writer was dead. Except that she couldn't be dead, because Catherine Swift was her real name.

She wished now that she'd used a pseudonym at the start of her career. It would have made it so much easier to reinvent herself. It also would have avoided awkward moments when she handed over her credit card in stores and people asked if she was *the* Catherine Swift. Occasionally she said, *No, I'm the other one*, and left while they were still figuring that out.

"Have you shown it to Daphne?"

"Not yet." She had no idea what her agent would say. She'd spent decades building a dedicated following of readers who loved her books. Her readers weren't going to love this book. They rushed to bookstores to pick up the latest Catherine Swift because they knew she would give them what they wanted, and she'd never let them down. Her books were guaranteed to deliver a strong heroine, a strong message and a happy ending. They could bite their nails at the emotional tension, laugh and cry with the heroine, safe in the knowledge that when they finally closed the book, they would be leaving the heroine in a good place. They would be uplifted and maybe a little inspired.

This book had a strong heroine, and a strong message—

when a man manipulates and controls you, consider murder as an option—but there was no laughter, and definitely no happy ending, although the heroine was alive at the end, which was more than could be said for most crime fiction. She considered that a nod to her former writing self.

"How long have you been working on this? And why didn't you tell me?"

"I didn't know that I could do it." People died in her books, of course. But her characters didn't cause each other's death. When they picked up a kitchen knife they were likely to chop an onion, not contemplate murder. Her characters had issues, but they weren't psychopaths. This was a departure for her.

"I'm amazed that you found time. You already have a full schedule delivering the books contracted to your publisher."

"I was inspired. But I've never written anything like this before. I've never killed anyone." She didn't meet his eyes, afraid that he might see something she didn't want him to see. "It was easier than I thought."

"Now you're really scaring me." But this time he was smiling as he reached across and took her hand. "You're magnificent. I'm in awe of your talent. I firmly believe that there is nothing you can't do, Catherine Swift."

It wasn't true—she couldn't sing, she'd never been able to run fast, she couldn't catch a ball—but the fact that he believed in her meant a great deal because, despite everything, she'd never been able to believe in herself.

"You don't think I'm foolish?"

"To write something different? No, of course not."

"I can't write both. I don't have time." She paused. "And I wouldn't want to. I think I'm done with romance."

"So what you're saying is that you intend to move to a life of crime." He grinned. "That could be fun. As long as you're doing it for the right reasons."

"What do you mean by that?"

"I know that it upset you not hitting number one."

She wasn't going to deny it. And she wasn't going to pretend she'd moved on and reached a point of acceptance. It stung. She still woke up at night and thought about it. *Number three.* The insecurity inside her was a monster. She tried to lock it away. Tried to ignore it. But it lurked there, always ready to pounce.

"The problem with always being number one," she said, "is that there is only ever one direction you can go."

"And I know it matters to you, but I wish you could separate it from who you are. You're not your book sales, Catherine. You are not your acceptances or your rejections. You are not your reviews, or your awards. Those are all just things going on around you. You are not your writing."

It wasn't true. Not the part about sales, acceptances, rejections and reviews. That was all true (although he made it sound as if those were easy to dismiss and they certainly weren't). But her writing? She *was* her writing, or rather her writing was part of her. As much a part of her as her hair, or her nose. Writing was her way of interpreting the world, of making sense of things.

But she hadn't been drawn to crime because of her dwindling sales; she'd been drawn for a different reason. Lately, she'd questioned her plots. Yes, she gave her characters challenges, but was she shortchanging women? Was she giving the impression that everything would always be all right in the end? Because that wasn't the case. Or maybe it was sometimes, but usually life was far messier. Life was unfair, and often it stayed unfair. She'd decided that the quality a person really needed was the ability to live comfortably alongside uncertainty, because life was full of uncertainty. To celebrate the good even in the presence of the bad. To find comfort in small things when they were overwhelmed by the big stuff.

She'd found it harder and harder to give her readers that simple happy ending they expected. Real life didn't come with the ends tied in a neat bow.

So with this book she'd looked at a different side of life. A darker side, but one no less valid. She'd done her research. She'd read several murder cases that had kept her up at night for weeks, then used those as inspiration for her story.

"I'm going to send it to Daphne and see what she says."

She knew what Daphne would say. Daphne would tell her to stick with what she knew. Daphne would tell her it was fine to be number three. She'd remind Catherine that some women found a happy ending in their lives, and there was no reason to focus on the ones who didn't.

But Catherine was ready for something different. She increasingly wanted to write a story for all the women out there whose lives didn't end with their future tied up in a neat bow.

"A new direction to your career, and a wedding." Andrew squeezed her hand. "This really is a fresh start."

Not really, Catherine thought. You never really started fresh, because whatever you did, you still had to drag the past along with you.

"I can't believe the wedding is only two weeks away. And the girls are arriving in a few days."

"I know." Andrew watched as a tiny bird swooped in and skimmed along the surface of the swimming pool. "You're sure you don't want to tell them about me before they arrive?"

"Not until they're on the island. Some things are better handled face-to-face."

He reached across and took her hand. "Why are you so afraid to tell them?"

"I'm not afraid. I think it's fair to say that the girls are going to love you." She leaned across to kiss him. It was going to be fine.

Was it going to be fine? She hoped so.

Andrew didn't seem convinced. "They can still leave, you know."

"Cassie wouldn't leave." She thought about her youngest daughter, always so warm and loving and supportive. *You're the best mother on the planet. I love you.*

"But you think Adeline might?"

Adeline? *You're the worst mother on the planet. I hate you.*

"I think that once she has met you, she'll be thrilled."

She hoped she was right. Hoped that this marriage was going to change everything for the better. That it would finally bring her family together.

It was what she wanted more than anything. Even more than she wanted a reboot of her career.

She wanted to mend things with Adeline.

7

Adeline

Adeline layered her neatly folded clothes into the suitcase. Dread was curled in a tight ball in her stomach. "I don't want to do this."

Mark glanced up from his phone, impatient. "Then why are you doing it?"

His reply upset her, possibly because she'd been asking herself the same question. "A little sympathy would be nice."

"Sympathy for what?" Mark looked genuinely puzzled. "I don't understand why you'd expect sympathy for something you're inflicting on yourself. You've made a choice. If you don't want to go, then make a different choice. Tell her no. You need to establish boundaries, Adeline. It's pretty simple."

It wasn't simple at all, and it frustrated her that he couldn't see that.

She didn't rely on him emotionally—she didn't rely on

anyone emotionally—but that didn't mean she wouldn't have welcomed a trace of empathy.

"She's my mother."

"So? There's no rule that says you have to spend time with any particular person, relative or friend. I broke off contact with my parents when I was eighteen, you know that. I don't return their calls and I don't open their Christmas cards." He had cut family from his life, like a surgeon excising a diseased body part.

And she had no idea why.

Mia's words popped into her head.

How well do you really know him?

That comment played on her mind. "You've never really talked to me about what happened."

"And I don't intend to."

"But—"

"It's in the past, Adeline." He didn't disguise his impatience. "The past has no relevance to the present. It's like thinking about an apartment you no longer live in. What's the point? Family or not, people have to earn a place in your life. They have to be worth the investment of time that goes into maintaining a relationship."

He made it sound as if he were buying stocks and bonds.

She imagined him studying a graph depicting his investment in their relationship, deciding if he should spread his risk.

"Am I worth the investment?"

"Of course. I wouldn't be here if I didn't think you were." He frowned and lowered his phone. "You're behaving strangely."

Perhaps she wasn't being fair on him, expecting him to understand when she hadn't given him the facts. "It goes back to my childhood…"

"You don't need to explain." He put his phone back in his pocket. "As I said, the past has no relevance to the present. And I'm sure you're aware of this, Adeline, but focusing on something that happened in your childhood when you're thirty isn't exactly demonstrating emotionally healthy behavior."

In other words, he didn't want her to explain. He wasn't interested. He didn't want to hear it.

The past has no relevance to the present.

As a psychologist, she knew that wasn't true. She also knew that examining the past could indeed be emotionally healthy behavior, but she didn't have the energy to argue with him. And maybe she wasn't being entirely fair to judge him. They'd both agreed that they weren't going to bring their past trauma into their current relationship, so she could hardly blame him now for not wanting to change those parameters. This was what she wanted. This was the relationship she was comfortable with.

Trying to move on, Adeline reached for the large box that had arrived that morning and tucked it into her suitcase.

Mark was watching her, wary, as if he wasn't sure what she'd say next. "What's that?"

"A gift from Mia. Clothes for my trip. It arrived this morning."

He stared at it. "And you're not even going to open the box and take a look?"

"She made me promise not to. I'm opening it when I get to Greece. It's a surprise."

"Is that sensible? Knowing Mia, I would have thought you'd want to check what she's sent you."

"What do you mean by that?" Adeline felt an immediate need to defend her friend. "She has a great sense of style." She knew that Mark didn't like Mia any more than Mia liked

Mark. *He's a robot, Adeline.* But that didn't worry her unduly, although occasionally she did find herself wishing that the two people she liked most were a little more tolerant of each other. She reminded herself that it didn't matter if her friend liked her boyfriend. It only mattered that *she* liked him.

"Style is subjective. Her appearance is a bit flamboyant and attention-seeking for my taste, but I can see she might appeal to some." Mark saw her expression change and sighed. "And now I've offended you, and that wasn't my intention. I was just pointing out that you and Mia don't have the same taste. You're more conservative than she is, thank goodness, so it might be wise to check what she has packed for you."

Was she conservative?

Was *conservative* another word for boring? And why was he relieved? Did he want her to be boring?

She glanced at herself in the mirror. The weather was overcast and dismal and she'd chosen to wear a tailored white shirt over jeans. Her hair was fastened in a neat twist at the back of her neck. She had to admit her look wasn't exciting. No one was going to stop her in the street and say *I love your dress*, as a woman had said to Mia last time the two of them had been out together. Everything about her said "safe." Some women stood out, and some blended. She blended.

And what was wrong with that? That was the way she wanted it.

She glanced at the box in her case. Maybe Mark was right. Maybe she should open it. At least then she'd know if she needed to supplement her wardrobe.

"If you don't check," Mark said, "you'll find yourself in Greece with nothing to wear that isn't revealing or borderline indecent."

There was every chance that he could be right, but still his comments were starting to irritate and upset her. He seemed oblivious to the fact that there was so much more to this than simply deciding what to pack. This wasn't a vacation. It wasn't a trip she was looking forward to. She was dreading it. He knew she was dreading it, so why couldn't he just say *poor you, this must be hard?* Or maybe give her a comforting hug and assure her everything was going to be fine.

"I'm not a child, Mark. I can make my own wardrobe decisions." When had he become so judgmental? Perhaps he'd always been that way and she hadn't noticed.

Or maybe something else was behind his words.

She was about to spend two weeks on a Greek island in summer, and he wasn't coming with her.

Maybe that was bothering him but he didn't like to say so because of the boundaries they'd set.

She closed the case and smiled at him. "Do you mind me going?"

"Why would I mind?"

"Because time off is precious, and we could be spending those two weeks together. I could ask my mother if you could join me." She wasn't sure why she'd said that. Did she even want him to join her? She couldn't picture Mark in Greece.

It was difficult to know which of them was more startled by the question.

He was looking at her as if she'd just asked him to jump from an aircraft without a parachute. "Why would you do that? Why would I join you?"

"Because it's Greece, and Corfu is a special place." It was true that the island stirred up uncomfortable feelings and memories for her, but that didn't mean she couldn't acknowledge its beauty. "We could spend the time relaxing. Swimming. Reading on the beach."

He pulled a face. "Beach holidays aren't my thing. You know I prefer city breaks. Museums. Galleries. Something more cerebral. It's what you enjoy too, which is another reason I don't understand why you're doing this. You're not a beach person either."

She thought back to her childhood. Once, she'd been a beach person. There had been nothing she'd loved more than swimming in the sea.

She frowned slightly. "I thought maybe it would be something fun to do together. We've both been so busy lately."

"Two weeks is a long time, and we don't need to live in each other's pockets, Adeline. I thought we both agreed on that. It's healthy to have separate lives."

Was it? Wasn't the whole point of a relationship the fact that your lives were woven together?

She tried to block out those thoughts. Normally, she wouldn't even have been asking herself this question, so why was she doing it now? Because of her mother. Ever since the letter had arrived inviting her to the wedding, she'd been unsettled.

But still—was Mark saying that two weeks was a long time for a beach holiday, or that he wouldn't be able to stand two weeks with her? "This is a family wedding." She cleared her throat. "My family. And I thought maybe it was time you…"

"Time I what? Why would I go to your family wedding? I don't even know why *you're* going. Your relationship with your mother is dysfunctional to say the least, and I don't understand why you would choose to continue it. You're a mature, evolved young woman. You've studied human behavior, and yet you still allow her to manipulate you."

His words were like a slap.

Had she really been hoping for comfort?

This conversation was making her feel worse, not better. "I'm not allowing her to manipulate me."

"No? Then why are you flying to Corfu, and spending two

weeks with people who cause you stress? Why do you even bother maintaining a relationship with your mother when it's so difficult? The adult thing to do would be to cut ties."

Was that the adult thing to do? Or would the adult thing be to drop hostilities and accept that all families came with complications?

"That would upset my father."

"He's an adult too. He shouldn't be using guilt as a lever."

"It's not that simple…"

"It *could* be that simple, Adeline." He made an impatient gesture. "You're the one who makes it complicated by creating an image in your head that doesn't match reality. I suppose that's to be expected, given who your mother is."

"Excuse me? What's that supposed to mean?" She had no idea how, or why, this conversation had deteriorated so rapidly.

"Do I need to spell it out? Your mother lives in a fictional world," he said. "She spins stories about romance. You do the same about family. Admit it, deep down you keep hoping she is going to turn into the sort of mother you'd like to have. The sort you read about in books. The type of books she writes."

Adeline swallowed. She didn't do that. Did she? Maybe she did.

"Why are you being like this?"

"Like what? We've always been honest. *You've* always been honest about everything except this. For some reason I haven't been able to figure out, you manage to lie to yourself about your family. You're spinning a fantasy, Adeline, if you're expecting this wedding to be anything other than stressful. And maybe you can lie to yourself, but don't expect me to lie to you because I won't do that."

"Enough. Stop." The back of her neck was sweating. Her

apartment suddenly felt airless and oppressive. "I'm finding this conversation upsetting and hurtful. I wanted a little comfort. A hug. Not a lecture."

"You're being oversensitive. It happens every time your mother comes up in conversation." He sighed. "But I agree we should stop. You're unsettled, which I understand, and that makes you needy, which isn't like you."

"Needy?" She licked her lips. "You think I'm needy?"

"Wanting me to comfort you for a decision that was entirely yours? Inviting me to the wedding because you need moral support? Asking if I mind you going? I understand what's going on here. You want the reassurance of a stable relationship because right now you're reverting to childhood. You're like a child on her first day in the playground. You're feeling unsettled, but this whole thing was your choice, Adeline. You're the one who decided to put yourself through this." He glanced at his watch. "We should leave. The table is booked for seven thirty."

Reverting to childhood? Was that really what he thought was happening here?

He didn't understand her at all. Worse, he had no interest in understanding her.

"I'm not hungry." She sat down on the edge of the bed and he looked at her in exasperation.

"Do you have any idea how hard it was to get this reservation? I booked the table two months ago. There's a waiting list. The chef makes the best noodles in London."

"Go without me."

"Adeline—" He seemed about to say something else and then took a deep breath. "Fine. I'll take someone else, but you need to have a long hard think about what you really want in life. And if you're going to persist with all this toxic family stuff, then I want no part of it."

She didn't know what she wanted, but she knew she didn't want noodles.

And right now, she didn't want Mark.

"Fine," she said. "Let's end it. Enjoy your noodles."

He paused. "You're being hysterical…"

"No, I'm not."

"You don't know what you want right now."

She did know.

She no longer wanted to be with Mark, and she wanted this wedding to be behind her.

Part Two

8

Cassie

"Hi, Adeline, great to see you. How are things?" Cassie practiced her speech as she drove from the villa to collect her sister from the airport. She knew the road well, having spent so much of her childhood living here. It was as familiar to her as the cobbled streets of Oxford. "No, I can't say that. She's not likely to tell me how things are because this is my sister, and my sister isn't exactly the confessional type. Her answer will be *fine* and then we'll be stuck with awkward silence. Nightmare." She pressed her foot to the floor and the little Jeep sped up the steep hill. "I could say *hi, how was your flight?*" She braked and shifted gears as she approached a hairpin bend. "But the answer to that could also be *fine*. Whichever way I approach this, I'm heading for the most awkward car journey of my life. Maybe I should just play loud music. Fill the silence that way."

A car sped past her, narrowly missing her wing mirror. A local, no doubt, because only the locals drove like that. Tourists were more cautious, wary of the narrow roads and the vertiginous drops. Cassie yelled something in Greek and then grinned. It felt good to be home and for Cassie, the island of Corfu was definitely home.

Her mother had purchased the villa more than two decades ago, and it was all thanks to a book called *Summer Star.* That particular book had been a game changer and catapulted her to the top of the bestseller lists. A major movie deal had followed and the release of the movie, which broke box office records, had driven another surge in book sales. Catherine Swift always said that *Summer Star* was the book that had changed her life, so perhaps it wasn't surprising that when she found the perfect villa on the stunningly beautiful north coast of Corfu, she'd called it *Summer Star.*

It was on the island of Corfu that Catherine had met Rob Dunn and fallen in love.

Cassie smiled as she thought about it.

It was the ultimate love story, and it turned out she wasn't the only one who thought so because a week earlier Cassie finally got the call she'd never thought would come. *We love your book.*

An agent loved her book! Not just *an* agent, but *her* agent, because she was now officially represented by Madeleine Ellwood. *The* Madeleine Ellwood. Cassie still couldn't believe it. She hadn't stopped grinning for the past week. And of course that still didn't mean that a publisher would actually buy her book, but Madeleine loved what she'd written (apparently, she'd cried! Actually cried at Cassie's book), didn't want to make any changes and for now that was enough. Cassie had signed a contract with the agency, and the next step was for Madeleine to approach publishers. She'd seemed particularly interested in the fact that the story had been inspired by Cassie's parents' relationship. *Would Cassie be prepared to talk about that? The human angle will make for great publicity.*

There was nothing Cassie loved more than talking about her parents' love story to anyone who would listen, so she was more than happy to agree to that.

She was trying not to get too excited. Just because Madeleine loved her book, didn't mean that a publishing house would and Madeleine had warned her that the process could take some time because editors everywhere were overworked, burned out and exhausted. But she felt Cassie's book was timely. Her story didn't have a happy ending of course, but it did have a hopeful ending and Madeleine had loved the fact that it was set on Corfu. It was obvious that Cassie knew it well. She'd praised the sense of place.

The setting had been easy for Cassie to handle because she'd virtually grown up on the island. Her first steps had been taken on the soft sand below the villa, she'd learned to swim in the ocean, attended the local school and learned Greek alongside English.

The road climbed upward and at the viewpoint at the top she pulled over and jumped out of the Jeep.

She had time to kill, and it was better to stop here for a few minutes and enjoy the fabulous view, than sit in the sweltering, dusty airport car park.

The sun was hot and she raised her face to it for a moment, enjoying the warmth on her skin. Then she grabbed a bottle of water from her bag and strolled to the edge of the road, which had one of the best viewpoints on the island. The land fell away steeply, deep green and verdant. Slim cyprus trees jutted up from dense olive groves and beyond that the sea, a sheet of endless sparkling blue stretching far into the distance.

It was one of her favorite spots and whether she was driving to the airport or the supermarket, she always stopped here.

She took a mouthful of water and then checked her phone. It seemed Adeline's flight was on time, which was more than hers had been. Her flight from London the day before had been delayed by several hours. By the time she'd finally landed in Corfu, it had been late afternoon.

She slid her phone back into the pocket of her shorts, thinking back to her arrival the day before.

Her mother had been waiting for her, arms extended and Cassie had walked right into them. This, for her, was home. She loved everything about it; the scents, the endless blue sky, the feel of the hot sun burning her skin, the intense flavors of the food and the relaxed pace of life. She had nothing but happy memories of living here with her mother. She was looking forward to spending time together, although maybe the preparations for the wedding would get in the way of their usual cozy chats. Certainly, there had been nothing cozy about the conversation in the car the day before.

She frowned as she thought about it.

As usual, her mother had driven too fast, occasionally taking both hands off the wheel to gesture to another driver or add emphasis to a point she was making. Cassie, who was only ever a nervous passenger when she was in a vehicle driven by her mother, had offered to drive but her mother wouldn't hear of it. *She'd just come off a flight! She must be tired! Her mother wanted to spoil her!*

So Cassie had clutched at the seat, breathed and hoped they'd both live long enough to go ahead with the wedding. She really should have been used to it after all these years. She'd lost count of the times her mother had suddenly slammed on the breaks and done an emergency stop, risking whiplash for her passengers. *I've had an idea for my book,* she'd say, ignoring the abuse from other drivers and franti-cally scrabbling for a pen and something to write on. Cassie had taken to stowing a pen and pad in the car, and also in her bag just in case. She'd grown up knowing that ideas should be treasured and immediately committed to paper in case they slid away and were lost, something she understood now that she was a writer herself.

But this time her mother hadn't slammed the breaks to cap-ture an idea, or talked about her current book—which was unusual—but instead had fired Cassie with questions, want-ing to know how she was doing and what she had planned. It was almost as if she didn't want to talk about herself.

Cassie had almost confessed that she'd got an agent (every time she thought about it, she started grinning) but some-thing had stopped her. What if Madeleine didn't manage to sell the book? Also, this was her mother's celebration, and she didn't want to be selfish and hijack it with her news.

So instead, she'd talked a little about the café and about Oliver, and then tried asking her mother about the man she was marrying. It had seemed like a reasonable question, but her mother had been evasive. All she would say was that she was sure Adeline and Cassie were going to love him.

Cassie was intrigued and a little amused by the secrecy.

Her mother had seemed nervous, but she couldn't figure out why. This was her home, and she was about to marry the man she loved. Why would she be nervous? It was al-most as if she was afraid Cassie wouldn't approve, but she couldn't possibly think that. Cassie had never fallen out with her mother about anything. She was totally nonjudgmental. She adored her mother and respected all her decisions. All she wanted was for her mother to be happy. If her mother was in love again, then that was *great*. She had less faith in

Adeline's ability to accept a new male presence in their lives gracefully and warmly.

Maybe that was the part that was making her mother nervous. Adeline.

For the millionth time Cassie thought how much easier it would have been for everyone if her sister had decided not to come, and then felt guilty for thinking that. Adeline was family. She deserved to be here. She *should* be here. But she should only be here if she was capable of celebrating their mother's happiness. Was she? Cassie had no idea, but whatever happened she would make it work. She planned on being enthusiastic enough for both of them. She had experience compensating for Adeline at her mother's weddings—she'd done it at the last one. She'd cheered and thrown her bridesmaid bouquet with such gusto that she almost knocked a guest unconscious.

Thinking of Adeline made her check the time again.

Deciding she couldn't put the moment off any longer, she slid back into the car and tucked her bottle of water back into her bag.

She headed down the mountain, the wind blowing her hair and the sun burning her face.

The next hour or so would be tense, being trapped in the car with her sister, but she had the evening to look forward to. Dinner on the terrace. A chance to *finally* meet the man her mother would be marrying. It was going to be great.

As she approached Corfu Town, the traffic grew heavier and the scenery changed from rural to urban. She turned onto the main road and saw the ocean and the harbor where ferries docked to take travelers on to other islands. This was where the tourists gathered. They spilled from cruise ships and ferries with their guidebooks, beach bags and fat tubes of sunscreen. They visited the Old Fortress, and congregated in the shady cafés that clustered around the Spianada, the big open square.

Cassie loved the Old Town, with its labyrinth of narrow sunbaked streets. Balconies clung to old buildings that blended together in shades of coffee, dusky pink and butter yellow, their walls adorned with the bright tangle of bougainvillea. A walk revealed hidden gardens, a historic church, a pretty square where locals gathered and swallows swooped from their nests in the rooftops. Even now, after years of exploring, she would stumble on a restaurant that she hadn't known existed, drawn by the scents of wild herbs and garlic sizzled in olive oil.

Trying not to think of all the more entertaining things she could be doing, Cassie took a shortcut and pulled over to grab a loaf of fresh crusty bread from her favorite bakery. Normally, she would have stopped and enjoyed a coffee at one of the shady tables, or maybe an ice cream. It would have been a race to eat it before it melted and dripped chocolate and vanilla over her fingers. But today she was too tense to allow herself either of those indulgences.

She arrived at the airport twenty minutes after Adeline's flight had landed, and saw her sister immediately. It wasn't hard to spot her. She was wearing a light-colored suit, teamed with a gleaming white shirt. Her hair was the color of polished oak and was pulled back and secured tightly at the back of her head. She looked as if she were ready to chair a board meeting or defend a client in court, not head to a beach villa. Surrounded by tourists dressed in an array of colorful shorts and sundresses that only ever saw the light of day during a summer vacation, she stood out like a zebra in a cornfield. But what really set her apart was the way she held herself. Whilst everyone around her was smiling and excited to be on the island, Adeline had the slightly martyred air of a prisoner about to be locked up for a crime she hadn't committed. Any doubts Cassie might have had about her desire to be here vanished instantly.

She was willing to lay bets that her sister would rather have been anywhere else.

How on earth had she cleared immigration so quickly? She'd probably frightened the officials with her ruthless efficiency.

Cassie sighed, closed the windows and switched on the air-conditioning. Her sister wasn't going to appreciate open windows and a breeze trying to tug at her perfect hair.

Please don't let this be as bad as I think it's going to be, she thought and leaned on her horn to attract her sister's attention.

Adeline turned her head (even that was a graceful movement), saw Cassie and headed toward the car with long athletic strides.

Now for the truly awkward part. How should she greet her? She was a hugger, but Adeline was as cuddly as a cactus. Shake hands? No, they were sisters, not business partners. Cassie refused to stoop that low.

She was still pondering her options when the driver she was currently blocking leaned out of his window and yelled at her in Greek, leaving her no choice but to act. With a wave of apology, Cassie leaped out and grabbed her sister's suitcase. "Hi there, we need to move quickly before the man behind us gives himself a heart attack. How was your flight? At least you're on time, which is more than I was." She was babbling. She needed to stop babbling.

"Thank you for coming to meet me." Adeline was scrupulously polite, but as distant as ever. It was as if there were a wall between her and the world.

"Of course. It's my pleasure." She didn't think it was going to be much of a pleasure, but she wasn't ready to give up hope.

Adeline removed her jacket and slid into the passenger seat. If she was stressed by this encounter, then there were no visible signs of it.

Cassie felt a stab of envy. She aspired to be that calm about everything, to meet the challenges of life with serene confidence (she also aspired to being able to wear white without immediately dropping food on herself, but some ambitions were never meant to be).

She'd spent *hours* worrying about this meeting, mostly at two in the morning when she should have been sleeping. She'd gone over and over it again in her head, imagining different scenarios. She'd conjured whole conversations, and then become stressed by them even though they'd only happened in her head. "Writer's brain," Oliver called it, and maybe it was but she wished she could switch that side of herself off when she wasn't working. She hated the way her mind could take a perfectly benign scenario and twist it into a crisis. She went from zero to disaster in less than two seconds.

And now the moment she'd been dreading was here, and yet Adeline was being perfectly civil. Maybe not *warm* exactly, but definitely civil.

It was her nature to be reserved. That could have been personality, or it could have been a result of her background, Cassie mused. Adeline's sense of security had been threatened at an impressionable age. The foundations of her life shaken. The experience had probably made her wary.

Cassie had examined the possibilities in detail. She knew that to understand the way a person behaved in the present, you often had to look at their past. It was something she did all the time when she was creating characters. She asked herself why a person would make the choices they made. Why they'd behave in a certain way. *What had happened to them?*

Adeline folded her jacket neatly and Cassie was conscious

of her creased shorts and bare legs. Her hair curled wildly thanks to the humidity, and her nose was pink because she'd been slow to apply sunscreen the day before. She'd chosen to wear shorts and a T-shirt, because she hadn't been able to face a car ride dressed in uncomfortable clothes that would stick to her skin. She felt like a mess next to her immaculate sister.

She reminded herself that this island was all about relaxation. "I went for a swim this morning before I left for the airport. You'll probably have time to settle in and have a swim before dinner if you fancy it."

Adeline fasted her seat belt. "I have work to do."

"Work? But you're on holiday."

Adeline settled her sunglasses on her nose. "Tomorrow is a deadline for me. And this isn't a holiday. It's a family wedding."

Family wedding. She made it sound like duty, and to Adeline that was what it was.

Cassie pulled into the flow of traffic, wondering what passed as a holiday to her sister.

"You're working on answers for your column? I liked the answer you gave to that man who didn't know how to tell his mother he was gay."

Adeline turned her head. "You read my column?"

"Sometimes. I mean, not always..." Remembering the letter she'd sent, Cassie floundered. Her face grew hot. Had her sister guessed it was from her? No. Of course she hadn't. *But what if she had?* "Your responses are always wise."

"Thank you."

"How do you pick which letters to answer? I've always wondered."

"I try to cover a range of topics. And if someone writes in about an issue that I know will affect a lot of people, then I might prioritize that." She placed her hands in her lap.

Her nails were neat, her choice of polish pale and discreet. "What about you? Have you decided what you want to do now you've graduated?"

"Not yet." She still wasn't ready to release her secret into the world. What if Madeleine couldn't sell her book? It might never happen and she didn't want to tempt fate. "I'm taking this summer to figure a few things out. At the moment I'm working in a café. People watching, and free cake. It might just be my dream job."

It was an easy answer, but not an honest one. She was a writer, and she knew that now. She was already more than half way through her next book. The words wouldn't stop flowing and she didn't want them to. Nothing in her life had ever been so dizzyingly satisfying as writing. With luck she would have finished a draft before she left Corfu. She'd stayed up late the night before, scribbling a plan for her next chapter in her notebook while sprawled on one of the loungers.

She would have done the same tonight, but she was sharing the cottage with Adeline, so maybe that wasn't going to work. Maybe she could say she was writing a diary.

Cassie took the road out of the airport, drove until the sea appeared in front of her and then took a left along the sea front. She knew the route so well she didn't have to think about it. The Old Fortress crouched on a hill, while all around was the sea, shades of turquoise and green under a cloudless blue sky.

Oh, how she wished she were diving into it right now, instead of being trapped in a hot car with someone who didn't want to be here.

She rooted around in her brain for a safe topic of conversation. Not the wedding, because that would inevitably be controversial. She needed to keep things neutral.

"A car drove into the wall here yesterday." She gestured to

the rubble that was still piled at the side of the road. "Mum and I were stuck here for an hour."

Adeline turned to look at her. "She met you at the airport?"

Too late, Cassie suddenly realized how that must look and feel. Their mother had stood in the baking heat, waiting for Cassie to arrive the day before, but she hadn't offered to make the trip to the airport to pick up Adeline. She'd left that to her sister.

And now she knew the true meaning of the word *discomfort*.

"She had to be in town anyway. She was seeing her lawyer." It was the truth, but both of them knew it wasn't the whole truth and Adeline didn't respond.

Cassie shifted in her seat. Guilt sat like a stone in her stomach. If she didn't have this almost unstoppable need to fill every silence, she wouldn't have said anything. She wished now that her mother hadn't come in person to meet her. Or that she'd insisted on meeting Adeline too. Maybe Cassie should have suggested it, but her mother had been hunched over her laptop, typing away frantically, and everyone who knew Catherine Swift knew better than to disturb her when her fingers were moving and her eyes were on the screen.

She knew that her mother and Adeline weren't close. It was something she'd just accepted as a fact. It was just one of those things. It happened. It was understandable. She'd assumed that Adeline didn't care, but now she wondered about that. What if she did care? What if she was hurt? It bothered her that she had no idea how her sister was feeling.

Cassie glanced at her briefly, but Adeline had turned her head away and was staring out the window, leaving Cassie with a view of the back of her head.

What did that mean? Was she admiring the view, or hiding her emotions?

Adeline wasn't an emotional person.

Or was she?

Cassie decided a law should be passed to compel people to at least give a *clue* about their emotions. If you didn't know how someone was feeling, how could you say the right thing? And she desperately wanted to say the right thing. In her mind, she imagined a scenario where Adeline said to her, *Thank you, talking to you has helped so much.* And then they hugged.

She almost laughed at herself.

Hugged. Like *that* was going to happen. Cassie couldn't remember a time when her sister had hugged her.

She stared at the road and tried to imagine how she'd feel if she were Adeline.

She hadn't been back to Corfu since her mother's last wedding, five years earlier, so clearly she didn't love it here. She didn't see the place as home, the way Cassie did.

And why would she? This was the place where her parents' marriage had disintegrated. She'd gone to live with her father when she was ten.

Cassie wanted to say something. She wanted to acknowledge that this was difficult, so that Adeline didn't feel alone. She wanted to say *I'm sorry if this is hard.*

Guilt washed over her. A small part of her felt that she'd ruined her sister's life, and it didn't matter how often she reasoned that she couldn't be held responsible for being born, she still felt bad.

She glanced at her sister again.

Adeline was still staring out of the window.

Cassie took a deep breath. "Are you okay?" She jumped right in before she could change her mind, like a swimmer plunging into cold water. Of course, everything wasn't okay. But she didn't know her sister well enough to know how to handle it. They were family, and yet they weren't family. They were like pieces of the same jigsaw that just didn't fit.

Adeline didn't respond and Cassie took another swift glance at her and saw her throat move.

Was she crying? *Crap, crap.*

Cassie felt her chest ache, and with a soft curse, swung the wheel hard and pulled into an empty space alongside the road. Horns blared in protest and she waved a hand by way of apology. Maybe she had more of her mother in her than she'd thought.

Nothing was okay and pretending that it was and trying to be normal was exhausting. It was time for honesty.

"Adeline…"

"What? Why have we stopped?" Adeline's voice was husky, as if she'd swallowed dust.

Cassie looked at her sister. She tried to search for clues, but her sunglasses made it impossible for her to see her eyes.

"This must be very hard for you."

"It's not hard. Why have you stopped? Do we have car problems?"

"No, but…"

"Are you feeling unwell?"

"Me? I'm fine." Cassie floundered. Maybe she'd imagined the emotion in Adeline's voice, because there was no emotion now. Or maybe Adeline was desperately trying to hide how she felt in front of Cassie. It wasn't as if they were close. *But she wanted to be close.* She wanted to tell Adeline that she understood. But did she, really?

"So why have you pulled over?"

It was like trying to squeeze juice from a pebble. "Look, I know our mother—" she emphasized the words, reminding her sister that Catherine was mother to both of them "—getting married again is probably a bit stressful for you."

"Why would it be stressful for me? She is responsible for her own choices. Those choices have no impact on me."

Yes they do, Cassie thought, *because you wouldn't be here if she weren't getting married.*

But it felt as if her sister was behind glass. She could see her, and hear her, but she couldn't touch her.

"I just wanted you to know that I'm here if you need anyone to talk to."

"I won't need anyone to talk to." There was a pause. "But thank you."

It was like standing on either side of a giant chasm.

Cassie had promised herself that she was going to stop trying to breach that chasm, and here she was doing it again. She could imagine Oliver rolling his eyes. *Give up, Cass!*

And she should give up. She'd been wrong to think her sister was upset. She obviously didn't feel anything at all. If she didn't know that she was made of flesh, she would have thought someone had programmed her.

Hurt, appalled to find that she was the one with a lump in her throat, she slammed the car into gear and pulled back into the stream of traffic.

Maybe she should write a fantasy book, where the heroine seemed human, but wasn't.

"The villa is looking gorgeous at the moment, particularly the garden. The bougainvillea is a picture. It's going to be the perfect setting for a wedding." If they weren't going to talk about anything meaningful, then she'd simply talk about boring everyday things with no emotional subtext.

There was a pause. "What's he like?"

"Who? Oh, you mean our soon to be stepdad? I don't know. I haven't met him." And she had to admit there was something strange about that. "I arrived late yesterday, and he'd gone to Athens for something. I didn't ask what."

"You haven't met him?" There was something in Adeline's voice. Surprise? Relief?

Cassie was encouraged to discover she was capable of an emotional reaction.

"I haven't met him *yet*. But we're going to meet him tonight. He's obviously a busy person."

"Busy doing what? What does he do?"

"I don't exactly know." She could feel Adeline's gaze on her.

"She hasn't told you anything about him?"

"Nothing. Not even his name." Which was also strange, now she thought about it. When she fell in love, she was pretty sure she was going to be dropping the guy's name into conversation at every turn. Or maybe it was just her mother being romantic. "She probably wants to surprise us. You know what she's like. Every birthday she buys you something that you wouldn't ever have thought of, but totally love."

"She gives me money," Adeline said and Cassie wondered whether she should just drive the car into the sea and have done with it.

A conversation with Adeline was like strolling down a road full of potholes whilst wearing a blindfold.

"I'm sure whoever he is, he's a great guy. He must be, if she wants to marry him."

There was a pause. "Or maybe he's a convincing con man, trying to take advantage of her money, like the last man she married."

Her mother's marriage to Gordon Pelling, husband number three, had been short-lived and ended acrimoniously when Catherine discovered his secret gambling habit and refused to provide financial support for that particular addiction.

"That was an unfortunate mistake. She's very trusting. And

I'm totally sure she wouldn't make the mistake again." Or would she? The thought hadn't entered her head. But now it was there, burrowing into her brain. "No, surely not. She'd spot a fake."

Adeline said nothing, but she didn't have to.

This is her fourth marriage.

Cassie pressed her foot to the floor and headed out of town. "I'm sure this time he's not a fake." She said it to convince herself as much as her sister. "He's back tonight and we're all having a special dinner, so we can get to know each other then. There's no secret. No surprise. Just a question of timing, that's all. I'm looking forward to it."

Still, Adeline said nothing. Presumably that meant she wasn't looking forward to it.

And now Cassie was starting to feel uneasy too. Why *hadn't* her mother told them anything about him?

She coaxed the Jeep up the steep hill that wound its way to the top of the mountain, retracing the route she'd taken on the way.

At the top, she glanced again at her sister because *surely* no one could fail to be moved by the stunning view.

Adeline said nothing so Cassie did what she always did and filled the silence.

"Did you know there are around four million olive trees on Corfu?" The olive groves stretched into the distance, plunging down to rocky coves and crystalline waters that sparkled like a jeweler's window. Dotted across the landscape were clusters of pastel cottages and the occasional ancient church. "Whenever I see this view, I immediately rethink my life. I tell myself I'm going to leave Oxford and start afresh here, but somehow once I'm back in the swing of things the urge fades."

Maybe it felt so appealing precisely because it was a dream.

Whenever she visited the island, she was basically stepping out of her life for a little while. That was what a holiday was, wasn't it? A break from real life. If this became real life, if she made it permanent, would she feel the need to escape from this too? Would it feel different?

She couldn't imagine ever wanting to escape from here. This was her place; she felt it in her bones.

She sneaked a glance at her sister, but Adeline was staring out the window, her expression revealing nothing. There was no smile, no *wow, look at that view*, no indication at all that this was anything other than a painful experience to be endured.

Was she traumatized by the place?

Giving up trying to figure out what her sister was thinking, Cassie headed for home. Whoever her mother's new husband was, she hoped he was chatty, otherwise dinner was going to be a painful experience for everyone concerned.

9

Catherine

Catherine gazed through the open doors of her office. From her desk, she could just see the roof of the guest cottage that nestled at the far end of her property. What were the girls doing? Were they chatting? Catching up? Wondering who their mother was marrying this time?

They'd arrived a few hours ago. She'd heard the squeak of the gates opening, the crunch of tires on gravel and then the slamming of car doors. Two doors, which meant that Adeline hadn't had a last-minute change of heart about coming.

The relief was intense.

Only now did she acknowledge just how nervous she'd been that Adeline might not come. She'd been afraid that the idea of her mother getting married *yet again* would repel her to the extent that she would want no part of it. And if that had happened, then Catherine would have lost this opportunity to finally mend the rift between them.

Because they *were* going to mend it.

Catherine was confident that this time her daughter was going to approve of her choice.

How could her daughter not love Andrew? She couldn't. It was impossible. She was so sure of it she hadn't allowed herself to consider an alternative.

Tonight was a new beginning. She'd planned it all so carefully and Andrew, even though he hadn't agreed with her decision not to tell the girls about him until they were on the island, had gone along with it because he loved her.

Because he loved her.

Just thinking of it gave her a thrill. At this stage in her life, after all that had happened, everything that lay behind her, it felt like a miracle. And maybe she was greedy, because now she wanted a second miracle. She wanted to heal her relationship with her daughter. And if only this part of her life would work out the way she wanted it to, she'd never complain about anything again.

Beside her on the tiled floor, his loyalty unwavering, was Ajax. He stretched himself out in a patch of sunlight, enjoying the warmth. She reached down and stroked him, earning herself a deep appreciative purr.

Pleasing the cats was delightfully uncomplicated. If only relationships with humans were as straightforward.

She knew she should have gone to greet Adeline the moment she'd arrived, but she'd stayed glued to her chair, telling herself that she had work to do even though that work hadn't stopped her taking an early morning swim and spending a satisfying hour in her garden. She was a coward when it came to emotional conflict. She had no problem putting her characters through emotional trauma, but when it came to

help
erine
guilt
her-
imis-
had
ences,
had

o any
rdinal
a, and
made
now
plenty
Swift
—but
umber
does the
out the
ft by a
ubbish,
nputer,
typo on
at the
to take
ke the

same
namely
er how

verything she could to avoid it. She was
s did when she was anxious or afraid,
fuge inside a fictional world. A world
ge and could control the outcome. A
fe.

feel anxious about meeting her own
lay between them that sometimes it
t it.

o composed, so mature, so *distant*. She
angry or even resentful—she showed
ehaved toward her mother the way she
r she was meeting for the first time.
out of her life. She didn't treat her like
erine thought, was the most painful
something she understood, because
ng herself. From the day her mother
oarding school, she'd found a way to
t maternal support. She'd told herself
other, and she worked hard to make
didn't need her, if she didn't care,
t. Her family network had fallen so
ons and dreams that she'd invented
ad and vowed that if and when she
she'd do better.

had taken her so long to understand
much more complicated than she'd
he chance to mend fences with her
d a decade before, but she was de-
up with her daughter.
hat Adeline was thirty and it could
ong past the age of needing her

mother, Catherine still hoped that this wedding woul¦
them forge a new relationship.

Despite the emotional upset of her childhood (Cat¦
couldn't bear to think of her role in that because th¦
would be unbearable), Adeline had built a good life fc¦
self. She was a respected professional. On her more op¦
tic days, Catherine liked to convince herself that Adeli¦
chosen that path precisely because of her own exper¦
in which case she could possibly assume that some go¦
come from bad.

Catherine closed her laptop. She hadn't managed to
work since the car arrived. Distracted, she'd made the c¦
mistake of wasting time scrolling through social med¦
checking some of the reviews of her latest book. Sh¦
a point never to read her reviews, but it was as if rig¦
she couldn't help punishing herself. There had been
of reviews with five stars—*I read everything Catheri¦
writes, Catherine Swift at her best, the woman is a geni¦*
also plenty of three stars (three was not her favorite ¦
right now)—*not her best, read as if she wrote it in a hurry,*
woman even have an editor? (most readers didn't think a¦
role of an editor, so she assumed that one had been ¦
writer), and a fair smattering of one and two stars—
she's lost her touch, this was written by a computer (*on* a co¦
Catherine thought, but not *by* a computer), *there's a*
page 49. She ignored the reviews that complained ¦
cover was torn (How was that her fault? She tended¦
the blame for everything, but even she refused to ¦
blame for a torn cover or late delivery).

She told herself to toughen up and gave herself t¦
advice she would have given to less seasoned writers,
that not every reader could enjoy every book no ma¦

much she might want them to. All she could do was write the best book she could, and after that it was out of her hands.

She needed to put the whole thing behind her. The book, the sales, the reviews. *Number three.* That part of her career was finished now. Catherine Swift the romance novelist was history. She was moving on.

After her early morning swim, she'd spent her time polishing her crime novel and had loved every moment. She'd felt energized and excited. She'd wanted to write, and *wanting* to write was an excellent feeling. It had been a while since she'd felt that way. People didn't understand that the "dream job" became just that after a while—a job. The "dream" part vanished once it became a reality. Thinking about something was much less work than actually doing it, which was why so many people said they wanted to be a writer but never actually managed to pin themselves to the keyboard for the length of time it took to produce a book. You could live the dream but Catherine was pretty sure that once you were living it, it was no longer *the dream.*

Catherine could no longer stare out the window and wait for inspiration to strike her; she had deadlines and people depending on her.

There were expectations, and nothing induced fear quite like expectations. There were days when the pressure of them threatened to crush her. When *the dream* almost became a nightmare. She felt unending sympathy for writers less successful than her, who labored over their work only to see it vanish from the shelves (if it even made it to the shelves) within weeks of release. They must have felt like Sisyphus, pushing the rock uphill.

The stress so easily eclipsed the joy, but lately she'd found the joy again. It took her back to the beginning, when she'd written for the sheer addictive thrill of creating, when the only pressure had come from within herself, from the stories unfolding in her brain. She took it as a sign that she was doing the right thing by making this change.

It wasn't that she *had* to do this. She *wanted* to do this.

She stood up and stretched to shake off the stiffness. She'd positioned her desk facing the garden, a decision that she found both uplifting and a distraction. Two walls of her office were floor-to-ceiling bookshelves, home to one copy of everything she'd written, along with translations. She gazed at them now, all those spines, all those words. All that work. Her life's work. Her purpose. She kept them there not to feed her ego, but to squash the self-doubt that never left her, no matter how many books bore her name. Sixty romances, and she knew now that she'd written her last. Her love affair with romance was over.

She closed the door of her office and headed to her bedroom to change.

Her phone pinged and there was a message from Cassie.

Can't wait to meet my soon-to-be stepdad! See you in half an hour xx

She felt a rush of warmth and gratitude (dearest Cassie, so easy, so loving, so accepting) followed by a flicker of nerves. Tonight was important. The most important night she'd had in a long time. She was glad Cassie was going to be there. She was always supportive of everything Catherine did.

She messaged back.

Just changing. See you on the terrace.

She changed out of her comfortable writing clothes into the outfit she'd chosen for the occasion, a wrap dress in the palest of blues, understated and elegant. She applied a minimum of makeup and was selecting a pair of oversized earrings to add a touch of drama when Andrew walked into the room.

"Sorry I'm late. Took longer than expected." He leaned down and kissed her on the neck, his lips lingering. "Mm, you smell good. Are they here?"

"Yes, but I haven't seen them yet. I'm about to join them on the terrace."

"Right." He straightened. "I'll take a shower and be ready in fifteen minutes."

"Don't rush. It will be good for me to have some time alone with them before you appear, and I need to check on the food with Maria."

Maria had worked for her ever since she'd bought the villa. She looked after the house, and her husband, Kostas, had looked after the pools and the garden before his untimely death a year ago.

Twice a year when Catherine went on book tours to the UK and US, Maria moved into the villa's guest cottage so that the place wasn't left empty. It was Maria who had taught her Greek when she'd first arrived. Maria who had helped her with baby Cassie when she'd been struggling. *Maria who had rescued her on that awful night she tried never to think about.*

Images flashed into her brain. Her own real–life horror story, but fortunately it was one story that no one else had access to.

Except Maria.

Maria was one of the few people who knew everything about her.

It should have made her feel vulnerable, but it didn't.

Maria was her family, in a way that her own family never had been, and this place was her home in a way that nowhere else had ever been.

Maria had spent the morning in the kitchen preparing a
variety of Greek dishes, and was back there now, putting the
finishing touches to the meal. Catherine had joined her for a
few hours and they'd cooked side by side, talking about everything and nothing. Cooking soothed her, and together
they'd made Cassie's favorite, spanakopita, the classic Greek
dish of wild greens and salty feta cheese flavored with dill and
encased in crisp golden pastry. They'd slow roasted lamb with
herbs grown in the gardens of the villa, and made bowls of
creamy hummus. Maria had already made a trip to the tiny
harbor to buy fish fresh from the boat. It lay in the fridge,
waiting to be flavored with olive oil, lemons from their own
trees and herbs grown in their own gardens. Then it would
be cooked on the grill, the skin slightly charred and the flesh
perfectly flaky and creamy.

Catherine had planned it all. Each mouthful would be perfect. The whole evening would be perfect. Catherine imagined that in years to come they'd look back on this evening.
She imagined them laughing together. It was going to be one
of those moments that you remember forever.

Even Adeline couldn't fail to be pleased by what lay ahead,
she was sure of that.

She wondered if the two girls were getting along.

One of her many regrets was that they weren't closer, which
was one of the reasons she'd put them both in the guest cottage. She was hoping that proximity might help. That this
visit might be a fresh start for all of them. The cottage had
two bedrooms, each with doors opening onto the little terrace and the small oval pool. It would be a rare opportunity
for the sisters to spend time together. Catherine imagined
them heading to a local taverna to eat one evening, or maybe
just enjoying an evening sprawled on the loungers outside

the cottage. Glass of wine, the warmth and scents of summer, the incessant chirp of cicadas—what could be better?

She stepped into the gardens and Ajax followed her like a feline bodyguard.

The gardens that surrounded the villa were her pride and joy. On one side stretched an olive grove covering dozens of acres, dense with trees, many of which were hundreds of years old. They'd stood firm through sunshine and storms, their trunks gnarled and knotted, their leaves a silvery green. People who reached for a bottle of olive oil in their supermarket rarely had any idea of the labor that went into producing it. Every year the local community gathered together to harvest the olives at Summer Star. And every year Catherine rolled up her sleeves to help. They used traditional methods, laying nets around the trees to catch the olives and then raking the branches. They pressed and produced their own olive oil, which she kept for her own consumption, and gave to favored guests.

The garden offered something different according to the months. Right now, the beds were bright with sunflowers, their golden faces beaming toward the sun. Bougainvillaea spilled from terracotta pots, providing a dazzle of color against the sunbaked paths that wound their way through the garden and down to the sea.

The garden calmed her, and she needed that because as she approached the terrace she saw that the girls were already there. They were standing a little distance apart, like two strangers at a party who had run out of small talk.

Cassie was wearing a pretty slip dress in a shade of bright pink that ended at mid-thigh. She had a touch of sunburn on her nose and her shoulders, and her short blond hair had been rough dried and fell in gentle waves around her face.

Adeline was also wearing a dress, but hers was a more formal shift dress, plain navy, structured and nipped in at the waist.

"Kalispera!" she greeted them both in Greek, and Cassie's smile was as bright as one of the sunflowers.

"Mum!" She almost bounced across the terrace, as if they hadn't already spent yesterday together talking about anything and everything (except for Andrew, of course. Also writing. In fact, now that Catherine thought about it, there was quite a lot they hadn't talked about) and pulled her into a warm hug.

Catherine was grateful for that hug but it didn't calm the anxiety that had come alive inside her. She'd been imagining this moment for weeks, months, but now it was finally here.

She drew away from Cassie and stretched out her hands to Adeline. Her heart jumped.

"Adeline—"

There was an excruciating moment where Catherine thought she might refuse to take her hands, but then Adeline stepped forward and gave her mother's hands a squeeze. Despite the heat, her fingers were chilly. Her smile was reserved and careful.

"You're looking well." She was polite, her tone hovering on the edge of warmth but not quite getting there.

My fault, Catherine thought. Adeline's childhood had shaped her, and she was responsible for that childhood.

"I'm great. Never better. It's being here, of course. The climate suits me. Not just the climate, the whole place. The people. This villa. The sea." *Oh, stop chatting, Catherine.* It was ridiculous to be nervous of meeting your own daughter. "How was your flight?"

"It was fine, thank you."

If she'd written this scene in a book, she would have deleted it. *Boring. Make something happen.*

Something was about to happen of course, but not until Andrew appeared. She was beginning to regret suggesting he arrive a little after her. She could have done with his support from the beginning, but she'd thought it might be best to ease into it.

"Maria has made a wonderful meal. She's made your favorite spanakopita, Cassie, and that lamb dish with herbs, and—"

"Stop!" Cassie was grinning as she scooped up Ajax and kissed him on the head. "Enough talk about flights and food. Where is he? Your new man! I am dying to meet him. Adeline is too. The suspense has been killing us."

"He'll be joining us soon."

Catherine glanced at Adeline and saw nothing more than a polite smile.

If she was feeling even a flicker of interest or anticipation, then it was well concealed.

How could she, the most emotional of creatures, have produced a child who was so calm and unemotional? Even as a child, Adeline had been more like her father. Thoughtful. Quiet. Happy in her own company. And then there was Cassie, who was so like Catherine it was unsettling to watch. She was impulsive, and romantic, and big hearted—all traits that made her vulnerable to making all the same mistakes as her mother.

The thought made her cold.

"Tell us about your wedding plans." Cassie put Ajax down and stroked him behind the ears. "How many people?"

"Just us, and Daphne is flying in from New York. And Maria, of course. Oh, and Stefanos."

Cassie straightened. "Stefanos? I thought he lived in Toronto?"

"He did. He worked in tech—I don't know exactly what

he did, but it was a good job. Flew all over the world. But he gave it up when his father died, and he came home."

"And he stayed? Why?" Cassie was ever-curious. She'd been the same as a child. *Why, why, why.* Another way in which she resembled her mother, although Catherine couldn't complain. That particular trait had enabled her to craft sixty novels.

"He wanted to be here for his family." And she knew Maria worried about him, but was it even possible to be a mother without worry? It seemed to her that children were born, along with a lifetime of anxiety. The worry didn't go away as the child grew; it simply changed. First, there were the baby worries—*is he sleeping? Is he eating?*—then the toddler worries—*don't fall in the pool, don't run across the road*—and the teenage worries—*don't take drugs, don't risk your life doing things your teenage brain tells you is safe but is demonstrably unsafe.*

Catherine had often wondered whether she would have had children if she'd known in advance how fierce the anxiety would be.

Adeline spoke finally. "He's living at home now?"

"Goodness no. He bought a plot of land up the coast. He's been renovating a villa up there over the winter. It was crumbling away, but not anymore. And he has been building up his father's boat business, which is useful. He's promised to take a look at our boat, which has been misbehaving." Catherine wasn't really thinking about Stefanos. Her mouth was forming words, but she was thinking about Andrew, and how the whole atmosphere was going to change once he arrived. How their lives were going to change.

She felt apprehensive, but also excited.

She was making a fresh start, and she wanted to make that start right now. She didn't want to wait a moment longer, and she didn't have to because she heard the sound of footsteps on the path and then Andrew appeared looking relaxed, and familiar and so handsome (why was it that strands of silver hair made a man look distinguished and attractive, and not simply old? Life was so unjust) that it took her breath away. Her heart flipped and she thought that although life could be unjust, it could also sometimes be miraculous.

She probably didn't deserve this, but she was going to take her good fortune anyway and hold it close.

"Here he is! I know this will be a surprise, girls, but I hope it's a good one." Feeling as nervous as a teenager introducing her date to her parents for the first time (although she had to imagine how that might have felt, because her parents had never been interested in any part of her life), she walked to his side and took his hand.

She braced herself for an explosion of joy and delight, and instead encountered a stunned silence.

She looked at Cassie first. Cassie, who could always be relied on to be smiling, enthusiastic and supportive in all things.

Cassie wasn't smiling. Her eyes were two wide pools of blue, her mouth a soundless circle as she tried to speak but failed to produce any words.

It was Adeline who eventually broke that silence, but only after taking several large gulps of air.

"Dad?" Her tone hovered somewhere between disbelief and incredulity. "What are you doing here?"

10

Adeline

Adeline was hit by a wave of dizziness. The heat pressed down on her and the atmosphere felt suddenly oppressive and airless.

Her father?

Here in Greece?

She felt disorientated. It had never occurred to her that her father would actually attend her mother's wedding. Shock turned to happiness. He'd come all this way to support her. He probably felt guilty because he was the one who had urged her to come, even though he knew she didn't want to.

Gratitude rose up inside her like the bubbles in a champagne glass. She couldn't have loved him more if she'd tried, and she was thrilled to see him. It was like spotting a lifeboat approaching when you were about to drown in stormy seas.

For the first time since she'd stepped onto the baking tarmac at the airport, she tho ught that maybe, just maybe, everything was going to be okay. That maybe she'd survive this.

"Dad!" She walked across the terrace and hugged him tightly. She felt a sense of peace and calm as she always did when she was with him. He was the opposite of her mother. His life was quiet, considered and drama-free. *Her dad*. He was the one person in the world who had never let her down. The one person who had always been there for her. The one person she trusted.

"Hi, Addy." He hugged her back with equal warmth and affection.

"What are you doing here?" She stepped back so that she could look at him. "Why didn't you tell me you were coming? You could have stayed with me in London first. We could have had a meal in that restaurant you love. We could have traveled together."

They could have given each other moral support.

She managed to not say that part aloud. Her father wouldn't hear a bad word about her mother, which was laudable of course, and mature, but also occasionally maddening.

She waited for an explanation and saw her mother reach for her father's hand. It was beyond inappropriate in her opinion, but she'd long since given up trying to understand her mother.

She waited for her father to gently extract himself from Catherine's grasp, but he didn't. Instead, his fingers folded over hers protectively.

Adeline decided that there were days when she didn't understand her father either, but presumably that was her mother's influence.

She took another step backward, uncomfortable with the physical display of affection between two people who had been divorced for more than two decades and had a tumultuous history.

It was fine that they'd managed to keep their relationship largely amicable, but holding hands went a little too far in her opinion.

And maybe he knew what she was thinking, because her father's face turned a strange shade of pink and he gave her what could only be described as a sheepish smile.

"I know this is probably a little surprising."

The understatement was reassuringly typical of her father and almost made her smile. "It's good to see you, Dad. But I don't understand why you didn't tell me you were coming." She tried not to sound accusatory. Tried to remind herself that her father was an adult, who didn't owe her an explanation for his movements. "When did you arrive?"

"On Corfu?" He looked awkward. "I've been here for the past two months."

Two *months*? How was that possible?

If she'd been puzzled before, she was completely confused now. "I spoke to you six weeks ago and you were at the cottage in Cape Cod."

"I never said I was at the cottage, Addy. You made that assumption."

Of course, she'd made that assumption. Why wouldn't she? It was where he lived, and she'd been given no reason to think he was staying somewhere else.

"I don't get it. Why didn't you tell me you were here?" Feelings awoke that had been dormant for a long time. A faint stirring of panic. Her relationship with her father had never been complicated. They didn't keep secrets. They both said what they meant and were respectful of each other. They both lived lives that were safe, quiet and predictable. There was none of the drama and theater that she associated with her mother. If her mother's life was a three-act play, her father's was a quiet sonnet.

Or so she'd always thought. But now it seemed she'd been wrong about that.

The fact that he hadn't told her the truth hurt her terribly.

She'd been worried sick about him. She'd lost sleep imagining him stressed and miserable as he contemplated his ex-wife's impending nuptials (although admittedly, he'd had plenty of experience in that area) and all the time he'd been here, and he hadn't told her?

"He didn't tell you, because I asked him not to." Her mother was still clinging to her father's hand.

"Why would you do that?"

"I thought it was better to tell you and Cassie in person. I wanted us to be together and celebrate as a family."

A family? Her mother's ability to spin real life into fiction never ceased to amaze her. If they were a *family*, then it was in the loosest sense of the word. Companies said that, didn't they? They said *we're a family*, but that didn't stop them kicking you out the door when it suited them.

And it was true that her father was the most forgiving, civilized man on the planet and that he seemed to harbor surprisingly little ill will toward her mother, but still the idea of him accepting an invitation to the wedding and agreeing to stay for such a long time in the lead up to the celebrations seemed a little *too* civilized to her. That was bordering on unnatural, surely? She wondered what her mother's latest man had to say about it all, and then she realized that her mother was gazing at her father with a dreamy look in her eyes, and he was gazing back at her with the same level of intimacy—

"No!" The word shot out of her mouth before she could stop it. And maybe she wouldn't have stopped it even if she could because what other reaction was there to what she was seeing? That look they were exchanging meant only one thing. They weren't just together—they were *together*. "You have to be kidding me."

She took several steps backward and would have fallen into the pool if Cassie hadn't grabbed her.

This couldn't be happening. They couldn't be serious. They couldn't possibly be thinking of doing this. It was inconceivable, which was why it had taken her a few minutes to realize what was going on. Her father wasn't a guest—he was the groom.

And now it all made sense. It was like a thriller where the clues had been laid but made no sense until the big reveal at the end. The reason her mother hadn't mentioned the name of the man she was marrying hadn't been a lapse of memory or an oversight, nor had it been driven by a romantic urge to surprise everyone. Instead, it had been a considered choice designed to lessen the chances of outside interference. She'd wanted to tell her daughters face-to-face because she'd known that there was no way Adeline would have agreed to be a witness to this car crash.

Nearby, a bee buzzed its way through tightly clustered blooms, and a tiny lizard scuttled from sun to shade.

Adeline was oblivious to the small details of life going on around her.

She'd thought she was past being shocked by anything her mother did or said. Past caring. But this involved her father too, and she definitely wasn't past caring about him.

She had plenty of examples of her mother's poor judgment, but her father had only showed poor judgment once—when he'd married her mother—and now he was thinking of repeating the mistake? It was like a toddler burning itself on a hot plate and then reaching out a hand to do the same thing again.

And she was supposed to be part of this circus. She was supposed to celebrate, and be delighted, and—

She couldn't breathe. Her heart was pounding so fast she thought she might pass out right here on the terrace.

She was an expert at handling stressful situations, she taught other people how to handle stressful situations, but everything she knew had abandoned her.

Her emotions were in a turmoil. Her vision blurred. She felt as if someone had flipped a switch inside her.

Her father stepped toward her, hands outstretched. "Adeline. I know this is a shock, honey, but everything is going to be okay. We need to sit down and talk, but all you really need to know is that your mother and I love each other. We want to spend the rest of our lives together. I hope you'll wish us well."

The sheer naivety of that statement unlocked the words that had been trapped inside her.

"Wish you *well*? She broke your heart, Dad!" She couldn't bear it. She couldn't bear the thought of her kind, gentle father exposing himself to that pain again. "Why would you do this? *Why?*" She prided herself in never reacting in an emotional way. She was rational and measured at all times, but she could feel control slipping from her fingers.

"Adeline—"

"I can't believe you're doing this. I can't believe you'd put yourself through this a second time. She cheated on you." She kept her voice low and steady. "She had an affair. She got pregnant and had a baby." She heard a choked sound from beside her and remembered too late that the *baby* was standing right beside her.

She'd forgotten about Cassie. From the moment her father had walked onto the terrace, she'd been unaware of anything but him. But this didn't just affect her, it affected her sister too. And gradually it dawned on her that Cassie hadn't said a word since her father had appeared. Not a single word.

Her half sister, who chatted incessantly about everything and had an almost unnatural ability to find the positive side in any situation, still hadn't spoken.

A waft of Cassie's perfume scented the air, but even that could do nothing to sweeten the atmosphere.

Mortified, Adeline turned to look at her sister, but before she could say anything—and she had no idea what she would have said—Cassie stumbled away from them across the terrace, bumping into the table in her haste. A bowl of olives fell to the floor and scattered. Ajax jumped and fled into the bushes, but Cassie didn't pause. Her flight was wild and uncoordinated as she headed for the path, stumbled again and then vanished from view.

Adeline, who considered the use of bad language to signify the ultimate loss of control, bit down on the profanity that hovered on her lips.

Guilt stabbed her hard in the ribs.

She got pregnant and had a baby.

If she could have snatched those words back, she would have done so. Not because of her mother, but because of her sister. It had been a thoughtless remark and saying it left her feeling deeply ashamed.

She felt a rush of frustration.

Being around her mother so often did this. It turned her into a version of herself that she didn't recognize and definitely didn't like. She liked calm and order in her life, but wherever her mother went, there was drama, disorder and chaos.

"That was a very cruel thing to say, Adeline." Her mother sent her a wounded look. "You've hurt me, you've hurt your father and you've hurt Cassie."

She felt a lump form in her throat. There was a strange pressure in her chest.

She hadn't meant to hurt Cassie and it was something she would deal with, but in the meantime, it was hard not to notice that her mother cared about everyone's feelings but Adeline's.

She appealed to her father. "You can't get married again. Why would you? It doesn't make any sense."

"Oh, Adeline, please stop." Her mother turned to her father in desperation. "Say something, Andrew. She listens to you. You've always been able to reason with her."

As if *she* was the problem.

"Don't reason with me. Don't handle me." She dug her fingertips hard into her palms. "Do you have no idea how I'm feeling right now?"

"I know how difficult it has been," her mother said. "I know it has been hard—it has been hard for me too—but I want to put the past behind us. I want us to start fresh, from this moment. I thought you'd be happy for us." Her mother's eyes were shiny and Adeline's own eyes stung because there were few things as frustrating as having your feelings ignored or dismissed. It said *you're not important.* Or, perhaps worse, *what you feel isn't important.*

It had been years since she'd allowed herself to be driven to this point.

She swallowed past the dryness of her throat and tried again. "You can't just ignore the past."

"Of course, you can. It's a choice. This is a chance for us to heal as a family, but you refuse to meet me half way and now you've upset Cassie." Her distress was visible and Adeline felt her own face grow wet with tears.

Bury it, ignore it, pretend it never happened. That was how her mother dealt with life's bumpier moments.

She had a ridiculous urge to behave like an insecure toddler and throw herself into her father's arms for comfort but at that moment her father, forced to make a choice between the women in his life, sent her a look of agonized apology and pulled Catherine into his arms.

"There. It's all right. Everything is going to be okay."

Adeline watched in disbelief as he held and soothed her mother.

He'd made a choice, and it hadn't been her.

She told herself that it didn't matter. That she was more than capable of soothing herself. After all, she'd had more than enough practice. She was old enough not to need a hug from her dad when things were bad.

She wasn't thinking of herself, she was thinking of him.

"Dad, everything is not okay—"

"It seems complicated. I understand, and maybe this wasn't the best way to handle it but there probably was no easy way. We'll talk about it, I promise, the way we always do, but not right now." He held Catherine against him. Protective. Solid.

Adeline stared at him in despair.

"But you can't just—"

"I'm asking you to trust me, Adeline, the way we've always trusted each other."

"How am I supposed to trust you? You didn't tell me the two of you were involved again. You didn't tell me you were here." Although she tried not to mind read, or make judgments without facts, it was impossible not to imagine them together, laughing over the secret they were sharing. Because at some point they had obviously decided not to tell their daughter. "Not telling me wasn't an accident or an oversight, it was a choice. And it was a hurtful one."

The pain was a thousand tiny knives, digging into all the sensitive parts of her.

Was there anything worse than a betrayal of trust? She didn't think so.

She stood alone and isolated, worried about her dad, and worried about her sister. Cassie was definitely not okay. And she felt guilty, because that was her fault.

"I should go and check on Cassie." Her mother was obviously thinking the same way, because she pulled away and blew her nose. "Cassie is very sensitive and emotional. She'll want to talk about it."

I'm sensitive, Adeline thought. *I want to talk about it.*

Her father kept his arm round Catherine. "Maybe give her some time."

Catherine gave him a despairing look. "I want this to work. This has to work. And Maria is about to serve the food. She's been in the kitchen all day. The champagne is chilled…"

Adeline saw her father put his hand on Catherine's arm.

"We need a pause, honey. Both girls are a bit shocked. They need time to digest our news."

"Cassie would have been fine, I'm sure, if it hadn't been for Adeline."

"You're saying this is my fault?" Adeline heard her voice lift. "Can you honestly not see why we might have been upset?"

"I can *see*. I know it's hard," her mother said, "but I was hoping that we could all sit down together at dinner and talk it through."

"Catherine—" this time her father spoke firmly "—we've sprung this on them. It's an adjustment."

An adjustment? Adeline, who made a living out of finding the right words in stressful situations, couldn't think of a thing to say. It was as if she'd been hit over the head with a hard object. Her brain was stunned. She had nothing.

"I don't understand what there is to adjust to. I thought

they'd be thrilled. Particularly you, Adeline." Catherine glanced at Adeline, bemused. "You were distraught when your father and I divorced. For months, you cried yourself to sleep. You clung to me and begged us to get back together."

"Stop." Every word her mother spoke sent her pulse rate hammering faster. She was a child again, witnessing her safe, secure life falling apart. The last threads of control finally slipped from her grasp. "I beg you, stop."

Why had she come? *What had possessed her to come?* Mark was right, she'd chosen to do this. She could have stayed away. She could have protected herself.

"All I'm saying is that this is what you wanted!" Her mother was defensive, as if she'd given Adeline the chocolate she'd asked for and now she'd changed her mind and asked for cake.

"It was what I wanted when I was *eight years old*!" All the emotions she'd been suppressing since the arrival of her mother's letter bubbled to the surface. "You can't turn back the clock and pretend nothing in the past happened. This isn't one of your books! You can't just edit out the bits you don't like. You can't delete a chapter and forget about it. It happened, and we're all living with the fallout of that. And moving on doesn't mean closing the door on it as if it's a messy child's bedroom that you're trying to ignore…"

"Adeline…" Her father stepped toward her, and for the first time in her life she stepped back from him.

"Don't." She raised her hands to keep him at a distance. "I can't believe you didn't tell me. You must have known I'd be hurt and shocked and yet you let me walk into this situation with no warning."

"Your mother wanted it this way."

"I know you were thinking of my mother, but you used to think about me. My feelings used to matter to you."

In indulging Catherine, he'd hurt his daughter and it felt

like a deep betrayal. Her father was the one person in the world she'd allowed herself to love unconditionally. He'd always been there for her, and she'd been there for him through all of the pain Catherine had caused him. When he'd said *I messed up, Adeline, I messed up* over and over again she was the one who had reassured him that none of this was his fault. Inevitably, perhaps, they'd formed a tight bond and that bond had stayed firm over the years. They were there for each other. They were a team.

But apparently not.

She'd always felt protective of him, and despite everything she still felt protective of him. She wanted to sweep him away from her mother and ask him what he thought he was doing? She wanted to sit him down and try to understand how they'd reached this point. What her mother had said to make him think this was a good idea.

She couldn't think clearly and her parents also seemed stuck for what to say next.

"I need to see Cassie," Catherine said faintly. "I need to apologize for Adeline's words."

Adeline's whole body felt numb. "I'll make my own apology."

Her mother seemed to relax a little. "Good. She'll forgive you, I know, because she's that type of person. She's warmhearted and generous. I'm sure when she calms down a little, she will realize you didn't mean to hurt her. She's not a sulker. Maybe she'll be back in a moment, and then we can all put this behind us and drink a toast to new beginnings."

They were supposed to sit down and drink a toast to celebrate what, in Adeline's opinion, was probably the worst decision they'd ever made (and that was saying something), and pretend to be happy about it? And they thought Cassie would be back to join them? It was like playing a starring role in a fantasy and realizing that the cast were reading from different scripts.

No wonder her sister had chosen to remove herself from the situation.

She needed to do the same. And yes, she needed to apologize to Cassie.

Adeline had never seen her half sister distressed before. If she was the cause of that distress, then fixing that needed to be her priority.

"You two should eat, and toast whatever you want to toast." She headed in the same direction as her sister, sidestepping as her mother tried to grab her arm.

"Adeline! Where are you going?"

"To find Cassie."

"Oh, well good." Her mother let her hand drop. "I hope you'll persuade her to come straight back with you."

"I won't be coming back. Please pass my apologies to Maria."

"But…" Her mother turned to her father. "Andrew, say something. *Do* something. We can talk about this. This was supposed to be a memorable evening."

It was definitely memorable.

Adeline kept walking, and to her father's credit, he shook his head and pulled her mother back.

"Give the girls some space, Cathy. I'm sure they'll have questions, but we need to give them time."

Adeline almost stopped. No one called her mother "Cathy." Even her father didn't call her "Cathy." Except, apparently, he now did. It seemed there was a great deal she didn't know about her father.

And they didn't know her.

Cassie is very sensitive and emotional.

What did they think she was? A piece of rock? Did they really think she didn't feel emotion?

Right now she was feeling more emotions than she knew what to do with, which might have surprised them if they'd managed to break eye contact for long enough to notice.

And yes, she had questions. She had a whole damn list of questions and at some point she'd be asking them.

But first she was going to check on her sister.

11

—

Cassie

Cassie sat in darkness on the beach that nestled below the villa. In the distance, she could see the blur of lights from the fishing village down the coast, and the occasional flash of light from a yacht moored in the bay. The sky was inky black and scattered with stars. She'd abandoned her shoes somewhere on the path and she could feel the sand, grainy and cool under her bare feet. This wasn't the way she'd expected to spend the evening.

She'd been excited to meet the man her mother had fallen in love with. She hadn't cared that she didn't know anything about him. It had seemed romantic to her, and she was prepared to love anyone her mother loved.

But Andrew? Adeline's father? Her mother's first husband? That was a plot twist she hadn't seen coming.

Her mother had left Andrew when she'd fallen in love with

Cassie's father because theirs was a love so huge and over-whelming that nothing, no force on earth, was going to stop it. She was the product of that love. She'd grown up know-ing that. It had cushioned her. The story of her parents' re-lationship had underpinned everything she believed about love. It had made total sense to her.

Until now. Now, it no longer made any sense.

The breeze cooled her skin and she shivered and rubbed her arms. Despite the darkness, the air still throbbed with heat. There was no reason for her to be cold, but she was. The cold came from the inside, creeping through this new tear in the fabric of her past.

Her mother was back with Andrew. What did that say about everything that had gone before? That she'd made a mistake leaving him in the first place? That her love affair had been a mistake? *That Cassie herself was a mistake?* If her mother hadn't become pregnant, what would have happened? Would she and Andrew have fixed things, stayed together? No, surely not. Her parents had been in love. Hadn't they?

She covered her ears with her hands, trying to mute the thoughts fighting for attention in her head. Everything Cassie had ever believed about her parents' relationship was now under question.

She kept hearing Adeline's voice.

She had an affair. She had a baby.

That was her. She was the baby. And standing there on the terrace, hearing it spelled out like that in calm logical tones, Cassie had felt truly awful. And like an intruder. This was her home, but for the first time in her life, she felt as if she didn't belong. And no matter how illogical it was for her to take the blame, she still felt at least partly responsible. An-drew, Adeline and her mother had once been a family, and now they were going to be a family again. People always said that you couldn't put the clock back, but it seemed Catherine and Andrew were going to do exactly that. So where did that leave her? Her part of the story would be deleted. She was definitely a mistake.

Her eyes stung with tears and she felt hideously homesick for Oxford. Which was ridiculous because Corfu was her favorite place in the world. It was *home*. When she was here, she never wanted to leave, but right now if there had been a way to easily leave the island she would have taken it.

All she wanted right now was to be back in the little terraced house she shared with Oliver.

To calm herself, she focused hard on that. What would they be doing if she were there now? They'd probably be in the garden, sprawled on a picnic rug on the small lawn that was sheltered from prying eyes by the trees and dense foliage that bordered the garden. Oliver would be leaping up to pluck a dead leaf from a plant or tug up a weed that had managed to sneak in when he wasn't looking. She teased him about it, but secretly she loved the garden and was more than happy to enjoy the fruits of his labor. Recently, he'd strung solar lanterns between the trees, and it had turned the garden into cozy sanctuary in the evening as well as daytime.

Whenever she was upset, he'd make her a large cup of tea and he'd sit and listen, giving her his full attention, plants forgotten. He was the best listener and always managed to make her feel better. Right now, she needed to feel better.

She pulled out her phone and messaged him, but there was no reply. She imagined him in a pub somewhere, the noise drowning out the ping of his phone. Or maybe he was on a date that was going so well he hadn't thought about his phone since he left the house. And even if he did see her message, he was hardly likely to ditch his date just because his best friend had messaged him. Dates over mates.

She sniffed and scrubbed her hand over her face. She *needed* him.

Some people preferred to be alone when their world fell apart, but she wasn't one of those. She was a people person. She needed friends like she needed air.

She could call Felicia, but although she was a good friend, she wasn't Oliver. Friendship, she'd discovered, was a complicated thing. She had a tendency to idealize friendship and to expect too much from people (she tried hard to be a brilliant friend herself, always ready for fun or comfort, whichever was required). Over time she'd learned to moderate her expectations. She reminded herself constantly that a friend couldn't be everything. There was the fun friend who was brilliant for a night out and any of the "light" stuff, but never showed up in a crisis. There was the friend who arrived armed with tissues and a bottle of wine when something went wrong, but never seemed to be around for the good times. There were yoga friends, and book friends, and friends who were brilliant shopping companions.

Felicia was the type of no-nonsense friend who told you the truth and always tried to "fix" things. She'd tell Cassie what she would do in her position (which wasn't at all what Cassie would do), and right now Cassie didn't need that. Felicia wouldn't understand how she was feeling. The only person who would understand was Oliver. Oliver was fun, caring, good in a crisis, loved books and wasn't completely awful as a shopping companion. It was rare to find everything you needed in one person, but Oliver was that person. Oliver was everything.

Her eyes filled. She was being pathetic and needy. It was a good thing for all their sakes that Oliver wasn't picking up his phone.

Why couldn't she be more like her sister? Aloof. Self-contained. Confident.

On days like today, she wanted to apply for a personality transplant. She'd always had high expectations, and the problem with high expectations was that there was a long way to fall. You bruised less if you didn't expect much from life.

She blinked away tears and checked her phone. Still nothing.

Where are you Oliver?

She'd never felt more alone in her life.

The other person she might have talked to in a crisis was her mother, but how could she do that when her mother was the cause of this crisis?

And that was upsetting too. How could her mother not have warned her? They talked about everything. Her mother always said that they were more like friends than mother and daughter and until now Cassie might have agreed. But this had clearly been going on for ages, and her mother hadn't said a word to her. They chatted most days, and not once had she said, *By the way, guess who is staying with me?*

It could have been a scene straight out of one of her mother's novels, one where she put the heroine through hell. Except in this case, the character wasn't fictional, and things weren't going to get fixed in the end. She should probably grab a pen and scribble down the way she was feeling right now so that she could use it in a story sometime, but she was just too raw.

"Cassie?"

Cassie heard Adeline's voice coming from near the cottage. She shrank, hoping to blend into the darkness, but blending hadn't been in her thoughts when she'd been dressing for the evening. There was no chance of making herself invisible, which was a pity. She didn't want to talk to Adeline who, for all her training and professional skills, was about as emotionally supportive to Cassie as wet lettuce.

She sat still and said nothing, hoping Adeline wouldn't come looking for her (she wouldn't try *that* hard, surely?), but the world evidently hated her because she heard footsteps on the path and then the sound of her name again. The only way to avoid her sister was to run into the sea, but then she'd ruin her dress. It was ironic, she thought, that she'd spent years longing to have a proper conversation with her sister, but now all she wanted to do was avoid her.

"Cassie? There you are." Adeline's voice came from the shadows at the edge of the beach. At one time, the "path" had been nothing but a steep, dusty track winding through wild vegetation. Reaching the beach had involved nerve, stumbles and scratches, but now the path was paved and studded with tiny lights.

Adeline stood in those lights, uncertain, paused at the point where the path met the sand. "I was looking for you."

Why? To make her feel worse than she did already?

Cassie wrapped her arms around her knees and pulled them into her chest. "Actually, I'd rather be on my own if that's all right with you." Words she'd never spoken before in her life. Oliver would have been concerned if he'd heard her because if there was one thing she hated, it was being on her own when she was upset. She was the sort of person who thought a problem shared was a problem halved, but not right now. She particularly didn't want to share it with someone who gave nothing back and didn't seem to experience normal human emotions, so she'd hold this problem by herself and hope it wasn't going to crush her.

Instead of turning back, Adeline stepped onto the sand and picked her way across the small beach. She was still wearing her wedge sandals. Anyone else would have tugged them off the moment their feet hit the sand, but not Adeline. And she still managed to look balanced and elegant.

"I don't blame you for feeling that way," she said. "I need to apologize. I'm sorry for what I said. Really sorry. It was thoughtless."

"It's okay. You were simply stating facts."

"No, I was upset and thinking about my parents and myself, not you. It was unforgiveable." Adeline hesitated and then sat down on the sand next to her.

Cassie shifted away a little, instinctively wary.

"The sand is damp. You'll ruin your dress. I bet it's dry clean only."

"It's just a dress." Adeline settled herself, smoothing the dress down over her thighs so that even here, on this tiny curve of beach, she was her usual elegant self. "How are you feeling?"

She felt terrible.

Her emotions were so close to the surface she almost let them spill, but then she remembered that this was Adeline and that they didn't do confidences.

"I'm fine." Presumably, that would be enough of an answer. When people said *how are you?* they were usually being polite. They didn't want to hear how you really were.

Adeline stayed next to her, staring into the darkness. "We both know you're not."

"So? It's the answer you gave when I asked you the same question in the car earlier. And I don't believe you were fine either." It wasn't like her to be confrontational, but she wasn't feeling like herself.

"You're right, I wasn't," Adeline said, "but mostly when people ask how you are, they don't really want to know the answer."

Cassie almost laughed, because her thoughts had gone in

the same direction. "That's true. But I do." She turned to look at her sister. "I asked because I wanted to know."

"And I appreciated you asking. But when I'm stressed, I tend not to talk about it." Adeline brushed sand from her legs. "It wasn't about you, it was about me. I don't find it easy to talk about my feelings."

The fact that her sister had feelings was news. "Why?"

Adeline thought about it.

"I suppose it's a bit like getting naked in public. There are some parts of me I don't want other people to see."

Cassie wondered what it said about her, that she had no problem with freely sharing her emotions. Maybe she was an exhibitionist.

Still, it was a relief to know she hadn't entirely lost her ability to read people. "So you *were* stressed? I thought maybe I was imagining things and that being here didn't bother you."

"It bothers me a great deal. It bothered me before my father showed up unexpectedly, and now? I can't think of a word to cover it."

Cassie felt the tight knot in her chest relax. She'd promised herself that she wasn't going to talk about anything personal with her sister, but that was before she discovered her sister might be human, after all.

"Did you really not know your dad was here?"

"I didn't know." Her voice was laced with hurt and bitterness, and Cassie recognized both emotions because she was feeling them herself.

"It was a shocker. I handled it badly."

"I think your reaction was entirely human."

"Maybe. But I should have been cool. Instead of running off and almost mowing down poor Ajax, I should have said congratulations and raised a glass. That's probably what you did after I left. But I'm not you." She felt her throat thicken and felt a rush of frustration toward herself. Her emotions were about as easy to contain as a litter of puppies. She would have given a lot to feel nothing, or at least to be able to pretend she felt nothing. "Unlike you, I'm terrible at hiding my feelings."

"Well, it turns out so am I in certain situations, and that was one of them. Maybe you didn't notice my reaction, but I didn't raise a glass. I didn't say congratulations. I guess one's ability to hide one's feelings depends on the circumstances." Adeline wrapped her arms round her legs. "I don't think you handled it badly, Cassie. Given the circumstances, I think you were restrained."

"You do?"

"Yes." Adeline turned her head. "You didn't know either, did you?"

"That your dad was the man she was marrying? No. Of course not."

"It must hurt that she didn't tell you. I know you're close to her."

Cassie felt emotion rise. "Apparently not as close as I thought. And you're close to your dad."

"Apparently not as close as *I* thought. And yes, it hurts. This is…" Adeline broke off and took several deep breaths. "It's difficult, isn't it?"

"Yes." The words were lean and sparse, an inadequate topping to the depth of emotions that lay beneath but it didn't matter because they both knew what they were feeling.

There was a long silence, which Adeline eventually broke. "We have to figure it out."

"I suppose we do." She liked the sound of the *we*. But what was there to figure out? It wasn't as if their mother had given them a choice. This was happening, whether they liked it or not. Her stomach gave a loud rumble, and she gave an embarrassed laugh. "Sorry. My stomach doesn't care about drama. All it knows is that it was looking forward to Maria's food."

Adeline scrambled to her feet and brushed the sand from her dress. "Wait there."

"Where are you going?"

"Some things can't be fixed, but others can. My first rule when I'm stressed or anxious is to make sure I'm not tired, thirsty or hungry. You missed lunch picking me up from the airport. It's no wonder you're hungry. We can't do much about tired, but we can fix hungry and thirsty."

"If you're thinking of joining them for dinner—"

"I'm not. And last time I looked, they weren't there anyway." She adjusted her dress, as if she were about to walk into an important meeting where she needed to make an impression. "Promise me you won't go anywhere."

"I promise." Where was she going to go? And was this really her big sister begging her not to go anywhere?

She was mystified by this new turn of events. She'd thought maybe her mother might come looking for her (why hadn't she?), but she hadn't expected her sister. And the fact that Adeline had admitted to finding the situation difficult was almost as surprising as discovering her mother was intending to remarry her first husband.

Adeline was back less than five minutes later carrying a bottle under one arm, glasses and a large plate loaded with food. She picked her way back across the sand.

Why didn't she take her shoes off?

"I raided the kitchen and piled as much food as I could onto this one plate so that I could carry it. I hope you don't have any allergies." She sat down, keeping both hands on the plate to hold it steady.

Cassie stared. "How did you do that without using your hands or falling over?"

"Pilates. I have excellent core strength. Allergies?"

"No allergies." That was the kind of thing sisters should know about each other, wasn't it?

And she was doing it again. Romanticizing and idealizing relationships.

Cassie focused on the food instead. Adeline had made good choices. There were slivers of tender lamb, slow-roasted with garlic and oregano, plump glossy olives from their own olive trees, creamy tzatziki and spanakopita.

Her stomach rumbled. "Did you see them?"

"No. No sign of anyone. And we're not going to think about them right now. Eat. Then we'll talk and make a plan. Here, have a napkin." Adeline removed two folded napkins from the pockets of her dress.

"You brought napkins?"

"I thought they'd be useful. I love a dress with pockets, don't you?"

"I do. And thanks." Cassie took a napkin and spread it on her knees.

Half an hour earlier, she never would have imagined that she'd be sitting here, side by side with her sister, sharing a plate of food. For a moment, they could have been just two people enjoying a beach picnic. Salty air. The soft sound of waves hitting the sand.

Adeline pulled a bottle from under her arm. "Drink?"

Cassie stared at it. "Champagne? Are you kidding? We're not exactly celebrating."

"I know, but I couldn't find the water." It was so practical, so Adeline, that Cassie laughed.

"That's funny."

"Hopefully we'll still think so in the morning. Can you hold the glasses?" Adeline handed them over. "I thought plastic was safer in case we feel like smashing them in a fit of fury. We don't want to have lacerated feet."

"Have you ever smashed anything in a fit of fury?"

"Never, but I'm starting to think it might be cathartic." Adeline eased the cork out of the bottle and jumped as it popped. Champagne fizzed onto her dress. "Oops. I'm not very good at this."

"What is there to be good at? The bottle is open. I give you an A-plus." Cassie held the glasses for her sister to fill. "I'm mad that they haven't come looking for us, but also relieved because I can't face talking to them. Does that sound weird?"

"No, it sounds logical. I can't face talking to them either. Probably because they're not making a lot of sense. And we don't have to talk to them. Not tonight. That is a problem for tomorrow and we're not going to worry about tomorrow today." She balanced the bottle on the sand.

"I always worry about tomorrow today." Cassie selected a piece of lamb and popped it into her mouth. It was tender and succulent, the edges charred from the grill. She could taste the herbs that grew wild on the hillsides all around them. "What happens next? Are you going to stay for the wedding?"

"I haven't thought that far," Adeline said. "I try never to make decisions when I'm feeling emotional."

It was news to her that her sister ever felt emotional.

"I make all my decisions when I'm feeling emotional."

Her sister glanced at her. "And how does that work out?"

"Mostly badly." Cassie helped herself to a slice of spanako-pita and moaned as the flavor exploded in her mouth. "This is delicious. Maria sent me the recipe for this once and I tried to make this at home. It was a disaster. Now I buy it from the deli near my house, but it's not the same. Do you think it's just because Greek food tastes better in Greece?"

"Maybe," Adeline selected an olive, "but I think it's mostly because Maria is a genius in the kitchen."

"She is. And I feel bad. She has been working all day preparing for this evening, and I ruined it." Guilt almost put her off her food, but not quite. She took another piece of lamb.

"You didn't ruin anything."

"I stormed off."

"And I stayed and yelled." Adeline took a careful sip of champagne. "I'd say that of the two of us, you handled it in a far more rational manner."

"You yelled? I can't imagine that."

Adeline lowered the glass and stared out across the sea. "I'm surprised you didn't hear me."

"I didn't hear anything." Cassie pondered. "There was nothing rational about the fact that I ran away. I didn't know what to do. It was impulse."

"It was an impulse that gave you space and time to think. Because you removed yourself from the situation, you didn't say things you might later regret. It was a sensible move. Your glass is empty."

"That's easily fixed." Cassie reached for the bottle and topped up her glass. She felt a flicker of guilt. "This was supposed to be for the celebration."

"Well, now it's for drowning our sorrows. Our mother owes us that at least after springing that surprise on us."

Cassie's stomach gave a flip as she remembered that the problem hadn't gone away. "Why didn't she at least warn us?"

"I don't know. Possibly because this is our mother and she expected us to be thrilled."

Cassie took an olive from the plate. "But how could she possibly have thought we'd be thrilled?"

"It's what she does. It's the way she thinks. You know her. She has a way of shaping life into the way she wants it to look. It probably didn't occur to her that we'd be shocked and horrified. She treats real life as fiction. She thinks we're her characters, and that we'll react the way she wants us to react. She wrote the story of this evening in her head."

"You're right, she does do that."

"Although there is another explanation." Adeline paused while she chewed. "It's possible that she was afraid."

"Afraid of what?"

"Afraid that if she told us," Adeline said slowly, "we wouldn't come."

"But what's the difference between telling us before we arrive, and telling us when we're on the island? It doesn't change the news."

"No, but now we're here, not exactly trapped, but certainly unable to leave easily. It's possible that she knew we'd be upset and thought that by being here, there would be a greater chance of us having time to calm down and think it through."

"You're very smart. I would never have thought of that."

"Not really. It's my job to think about why people do the things they do."

Cassie did the same, only Adeline dealt with real people and she dealt with fictional people.

She topped up her sister's glass. It felt strange to be sharing like this. "You never struck me as the sort of person who drowns her sorrows. I thought you were always rational and calm."

"I thought that too until tonight." Adeline took a mouthful and then rested the glass in her lap. "Turns out I was wrong."

"Did you say things you now regret?"

"I said things. So far I'm not regretting them, but I'll let you know if that changes in the morning." Adeline helped herself to lamb. "Actually, that's not true. I do regret one thing, and that was reminding my mother that she had an affair and got pregnant."

"Exhibit A sitting right here." Cassie drained her glass and Adeline looked at her.

"I'm sorry. It was a terrible thing to say."

"It was the truth. She did have an affair. And then she had me."

"But what I was trying to point out to my father was that she'd crashed the relationship before, so why would he trust her not to do it again." Adeline wiped her fingers on a napkin. "If it was wrong last time, why is it suddenly right?"

Cassie had been asking herself the same thing and no matter which way she looked at it, it wasn't good.

She voiced the thought that had been simmering inside her. "If leaving your dad was a mistake, then having me was a mistake."

"I don't think those two things are connected." Adeline tipped more champagne into Cassie's glass.

"But maybe they are. And I'm sorry."

"Why are *you* sorry?"

"If I hadn't been born, maybe your parents wouldn't have broken up in the first place."

"You cannot be serious." Adeline gave an astonished laugh. "People often take responsibility for things that aren't their fault, but I don't think I've ever heard anyone blame themselves for being born."

"I know it's ridiculous, but it's how I feel."

"Well, you shouldn't." Adeline rested the bottle back on the sand. "The truth is this isn't about us at all. It's about them. They were thinking about themselves, and we were collateral damage."

"You're not pleased then?" Cassie felt herself blush. "I

mean, they are your parents. I could see a scenario where you'd be pleased."

"Pleased?" Adeline shot her an incredulous look. "They've been divorced for more than two decades. They decided their marriage was a mistake. That they weren't meant to be together. But despite that—despite twenty years where they have functioned perfectly well apart—they seem intent on making that mistake again. It's perplexing and upsetting."

It was comforting to know that her sister was thinking all the same things she'd been thinking.

"I've never seen you like this before. Sometimes it seems as if you don't feel anything."

"Does it seem that way?" Adeline frowned. "I feel plenty of things, but I've learned to hide it."

"I can't hide how I feel. I wish I could." Her phone pinged and she glanced at it. A message from Oliver flashed up on her screen.

You okay, Cass?

If he'd asked her an hour ago, the answer would most definitely have been *no*. But now?

She hesitated and then typed her reply.

Yes thanks. Just wanted to say hi.

"Who was that?" Adeline ate another piece of lamb. "If you need to make a call, go ahead. But be warned, I might finish the lamb while you're distracted. It's so good."

"I know, although I'd probably choose the spanakopita for my last meal on earth. I don't need to make a call. It was just Oliver."

"Boyfriend?"

"No. Best friend. We live together. I mean, not actually *together* in a romantic sense. We share a house in Oxford." A short time ago, she'd desperately wanted to be back there, but now she was glad she was right where she was. "How about you? Are you seeing someone?"

Adeline stared out at the ocean. "I was. His name is Mark."

"Was?"

"We didn't part on the best of terms. I broke up with him recently."

Cassie finished her drink. "Sorry. I shouldn't have asked."

"Why not? I asked you about Oliver."

"But Oliver is just a friend, it's different. Were you in love with Mark?"

"I don't know," Adeline said. "I don't think so. He hasn't been in contact since that night, and I don't care. That can't be a good sign, can it?"

Cassie tried to imagine her sister madly in love. Giggling. Passionate. "Were you together a long time?"

"A year."

"That's *ages*. So he can't have been the one. I mean, if someone is right, then you know, don't you think?"

Adeline frowned. "I don't believe in *the one*."

Cassie didn't know what to say to that. If they'd been having this conversation the week before, she would have said she absolutely believed in "the one" because look at her parents, but now she didn't know what to think. If her father had been the love of her mother's life, where did Adeline's father fit into that? How could he have been the wrong person, if he was back on the scene? It was so confusing.

Her brain couldn't decipher it, so she focused on her sister instead. "You said you and Mark didn't part on good terms. You had a fight?"

"Not exactly a fight. More a disagreement." Adeline finished her champagne and put the glass down on the sand next to the bottle. "He said he was seriously concerned about my judgment."

"He actually said that?" In her mind, Cassie tried putting those words into the mouth of the hero she was writing, but they didn't work. No matter which way you looked at it, that wasn't a heroic thing to say.

"It was about me coming here, to my mother's fourth wedding. He had a point. And if it hadn't been for Dad, I probably wouldn't have done." Adeline's laugh was devoid of humor. "Dad wanted me here. And I admired him for behaving in such a civilized way toward someone who broke his heart all those years ago. It didn't occur to me that there was anything else going on."

"Why would it? Why would either of us have thought that?" Cassie realized that Adeline felt as betrayed as she did.

"It's always a shock to discover you don't know someone as well as you thought you did."

Cassie scrunched the napkin in her lap. "I don't know what to do now. I don't know what to say to our mother."

"I don't know either."

"But you're the psychologist. You're trained for things like this."

"It doesn't make it any easier when you're the one in the middle of it."

Cassie didn't know if that was comforting or alarming. "Are you going to leave?"

"Leave the island? I don't know."

Cassie thought about how it would feel if Adeline left and her heart flipped. "Please don't." She felt suddenly awkward and wished she could snatch those words back. She had no right to say them. They didn't make sense, even to her. Up until today, she'd been hoping Adeline wouldn't come. And now she was hoping she wouldn't leave. "You must do whatever is right for you, of course. Ignore me."

"Why would I ignore you? We're in this together. We'll figure it out together." Adeline shifted closer to Cassie.

Their arms brushed and Cassie felt the first flickers of warmth. They'd never been in anything together before.

It felt good.

12

Catherine

Catherine sat on the lounger in the darkness. In front of her the pool lay empty and still, a slash of bright turquoise, illuminated from beneath by tiny lights. It was three in the morning and she'd given up on sleep.

When was she going to learn that real life wasn't like fiction? You could never predict how people were going to react.

If this were a scene in her book, she would have deleted it (always a painful experience, but occasionally necessary. Once, she'd deleted thirty thousand words and had to lie down for an entire day to recover). She would have hacked out those words and started again because the whole thing wasn't working the way it should.

She stared at the pool. The air was oppressively warm and scented sweet from the flowers that tumbled from terracotta pots around the terrace. Apart from the rhythmic call of cicadas and the sound of the sea, everything around her was still and quiet. Inside, her emotions churned like the ocean in the middle of a storm.

Andrew was fast asleep in their bedroom (it was one of the many injustices of life that whatever the crisis, men always seemed able to sleep) but Catherine's mind had been as active as an elite athlete in a training session. She knew from experience that the chances of sleep were zero, so she'd chosen to get up.

Why her brain always chose to be active at night she had no idea, but the moment she closed her eyes, her mind raced into overdrive. Dark thoughts nudged at her brain, refusing to allow her rest. During the day, she managed to keep reality at a distance, but at night it descended, ugly and undisguised, pressing itself into her consciousness. *Avoid me if you must, but that doesn't mean I'm not here.*

The evening had not gone as planned, which shouldn't have surprised her because since when did life ever go according to plan? But this time, she couldn't blame fate. The blame, if that was the right word, lay entirely with her. Her weakness had always been her tendency to reshape reality into something she found palatable. She'd had a clear image of how the evening would go and only now could she see how naive she'd been. She'd gone straight for the happy ending and tried to skip all the conflict and tough stuff that came before.

Adeline had said that to her once. *Your whole life is fiction!* And maybe that was true. When she didn't like what was happening, her brain imagined a different reality. She saw things the way she wanted them to be, rather than the way they were. It was the reason she was about to embark on her fourth marriage, and the reason her daughters weren't currently laughing together and enjoying their second or third glass of champagne while they celebrated the happy news.

Instead of considering the possibility that her daughter would be upset by the revelation that her parents were planning to remarry, she'd pictured Adeline's delight. She'd thought, optimistically, that her eldest daughter would be thrilled. Adeline and her father were close. She'd hoped that Adeline's unconditional love for her father might spill over and land on her, drawing them together. She'd imagined Adeline thinking, *If my father forgives her, then I forgive her.*

That wasn't what had happened.

Adeline's voice rang in her head. *I can't believe you'd put yourself through this a second time. She cheated on you! She had an affair. She got pregnant and had a baby.*

Catherine winced as she remembered those words. They were all true, and when you distilled it down to a few bare facts, it sounded awful. But life was always more than a few bare facts just as a human body was more than a skeleton. Flesh, blood, mistakes. Those were the things that made someone human. She'd made more mistakes than most.

It was embarrassing to admit that she wasn't good at relationships, given that she made her living writing about them, but writing about them gave you the chance to delete scenes and change the past. That wasn't an option in real life.

Three, soon to be four, marriages and two daughters, neither of whom were currently speaking to her. Even her brain couldn't reshape that into a scenario where she was a blameless victim.

In hindsight, perhaps it had been *too* optimistic of her to assume Adeline would be delighted. Perhaps it wasn't so surprising that it hadn't turned out that way.

Still, she wished her daughter had chosen her words more carefully.

Cassie had obviously been hurt badly by her sister's thoughtless outburst or she wouldn't have gone running off.

Catherine had wanted to go after her, but she'd had Adeline to deal with, and when Adeline had also stormed off, Andrew had insisted on giving both girls time to settle down and digest the news before having further conversation.

It had almost killed Catherine thinking of Cassie alone with her distress, but she knew that given time Cassie would accept the situation. Cassie was always fine with everything. She'd been the easiest child and seemed to find happiness and hope in every situation.

Adeline was more difficult.

Catherine felt a pang of guilt because she knew that the reason for her daughter's strong reaction could be traced right back to childhood.

She was responsible for the upheaval Adeline had experienced at a young age. But for how long was she going to punish herself for doing what she'd had to do? She'd had no choice, at least none that she'd been able to see. And that one decision had affected both her life and her daughter's.

Because of her, Adeline was wary of relationships. Her own and, it turned out, her mother's.

Adeline didn't understand of course, and neither did Cassie. Not only did children rarely see their parents as people with their own complicated lives and flaws (in her case, so many flaws) but it was human nature to form judgments based on the facts available, and she hadn't given them all the facts and she didn't intend to. And the ones she *had* given them, didn't begin to hint at the whole picture.

Fortunately, most people didn't bother looking for more. They didn't ask themselves, *What else could be going on here?* It was something she thought about all the time when she was writing, the fact that a person's actions were almost always motivated by something bigger than the moment. That behind every action was a chain of events that could stretch back into the far distance. There was always something *more*. When a woman snapped at a colleague, they might dismiss her as short-tempered, but maybe the truth was that things were terrible at home, her teenager wasn't speaking to her, she was caring for elderly parents, she was so oppressed by the pressures of her life that there were days when she could barely breathe. And then she arrived at the office stressed by her life, emotionally stretched to the point of snapping, unable to handle one more thing, and a colleague asked her when she would finish a piece of work because the deadline was yesterday, and that was it. *Snap*. It wasn't about the deadline or the colleague. It was all the things that had gone before.

But the people she worked with didn't know that. They didn't see how hard she was working to keep her family safe and together. All they saw was a missed deadline and a short-tempered colleague.

And when the world looked at her, Catherine Swift, they saw a wealthy, successful woman remarrying a man she'd divorced two decades before. They had no idea of the events that had brought her to this point.

Catherine took a sip of her drink and let her mind travel back to the day she'd first met Andrew Swift.

She'd been eighteen and working in a coffee shop. Unlike her school friends, she'd had no wish to go to university. All she wanted to do was tell stories. She wanted to write. Her first book had been accepted by a publisher (and she was only eighteen! With the optimism of youth, she'd truly believed she had this sorted). She'd assumed it was the start of a brilliant future.

She'd been woefully ignorant.

The publisher had paid her a small advance, but it would be another eighteen months before they published her book. She'd had no idea it would take that long. The idea of being paid to do what she loved was exciting, until she'd figured out that her advance would only cover her rent and food for two months. After that, she'd have to find another way to make money because writing wasn't going to feed her.

She needed to get a "proper" job. But she wasn't qualified for anything. And how was she going to write if she had a job? Where would she find the time?

She liked coffee and she drank plenty of it, so she walked into a fancy coffee shop in Covent Garden and talked them into hiring her. She figured that she could listen to conversations, observe people, develop ideas and scribble in her notebook on her breaks.

She'd been working there for a month when Andrew had walked in.

She'd been struck by two things: his American accent and his confidence. He had a sophistication that she hadn't encountered before, and she'd immediately rethought the hero she was currently writing. *He'd be American*, she thought. *With a warm smile and great eye contact*. But behind that smooth exterior and apparently perfect life, he would be hiding a secret.

Her creative brain was alight with ideas as she'd delivered Andrew's order to his table by the window. He'd thanked her (impeccable manners) and asked her to join him. She'd badly wanted to but hadn't dared. The job was barely covering her rent and she couldn't risk losing it, so she'd declined regretfully but served him an extra coffee on the house to make up for it and to show she was interested.

He'd come in the next day and then the next, and by the end of the week he'd asked her out.

She'd never had a real boyfriend before (she'd had plenty of fictional ones) and she felt as if she'd struck gold.

He was ten years older than her and rising through the ranks in his job in the city. She didn't know exactly what he did, but whatever it was paid him enough to own his own apartment and take her to dinner in restaurants with fancy French names and incomprehensible menus.

He was glamorous, sophisticated (he ate oysters! Catherine had never met anyone who ate oysters) and fascinated by her. He told her that what he'd always wanted was to be an artist, but he came from a wealthy Bostonian family who had worked in finance for three generations and Andrew Swift was expected to follow the same. He'd told himself he could paint as a hobby, but his work left virtually no time for hobbies so in reality he rarely picked up a paintbrush.

He admired Catherine's creativity, and was impressed that she had already written a book that was going to be published. She'd only realized much later that in her he'd seen the life he could have been living.

They'd married, and he'd insisted that she give up her job so that she could concentrate on being creative and writing full-time. He didn't want her to work in the coffee shop. He wanted her to write. It didn't matter that she didn't earn much money. He earned more than enough for both.

His generosity had floored her. She was desperate to write and here he was presenting her with the means to allow her to do it. Not only that, but he believed in her.

Her first book was finally published (with the name Catherine Swift on the cover), and by traveling half way across London, she managed to find it in one store. But still that was a thrill. Her book! For sale. It was the biggest high. She'd stood in the store for two hours and finally someone had picked up her book from the shelf and bought it. It had taken all her self-control not to tap the woman on the shoulder and say, *I wrote that.*

And it was true that being a published author hadn't at that point come with either fame or fortune, but still it was an unbeatable feeling. She'd felt vindicated in her life choices.

Andrew had continued to encourage her, and Catherine had continued to write. She had another book published, and then another. By publishing standards, she was doing well, but still she didn't earn enough to make more than a trivial contribution toward their expenses. Writing, it turned out, wasn't a route to riches although the public rarely understood that. For every author who made serious money, there were thousands of others barely able to subsidize their coffee habit.

It didn't matter to Andrew, and because it didn't matter to him, it didn't matter to her either. They were happy. They laughed a lot. He immersed himself in her creative world, and in the evenings, they'd sit in their tiny garden and she'd talk to him about her plots and characters. He relished any conversation that didn't involve the boring world of banking, which he increasingly loathed. A few years into their marriage, Adeline arrived, and Catherine somehow navigated the challenge of writing while caring for a child.

And then her books had started to sell. It wasn't an overnight thing, more of a slow build as a reader discovered one of her books and then went back to read everything else she'd written. It snowballed. Finally, she was earning money, which delighted her after years of feeling like a drain on Andrew.

That was the point where things had gone wrong.

To be precise, she changed.

Success, she discovered, altered things in a way that wasn't always immediately visible. She couldn't look back and identify the exact moment it all started to go wrong. The decline of a marriage wasn't always a seismic event. Often it began with small virtually undetectable ripples of discontent that shook the foundations of a partnership. Cracks appeared. The change in their circumstances chipped away at them.

She was relieved that she was no longer dependent on Andrew. The guilt that had always niggled melted away.

Now when they went to dinner parties, people asked her about her work and congratulated her. They joked that Andrew would soon be able to give up work and be a kept man.

She should have noticed sooner that Andrew was the only one not laughing.

It was on the way home from an evening with friends that they'd had their first proper fight. She'd wished many times since that night that she'd handled things differently. Maybe if she hadn't had that extra glass of wine, or hadn't just received the news that her sales had grown beyond all expectations, she might have paid more attention to him. She might have listened more carefully to what he was saying.

Instead, she'd interpreted his moodiness as envy. After all, hadn't he always longed to pursue an artistic career? She'd thought he was resentful of her success and she'd been upset that he couldn't celebrate what was, to her, the culmination of her hard work and dreams.

He'd tried telling her that night that he'd always felt that his job had a purpose, and that was to support her so that she could pursue her dream. Now she no longer needed his financial support, his job had ceased to have purpose. He'd confessed that he missed the old days, when struggle had bonded them. She knew now that what he was trying to say was that he no longer felt needed or important in her life, but at the time what she'd heard was him saying he wished her success had never happened.

The success of *Summer Star* was to be the final straw.

With the money she earned from the book and the movie, she bought the villa on Corfu (Andrew had said that it was her money, so of course she should do what she wanted with it). It was impossible for her to describe what the place meant to her. Not just the villa and the view, both of which were spectacular, but what it symbolized. She thought about her father (long dead, thanks to a collision between his skull and a cricket ball). She thought about Miss Barrett.

How could she be worthless when she had this tangible proof of her worth?

She spent as much time at the villa as possible. Andrew joined her when he could, but she was always in demand. She was expected to record interviews, to tour, and she arrived home one night to find that he'd flown back to London because there was no point in him being in Greece when she was somewhere else.

She'd felt resentful (she wished she could put the clock back and give her young self a sharp talking to). What was she supposed to do? Of course, she had to travel if she was asked to. This was her career. Having supported her for so long, why could he no longer understand that?

Their relationship, now fragile and newly brittle, had started to crack.

On the surface, it was her success that had broken her, but deep down she knew it wasn't that simple. *She'd* broken them. By not listening to Andrew properly. By not spending more time hearing what he was saying. By not thinking about what *he* needed. For jumping to conclusions.

She wished she'd told him that it wasn't his financial support that had made the biggest difference to her (although she didn't underestimate that), but his belief in her. She should have made it clear that it was *him* she needed, not his money. From her point of view, the fact that she no longer needed his money was a good thing, and she didn't see it that way.

Would she have had an affair had things been going well in their marriage? Definitely not. But she'd been lonely and struggling and missing Andrew when she'd met the charming and charismatic Robert Dunn. He'd arrived in her life at her weakest, most vulnerable moment. He'd given her exactly what she needed, and in doing so had delivered the fatal blow to her marriage.

With a shiver, Catherine stood up. How long had she been sitting on the lounger? Her skin was chilled, and she hadn't even noticed. She rubbed her hands over her flesh. She'd lost track of time.

She didn't want to think about Rob right now.

She couldn't.

Her priority was her girls.

How was she going to handle this?

The girls couldn't comprehend how two people who had chosen to live their lives apart, could suddenly want to be together again. They didn't understand that life wasn't static. That people weren't static. That they were formed and changed by their experiences, and she and Andrew had been changed by theirs. Maybe if they'd been better at communicating, maybe if her success hadn't come as hard and fast as it had, maybe if she hadn't needed her career to soothe her deep-seated insecurities—

Maybe, maybe, maybe…

Andrew, who had been a casualty of staffing cuts at the bank, had finally used that as an excuse to walk away from a career he hated. Instead of spending long days in a glass-fronted office doing a job that gave him no satisfaction, he'd done what he always wanted to do. He'd taken the severance package they'd paid him and rented a studio. He spent his days painting. Finally, he'd found his own passion instead of working to support hers.

They'd stayed in touch over the years, at first because of Adeline and later because they chose to.

When their relationship had blossomed again, no one had

been more surprised than Catherine. It had happened gradually. Their occasional lunch dates had become more frequent. Conversation that had barely skimmed the surface of their lives had plunged deeper. Lunch had blended into dinner until they were spending more and more time together. Casual had become intimate. They talked, really talked, in a way they never had when they were together the first time. And then she'd spent that wonderful week at his home in Cape Cod. And that had been it. They'd been together since. She hadn't thought she was capable of trusting again after everything that had happened. It had turned out that with the right man, she could. And Andrew was the right man.

What she needed to explain to the girls was that this wasn't a resurrection of an old relationship, but the beginning of a new one. She was different. Andrew was different. Their relationship was different. As a couple, this time around they were *better*.

Tired and stressed, she walked to the edge of the terrace. She could see the lights illuminating the path to the guest cottage. The cottage itself was in darkness. Were the girls in there? Had Adeline apologized or had they gone to bed, each nursing their wounds separately? Andrew had insisted that they give the girls space, so that's what they'd done but that didn't mean Catherine was comfortable with it.

She should have anticipated that rekindling her relationship with Andrew would trigger all manner of awkward questions.

She wished now that she'd told Cassie about Andrew in advance. But maybe that wouldn't have helped. And what would she have said?

"Catherine?"

She turned, guilty, as she heard Maria's voice.

"Sorry, Maria. Did I wake you?"

Maria had stayed the night in the house, which she sometimes did when she was cooking and the guest cottage was occupied.

"I wasn't asleep. I guessed you wouldn't be either." Maria put an arm round her and Catherine turned and leaned her head against her shoulder, breathing in the scent of lemon soap and comfort.

She felt a rush of love and gratitude. Maria was the best friend she'd ever had.

"I'm sorry——" Her voice cracked. "Your beautiful meal. All that work."

"The meal will keep. It's you I'm worried about. Tonight was difficult."

"Yes." She'd never lied to Maria and she wasn't going to start now.

Maria knew everything. All of it, even the dark parts that Catherine had hidden from everyone else. She'd been with Catherine through thick and thin, through three husbands, through death and divorce. She'd seen her at her worst and her best. Lived through the highs and the lows and through it all she'd been rock-solid. Even on that awful night, she'd been rock-solid. A lighthouse in a storm.

We never talk about this again, Catherine. Never. Not to anyone. It's our secret.

And so it had remained. Their secret. And they never had talked about it. Not once.

And she knew they weren't going to talk about it now. They'd do what they always did, and pretend that it had never happened.

"What if they don't accept this?"

"They will. Give them time."

"But what if time isn't enough?" It was something she hadn't allowed herself to consider until now.

"It will be."

She would need to find a way to help them understand.

People thought that you fell in love, got married and that was it. They didn't know that the real story began there.

They didn't realize that the really juicy stuff was what happened after.

13

Adeline

Her head was being hammered by a sharp object. Someone was removing her brain and had forgotten to give her an anesthetic. She was going to sue them.

Adeline opened her eyes, forgetting that when she'd eventually fallen into bed she'd been too tired to close the shutters. Sunlight dazzled, hitting bright white walls and bouncing off the cheerful blue paintwork. It was like being prepped for an interrogation.

She closed her eyes again. Exhaustion and anxiety clung to her brain. Through the open window, she could hear birds and the soft sounds of the ocean. It should have soothed her. This was what people did when they were stressed, wasn't it? They listened to the steady sound of rainfall, or the rush ocean waves. And here she was, listening to actual ocean waves, and she'd never felt less relaxed in her life.

Her chest was tight, her muscles were tense, her head was crowded with something close to panic. None of those feelings had anything to do with the champagne she'd drunk, and everything to do with the events of the night before, which had destroyed all chances of meaningful rest. She'd thought she could make it through another of her mother's weddings. After all, she'd attended her fair share. She'd thought she'd be able to grit her teeth, force a smile and maybe even say congratulations as she had on those other occasions. She hadn't really cared who her mother was marrying because it hadn't mattered to her.

It mattered to her now. And she cared.

Her father. Her mother was marrying her father.

She groaned and pressed her face into the pillow. The whole thing felt as weird as it sounded.

Anxiety sliced through her.

For the past weeks, she'd been imagining her father pottering around his beach house in Cape Cod, keeping himself busy, painting alone or with his artist friends, strolling barefoot along the sand, filling his day and his mind so that he didn't have to think about the woman who had once been his wife getting married again. She'd imagined him awake at night, solitary and sad.

Now she was imagining him laughing with her mother. Kissing her mother. *In bed with her mother.*

Swamped by a rush of hot and then cold, she sat upright.

She didn't want to imagine that.

She didn't want to think about that.

She rubbed her fingers across her forehead, trying to chase the thought from her brain. Why would he choose to do this? She didn't understand. It wasn't right, or reasonable. She needed to talk to him, without her mother there. She had to reason with him. She had to give him the opportunity to explore his feelings. Was he trying to go back to the past?

Giving up on rest, she stood up and walked to the bathroom.

Through the large window, she could see the sea, shimmering turquoise and silver in the morning sunlight.

She'd been seven years old when her mother had bought the villa. That had been the first clue as to just how successful her mother had become. Before that, Adeline hadn't thought about her mother's career. Her family had seemed no different to anyone else's. Her father worked in a bank, doing something that required him to wear a suit and leave their small house in the west of London before Adeline was awake. Her mother spent her time writing, which meant she was home with Adeline. Being home didn't always mean being present, but Adeline understood that her mother's work was different from other people's. She learned that when the door to the spare room was closed, she wasn't to go inside. Eventually her mother would emerge (smiling or stressed, depending on what sort of writing day she'd had) and they'd spend time together. They'd walked through parks, along the River Thames, through the historic streets of London and Adeline had treasured those moments when she'd had her mother to herself. Most of all, she'd treasured the moments when they read together, side by side on the sofa, listening to the rain hammering against the window. Sometimes her mother had made up stories just for her and those were some of her favorites. She'd felt happy, warm, loved.

And then came *Summer Star*, the book that changed all their lives.

Adeline had often wondered how her life might have looked if her mother hadn't written that book, or if the public hadn't been hungry for a book exactly like that one. The timing had been perfect. Publishing, she knew now, was fickle but that book had struck a chord. It was a time before social media, and yet that book had sold and sold, its growth fed by word-of-mouth recommendation from friends, family and bookstore owners. *Summer Star* had spent week after week at the top of the bestseller lists in multiple countries. The money had followed.

Memories flashed up from that time. Random. Disconnected. She'd been young, focused on herself, school, friends, their new puppy, but there were things she remembered. Her mother, coming out of the spare room after a phone call with her agent, tears rolling down her face and a look of excitement in her eyes. She'd been mouthing something indistinctly and it had taken Adeline a moment to understand what she was saying.

You have no talent.

She'd repeated the words over and over again, and Adeline hadn't had a clue what her mother was talking about or why she was smiling and crying at the same time.

It was clear to her that her mother did have talent, so it didn't make sense.

She'd grabbed Adeline by the shoulders, her grip tight and her eyes fevered. *Never believe anyone who tells you that you can't do something. Promise me.*

Adeline had promised, having no idea what she was promising but willing to say anything because this slightly wild version of her mother was unnerving.

It's a new beginning, her mother kept saying. A new beginning.

It had taken Adeline a while to realize that beginnings followed endings. In this case, the thing that was ending was her parents' marriage. She'd been too young to understand the details, but not too young to feel the tension. The atmosphere in the house changed. Her mother's routine changed. She no longer spent all day locked in her office writing her latest book. She was expected to tour, and do book signings in multiple countries.

On the nights she was away, Adeline would often find her father sitting alone in her study, staring at the shelves stacked with her mother's books. On one occasion, she'd crawled onto his lap and he'd hugged her tightly and muttered, "I wasn't enough."

She had no idea what he meant by that, but she knew it wasn't good.

And then her mother had bought the villa in Corfu.

The first time Adeline had seen it, she'd felt as if she'd stepped into another life.

The villa clung to a steep hillside that sloped down to the sea. It was built from local stone and a brief glimpse might have suggested that it was rustic, but that idea vanished the moment you stepped over the threshold. From the beautiful curved living room that opened onto the terrace and the infinity pool to the peaceful, calm bedroom suites, each with its own terrace, the villa was pure luxury. It was furnished in creams and pastel tones, with accents of blue and violet, which picked out the colors of the ocean and the sky. White marble floors reflected the light. Large bold canvases hung on the wall, but most visitors focused not on the art, but on the view.

Adeline had been both impressed and intimidated. Mostly she'd been homesick for London and their tall townhouse with her cozy attic bedroom stuffed with her toys and books. Her father had seemed equally unsure, although she was starting to sense there was something more complicated happening between the two adults in her life. Her mother was swanning around in caftans, staring wistfully out across the ocean like a heroine from one of her novels. Her father was staring at her mother, as if trying to recognize and understand this person he was married to. Laughter gave way to sharp words and raised voices.

It was the first hint she'd had that relationships didn't always stay the same. That love wasn't a constant thing. That it could be withdrawn as easily as it had been given.

With a sigh, Adeline turned away from the window and stepped under the rainfall shower. She shouldn't be thinking about that now. There was enough to deal with in the present without going back to the past.

In the calm of her London apartment, it had been easy to tell herself that she'd be able to handle it, that she'd moved on. She was *trained* for this.

The reality wasn't so simple.

It was jarring that somewhere so beautiful, so perfect, could shake up her insides like a cocktail mixer.

She closed her eyes and let the water flow over her, feeling the sting of heat against her skin. Gradually, she felt her muscles relax and by the time she stepped out of the shower, she was feeling more in control.

She wrapped herself in one of the large soft towels that had been left for her use. Her clothes were still in her suitcase, and her suitcase was by the door where she'd abandoned it the moment she'd walked into the cottage. Unpacking had seemed a stressful acknowledgment that this version of family hell wasn't going to end anytime soon, so she'd left it, telling herself that she could grab that case and go whenever she chose. She could be back in London in a matter of hours, leaving all this behind. There was nothing keeping her here. She did not have to stay for this wedding.

That was before she'd discovered that the groom was her father.

How could she walk away now?

She pulled on a swimsuit, intending to try to work off some of her stress in the pool.

"Adeline?"

She heard Cassie's voice through the door of her bedroom and felt something tug inside her.

It wasn't only her father that she had to think about. If she left, then Cassie would be on her own with this.

Mark would say that wasn't her problem. He'd point out that she and Cassie didn't have a relationship. That she didn't owe her anything.

But she didn't feel that way. She couldn't forget the sight of her sister sitting on the beach.

Cassie had felt rejected. Alone. Adeline knew how that felt.

Ignoring the ache in her chest, Adeline pulled shorts and a linen top over her swimsuit.

Scooping her still wet hair into a ponytail, she opened the door of the bedroom.

"Good morning."

Cassie was hovering by the door, holding two oversized mugs brimming with coffee. She was wearing a loose T-shirt in a bright shade of coral over a pair of cutoff shorts. Her cheeks were pink from the sun and dusted with freckles. Her eyes were tired and her hair was caught up in a scrunchie. She looked young and vulnerable.

"You're already packed?" She eyed the open suitcase. "You don't have to leave. If anyone is leaving, it should be me, so that you can spend some proper time with your parents." It was said casually, but Adeline knew there was nothing casual about it.

Her half sister was as hurt and confused as she was, possibly more so. Cassie seemed to be picturing Catherine, Andrew and Adeline putting the past behind them and reverting to a cozy little family unit with herself on the outside.

Adeline wasn't able to picture that at all, mostly because she knew it wouldn't happen. They'd had their shot at being a functional family and failed. So what did that make them this time? She had no idea.

"I haven't packed. I didn't bother unpacking."

"I'm not sure if that makes it worse or better." Cassie gave a half smile. "I wanted to say thank you for last night. For coming to find me. For listening. I was feeling horrible and you made it easier. Sorry I was pathetic."

"You weren't pathetic. Your reaction was valid and understandable." She met Cassie's anxious gaze and some long-forgotten emotion uncurled inside her. A bond that she'd rejected. "Did you sleep?" She probably shouldn't have asked. She was struggling to handle her own feelings, without taking on anyone else's.

"Not much. You?"

Adeline shook her head. "No." She glanced at her open suitcase. The box that Maya had sent her was still unopened. Figuring that this was as good a time as any to see what her friend had picked out for her, she slid her finger under the seal and opened it.

She blinked, dazzled by the rainbow of colors that greeted her.

"Damn it, Maya." She muttered the words under her breath. "Mark was right. I should have checked."

She picked up a sundress in a shade of pale lemon, and then another that was bright coral and hung from straps so thin they looked as if they'd snap at the faintest pressure.

"Wow. I love that." Cassie was still in the doorway, and she was staring at the dress Adeline was holding up. "It will look stunning on you. Sorry, I didn't mean to disturb you, but do you have painkillers? I don't think I'll survive the next few hours without medicinal support."

Adeline reached into her suitcase and held out a small box. "Take them. I have more."

"Thanks." Cassie put the mugs of coffee down on the table and slipped the painkillers into the pocket of her shorts. She was still staring at the dress. "Why are you looking at it so doubtfully?"

"Because I don't wear dresses like this."

"So why did you buy it?"

"I didn't. I have a friend who works for a fashion magazine, and she sent me a box of clothes as a gift. I should have checked what was in the box before I packed it."

"That's an amazing gift." Cassie stepped closer so that she could see the contents of the box. "There are some fabulous pieces here. I need to rethink my friends. None of mine would send me stuff like this." She held up a floaty nearly transparent beach wrap in a shade of turquoise. "I don't understand the problem."

"The problem is that she has picked out clothes that suit her life, not mine."

Cassie put the wrap down and grinned. "As your sister, I owe it to you to tell you that if your life doesn't suit these clothes, then you need to change your life."

Adeline hung the dresses up. "Maya would agree with you." She didn't know why she was bothering to hang them, but she didn't want Cassie to think she was going to leave the moment her back was turned. Hanging them up hopefully signaled that she was here for the duration.

"I don't know if you're a coffee drinker." Cassie picked up a mug and handed it to her. "It's strong."

"I'm a coffee drinker, and strong works for me. Thanks."

Adeline tucked the empty suitcase under the bed and took the mug. "My head is killing me. Yours obviously is too."

Cassie gave a brief smile of recognition. "Why do you think I was begging for painkillers? I can leave you alone if you prefer."

She did prefer. She had so much to think about, and she always did her best thinking by herself. On top of that, she wasn't sure that right now she could handle Cassie's emotions as well as her own.

And then she glanced at her sister and saw the look in her eyes. Uncertainty.

Her lips moved, forming the words she hadn't intended to say. "Let's take our coffee onto the terrace."

Cassie's face brightened. "Really? Are you sure?"

Adeline felt an ache build inside her. She knew that emotion. Insecurity. The voice of someone who wasn't sure they were wanted.

"Yes. We're in this together, Cassie." She emphasized the word *together* and saw her sister's eyes glisten in the few seconds before she blinked.

"Right. Good." Cassie handed her mug to Adeline to hold while she opened the doors that led from the bedroom to the terrace.

They settled on sun loungers with their coffees. Immediately below them the sea sparkled, turquoise blue and inviting.

"It feels strange, doesn't it, being here in this stunning place and being so stressed." Cassie settled on a sun lounger and stretched out her legs. Tiny flecks of coffee spilled onto her T-shirt as she moved, and she cursed and put the cup down on the terrace. "My head is thumping. Probably shouldn't have drunk that champagne, but in our defense, it was a very low point in our lives."

"I know. Although generally I don't overindulge when I'm

at a low point. I don't believe in using substances as a mood regulator." But last night she had. Last night, she'd done and said all sorts of things she wouldn't normally have done and said. She'd even talked to Cassie about Mark. Why would she have done that?

Cassie glanced at her. "You never overindulge?"

"No. I think it's important to acknowledge your emotions and deal with them, not numb them."

"I think of it more as numbing them until you're ready to deal with them." Cassie took a sip of her coffee. "And I think it's a good thing you overindulged."

"I don't." Her head throbbed. She slid sunglasses onto her nose. "The very worst thing you can do in a low moment is turn to alcohol, or sugar, or drugs."

Cassie gave a fatalistic shrug. "Well, we didn't do any drugs, so I guess that's a win."

"I shouldn't have come. Mark was right."

"Mark's the guy who thinks you need to rethink your priorities? I don't like the sound of him."

What did it say about her relationship that she didn't even feel the urge to defend him?

She was starting to wonder why she'd stayed with him for so long.

"Why do you think it's a good thing that I overindulged?"

"It was good for me. It made you seem less intimidating. More human."

Adeline couldn't have been more shocked. "You find me intimidating?"

"A bit. You're very composed and in control. But last night you were a little unbalanced by everything, and also very honest. That was refreshing. And it made me feel a lot better at a point in my life when I was coming unglued. Did you take something for your headache?"

"No, but I'm hydrating." Adeline was reeling from the revelation that she was intimidating.

"If you don't usually drink, or stuff yourself full of sugar, how do you deal with stress?"

"Meditation. Controlled breathing. Yoga. Exercise if it's convenient and safe to do so."

"And does that work?" Cassie was staring. "As someone who tends to dive head first into chocolate, I find that impressive. And a little daunting if I'm honest."

"It works, depending on the level of stress." Adeline put her coffee down. Maybe caffeine hadn't been such a great idea. "Is it me or are those plants really bright?"

"The bougainvillaea? They're bright, but even brighter after a bottle of champagne. Shame there isn't a way to mute them until we've recovered." With her tumbled hair and sleepy eyes, Cassie reminded Adeline of a kitten, fluffy and comfortable.

"You love it here, don't you?"

"Yes. Particularly this cottage. My room is so peaceful. I love the little desk under the window. I've spent so many hours writing in that spot. Distracting though, with the ocean right there and the garden and the birds."

"Writing?"

"Essays. Homework. That kind of thing." There was a tinge of pink on Cassie's cheeks. She seemed about to say something and then stopped herself. "Boring stuff."

Not boring, Adeline thought, just something she didn't want to share.

She realized how little she knew about her sister. "You're not tempted to stay in academia?"

"No." Cassie was vague. "I'm waiting to see if something pans out." Her phone rang and she snatched it up and checked the caller display.

"Oliver?"

Cassie shook her head. "Number withheld. Which probably means it's a scam or a sales call. Someone trying to catch me off guard and persuade me to transfer all my money into their bank account." She put her phone down. "How about you? When did you decide you wanted to be a psychologist?"

"I was ten."

"What happened when you were ten? Was it the divorce? No, you would have been eight when that happened." Cassie flushed. "You probably don't want to talk about it. It's just that I've always felt as if there is a big missing part of my life where you should have been. Our mother doesn't really talk about that time much."

Adeline didn't talk about it either.

She wasn't sure she wanted to talk about it now when her feelings were all over the place and she didn't feel entirely in control.

But Cassie was looking at her with hope and expectation and memories flashed into her brain. Cassie, aged eighteen months, her chubby arms outstretched for Adeline to pick her up. Cassie snuggled on her lap while Adeline read to her. Cassie by her side wherever she went.

She swallowed. "At ten, I was sent to live with my dad."

"Oh." Cassie frowned. "You make it sound as if you didn't have a choice."

There had been no choice.

People said memories faded, but that one hadn't. She still remembered the agonizing, wrenching sense of loss as her world had changed again. That was the point where she'd realized that emotions were so much more than just strong feelings that rushed in and retreated like sea on sand. They were so much more than love, joy, excitement and fear. Emotions had power. Emotions could change you. Deep down, from the inside out, they could reshape you as a person.

"Adeline?" Cassie's soft prompt dragged her back to the present.

And now it was her turn to frown, because did Cassie really think she'd chosen to leave?

"Is that what she told you? That I chose to leave? It isn't true."

It was obvious that this was new information to Cassie. "Would you tell me all of it? From your side of things? If you'd rather not, then I understand. We'll drop the subject and never talk about it again."

Her sister was as warm and kind as she'd been as a toddler, and Adeline was relieved that life hadn't changed that about her. That experiences and emotions hadn't yet sharpened that softness.

But what would hearing her story do?

"It's the past," she said finally. "We should probably leave it there."

"If you want to leave it, we'll leave it. But if you're worried about me, then don't be. I'd like to know. Until last night, I had a really clear picture of my past, and it's growing murkier by the minute. There is so much I don't understand. All I want is the truth."

Adeline felt a pang of sympathy because she was feeling the same way. There was so much that the pair of them didn't understand about what was happening. The least she could do was throw clarity on the parts she was sure about.

"You're right that I was eight when they divorced. Like most kids, it hadn't occurred to me that my life could change with no warning. At that age, you're very focused on self. If I'd been older, maybe I would have seen signs, but I didn't."

Cassie listened carefully. "It must have been a terrible shock."

"It was. I won't bore you with the details because they aren't relevant, but to begin with, I carried on living here, and stayed with my father during the holidays. For almost two years, that was the arrangement. Then overnight everything changed and she sent me to live with my dad permanently." It was easier to talk about it than she'd thought it would be. Perhaps it was because her emotional outburst of the night before had cracked something open inside her. Or maybe it was simply that her sister was surprisingly easy to talk to. "She said it was the best thing for me. What she really meant was that it was the best thing for her. She had a new husband and a new baby, and I was in the way." It was impossible to describe how that had made her feel, but perhaps it wasn't necessary because Cassie made a distressed sound.

"I don't get it. She always told me you wanted to live with your father. She told me you'd chosen that. I remember after one of your visits, when you were older, she cried after you left. I mean, really cried. She sobbed in a way I'd never seen before. And when I asked her what was wrong, she told me that life could sometimes be very complicated. She said she missed you."

Adeline digested that. "That can't be right."

"It is. I remember it well because it was so upsetting. I felt sorry for her, because I thought you'd chosen to leave. And I felt guilty, because I assumed I was the reason you'd chosen to leave." Cassie gave an awkward shrug. "I thought you probably didn't want to be near me."

"You couldn't be more wrong." She'd been ready to close down the conversation after delivering a few facts, but there was no way she could do that now. "You were the best part of my new life. I fell in love with you the moment I saw you."

Cassie sat a little straighter. "You did?"

"Yes. And no one was more surprised than me. Before you were born, I resented you." It felt strange, voicing thoughts she'd kept to herself for so long. "I believed that you and your dad were the reason my family had been blown apart. That if she hadn't had you, my parents would still be together. Not true, of course, but eight-year-olds don't have a sophisticated understanding of adult relationships. I was ready to hate you, but then there you were in your crib with your fuzzy hair and your big eyes." She smiled, remembering. "You were such a cute little thing."

"You thought I was cute?"

"You *were* cute." Adeline glanced at her. "I swear you were born smiling. Instead of wanting to smother you, I discovered I wanted to hold you and cuddle you. I did that a lot. You were the reason I started to accept this new life and my parents' divorce. You did a lot to calm my stress levels."

Cassie let out a long breath. "I always assumed you blamed me."

"How could I blame you? You were a baby. Even eight-year-old me knew it wasn't your fault. Before you were born, I didn't feel too much goodwill toward you, that's true. But afterward? The world seemed like a better place after you arrived." She rarely allowed herself to think about that time, but she did it now, and in doing so, she felt the emotion form a solid lump in her chest. "Once you started crawling, I rarely left your side. I made sure you didn't get into something you shouldn't. I was there when you took your first steps. You managed three, and then you fell on my lap. Your first word was *Adda*."

"The first thing I talked about was a snake?"

"Not adder." Adeline smiled. "Adda. You were trying to say *Adeline* but you could only manage Adda."

"Adda." Cassie smiled as she repeated it. "I like it."

"Our mother didn't. She kept trying to get you to say *Dadda* instead. I suppose she thought your father would like it. You loved books, although back then you mostly chewed them. My favorite book was *Matilda*. I still have it. It has tooth marks in one corner."

Cassie gave a laugh. "Sorry."

"Don't be. It's a good memory." But also a painful one. Adeline turned to look at her. "I imagined us growing up together. You loved me unconditionally, and I felt the same way about you. I was going to teach you everything. I was going to take care of you when the world was horrid." It was the last time she'd let herself feel like that. The last time she'd given her love without reservation.

"I didn't know." Cassie's eyes were shiny. "I didn't know any of this."

"You were too young to remember. And then one morning we were eating breakfast together, you and I..." She took a deep breath as she allowed herself to remember that morning. "Maria had made you eggs. I was teaching you to dip toast in them. And our mother suddenly appeared, all flustered, and told me that Kostas was going to drive me to the airport and I was going to stay with my father. I kept saying *for how long? How long will I be there?* I was upset, because it was the summer holidays and I'd been looking forward to spending all my time with you. I argued with her. I begged her. But she said I had to trust her, and that she was doing what was right for me." There had been something so strange about her mother that day. A memory flickered into her brain. Something she hadn't thought about in a long time. "I was crying, but it made no difference to her."

"Oh, Adeline..."

"It took me a while to figure out that it was permanent.

I wasn't going to live with her anymore. And that meant I wasn't going to live with you either. That was the part that upset me the most."

And she'd wanted to be an adult so that she could make her own decisions and not have her life upended for reasons that made no sense to her.

"I don't remember, obviously." Cassie blew her nose. "All I remember was those later years when you came to stay, and you were distant and aloof. I wanted you to play with me, but you were never interested."

"That wasn't it. After I went to live with my father, I missed you." Those three simple words, *I missed you*, didn't begin to describe the trauma she'd felt. "I was a mess. I couldn't believe she'd sent me away. I was so upset with her. I had no idea what I'd done to deserve it. It didn't make sense to me. After that, I withdrew emotionally, although at the time I had no idea that was what I was doing. It was fear, of course." That most powerful of all the emotions. "I was afraid of getting close to you again. I suppose I thought I could make life easier on myself if I didn't have those strong attachments. It took me years to understand that I had abandonment issues and everything that came with that. Anger, anxiety, failure to sustain relationships." Adeline paused and cleared her throat. She understood her issues better than most, but that didn't make them any easier to handle. If anything, it made it more frustrating that she found it all so challenging. "It was a horrible time. It didn't help that my father had no idea how to deal with me, and he was struggling too. He was devastated when she divorced him. Crushed. He could barely handle his own emotions, let alone mine. So he did what he always does when he doesn't know what to do. He called an expert. Fortunately for me, that expert was Tanya."

"Tanya?"

"She was a child psychologist. The wife of someone my father worked with. I guess he must have talked about how difficult I was to handle. I was a scared person back then. I didn't allow myself to feel settled because I knew everything could change in a moment. I was braced for it. If Dad left the house, I assumed he wasn't coming back. If I broke a plate or washed a red sock with his white shirts, I assumed he was going to send me away. I didn't want to go to school in case he took advantage of my absence to pack up the house and leave." It had been years since she'd allowed herself to really think about that time, and it wasn't easy. As well as navigating her own pain, she felt more than a little guilty for what she'd put her father through. "To say that I was clingy would be an understatement. I was so afraid he'd abandon me."

"But why would you think he would do that? He loves you."

"But my mother loved me, and she sent me away." Adeline stared straight ahead. "At ten years old, it seemed like logical thinking. It was Tanya who helped me see that it wasn't my fault. That I hadn't done anything. And she talked to my father too, and helped us communicate. We'd both been avoiding difficult conversations, but it turned out that having those conversations made things easier. She was brilliant and she made a huge difference to me. In a way, she saved me. I decided I wanted to do the same job Tanya did. I wanted to make a difference to someone's life."

"And that's why you studied psychology." Cassie stood up and pulled her sun lounger farther into the shade. "I didn't know any of this, and I've been filling in blanks from my own imagination and getting it wrong. What about my father? Do you remember him?"

It was obvious that her sister yearned for some rich detail, a nugget of information that she could add to the other things she knew about her father.

Adeline felt bad that she wouldn't be able to give what was needed. "Barely. A few hazy memories. Silly ones. I remember him breaking our mother's favorite vase and feeling relieved that it was him and not me. He felt awful about it. I remember him saying sorry about a thousand times. And I remember our mother had a fall, and he was so caring. So attentive. He wouldn't let us in the room to see her because he wanted her to rest."

"How did she fall?"

"I don't remember. I only remember that she had a nasty cut on her head and a bruise. You wanted to cling to her, but he wouldn't let you crawl on her in case you hurt her. He asked me to take you away and play with you."

"He loved her so much. He was being protective."

"Yes." Adeline hadn't thought about the incident for years.

"Do you remember anything else? I have about a million questions. Shall I make more coffee? Toast?"

Adeline was about to confess that she remembered little else about her first stepfather when she heard footsteps and her own father appeared.

Both of them stopped talking. The atmosphere shifted from the past to the present.

"Dad." She stood up, all her anxieties rushing back when she saw him.

"Hi, girls." Her father looked about as uncertain as she'd ever seen him. He also looked different. Younger. He'd cut his hair, she realized. Smartened up his clothes. There was no sign of the paint-stained shirt and old jeans he usually wore when she was staying at his house in Cape Cod. Presumably, that was her mother's influence.

Adeline felt another rush of hurt that he hadn't told her, and banked it down. Her own feelings could wait. Right now, her priority was him. Understanding him. Helping him see what a bad idea this was.

"I'm going to take a shower," Cassie said and disappeared before Adeline could stop her.

And maybe she wouldn't have stopped her.

There were things she needed to say to her father that she wouldn't be comfortable saying in front of her sister.

"Sit down, Dad."

Last night, she hadn't been able to control her emotions. She'd been transported right back to her childhood, but today she intended to do better. She wanted to understand. She *needed* to understand. No matter what, she was going to stay calm.

Instead of sitting, he held out his hand to her. "It's a beautiful morning. Why don't we walk?"

There was a path that followed the curve of the beach to a village. Off the beaten track, it was popular with locals and with tourists keen to avoid Corfu's busier hot spots.

Maybe walking would make the conversation easier and more natural. It was something they often did together when she was staying in Cape Cod. They strolled until the sun hit the sea and the sky darkened, talking about anything and everything.

"All right. Let me grab a hat and shoes." She went back to her room, pulled a hat with a wide brim onto her head and slid her feet into her sandals.

Her heart pounded and she stared at her palms. She was nervous. Her father's happiness was at stake here. It had never been more important that she say the right thing. She needed to help him see what a terrible mistake he was making. And she needed to do it in such a way that he came to that conclusion by himself.

She grabbed her bag, took a deep breath and joined her father.

"So how's my girl?" Her father tucked his arm into hers and they started to walk. "It's good to see you."

My girl.

Emotion jammed in her throat. She loved him so much. She would have thrown herself into the ocean to prevent him from being hurt.

"Worried about you, obviously."

He shortened his stride to keep pace with her. "You think I'm making a mistake."

"Yes."

"You sound very sure." He seemed almost amused. "Do you think I'm not old and wise enough to know my own mind?"•

She swallowed, uncomfortable. "Dad…"

"Let me save you the trouble of saying what you want to say." He stopped walking. "You're about to list a hundred reasons why this is a bad idea. You're going to tell me that if your mother and I couldn't live together before, then we won't be able to live together now. You're going to tell me that she'll break my heart again and that I'm going to regret this. Isn't that right?"

She'd worried about saying exactly the right thing, and he'd done it for her. It was a relief. "That's right."

Even though it was still early, she could feel the heat pressing in on her and the hot burn of the sun on her legs.

Here, close to the beach, the salty tang of the sea mingled with the scent of sun cream.

He eased the brim of her hat back so that he could see her face. "The one thing you probably won't mention is the most important factor of all. The reason we're doing this."

"Dad…"

"Love." He said the word quietly but with emphasis, as if he wasn't sure it was a word she knew. "We're doing this because we're in love. I fell in love with your mother when she was eighteen years old, and I have loved her every day since then. And I still love her."

She wanted to scream with frustration.

Love, she thought, had to be the biggest source of bad decision-making and misery for humankind. It was mystifying to her that people would ever think that was enough. Where was the logic?

She took a breath, and then gave him logic. Facts to puncture fantasy. "Dad, she had an affair and left you. You've been apart for two decades."

"That's true. And I never said that loving her was easy, or that our relationship has been some sort of fairy tale, but very few things worth having are ever easy. I know you think the divorce was her fault, but I was to blame too."

She sighed. "I don't think—"

"It's true. A child never gets to see the inside of their parents' relationship, and that's probably just as well because they'd see that they are as human as anyone else. We're capable of making mistakes. Big ones. Your mother and I both changed a lot over the course of our marriage."

"You mean she hit the big time and no longer had room for you in her life."

"She found her own success, that's true. But I didn't handle it well. I no longer felt needed, you see." He gave a half smile, half-despairing and half-amused by his old self. "I'd supported your mother in those early years. I was the reason she was able to stay home and write, and I felt good about that. We were a team. Then your mother's career took off. She was the one working long hours. She was in demand, flying all over the world. Her books were everywhere. Studios were fighting over the movie rights to her books. The money rolled in. I should have been grateful for that, but instead I felt unnecessary."

She frowned. "Unnecessary?"

"It happens sometimes, I believe, when people have defined roles in a marriage and those roles change." He patted her arm gently. "You'll know more about that than me, of course. I don't pretend to be an expert."

She didn't feel like an expert either.

She said nothing, but she didn't need to because her father was still talking.

"The way I saw it, if she didn't need me for my money, maybe she didn't need me at all. What was my role? Things shift in a relationship, and we didn't shift together. I didn't handle it well, not least because I didn't much enjoy my job but knowing that it gave your mother freedom to create gave me a purpose." He paused. "Your mother didn't handle it well either. We weren't communicating properly. If I had my time again, I suppose I would have said *this is how I feel*, but in those days I wasn't used to talking about how I felt. It wasn't something I did. I assumed she'd just know. I thought it was obvious, but it wasn't. If we had been communicating, then maybe when she met Rob that night, she would have walked straight out of the bar without talking to him."

Was he really blaming himself?

She bit her lip and forced herself to listen as he talked.

"Those years after we divorced were hard," he said, "but we stayed in touch, as you know. And maybe it was a good thing because I found a new direction for myself. One that made me happy. And now here we are. Somehow, we found our way back to each other. We've talked a lot about what happened back then. We both know where we went wrong, took that wrong turn. I can't believe we've reached this point again."

She couldn't believe it either. "I wish you'd think hard about it."

"I have. Life doesn't always give you a second chance, Addy, but when it does—" his face glowed with happiness and contentment "—well you don't turn your back on that. You grab it. And that's what I'm doing. I'm choosing happiness." The dreamy look in his eyes worried her almost as much as his words.

She wanted to shake him and wake him up.

"You're choosing misery and heartache, Dad. Just like you did before. It seems great now, but how long before it starts to unravel?"

"There are no certainties in life."

"I think this is a certainty. She hasn't stayed married to anyone, Dad." Although Cassie's father had died, and even her mother couldn't be held responsible for that.

"Those relationships weren't right. It's complicated."

"But one of those relationships was *you*." What did she have to say to make him see sense? She couldn't stand this. Already she was picturing the future—her father brokenhearted again, and her picking up the pieces, biting her tongue to stop herself saying, *I warned you.* "You're asking me to stand by and watch you be hurt again, and I can't. I don't understand how you would even think of putting yourself through this again. It will all go wrong, just as it did before."

"I don't believe it will. I hope it doesn't, but if it does, then I'll survive it just as I survived the first time."

She felt pressure in her chest as she thought about the first time. Panic rose and threatened to swallow her.

Maybe he'd forgotten. Maybe he'd blocked it out. People did that, didn't they, with trauma?

"There were days when you didn't want to get out of bed. You were in a terrible state." She felt cruel reminding him, but these were desperate times.

"Yes." He started walking again, his pace slow to accommodate the heat. "And it is one of the biggest regrets of my life that you witnessed that."

"Don't worry about that side of things because I'm fine. We're not talking about me."

"You're not fine. And maybe we should talk about you," he said. "I know you worry about me, but I also worry about you because I know that what you saw, what you witnessed, has affected you deeply."

They'd reached the road that led into the village. To their right was the beach, already scattered with people. A mother rubbed sunscreen onto the limbs of a wriggling toddler, while a man wrestled with a sun umbrella. There were two young women in the water, splashing, shrieking as they plunged into the tempting shimmer of turquoise blue.

She felt a stab of envy at their total enjoyment of the moment. Whatever else was going on in their lives beyond this beach, right now their world was light and carefree. "Why would you worry about me? My life is steady and predictable."

"I know. That's why I worry." Her father glanced at her. "When did you last do something even though you were uncertain of the outcome?"

She watched as a mother scooped up her toddler. "There is never any certainty in life."

"True. But you try your hardest to remove it. Particularly emotional uncertainty. Are you still seeing that guy who refuses to meet me?"

She looked at him. "His name is Mark. And he didn't refuse to meet you. You gave us barely any notice that you were coming, and the timing just didn't work out." In fact,

Mark *had* all but refused to meet her father, but she wasn't going to admit to that.

She really ought to tell her father that she and Mark had ended their relationship, but she didn't like the way the focus of the conversation had shifted.

Unfortunately, her father wasn't ready to drop the subject. "Does Mark make you happy?"

This conversation wasn't supposed to be about her relationship. It was supposed to be about his.

"Can we focus on this wedding? I didn't even know you and Mom were seeing each other. You didn't mention it." And that was one of the biggest hurts of all. Her emotions felt bruised. "When did it start? How?"

"It's hard to say. We've always stayed friends, as you know."

And she'd always found that part difficult to understand. She found the entire history of their relationship difficult to understand.

"There's a big shift between friendship and a romantic relationship."

"It was a gradual thing. We saw each other more frequently. I suppose it started to change last winter. Your mother was in the States on one of her book tours, and when it finished she spent a week with me at the house in Cape Cod."

Her mother had *stayed* with him? It was the first she'd heard of it.

She thought back, tracing the timeline. "I saw you after her book tour. You never mentioned it."

"There was nothing to tell at that point." He paused next to a pretty taverna that had tables overlooking the water. "Breakfast?"

"I—yes, I guess so." She wasn't particularly hungry, but she wanted the excuse to have more time with him, so she sat down and waited while he ordered for them both.

"I probably should have mentioned it, but I knew you'd be upset and worried and at the time I didn't know it was going anywhere. After she left, we realized we missed each other. We started talking on the phone every night."

"You hate the phone."

"I learned the art of video chat." He looked sheepish and Adeline digested the fact that for Catherine Swift, her father had been willing to embrace new technology.

"You have a smartphone now?"

"I do. Your mother persuaded me that it was a good idea. I'm glad she did." He reached into the pocket of his shorts and put it on the table. And there, on his home screen, was a photo of her mother. She was standing on the beach in Cape Cod looking windswept and happy.

Her father had a picture of her mother on his phone.

She tried to get past that so that she could finish the conversation. "But once you knew—and that must have been some months ago unless Mom sent out a speculative wedding invitation—why didn't you tell us?"

Her father sat back in his chair. "It was something your mother felt strongly about. She wanted to do it face-to-face, and I respected her wishes. I actually agreed with her that telling you in person would be better. I wanted us to be able to have this conversation."

She tried not to mind that he'd prioritized her mother over her.

She tried to stay calm and not let her emotions nudge her in directions she would later regret.

Their food arrived. Chunks of juicy watermelon, bowls of thick creamy yogurt topped with a generous swirl of golden honey and strong black coffee.

Adeline stirred honey into her yogurt until it was streaked

with gold. "There's nothing I can do or say to change your mind?"

"I don't want to change my mind."

She felt a rush of deep despair. He was going to do this. No matter what she said, he was going to go ahead and marry her mother again. And she couldn't bear it. She couldn't bear seeing him hurt again. Just thinking about him broken and struggling took her right back to that time. Her heart started to pound. Her fingers felt sweaty on the spoon she was holding.

She knew him better than she knew anyone, but right now she felt as if she didn't know him at all.

She put her spoon down. "Aren't you at all scared?"

"A little. I'm not focusing on that part."

She wished he would. "How can you bring yourself to risk it again after what happened last time?"

"Hope and courage. Those two human qualities that help us lead a full life. The two qualities needed to truly love, because love is always a risk but it's a risk worth taking in my opinion. A life without love is like a salad without dressing." He blushed awkwardly and stabbed a chunk of watermelon with his fork. "Sorry. It's your mother who is the wordsmith, not me. And she's the best example of hope and courage I've ever encountered. Despite everything that has happened, she has never been afraid to love and live life to the fullest."

She couldn't believe what she was hearing. His admiration for her mother. His belief that he loved her. He didn't seem able to see that it was going to end in disaster.

"I wish you'd protect yourself."

"Protect myself from love? From life?" He put his fork down. "What does that look like? Do I shut myself in a room and never leave in case I get hurt? The ceiling could fall in. I could trip and fall down the stairs."

She shifted uncomfortably because of course that was exactly what had happened to Cassie's father. He'd got up to
use the bathroom in the night and tripped over one of her
mother's shoes. An unfortunate accident, a twist of fate, and
his life had ended, leaving Catherine without a husband and
Cassie without a father.

"What about Cassie? Have you considered how all this
will make her feel?"

"I knew it would be a shock for her too. It's an adjustment, but I'm confident we can forge a strong relationship,"
he said. "Your mother is talking to her now, or that was the
plan. And once we've cleared the air, we will find a way to
move forward as a family. We're on this journey together."

But not through choice. There was no way she would have
chosen to buy a ticket for this particular journey.

"Dad…"

He reached for his coffee. "If you always try and protect
yourself, if you always take the safe route, imagine all the
experiences that you'll miss."

"And imagine all the misery you'll avoid."

He took a sip of coffee and put his cup down slowly.
"Would it help if I told you that I'd go through all that pain
again to enjoy one more day with your mother?"

But it wasn't only about him, was it?

He'd be asking her to go through the pain too. He'd be
asking her to suffer, and to watch him suffer. And she definitely didn't think it was worth it.

There was clearly something wrong with him. Or maybe
there was something wrong with her because she just didn't
get it. The whole thing was mystifying.

He talked about hope and courage, but when was hope
naivety? When was courage stupidity?

"So that's it? You've made up your mind."

He reached across the table and took her hand. "Sometimes you just have to take a risk, Adeline." He held her gaze and she shifted uncomfortably.

Why was he looking at her that way?

What exactly was he implying? That she was missing out on life because she was careful and sensible?

It was maddening that he seemed to think *she* was the one with the problem.

She felt a rush of frustration. Normally when she felt this unsettled, she'd do something practical. Go for a swim. Take a boxing class. Open a meditation app.

She probably needed to do all three because one thing was clear to her—her father was determined to go ahead with this wedding and nothing she said or did was going to stop it.

14

Cassie

The text from her mother pinged onto her phone about five minutes after Adeline had disappeared toward the village with her father.

Join me for yoga on the terrace. Please!

Cassie stared at her phone.

Even today, with her daughters thrown headfirst into emotional chaos, her mother didn't miss yoga. It shouldn't have surprised her. Catherine Swift was ruthlessly committed to routine and discipline. She talked about that side of her life in interviews. *How else do you think I've written so many books?*

Cassie had always admired that about her. It was, she knew, the key to her mother's success. She'd learned from her mother that inspiration, talent and ambition were nothing without hard work and commitment.

When she was staying on the island, Cassie often joined her for yoga but right now she wasn't in the mood. She wasn't sure of her mood at all. She felt restless. Tired and hurt. Also confused. Her mind was in a turmoil, her thoughts jumbled and tangled after the events of the night before and her conversation with her sister. She'd had a very clear picture of her past, and now that picture was blurry and indistinct.

She had more questions than she had answers. Nothing made sense to her and given that the only person who could help her make sense of it was her mother, she knew she should probably get this conversation over with. Part of her wished that Adeline was here and that they were doing it together. She'd been learning things about her past that were new to her. Learning things about Adeline.

She felt a twist of guilt because she knew her life had been easier than her sister's. She'd lost her father of course, but she had no memory of him, so for her the loss had always felt abstract. She didn't miss him as a person, because she'd never known him as a person. It was more that she missed the *idea* of him. When she met friends' fathers, she sometimes felt a tug of envy and found herself wondering how it must feel to be able to say, *Meet my dad*. At her graduation, she'd glanced up and seen her mother's proud face and wondered how it would have felt to see her father there too.

But for the most part, you didn't miss what you'd never had. Maybe it would have been different if she and her mother hadn't been so close, but they were. They were a happy family, and she'd never once felt anything other than loved and secure. Families came in all shapes and sizes, and just because hers was leaner than some didn't mean it didn't function well. They were a unit. A team. A pair.

She'd been lucky. Compared to her sister, she'd had a smooth, easy life. She'd never had to weather rejection. Even her mother's failed marriage to Gordon Pelling hadn't shaken their bond.

She'd never felt the deep wrenching grief that Adeline had felt when her family had fallen apart. You didn't need to study psychology to understand the impact that could have on someone.

A lump formed in her throat. If Adeline hadn't gone to live with her father, what would her life have looked like? She would have grown up with a sister. Of course, the age difference would always have been there and Adeline would have left home long before Cassie, but they would have stayed in touch. Maybe they would have grown closer as Cassie grew up and the age difference had mattered less.

Her mind raced ahead, imagining a world where she'd called Adeline whenever something bad happened. *I flunked an exam, I met a boy...* And Adeline would have been calm and wise and reassuring. There had been so many situations where it would have been comforting to have someone older and wiser in her corner. She'd always been close to her mother (or so she'd thought), but there were plenty of things she would never dream of discussing with a parent. And maybe she could have supported Adeline too. Maybe, as she'd grown up, Adeline would have confided in her.

If she'd been confused before, she was even more so now and running through that emotion was a seam of anger.

Why hadn't her mother told her any of this?

She had so many questions, and with Adeline and her father having their own heart-to-heart, this was the obvious time to ask them.

She gave her mother time to finish her yoga session, and then headed up the sunbaked path to the main villa.

Her mother was on the terrace, rolling up her mat. She was wearing sky blue yoga pants and her hair was caught in a ponytail. From this distance, she could have passed for a much younger woman.

As she straightened, she saw Cassie and smiled. "There you are. You should have joined me for yoga. It's glorious in the shade with the breeze coming off the sea. It's the perfect start to the day."

Cassie felt a sizzle of frustration. Her mother was behaving as if nothing out of the ordinary had happened. "I didn't feel like it."

"I don't ask myself if I feel like it. I just do it. Did Adeline apologize? I know she upset you." Her mother put the yoga mat down and held out her arms. "Give me a hug."

Cassie, who would normally have walked straight into those arms, didn't move.

Did her mother really think she was upset because of Adeline?

"Adeline was simply stating facts. You did have an affair and get pregnant. I am the baby." Cassie swallowed. She had so many questions and she didn't know which one to ask first. It felt wrong to be interrogating her mother, but she needed answers.

Her mother waved a hand toward the table. "I thought perhaps we could have breakfast before we—"

"No. I want to talk about this now. You told me that you and Andrew weren't right for each other. You always told me that my dad was the one. That you were in love with him. That's what I've always believed."

"Oh, sweetheart—" her mother moved toward her but Cassie took a step back.

"Gordon was different. You were lonely. Vulnerable. He was a mistake, you told me that. But you always told me Andrew was wrong too, so why would you be marrying him again?"

"You're upset, and I don't blame you. I should have told you about Andrew before now. It's all come as a terrible shock and I'm sorry. I misjudged everything, I see that now."

Cassie felt a rush of frustration.

"Why didn't you tell us? It's not as if you're marrying a stranger. This is complicated."

"That's why I thought it was better to have a conversation face-to-face. And to be honest, I thought Adeline would be thrilled. She loves her father and was horrified when we broke up. But I can see I was overly optimistic."

Cassie thought about what Adeline had said. *She spins things the way she wants them to look.* "She's concerned." It was an understatement, but she didn't want to throw fuel on the fire by being her usual emotional self. She aspired to be more like her sister. Calm. Measured. In control.

"She has no reason to be concerned, and hopefully her father will be able to reassure her this morning. They've gone for a walk. It will be good for them to have some time alone to talk." Catherine sat down at the table and Cassie hesitated for a moment and then joined her because standing in the hot sun after a sleepless night didn't seem like a great idea.

"Is it really surprising she's worried? You and Andrew have been divorced for decades." She glanced at her mother. Close up, she saw now what she hadn't seen from a distance. Shadows and stress. Tiredness. So maybe she wasn't finding this as easy as she seemed to be.

"That's true," her mother said. "People tend to view relationships through a simple lens. Because our relationship didn't work out the first time, Adeline can't understand why we'd be giving it another go."

"I can't understand that either." Not only did she feel compelled to defend her sister, she felt the same way. "You always told me that your marriage to Andrew was already over when you met my dad. You said that meeting him didn't break anything that wasn't already broken."

"That's true."

"You told me that Dad was your big love. You said he used to tell the story of how you met. *I went into that bar for a drink, and left with the love of my life.* You said it was only when you met him that you realized what love really was. You said that the two of you shared something so powerful it was like nothing you'd ever experienced." The stories her mother had told her had stayed with her. She'd painted a picture. From her mother's words alone, she'd been able to feel the love they'd shared. It had been her goal to one day have a relationship exactly like theirs. Everything she believed about love was because of her parents.

"That's true. I had never experienced anything like it before. It was—overwhelming." Her mother spooned fruit into a bowl and passed it to Cassie. "Eat. I know what you students are like. Your diet is mostly carbs and sugar."

She honestly didn't care what she was eating. The shape of her world had changed, and she wanted to make sense of it. "You said that you realized that you and Andrew were wrong together. That you'd grown apart. That you weren't in love anymore."

"That's true too. I did feel that way."

"And yet now here you are preparing to marry him again?" Couldn't her mother see the lack of logic? "What's changed?" It didn't make sense. She had a feeling that she was missing something big. It was like reading a book and realizing that you'd somehow jumped ahead and missed a huge chunk of the plot.

"*We* changed," her mother said. "I was very young when

I married Andrew. Our lives were different then. I suppose you could say we grew up together and as we grew up, we also grew apart. We wanted different things. Suddenly, we were both headed in different directions and our relationship no longer worked. It happens all the time. But just because a relationship ends, doesn't mean it was wrong. I had no regrets about marrying Andrew. And he and I were already living separately when I met your father."

Achilles emerged, tail flicking as he stalked toward her and then sprang onto her lap.

Cassie stroked him, feeling the comforting warmth of his body press through her shorts.

"So you did love him?"

"The cats are not allowed at the table when we're eating. You know that."

"Don't change the subject." Cassie kept stroking the cat, her fingers buried in the softness of feline comfort.

"What? You were asking about your father." Her mother stirred her coffee slowly. "That man could charm the birds from the trees. He had the most compelling, irresistible smile. Being with him was the most intense, dizzying, all-consuming feeling—I can't even describe it." She put the spoon down. "He made me feel adored."

She'd heard that part so many times. She'd written about it.
He made me feel adored.
She'd used that exact line in her book.
But still…

"If he hadn't died, do you think you'd still be together?"

The air throbbed with heat and tension.

Or maybe she was the only one feeling the tension. She was so afraid she might not like the answer to that question.

Her mother gestured to Cassie's bowl. "Eat something. The orange juice is freshly squeezed from the oranges on our trees, and the honey is from our own hives. Maria thinks it is the best we've ever had."

Either her mother hadn't heard her question, or she was choosing to ignore it. "Would you and Dad still be together?"

"Goodness you're asking so many difficult questions today. I'm sure we would. Of course, it's impossible to say for sure." Her mother poured orange juice into glasses and it swirled around shards of ice, bright as the sun. "This is delicious. You must try it."

"Did you ever regret leaving Andrew?"

Her mother took a sip of juice. "Why would I regret it? I was with your father. I had you."

"Would you have married my father if you hadn't been pregnant, or would the affair have fizzled out?"

"Cassie…"

"Was my dad pleased when you told him you were pregnant?"

Her mother put the glass down, her smile absent. "This is starting to sound like an interrogation."

They'd rarely exchanged a cross word in their lives. Their conversation was often lively, but almost always aligned, but now there was a tug of antagonism. Her mother was trying to protect her secrets and Cassie was trying to uncover them.

"Surely I have a right to some answers."

"Of course, you do. What was the question again? Was your father pleased that I was pregnant?" Her mother drizzled honey onto a bowl of creamy yogurt and reached for a spoon. "Yes. I can honestly say that he was thrilled."

A whisper of relief licked through her. "So he liked children."

"He loved you very much, Cassie. You were his pride and joy."

"So if he liked children, why did you send Adeline away?"

The spoon slid from her mother's fingers and clattered to the floor. Startled by the sound, Achilles sprang off Cassie's lap, his claws leaving dents in her thighs as he dived for cover.

"Oh, look at me. Clumsy." Catherine bent to retrieve the spoon. When she sat up again her cheeks were flushed. "I didn't send her away. Like everything, it was complicated. Adeline missed her father. I was spending most of my time in Corfu by then, and we thought she'd be better in London back in the house she knew, with her friends. There was her education to think of. We thought it would be the best thing."

Adeline hadn't thought that, but it seemed she hadn't been consulted.

Her mother reached for a fresh spoon.

"I don't know why we're focusing on the past. It's the present that matters. Let's talk about that."

Cassie was torn. Her mother obviously found it painful to talk about Cassie's father, which surely meant that their love had been deep and real.

Still, there was something about this whole situation that didn't make sense.

Her mother glanced at her. "Andrew is a wonderful man. I think you're going to love him if you take the time to talk to him and get to know him."

That wasn't really the point, was it?

"And how does he feel about me?" Couldn't her mother see how awkward this situation was for her?

"He is looking forward to spending time with you. He's a warm, funny, generous man, Cassie. You won't meet better."

So why did you leave him?

"If my dad hadn't died, would you have divorced him and remarried Andrew?"

"You are making this whole thing more complicated than it needs to be." Her mother was stubborn, but Cassie discovered that when there was something important at stake, she could be stubborn too.

"I'm trying to understand."

"It's impossible to know what would have happened in that situation. None of us can see down the road we don't travel." Her mother put her spoon down. Gave up on eating. "Relationships are complicated, that's why I've managed to make a career writing about them. If they were simple, predictable and always stayed the same, there would be only one story to tell and I wouldn't have had the career I've had. The reason I can write book after book is because no two people are the same, and—this is the important thing—" her mother leaned forward "—no two relationships are the same, even when it's between the same two people. No one stays the same throughout their life. We're all shaped and molded by the events we experience. I'm not the same person I was when I was married to Andrew the first time around. He's not the same person either."

Cassie thought about Adeline and the way she lived her life. Safe. Protected. Her childhood experiences had shaped her into the person she was.

She felt a pang as she thought of her sister.

"So marrying my father wasn't a mistake?" She needed to know that. She needed to believe it, because otherwise what did that say about her? *That she was a mistake too.*

"How could it have been a mistake? I had you. And you and your sister are the two most important things in my life. Now, let's eat some breakfast or we risk offending Maria twice in twenty-four hours and we don't want to do that."

Cassie poured herself a glass of juice. She'd asked her questions and her mother had answered them. Or most of them. Her answers had made sense. Of course, people changed. Of course, it was theoretically possible that you could fall out of love with a partner, and then back in love with them again. Complicated, but possible.

Cassie should be feeling better about everything. She should be feeling reassured.

So why couldn't she shake the feeling that there was something her mother wasn't telling her?

15

Adeline

Adeline paced to the end of the jetty, past her mother's boat, which bobbed quietly on the crystal clear water, its blue-green paint gleaming in the hot sunshine.

She took slow deep breaths. *Calm, calm, calm.*

The sun blazed and her linen shorts, which had seemed cool in the villa, stuck to her thighs. Her loose shirt felt like a fur coat.

She removed her hat and lifted the heavy weight of her hair off the back of her neck. Here, right by the edge of the ocean, a faint breeze cut through the almost oppressive heat.

Her father had gone back to the villa, apparently unable to face being apart from Catherine for more than an hour. He'd urged her to join them, but she'd told him she needed to check her emails and send in her copy for her Dr. Swift column. Which was all true.

She also needed time to get her thoughts straight.

The conversation hadn't gone the way she'd hoped it would. Nothing she'd said had made her father question what he was doing. He believed that life was giving him a second chance and he was determined to grab it. The wedding would be going ahead.

He was making a mistake, that was obvious, and yet he seemed to think *she* was the one with the problem.

She relaxed her muscles and closed her eyes.

"I am not going to scream."

"Scream if you need to. Don't mind me." A man emerged from the boat. His hair was dark and rumpled by the breeze and he was wiping his fingers on a rag smeared with oil. There was a smudge of oil on his cheek and on the shoulder of his T-shirt. He stood on the deck, his board shorts riding low, his legs planted apart as he steadied himself against the gentle rocking of the boat. He looked like someone who was entirely at home on the water.

Adeline was mortified that he'd witnessed what she'd thought was a private moment. "I didn't realize anyone was on the boat."

"You had things on your mind. Bad day?"

Her defenses snapped back into position. She wasn't about to share her deepest emotions with a stranger.

"Everything is fine. It's a good day."

"You scream on your good days?" He stepped off the boat in a single athletic stride and she took an involuntary step backward.

She didn't want company. She wished he'd just stay on the boat and get on with whatever he'd been doing, and let her get on with…

With what?

"I wasn't screaming."

"But you wanted to scream. Don't hold back on my account. It's not the first time I've seen you upset." He tucked the rag he was holding into the pocket of his shorts and she stared at him.

"I have no idea what you're…" She studied his face, taking in raven dark hair, those angular cheekbones and the smile that curved his mouth and creased the corners of his eyes. There was something familiar about the angle of that smile. A memory stirred deep inside her. "Stefanos?"

His smile widened. "I don't know whether to be offended that you didn't recognize me or flattered. I'll go with flattered, because no one wants to look the way they did at twelve years old. You've changed too, by the way."

"I wasn't expecting—oh, it's good to see you." She took a step forward and then stopped herself just in time. What was she thinking? She'd almost hugged him! She must be feeling worse than she'd thought. "My mother mentioned that you were here but I didn't…"

"You were focused on other things." He paused for a moment. "You're here for the wedding. That must be a little strange in the circumstances. How do you feel about it?"

Sick. Stressed. Panicked.

She curled her fingers into her palms. "It's exciting," she said. "I'm very happy for them."

"Yes?" His gaze connected with hers and she saw the sympathy there. "That's why you were pacing the jetty looking for a place to scream?"

Perhaps it wasn't altogether surprising that he didn't believe her given that he'd witnessed her reaction to her parents' divorce. It was the first time she'd discovered the true power of friendship. The matchless comfort of having someone in your corner. Someone who cared and understood.

"It was a shock." She was willing to admit that much. "I'm still processing it."

"A shock?" He frowned. "You didn't know? They didn't tell you?"

"Not until last night. Apparently, my parents thought the best plan was to wait and tell us in person."

He muttered something in Greek and she smiled because although her Greek was limited she understood what he'd said.

"Exactly. We gathered together on the terrace for dinner and then my mother produced my father like some sort of conjuring trick. The big reveal. We were probably meant to applaud, but it didn't quite work out that way."

The look he gave her was sympathetic.

"I'm starting to understand why you're feeling the need to scream."

She was embarrassed. "I don't know why I'm telling you this."

"Perhaps because we were once good friends and told each other everything. We're not strangers, Addy." The warmth in his eyes and his easy use of her childhood nickname stirred something inside her.

The world tilted.

She felt as if she'd been pushed off balance.

"How about you? My mother mentioned that you'd moved back here permanently."

"I moved back last summer after my father died." There was a shadow behind his eyes, a hint of pain behind the smile.

"I was sorry to hear about your father." And now she had another reason to feel embarrassed. "I should have contacted you."

"How? We lost touch, although why that happened, I'm not sure." His gaze lingered on hers and she felt almost breathless.

"We were just kids. I was eight years old when we met. You were ten."

"But for two years we were the best of friends."

The best of friends.

At eight, she'd been handling turmoil and he'd been there. They'd clambered over rocks together. Swam in the shallow waters of the beach beneath her mother's house. He'd taught her some words of Greek and held her hand as they'd explored some of the trails along the beautiful coastline. He'd been the one predictable thing in her rapidly changing world.

She pushed the memory aside. There was no point in being sentimental about something that had happened so long ago.

"How is your mother doing? I haven't seen her yet." She felt a twinge of guilt thinking about how hard Maria had probably worked to produce the meal they hadn't eaten, although in the end she and Cassie had eaten some of it, of course. Not at a table with silverware and freshly ironed linens, but quietly on their laps on the beach, like two children sneaking out to have a midnight feast.

"She's surviving. It's been hard for her. My parents had been together for more than thirty years, side by side through everything. Losing him has rocked her whole life. It's a big adjustment." He paused. "Catherine has been a wonderful support. Their bond is extraordinary. She's been there for my mother throughout the whole thing. She was the one who called me when my father was taken to hospital. She kept me updated right through my journey home from Canada and stayed with my mother the whole time until I arrived."

"I didn't know that."

She thought back to the message her mother had sent.

Kostas died suddenly this weekend.

She'd felt a stab of sadness because she had fond memories of Kostas, and had thought then about Stefanos and wondered how her old friend was doing. But she hadn't reached out. It had been twenty years. She'd told herself that her words were unlikely to bring comfort, but she'd been lying to herself. The truth was that thinking about Stefanos took her back to that time.

Now she wished she'd contacted him personally instead of sending a message of condolence via her mother.

Stefanos was watching her. "Why don't we sit for a while?" He gestured to the bench at the end of the jetty where her mother sometimes sat with a notebook and wrote her books undisturbed.

She'd thought she wanted to be on her own, but now she discovered that she didn't and she walked to the end of the jetty and settled herself on the bench.

Stefanos grabbed a bottle of water from the boat and joined her. "Did you know that Catherine cancelled a book tour so that she could stay close to my mother? She refused to leave her side."

That didn't sound like her mother. Catherine Swift never let anything get in the way of her work. When it came to anything to do with her writing, she was a machine.

Memories dug into her, sharp and uncomfortable.

How many times had she begged her as a child? *Don't go away. Please stay.* And her mother had replied, *This is my job, honey, and I have responsibilities. We wouldn't want to let people down, would we?*

When Adeline had been sick with chicken pox the week before a tour of the US, her mother had stayed away from her in case she caught it before her trip. It had been left to her father to comfort her in her itchy misery. And then Cassie had arrived and her mother hadn't left her alone. She'd said that it was impossible to tour when she had a baby and Adeline had wondered why it had been so easy for her mother to leave her, and yet impossible for her to leave her little sister.

What was she lacking?

It was only after Cassie's father had died that she'd started touring again, apparently happy to leave Cassie in the care of Maria. That had seemed a little strange to Adeline, but by then she'd long since given up trying to understand adults.

And now Stefanos was telling her that her mother had cancelled a tour for Maria. He had to have that wrong.

"You mean she cancelled a signing."

"No. The whole book tour," he said. "She only allowed it to be rearranged when she had my assurance that I was back for good and wouldn't be leaving. Her loyalty to my mother is extraordinary. Their friendship is inspiring."

His warmth and gratitude jarred with her current feelings toward her mother.

Her mother was there for everyone else, it seemed. She picked Cassie up from the airport, she supported Maria—

She shouldn't be feeling hurt or envious. She was past the stage of needing comfort and attention from her mother. If anything it was good to know her mother was capable of offering comfort.

"I'm glad she helped. And I really am sorry you lost your father. He was a lovely man." She'd been envious of Stefanos's stable family life, and the close, loving relationship between his parents. "So you came home and stayed, instead of going back to Canada."

The air was slightly cooler right here by the sea, and she glanced down and saw a shoal of tiny fish dart through the clear blue water.

She felt calmer, although whether that was due to the tranquilizing effect of cloudless blue skies and an endless shimmering ocean or being with Stefanos she wasn't sure.

She'd always found him easy company.

"There was so much to deal with." He stretched out his legs. "When I wasn't handling paperwork and checking on my mother, I was sorting out the boats. I fixed them up, planning to sell them, but then I took one of them out on the water and that was it."

"That was what?" She felt the sun burning her cheek and altered the angle of her hat.

"The moment I decided I wasn't going to sell anything. I wanted to run the business. No one was more surprised than me." He glanced across the water. "Growing up, I couldn't wait to leave this place. I kept thinking of all the things out there that I was missing. I was hungry for anything and everything that wasn't what I had."

"It's human nature to want to explore."

"Maybe. And I don't regret leaving, because it's only by trying different things that you find out what's important to you and what you really want. But people change, don't they? Life happens and you have experiences—good and bad—and discover that the things that matter most don't really matter at all, or the place you're spending time isn't where you want to be. You start to appreciate things you didn't appreciate before." He gave her an apologetic smile. "And that was far too much information to load onto someone I haven't seen for two decades. I'm not sure why I told you all that."

"Because we were once best friends," she said, "and because I understand. I'm glad you told me."

"Yes, well—" he twisted the cap off the bottle of water "—you always were easy to talk to. That's something that hasn't changed." He offered her water, but she shook her head.

"I'm fine, thanks. You always did love the ocean. That's something else that hasn't changed. It's not so surprising that you're back here." She remembered him, barefoot and bronzed, plunging into the sea without hesitation. Working on the deck of his father's boat, or heaving a heavy anchor overboard. "Almost every memory I have of you has the sea in it."

"I didn't realize how much I missed it until I came back here. If you'd asked me if I was happy with my life in Canada, I would have said that I was. I had a great apartment, a job that paid well and that I was good at. I commuted to my office, worked, socialized with friends. It was predictable."

"You don't like predictable?"

She thought about her own life, and how hard she'd worked to make it exactly that. Predictable was her lifestyle of choice.

"I don't think I asked myself that question until I lost my father," he said. "Then I realized that sometimes the way you live your life is more down to habit than choice. You rarely stop and ask yourself if this is really how you want to be spending your time, or if you do, you dismiss it because you're deep in your career and humans are wired to prefer certainty and why would you give that up for something uncertain?"

Why indeed? She felt her heart beat a little faster.

"But you did."

"Yes, but only because it was forced on me. If my father hadn't died, I've no doubt I'd still be in Canada sitting at my desk or heading into another meeting. And that's scary, because I finally feel as if I'm exactly where I want to be. I don't like the idea that I arrived here by accident."

She felt a twinge of something that could have been envy.

"No plans to go back?"

"None. I am now the official owner of my father's business."

"What does that involve? You take tourists out? You're the skipper?"

"Sometimes, if that's what they want." He screwed the cap

back on the bottle. "More often they just want to take the boat on their own and providing they're prepared to follow my safety rules and don't seem about to party hard and drown themselves, I let them. I have one yacht and five speedboats for hire. And my own boat, which I use as the rescue boat." His gaze connected with hers. "Remember when we took my dad's boat out together?"

She felt a twinge of guilt. "He was so angry!." It was something she hadn't thought about in years. "You were grounded for a week, my dad yelled at you and I felt terrible because you'd done it for me."

"We scared them," he said. "You were only eight. If I'd been your dad, I would have yelled at me too. But it seemed the right thing to do at the time. All I knew was that life felt better when I was on the water. You were upset, and I thought it might make you feel better too."

"It did make me feel better."

She thought back to that afternoon. Her parents had told her they were no longer going to live together. That her mother was marrying someone else. That she was going to have a sibling.

She'd run away, trying to escape from this change to her life. She'd gone straight to Stefanos who had been earning pocket money scrubbing the deck of his father's boat.

It had been her idea to go out on the water so that she could have some time to think and digest without an adult coming and trying to reason with her. He'd complied without question.

She'd sat shivering in the dinghy while Stefanos had taken the boat around the coast. She remembered the look of concentration on his face and his skinny arms and legs straining with the effort required to keep the boat steady. He'd steered the boat into one of the sheltered coves that peppered the coastline and killed the engine.

Her eyes had stung from crying, and the breeze had been cool against her sore skin. She remembered the way he'd listened to her, and squeezed her hand in wordless comfort. She might have wondered how she could remember something that had happened so long ago, but she knew that great kindness often stayed with a person and Stefanos had shown her great kindness.

He gave her a thoughtful look. "What are you doing for the rest of the morning?"

"Excuse me?"

"I'm a better sailor than I was when I was ten years old, but some things haven't changed. Life still seems better on the water. When I feel the need to scream, I usually take the boat out. A few hours away from things, feeling the sun on your face and the wind in your hair, calms the mind I find."

Sailing? Right now?

She couldn't do that. It would feel like running away, and she wasn't eight years old anymore. "I can't but thank you."

"Why not?"

"I need to talk to my mother." And after the way the conversation had gone with her father, the thought of repeating it with her mother made her stomach churn.

"I've always thought that when you're upset, it's best to take some time before having difficult conversations."

"True. But I also have work to do. I'm sure you do too."

"My work is to take the boat out, to check everything is okay." He glanced at the boat and then back at her. "Company would be nice."

Temptation tugged at her, but she tried to ignore it. Her emotions were too unsteady. She'd already told him far too much. Like a purse that had been left open, contents spilled, she wasn't sure what else might fall out. She needed time to settle herself.

"I have a deadline."

"Surely people can handle their own problems for a couple of hours, Dr. Swift?"

Her curiosity sparked. "You know what I do?"

"Your mother told me. She's proud of you, and everything you have achieved."

"She talks about me?"

"All the time. She has several files, full of everything you've written. She prints the pages off so that she can read it whenever she likes. And she shares them with my mother, who then shares them with me." He seemed surprised by her reaction. "You didn't know?"

"No." It was a revelation that her mother kept a file of her work. That she talked about her. That she was proud.

"It's always embarrassing when a parent boasts about you. My mother does it. Her standard introduction at the moment is *this is my son, he owns his own house and he's single.*"

Adeline laughed properly for the first time since she'd arrived on the island. "Ouch."

"Exactly…" He spread his hands. "According to my mother, whatever you achieve in life is worth nothing if you don't have a family. You are looking at a failure." He looked relaxed, content and as far from a failure as it was possible to be.

The sun was scorching and she removed her hat to let the breeze cool her head. She thought back to the conversation with her father and his comments about Mark. "It's funny that no matter what we do, our parents measure us by the success of our romantic relationships."

"You too?" He gave her a sympathetic smile. "Whatever the limitations of my romantic life, I'm good with boats.

Come out with me for a few hours. Work can wait. When is your deadline?"

"Four p.m." She glanced at him, and then over her shoulder at the boat, bobbing on the surface of the water, its paintwork gleaming, a shiny aquamarine in the bright light.

The sea sparkled and beyond the dock the coastline stretched temptingly into the distance. She thought of the beaches and the hidden inlets, the breeze and the spray of salt water against her skin.

He glanced at his watch. "I promise to have you back by two. I'm sure that whatever problems you're solving for them, you can do it in two hours. We can draft your answers together on the boat if you like."

It made her smile. "You want to give advice on other people's problems?"

"Why not? No one has to take it. I'll probably just say come to Greece, and all your problems will vanish."

If only it were that simple.

Her phone pinged at that moment and a message from her mother appeared.

Join me on the terrace.

The moment of lightness passed. It was as if the world was testing her, placing two options in front of her. What she wanted to do, and what she knew she ought to do.

She stared at her phone, wishing the message would disappear so that she didn't have to do anything about it.

"My mother wants to talk to me."

"But you're not ready to talk to her."

"I'm not sure I'll ever be ready." She put her phone back in her pocket and stood up, her mood plunging. "It was good to see you, Stefanos."

"Wait…" He stood up too. "Are you really going to be able to have a calm and productive conversation with your mother feeling the way you do? Maybe you do need to have this conversation, but you can choose when to have it."

Her choice.

It made her think of Mark, and she felt tension ripple through her. "You probably think I'm foolish to have come home."

He frowned. "Why would I think that? This is your family. Of course, you have to be here. Family can be infuriating, and irritating and confusing—also misguided—but it doesn't mean you abandon them. Not that my opinion should matter to you, but for what it's worth, I think you're right to be here. These are the people you love. The fact that the situation is difficult to navigate doesn't change that. But that doesn't mean you can't also take care of yourself."

He didn't think she was foolish being here. He didn't think she was making bad choices.

She glanced at his face and then toward the villa.

She imagined her mother sitting at her favorite table on the terrace, waiting.

Stefanos was right. The conversation would be better if she had a chance to calm down first.

Digging her phone from her pocket, she replied to the message.

Will join you for tea at 4.

She pressed Send, stuffed her phone back into her pocket and took a calming breath.

"Let's do this right now, before I change my mind."

She walked back to the boat, stepped aboard and watched while he untied the rope.

"I take it you're not usually spontaneous these days." He stepped onto the boat and it rocked gently.

"Never." She steadied herself. "I'm a planner."

He raised an eyebrow. "What happened to the girl who urged me to steal my father's boat?"

"Borrow," she corrected, "not steal. We were always going to return it." But it was an interesting question. What had happened to that girl? "I think she had a bit too much of the unpredictable."

He nodded. "So now you try and control everything."

"As far as life can ever be controlled, yes. According to my father, it's a trait that is ruining my life. Apparently, it's not them who are being reckless and acting in an illogical fashion, despite the undeniable fact they decided they couldn't live with each other last time, it's all me." She settled herself on the seat and secured her hat. The boat rocked on the water and the sky was a vast swathe of brilliant blue. "This morning my father made a point of telling me that I have my priorities all wrong and need to rethink the way I live my life."

Instead of starting the engine, he sat down opposite her, giving her his full attention. "I'm starting to understand why you felt the need to scream."

"Exactly. But I've said more than enough. I shouldn't be talking about this."

"Why not? There was a time when we told each other everything."

The wind caught her hat and she slapped her hand onto it to stop it blowing across the water. "We were children. It's not the same."

"Don't you believe it. I know things about you, Dr. Swift." He started the engine and eased the boat away from the dock. "Big things. Small things. I could bring you down."

"Is that right?" It made her smile. "Which piece of inside

knowledge do you think would have the most devastating
effect on my career?"

He increased speed and headed out into the bay.

"Tough one." He kept his hands on the wheel and his eyes
straight ahead. "There was that time when you broke your
dad's watch and buried it in the sand so he wouldn't find out."

"I dug it up again."

"Or the time you let that stray cat sleep in your bedroom
because you felt sorry for it?"

"It destroyed the room." She gave a groan, remembering.
"That was awful. I told my mother it must have crept through
the window when I was asleep." The truth was she'd wanted
the comfort. She'd felt as alone and abandoned as that kitten. "You think I should add that to my résumé under life
experience?"

"I think it might give you an edge. You probably shouldn't
mention that when you get stressed, you scream."

"I didn't scream."

"You were about to scream. The air was pulled into your
lungs, ready. There's not a lot of screaming around here," he
said, "although I've been known to yelp occasionally if the
water is really cold. I probably saved you from intrusive questioning by the Greek police. You're welcome."

His teasing was a balm, and she felt some of the tension
leave her.

"All I wanted from that conversation with my dad this
morning was to understand." It wasn't quite true, of course.
What she'd really wanted was for her father to change his
mind. For him to look at her across the table and say, *I'm sorry,
Addy, it was a moment of madness but it's finished now. You're
right. This can never work.* "I was hoping for a rational explanation as to how something that didn't work last time could
possibly work this time."

Stefanos glanced at her. "And did he give you one?"

"No." She frowned. "Well, he said it was love. As if that explained everything. As if that was enough, even though they'd presumably felt *love* before but it hadn't been enough for them to work out how to be together. He seems to think I'm the one behaving oddly for not believing in the all-healing, all-consuming power of love."

He headed along the coast, the wake of the boat leaving a trail of sparkling silver behind them.

After a few minutes, he slowed down and steered the boat into a little cove accessible only from the water.

Cliffs plunged steeply into the sea on either side, forming a horseshoe. A strip of white-gold sand nestled at the tip. The sea sparkled, jewel-toned and dazzling in the sunlight.

Stefanos cut the engine, and now the only sounds were the water lapping the sides of the boat and the soft rush of waves as they hit the beach.

"I'd forgotten how beautiful it is here." She leaned down to trail her fingers through the crystalline waters. Far below, tiny fish darted between the rocks. The air tasted salty and fresh and she felt the cool breath of the breeze brush her heated skin.

"It's one of my favorite places. And it's always quiet. No access from the cliffs or the road, and the approach is tricky so only the locals come here." He hauled the anchor from the bow and dropped it over the side. "So you don't think your parents love each other?"

She withdrew her hand from the water. "I don't know, but I think relying on gut instinct and emotion is an unreliable way to make what is one of the most important decisions of your life. If more people applied logic to their choice of partner, there would be fewer divorces."

"Logic?"

"People focus too much on *romance* and not enough on practicalities. It's important to identify your core values. If you value honesty, then don't choose someone who has a loose relationship with the truth. If family is important to you, then don't choose someone who has no interest in fostering family bonds." *Like Mark.* How could she ever have thought that might work? "My father values loyalty, and yet he's choosing to be with my mother again even though this will be her fourth marriage." She saw his expression change. "You think I'm wrong?"

"I think the theory is good, but I don't think human beings can be boxed as easily as you imply. For example, your mother may not have shown loyalty toward your father, but she has shown extreme loyalty to my mother."

"That's true."

"And although I agree with much of what you say about the dangers of making a decision based on emotions," he said, "I know many people who share my values but not for anything would I choose to spend the rest of my life with them."

"I agree it's not all about compatibility. There is an extra factor that isn't so easy to define." She looked at him. "You're going to tell me that's love."

"I'm not telling you anything." He reached into the cooler by his feet and pulled out two bottles of water. "But I think there's plenty of evidence that emotions can bind people together strongly. Take my parents. Married for more than thirty years. Over a period that long, there are going to be times when a partnership faces challenges. Illness. Bereavement. So many things can go wrong. Times when logic alone would tell you to walk away. And yet people don't." He leaned across and handed her the water. "I'm saying that love can be the thing that holds people together. And I'm guessing that for a planner like you, love is a scary concept because it's difficult to define and impossible to control."

She took the water from him and pulled her hat from her head. The sun was baking and her hair was damp from the heat. She had a sudden urge to just leap over the side of the boat and plunge deep into the water.

"So I'm expected to forget logic and reason and accept that love is a sufficient explanation for this questionable decision my father is making?" She twisted off the cap and drank, the water soothing her dry throat. "Not that he wants my opinion. I'm supposed to greet his news with joyful acceptance, and I confess I'm struggling with that. I love him, and I don't want to see him hurt."

He lowered the bottle. "Are you sure it's just about him?"

She put the rest of her water back in the cool box for later. "What do you mean?"

"Your parents' divorce had a profound impact on you. I witnessed it. Your world ceased to be safe and predictable at an age when everyone needs that. I'm guessing from what you've said that since then you've done what you can to redress that. To make your world as safe as possible."

"You're taking sides with my father and telling me I need to rethink my life? I might push you overboard."

"I'm not telling you that. I'm saying that it's no wonder you feel the way you do. It's human nature to avoid pain, and you're afraid that what happened last time will happen again," he said. "And even if their marriage works this time, it's still a big change for you. It's been your father and you for so long, but now things will be different."

She stared at him, thrown by his words.

She was supposed to be the psychologist. She prided herself on self-insight and never hiding from difficult truths.

But she hadn't registered that as well as being anxious for her father, she was anxious for herself. That it wasn't just his life she was worried about, but her life. Her future.

She associated her father with security. Consistency. Their relationship had been the one sure, safe thing in her life and the idea of that changing shook her more than it should.

She glanced toward the beach. The sweep of sand gleamed pale gold. Between the boat and beach the sea stretched, deep and inviting, ribbons of sunlight glistening on the surface.

"You're right," she said finally. "Everything you just said is right, and I didn't see it."

Why hadn't she seen it?

He shrugged. "Understanding the origin of your feelings doesn't necessarily change them."

"But it should. Maybe I'm being selfish." It troubled her, the idea that she might have been thinking about her own needs and not her father's. "I genuinely thought I was protecting him, and guarding his best interests."

"You were. Are. It's possible to feel more than one thing. To care about more than one thing. And you're allowed to care about yourself too. It's hardly surprising that what's happening would affect you so strongly. The situation sucks. And you're allowed to say it sucks."

He was trying to make her feel better, but she didn't feel better. She felt awful.

The boat drifted slightly, tugging on its anchor.

She gave him a shaky smile. "Ever thought of being a psychologist?"

"I'd be a terrible psychologist. And I'm starting to wonder about you, because I'm pretty sure no decent psychologist would be beating herself up for having normal human feelings. Do you know what you need?" He stood up and she looked at him, feeling exposed and vulnerable.

"A large drink? A do-over?"

"No, a swim. It cures everything." He stripped off his shirt and she caught the ripple and flex of muscle before she turned her head, frustrated with herself. She wasn't eighteen. She should have moved beyond staring at a man's abs.

"You're going to swim now? Here?"

"Yes. And so are you. You might want to take some clothes off too, unless you fancy swimming fully clothed."

She sat up a little straighter. "I'm not in the mood."

"Trust me, the moment your toes hit that water, you'll be in the mood," he said. "This is a great place to swim. If my memory is right, you're a good swimmer. The water is perfect, and we have the bay to ourselves. It would be a waste not to use it. I could throw you in if that would help your decision-making."

As a child, being with him had always felt comfortable. Easy. They slid into their friendship like pieces of the same puzzle, fitting perfectly. It still felt comfortable, but now that feeling mingled with other sensations. Watching him strip down, ready to swim, she felt a slow unraveling inside her and a throb of heat low in her belly.

"I haven't swum in the sea for years. You go ahead." She felt lightheaded and a little strange, and he gave her a long look.

"You're intending to sit in the boat and watch?"

"Yes."

He didn't attempt to persuade her. Instead, he stepped onto the side of the boat, stood for a moment, poised, and then plunged headfirst into the sea. Too late, she remembered that he'd always loved to splash her, dunk her, shower her in water. It had been one of their games.

She gasped as salt water soaked her shirt and dampened her hair. She peeled her shirt away from her skin and wiped her eyes with her palm.

Stefanos surfaced, wearing that wicked smile that reminded her of the boy.

"Thanks," she muttered, and he grinned.

"You're welcome." His hair was sleek against his head and droplets of water clung to his cheeks and his wide shoulders. "You're right. It's terrible in here. Good decision to stay there safe in the boat. Don't leave without me."

He disappeared under the water again and then turned and headed for the beach, covering the distance in a strong, steady crawl.

She reached down and dipped her fingers into the water again. The surface was warm, heated by the sun, but as she plunged her hand deeper, she felt the cooler water. It reminded her that things were rarely the way they seemed on the surface.

Was Stefanos right? Was she standing in the way of her dad's happiness because she was trying to protect herself? Maybe that wouldn't make her an awful person (she tried always to challenge such extreme views), but it certainly didn't make her a person she wanted to be.

She glanced back at Stefanos and saw that he'd almost reached the shore.

Was she protecting herself now, by not following him?

He reached the beach and she saw him stand up and swipe the water from his face with his hand.

He raised his hand and waved at her, and she felt regret nudge her.

Why hadn't she followed him into the ocean? What exactly was she risking by going for a cooling swim in these crystal clear waters with an old friend?

Without stopping to question herself any further, she stood

up and stripped off her linen shorts and her top, grateful that she'd thought to wear a swimsuit underneath.

Before she could change her mind, she dropped her hat onto the deck of the boat, held her breath and plunged.

16

Cassie

Cassie closed her laptop (she'd written four thousand words! A brilliant morning, particularly when you considered the emotional turmoil doing its best to distract her) and glanced up as she heard a motorboat heading into the bay below the villa.

Presumably, Stefanos. Her mother had mentioned that he had done some work on the boat.

She watched as he cut the engine and then steered the boat skillfully alongside the dock.

She'd met Stefanos a few times over the years when she visited and had always thought he would make a perfect romantic hero. Or was he, perhaps, too physically perfect? It didn't do to make one's characters too perfect and Stefanos fit the "tall, dark, handsome" description a little too well. If she wasn't careful, readers might dismiss him as a cliché.

Also, in her experience, exceptionally handsome men often knew they were exceptionally handsome and that tended to make them exceptionally irritating.

Besides, the real appeal for her, the trait that she found sexiest in a man, wasn't looks—it was competence. She'd rather have a man who would step up in a crisis, than one who was preoccupied with his appearance. Take Oliver, for example. There was that time she'd fallen into the river while trying to photograph ducklings (not her fault—it had been raining and the bank was soft). The water had been deeper than she'd thought, and Oliver had jumped in and hauled her out without giving a single thought to what it would do to his jeans. And he'd been remarkably good-humored as he'd removed pond weed from his hair and hers, and calming as he'd assured her that they weren't going to die of some terrible waterborne disease. And then there was the time she'd locked herself out of her college room and he'd shimmied along a wall to squeeze his way through her open window, ripping his favorite shirt in the process. The point was Oliver could always be relied on to come through in a crisis, even a messy one. In her opinion, that was the true definition of *hero* and beat razor sharp cheekbones and broad shoulders, although broad shoulders did come in handy. She'd discovered that when she sat on Oliver's during a summer festival when her favorite band had been playing and she couldn't see a thing.

So in fact, Oliver did have broad shoulders, but his shoulders weren't the reason she liked him.

She watched as Stefanos secured the boat and it was then that she noticed that he wasn't alone. There was a second person in the boat. A woman.

Interesting.

Telling herself that it was a novelist's job to observe people, she leaned forward, craning her neck to get a better view.

Stefanos stepped back toward the boat and held out his hand to the woman, who took it and stepped onto the dock with cautious grace.

She was tall, although not as tall as Stefanos. A red swimsuit clung to her long lean body and her hair fell in damp dark waves past her shoulders and half way down her back. Her sun hat half-covered her face. In her free hand, she appeared to be holding a bundle of clothes.

She was beautiful, Cassie mused. In fact, this exact scene might fit perfectly in her current book. Stefanos leaned closer to say something and the woman laughed, clearly amused by whatever it was he'd murmured in her ear.

Cassie felt a twinge of envy. This was intimacy. She could *feel* the deliciousness of that deep connection. The way they understood each other and communicated with the brush of fingers or a glance. Those were the things she was trying to convey in her current novel, but it was hard to convey in the written word what she was witnessing right now.

She was wondering why her mother hadn't mentioned that Stefanos was dating someone and who she could possibly be when the woman turned her head.

Cassie felt a jolt of surprise. *Adeline?*

Adeline had been out on the boat with Stefanos? Even more surprising, Adeline was wearing a knockout red swimsuit? And judging from her damp tangled hair, she'd been swimming.

Cassie wondered how many more surprises this trip was going to deliver.

She should probably give them some privacy, but she couldn't look away and consoled herself with the knowledge that people-watching was part of her job. Also understanding human behavior, although she had to confess that she often failed at that part.

When she and her sister had parted company that morning, both of them had been feeling anxious and, given the circumstances, Cassie hadn't anticipated that things were going to return to normal anytime soon. But here was Adeline, smiling and talking to Stefanos as if they were a couple on vacation.

She watched, hypnotized by the scene unfolding in front of her, until she saw Adeline turn and start walking up the path to the guest cottage, at which point she grabbed her laptop and pretended to be engrossed in something important.

"Hi there." She closed the laptop casually as Adeline arrived. "You've been swimming?"

"Yes." Adeline sat down on the lounger closest to her. "It was impromptu. I bumped into Stefanos. He invited me out on the boat. Given the way my morning had gone, I thought some breathing space might be good before the next difficult conversation."

Cassie wasn't interested in the difficult conversations, but she was interested in what had happened between Adeline and Stefanos. It was the first time she'd ever seen her sister anything other than immaculate. And it suited her. If anything, she looked more gorgeous now that she was rumpled and casual. "I didn't realize you knew each other so well."

"We haven't seen each other for decades. But I was standing on the dock this morning—" she paused and then gave a brief smile "—enjoying the view. And he was in the boat. I didn't know he was there. We got talking."

Cassie studied her. "You weren't really enjoying the view, were you?"

"No," Adeline said. "I was trying to decide between screaming and swimming out to sea."

Cassie nodded. This was becoming more and more interesting. "And he saved your vocal cords?"

"Something like that."

"So you went for a trip in the boat, and he took off his shirt, and you took off your shirt, and suddenly life seemed a whole lot better," Cassie offered. "And now you're living happily-ever-after. The end."

Adeline gave her a look. "We swam."

"That must have been a treat. A visual treat at the very least. He has an incredible body."

"Does he? I didn't notice."

Cassie grinned and put her laptop down. "Were you swimming with your eyes closed? He's a great swimmer, isn't he?"

"You've swum with him?"

"He was the one who taught me. He was seventeen, or maybe eighteen—I can't remember. Just before he left the island to go to college. I was eight at the time, so don't be jealous."

"Why would I be jealous?"

"You wouldn't be. I was teasing. But the two of you seemed to be having a good time." She saw Adeline's guarded look and felt a stab of panic. "I'm sorry. I'll stop teasing. Please don't do that."

"Do what?"

"Shut me out. I hate it when you hide behind that barrier you've built."

"I have a barrier?"

"Yes. It's right there between you and the world and I've never been able to see over it, but the last few days you let me in."

Amusement flickered in her sister's eyes. "You found a door in my barrier?"

"I don't know." She thought about the way Adeline had smiled up at Stefanos. "Maybe your barrier isn't as strong as you thought. But please don't reinforce it. I've had a horrid morning and I need to dilute it with happy and uplifting things."

Adeline put her bag down next to her and pulled her top over her swimsuit. "I assume that means you talked to our mother and it didn't go well. I don't suppose you were able to reason with her?"

"No. She kept saying that she and your father had both changed in the past two decades and that this was almost like a whole new relationship."

"Well let's hope so, given that the old one didn't turn out to be such a success." Adeline flipped her hair free from the neck of her top. "Did you ask her everything you wanted to ask her? Did she talk about your dad?"

"Yes." Cassie hesitated. "She said all the things I would have expected her to say."

Her sister looked at her. "But?"

What was she going to say? That there had been something not quite right about the conversation with her mother? It probably wasn't anything. She was just being oversensitive and was looking for things that weren't there. Overthinking. She did that a lot.

"But nothing." Cassie tucked her legs underneath her. "How did your chat with your dad go?"

"About the same as yours with our mother from the sounds of it. We had a frank conversation, but no amount of logic or reason made him change his mind. Apparently, it's my fault for not understanding, not his for behaving with an alarming lack of logic."

Cassie felt a stab of anxiety. "I guess this wedding is going ahead then."

"Seems that way."

What would that mean for her? No more long lazy weeks at the villa, just her and her mother, chatting about everything. No more messaging late at night. The shape of her life was going to change, and she wasn't sure where she fit. And how did Andrew feel about her, really? Her mother expected everyone to live happily-ever-after but was that possible given who she was?

Adeline stood up. "I am going to take a shower, write my Dr. Swift column, and then go and talk to our mother."

Her tone suggested she wasn't looking forward to it.

"Do you want me to come with you? Moral support?"

Adeline's expression softened. "No, but thank you for offering. She messaged me to say we'd all be having dinner together again tonight. A second attempt at a celebration."

"Right. And I am not going to run off, or tread on Achilles, or have a single drama moment. We are going to have a peaceful, civilized evening and no matter what they say, I'm not going to get upset." Cassie flicked away an insect that was hovering. "I will drink water, so that I don't say something I'm later going to regret."

"Water it is," Adeline said. "Sounds like a plan."

Cassie decided that however difficult this was, it did have an upside. She and her sister had connected in a way they never had before.

"I'm glad you're going to be there." Immediately, she felt embarrassed for being so effusive. "Go and write your column. Someone, somewhere, is probably desperate and hoping you'll choose to answer their question. And wear one of your friend's choices tonight because it's cruelty to dresses of that quality to keep them shut in a closet. They should be living an exciting life."

"You sound uncannily like Mia." With a shake of her head, Adeline headed into the villa and Cassie picked up her phone and sent a message to Oliver.

Hope you're having lots of great sex with someone who deserves you x

His reply came moments later.

Working hard. Too tired for sex.

She grinned and messaged back.

Wimp.

She was waiting for his reply when her phone rang.

The call display said *New York*.

New York? She didn't know anyone in New York.

The phone was on its third ring when she realized that she *did* know someone in New York. Her agent.

Obviously, she was calling to say she hadn't been able to sell Cassie's book. Everyone thought it was rubbish. She'd decided she no longer wanted to be Cassie's agent and was going to advise that Cassie consider a different job.

But if that was the case, wouldn't she simply have sent an email? Maybe she'd decided that bad news was better delivered by phone than email.

Hands shaking, she answered her phone.

"Hello?"

"Cassie?" Madeleine ("call me Maddy") was crisp and businesslike. "I hope you're sitting down."

"I'm sitting down. I'm in Corfu, staying with my mother and currently gazing at a stunning view."

"That's perfect, because you're going to remember this moment forever."

Cassie's heart started to thud. "I am?"

"Yes. And the fact that you're with your mother is also good, because you'll be able to celebrate together."

"Celebrate?" As well as her hands, Cassie's legs were now shaking too. "I have something to celebrate? Are you saying a publisher is interested in my book?"

"More than interested."

Cassie listened to the rest of the conversation in a daze.

She'd had not just one offer, but several. Publishers were fighting over her story. This so rarely happened.

She felt dizzy. She wanted to message Oliver, but she was afraid that with her fumbling fingers she might cut off the call.

Her agent was still talking, but Cassie heard only random words. *Exciting new voice…romance market buzzing right now… they think you're going to be the next big thing…lead title for next year…two book contract…*

And then she named a sum that almost made Cassie fall off her lounger.

"How much?"

Her agent repeated it. "The top bidder is excited, they want your book and they're willing to pay. If you agree, then we need to have a meeting to firm up details and I'll want to see more on their plans for the book before we formally accept their offer, but I wanted to let you know where we are right now. It's exciting, and you deserve to be part of that excitement."

"I don't know what to say." Cassie felt her eyes fill. People said dreams didn't come true, but hers just had. She was a writer. A real writer. Her book was going to be in bookstores.

And what better way to honor her parents' love affair than to immortalize it in a story?

She couldn't wait to tell her mother. She was going to be thrilled.

"They're already planning a major campaign to support the book," Maddy said. "They'll want you involved, obviously. They'll probably want you to tour."

"Tour?"

"Yes. Connect with readers, booksellers and librarians. Everyone loves the fact that this book was inspired by your parents' love story. It adds an authenticity, and that personal touch that always speaks to readers. They're going to want you to talk about that."

Cassie felt a flicker of doubt. Her mother was about to get married. It might not be massively tactful for Cassie to be talking to strangers about another of her marriages.

On the other hand, Cassie wasn't *Swift*, so who was ever going to know?

"One more thing, before I leave you to open that bottle of champagne," Maddy said, "they don't like your name."

"Excuse me?" Cassie blinked. "It's my name."

"Yes, but Cassie Dunn just doesn't work. It doesn't have the right ring to it. Hard to be specific. Just one of those instinct things. They wonder how you'd feel about using Cassie Swift."

She was showered with cold. "They know who my mother is?"

"Catherine Swift is famous. Everyone knows she has two daughters. You were never going to be able to hide this, Cassie. And why would you?"

There were many reasons.

A minute hole, the size of a pinprick, appeared in her bubble of happiness.

"But I'm not Cassie Swift."

"That doesn't matter. We're talking about a name—call it a pen name if you prefer. No one is suggesting a legal change of name."

Maybe not, but still—

"Are you saying they're only giving me this book deal because of my mother?"

"No. They're offering you the book deal because your book is brilliant, but we need to be honest here, and when it comes to marketing that book, it's not going to hurt that your mother is Catherine Swift. That's something they're going to want to use."

It was like swimming in crystal clear water, and then discovering pollution.

"But what if I don't want to use it? I want to do this by myself, on my terms. I want to know that any success I have is because of me."

"Of course, but, Cassie, this is the real world and selling books is hard. Don't be fooled by the occasional fairy-tale moment. This is business, and it's a brutal business. If you have an edge—and let's face it, being Catherine Swift's daughter gives you an edge—then you have to use it."

Cassie Swift.

She swallowed. She didn't like it. She was pretty sure Andrew wouldn't like it (and the name belonged to him, after all). She had no idea how her mother would feel.

What if she thought that this was all Cassie's idea? That she'd cashed in on her mother's success without even having the courtesy to mention it?

It was mortifying.

"That doesn't feel right to me."

"Reflect on it." Her agent had a brisk no-nonsense tone that suggested not only should Cassie reflect on it, but that she should then make the decision that the publisher wanted her to make.

"Are you saying that if I want this deal, I have to call myself Cassie Swift?"

There was a pause.

"Not necessarily. I'm saying it would give you a boost. This is the deal of a lifetime," her agent said. "Think about it."

The call ended and Cassie stared at her phone, her thoughts and emotions in a tangle.

She was going to be a published author.

Whatever happened, whatever she ended up calling herself, nothing was going to change that. And her agent hadn't said she *had* to call herself Cassie Swift, just that it would help. So she could refuse. If Cassie Dunn didn't work, then she'd think of another name herself.

It really wasn't a big deal. She was not going to ruin this special moment by overreacting.

She was delighted. And she was sure that despite the fact they needed to sort out the name issue, her mother was going to be delighted too.

Cassie felt a rush of pride.

The best part of this was that the whole world was going to hear her parents' love story.

How wonderful was *that?*

17

Catherine

"Second time lucky, I hope. I want this evening to be perfect." Catherine surveyed the table. Silverware gleamed against snowy white linen and the tall glasses caught the last of the amber sunlight. A simple bunch of white daisies formed a centerpiece in the middle of the table. It would have made a perfect shot to share on her social media—*#dinnerwiththefamily*—but she had no intention of sharing this moment with anyone. She shared snippets of her life (it was a requirement these days, and occasionally she longed for the early years of her career where her sole responsibility had been to write the book), but she selected the snippets carefully. There was a wide gap between reality and the truth, but these days everyone knew that social media images were carefully curated. And although her publisher was always telling her that her readers wanted insight into her real life, Catherine was pretty sure they didn't. She treated the darker parts of her life the way she did her laundry. She hid them away in the hamper and didn't show them to the public.

Satisfied, she glanced at Andrew. "No repeats of last night, I hope."

They shared a smile of understanding.

It had been an exhausting twenty-four hours. She felt emotionally drained. Picking through the past did that to her, which was why she tried not to do it. She'd selected the parts she could share with the girls, and buried the rest which, now that she thought about it, was very like her social media feed.

"There won't be any repeats." He pulled her against him and kissed the top of her head. "We've both spoken to Adeline, and you've spoken to Cassie. There's nothing more to be said. Nothing that can go wrong."

"I hope you're right."

"Why the doubt? I thought your conversation with Adeline went well?"

"It was perfectly civil." It was hard to explain exactly what she was feeling, maybe because she didn't really understand it herself. "I was hoping for more." She wanted to rebuild her relationship with her eldest daughter. She didn't want them to be like two polite strangers making small talk. She'd lost her, years before, but now she wanted her back.

Andrew took her face in his hands. "Maybe you should tell the girls the truth, Catherine. All of it. If they understood…"

"No." She stepped away from him. "I won't do that to Cassie." She wouldn't risk damaging her relationship with one daughter in order to try and fix her relationship with the other.

"It's your decision, of course," he said, "but you're not going to fix this in a few days, Catherine. Adeline was very young. She was bruised by everything. You have to give it time. Build up trust again. It will happen, I'm sure of it."

His confidence settled her.

"Yes, you're right."

Finally, the past was behind her. She could move on.

There was no time to discuss it further because at that moment Adeline and Cassie appeared.

Cassie was wearing a sheath dress in a shade of hot pink that matched the bougainvillea that frothed and tumbled around the paths of the villa. It fell from two narrow straps and ended half way up her thighs.

She was also wearing an enormous smile. The smile helped Catherine to relax. After their conversation that morning, she'd been worried. She'd had an uneasy feeling that Cassie knew she was hiding something. And she was. But didn't parents always keep things from their children? How many times a day did a mother say, *I'm fine, honey*, when the truth would have been, *My life is falling apart but I'm the adult and it's my job to protect you and make it look as if I've got this.*

And that was what Catherine was doing. She was protecting Cassie, just as she'd protected Adeline. And she'd done her best, even if her best had fallen short of what she would have wanted it to be.

Children didn't need to know that their parents didn't have all the answers.

People didn't always understand that you could love your children deep down to the bone, and still make mistakes. That you didn't always know a choice was a bad one until after you'd made it. That although you might try to control everything, in the end you controlled very little.

After Cassie had left her that morning, she'd fretted that her answers hadn't been good enough and that the questions were going to start again over dinner. But judging from the smile on her face, Cassie seemed to have accepted everything her mother had said, and all was right with the world again. She'd been careful to give exactly the same facts to Adeline.

She felt the tension in her shoulders ease a little.

Maybe Andrew was right. Maybe everything was going to be fine. The rocky part was behind them. All they needed now was time and patience.

She hugged Cassie and smiled at Adeline. "You both look wonderful."

Adeline was wearing a dress in a pale shade of lemon that looked perfect with her coloring. Her face and shoulders were showing a touch of the sun. Tonight, she'd chosen to leave her hair loose, and it slid past her shoulders in soft waves. She looked younger somehow, more relaxed, and Catherine finally relaxed too.

Hopefully, this evening would be fun.

The first few moment felt a little awkward, all of them were reliving what had happened on this exact spot just twenty-four hours earlier.

It was Andrew who smoothed it over. Andrew who greeted Cassie warmly, making it clear that whatever her reservations about them becoming a family, he had none.

They talked about nothing in particular while Andrew filled their glasses and they admired the gardens and the view across the sea.

The scent of wild thyme and garlic wafted from the kitchen, mingling with the sweetness of flowers. The infinity pool merged with the sea beyond, blue on blue, the view stretching forever.

My place, Catherine thought. *My special place.*

As the evening cooled, they sat down to eat, this time fresh fish baked with lemon and herbs that grew wild on the hills around them. There were tiny potatoes, fried crisp with salt, and greens picked fresh from the gardens.

The girls greeted Maria with hugs and genuine warmth and she lingered for a while, catching up on their news. Maria knew how much their presence meant to Catherine and she was all smiles, her own sadness pushed aside as she celebrated the moment.

And then she returned to the kitchen to tend to the elaborate dessert she'd been planning all day.

"And how did you girls spend the afternoon." Catherine passed Adeline a basket of freshly baked bread. "Whatever it was, you caught the sun."

Adeline paused while her father filled her glass. "I went out on the boat with Stefanos."

Catherine felt a spark of interest but knew better than to show it. She also knew that if she'd suggested such an activity, it would have been rejected. "It's been a beautiful day for it. Hot, but not too hot. Did you swim? You always did love to swim."

"Yes, I swam." Adeline glanced up from her food. "We went to that pretty bay up the coast. I can't remember the name."

"I know the one you mean, it's one of my favorites. It has a Greek name, but I usually call it the horseshoe beach. And the boat behaved? She broke down on Andrew last week and Stefanos had to rescue him."

"He's handy to have around." Andrew helped himself to more potatoes. "He messaged me earlier to tell me that he'd fixed the motor, Catherine. I forgot to tell you."

"Excellent. Did you go too, Cassie?"

"No. I was…" Cassie paused. "I was doing something else."

What else?

It was unlike Cassie to be vague. Normally, she told Catherine everything, which did make for a simple life.

"Something relaxing, I hope." She nudged gently. "Not job hunting."

"Not job hunting. At least, not exactly." Cassie hesitated and put her fork down. Achilles jumped into her lap, ever hopeful that he might be fed. "Actually, I have some news of my own. Something I'm very excited about."

Catherine's heart lifted. Suddenly, the evening felt almost close to normal. Exchanging news. Sharing. "Wonderful! We can celebrate together. It's the perfect night for it. Tell us."

Cassie's cheeks were tinged pink. "I haven't mentioned it before, for all sorts of reasons, but I've been writing. Fiction."

Catherine felt surprise, closely followed by delight and pride.

"Cassie! Why didn't you tell me?"

"Because you're brilliant at what you do, the best, and I was scared you would hate what I'd written and kill my confidence."

Catherine was affronted. She wasn't that bad of a mother, surely? "I'm sure I'll love anything you've written. The last thing I would do is kill your confidence."

But others would.

She felt a stab of concern. A good mother would probably encourage Cassie to be anything else but a writer. Cassie was gentle, soft-hearted and an optimist. Publishing was a brutal industry. Catherine couldn't bear the idea of all that enthusiasm and spark gradually oozing out of her daughter.

People thought it was glamorous. Everyone wanted to be a writer—if she had a dollar for every time someone had said to her *I'm going to write a book one day*, she could have bought the whole of Greece, not just this idyllic corner of Corfu— but most people said that because they had no idea what being a writer truly involved. They imagined a romantic scenario where they spent endless days caught in a blissful froth of creativity, embracing the joy of being their own master while being paid a small fortune. The reality was that most writers could barely scrape a living. If indeed she was ever published, Cassie would be stabbed by reviews, crushed by rejection, demoralized by sales and the ever-increasing competition (Miranda! Everything came back to Miranda!), and she would discover that once the book left her hands, she had almost no control over its fate.

People assumed it became easier the more successful you were, but it was never easy.

A writing career was like the Twelve Labors of Hercules.

Cassie leaned forward, her excitement undimmed because fortunately she wasn't able to read her mother's mind. "Exactly! You're my mother. You would have said you loved it, even if you'd hated it. I needed an honest opinion."

Should she point out that opinions were just that? Opinions. They were subjective? One publisher's rejection was another's lead title. One reviewer's *best book ever* was another's *worst thing I've ever read*. There were big-name authors who had been rejected multiple times before finally snagging a deal for a book that went on to be a global bestseller. Publishing was often a gamble. A throw of the dice. A flip of the coin. Who could predict what the public would want next?

She often thought that a writing career was a little like boxing. It wasn't just about the punch; it was about how many times you could haul yourself back on your feet when you were knocked to the ground.

But she would not kill her daughter's dream. If you couldn't be excited at the beginning, then when could you be excited?

Catherine envisaged a future where she was there for her daughter at all the low points (Andrew had been there for her, but he wasn't a writer so he didn't completely understand that indefinable seam of terror that was ever-present when you were trying to pluck creativity from thin air). She'd be able to give her the benefit of her wisdom and perhaps try to give her career a boost. Why not? Maybe it was unfair, but life was unfair. If you were thrown a rope, you should grab it.

"You can send it to Daphne. She'd be delighted to read it, I'm sure." She sent a silent apology to Daphne who would of course read it to please her most successful and bankable client, and would then have to find a tactful way to tell her that she didn't think Cassie's work was up to publishable standards. Maybe she should at least inject a note of reality. "Even if it's a rejection—and those are so common, even amongst the most successful of writers, so you really have to brace yourself for that—she will give you excellent and useful feedback. Daphne always has tremendous insight."

"I don't need to send it to Daphne." Cassie was fiddling with her glass. There was a sparkle in her eyes. She was positively alive with excitement. "I already have an agent."

"You have an agent? Since when? Who?"

"Madeleine Ellwood." She didn't explain who Madeleine Ellwood was. She didn't need to. Every writer knew her, or knew of her. In literary circles, she was as famous as the writers she represented. Her nickname was the Mighty Madeleine.

Catherine felt a stab of emotion she didn't immediately recognize.

Madeleine Ellwood was Miranda Patterson's agent. Madeleine was known industry-wide as a sharp, savvy agent and was as hot right now as Miranda herself. Everyone wanted to be represented by Madeleine. If Catherine hadn't been with Daphne, *she* would have wanted to be with Madeleine.

And Cassie, her own daughter, was with Madeleine.

And now she recognized the emotion. It was envy. Envy

that her daughter was at the start of something that seemed so exciting and full of possibilities. She saw the future full of blue skies and sunshine, with no dark clouds in sight. It was all dreams, and hope, and anticipation.

Oh, how Catherine would have loved to have been back there again, at the start of the upward journey, with no insecurities.

When had she lost that joy? The simple pleasure of creating a story and living every day with those fictional people? When had it become about numbers, about chart positions—"hitting the list"—about competition, about success and failure?

Number three.

She ran her tongue over dry lips. She wanted to recapture all those early feelings.

She made sure none of her thoughts showed on her face. This was Cassie's moment. She would not dilute it or tarnish the shine.

"When did this happen?" Why hadn't Cassie mentioned that she had an agent? Or maybe she didn't understand how big it was. Maybe she thought finding an agent to represent her was easy. Maybe she wasn't aware of the number of submissions and rejections that most writers endured in their quest to see their words in print.

"I sent it to her months ago, but didn't hear anything. I'd given up. Then she called me last week to say she'd read my book in one sitting and loved it. She offered to represent me, and of course I said yes."

Of course, Catherine thought. Because who would turn down the opportunity to be represented by the Mighty Madeleine?

Had Madeleine taken her on because she knew Cassie was

Catherine Swift's daughter? Was it cynical of her to allow that thought into her head?

Whether it was true or not, she had no intention of voicing it.

"Has she told you which publishers she plans to approach?"

"She sent it out to a few people last week."

"Only last week?" Catherine gave her a sympathetic look. "Then you need to brace yourself for another long wait."

"That's what I told myself, but then she called an hour ago." Cassie sat up a little straighter. "She's had three offers."

"Three?"

What was it with the number three?

"Yes. And I've been offered a two-book deal." Breathless with disbelief and excitement, Cassie shared what her agent had said, naming one of the biggest publishers in the game. "They think I'm an exciting new voice. They told me they think I'll be big. I can't believe it!"

Catherine couldn't believe it either. Pride grew inside her until she almost burst with it. Her baby! A major book deal. A soon-to-be-published author. Who would have thought it?

She sprang from her chair and hugged her daughter.

"Congratulations. This is incredible news."

"I know! I can't believe it." Cassie hugged her back. "Thank you."

For a moment, Catherine stood like that, breathing in the sweet scent of her daughter's hair and bathing in her child's happiness. It engulfed her like a wave, lifting her spirits. It had been a shock to her to discover that as a mother she was intrinsically connected to her child's mood. Maybe it wasn't that way for everyone, but it certainly was for her.

Cassie's happiness was her happiness.

Adeline's pain was her pain.

She gave her daughter a final squeeze and returned to her

chair. The evening was going better than she could possibly have hoped for. And they weren't even talking about the wedding. They were just a normal family, celebrating the success of one of its members. "Do you have any idea what an achievement this is? Andrew, we must open more champagne."

He was already on his feet and smiling. "We must. I'll fix that right away. Congratulations, Cassie." He headed to the kitchen, along paths lit by tiny lights and bordered by flowers.

Adeline leaned across the table and tapped her half-empty glass against her sister's.

"Go you! Why didn't you mention it before?"

"Because I didn't think it was going to happen," Cassie said. "I thought I'd jinx it. And when it's something you've created, rejection is so personal. If it turned out everything I'd written was crap, I didn't really want to announce it. It's hard enough believing in yourself without anyone else casting doubt."

Welcome to my world, Catherine thought.

"This explains why you were cagey whenever I asked you if you'd had any thoughts about what you might do next," Adeline said. "Presumably this is what you're doing next."

"Yes." Cassie looked a little dazed, as if she still didn't quite believe it herself. "Yes, it looks as if I'm going to be a full-time writer."

"You can give up your job in the café," Catherine said, "and maybe I can help set you up in an apartment of your own so that you don't have to share with Oliver anymore."

Cassie gave a little frown. "I hadn't thought…" She stopped. "That's generous of you, but there's no rush to think about that. I like my job in the café. And I like where I live."

Her daughter's living arrangements had been a constant source of anxiety.

Catherine had met Oliver on one of her trips to Oxford, and liked him enormously. He was handsome, smart and kind. A man like that was unlikely to stay single for long.

What would happen when Oliver finally had a serious relationship? Surely, he wasn't going to want Cassie in his spare room then?

"Tell us about the book," Adeline said. "I want to hear all about it."

Andrew had reappeared, a fresh bottle in his hand.

"I want to hear all about it too." Catherine smiled her thanks to Andrew as he topped up their glasses. She felt a rush of love and gratitude. Cassie wasn't his daughter, and yet he was treating her as if she was. He was a kind and generous man. "But first a toast. To having another author in the family." She raised her glass and Andrew and Adeline raised theirs.

It was funny, Catherine thought, that this achievement of her daughter's had brought them together in a way that the wedding hadn't. It was unexpected.

Even Adeline was smiling and relaxed.

Cassie took a sip of champagne and then put her glass down. "I'll need all the advice you can give me."

"My best advice?" *Grow ten skins, and make one of them solid steel.* "Enjoy every moment! Now tell me about the book."

"It's a love story."

"That doesn't surprise me," Catherine said. "You always loved romantic stories."

Adeline relaxed in her chair. "Following in the family tradition. Kissing not killing."

Catherine thought of her current manuscript, full of gruesome detail, and said nothing. The only kiss was when the heroine kissed goodbye the man who had been tormenting her and that had been approximately two seconds before she'd used the blade in her hand to open an artery. She'd spent two days researching blood spatter, which had proved to be a complex and surprisingly fascinating topic. Who knew that you could learn so much from the pattern that blood made when it hit a wall?

But this wasn't the time to reveal her own change in direction.

"I'm not exactly following in the family tradition," Cassie said. "This isn't a romance, as such. Romance always has a happy ending, doesn't it? Mine doesn't. But it's definitely a love story."

Catherine was intrigued. "Your romantic leads don't get together?"

"Oh, yes, they're very much together. But then he dies. He was her big love, but she picks herself up and survives. It is romantic, although it's not a romance. And it has a hopeful ending."

"Oh?" She felt a warning prickle behind her neck. An instinctive reaction to a threat yet to be identified. "The market for love stories is hot right now. Do you have the manuscript with you? I'd love to read it. And now it's already been accepted and you're on your way, hopefully you won't be too shy to share it with your own mother."

"I can email it to you right now." Cassie dug out her phone and opened her emails.

"Email it to me too," Adeline said. "I'd love to read it."

Cassie glanced at her. "I'm not sure if you'll like it. What do you normally read?"

"I read a variety of things. Please…" Adeline leaned forward, "I'd love to read it if you'll let me."

"Okay. This is nerve-wracking." Cassie's fingers flew over the keys and then she pressed Send. "My book, currently entitled *Without End*, should now be sitting in your inbox."

"I'll print out a copy and read it the old-fashioned way," Catherine said. "I spend too long staring at screens. Where is it set?"

"Right here on Corfu." Cassie put her phone down and reached across to her mother. "I'm dedicating it to you. I hope you're going to love it."

"I'm sure I will." And if she didn't, she would never say so. "And I'm touched that you're dedicating it to me."

"I've said *to my mother, for teaching me all there is to know about love.*"

Catherine kept her smile in place, even though the idea of her being called an expert in love was close to laughable. Still, the truth wouldn't work.

To my mother, who stuffed up love at every opportunity.

The book was fiction, so why shouldn't the dedication be fiction too?

"Perfect." She squeezed Cassie's hand. "Thank you."

"It seemed appropriate. If I hadn't grown up seeing you write, maybe I wouldn't have thought it was even possible as a career."

It felt good to know she'd inspired her daughter. "So it's a love story, underpinned by tragedy."

"Not just any love story. It's *your* love story."

Catherine's smile froze on her face. The world around her seemed to slow down. The sensation behind her neck went from a warning prickle to a freezing shower. "Mine?"

"Well, yours and my dad's. This is a little bit awkward under the circumstances." Cassie sent an apologetic look toward Andrew. "Obviously, I had no idea that the two of you were together again when I wrote it. I didn't mean to be insensitive. I hope you understand, Andrew. It was all in the past, obviously."

Well, obviously, Catherine thought, *given that Rob was dead.*

To his credit, Andrew's smile didn't slip but there was caution in his smile too, as if he was working out the full implications of what Cassie was telling them. "I'm proud of you. I know your mother is too. I have no problem with it, Cassie."

Cassie turned to Catherine. "Mum?"

She had a problem with it. *She had an enormous problem.*

Cassie had written a love story inspired by her relationship with Rob Dunn?

A *love* story.

She put her hand across her mouth to stop a hysterical laugh escaping. If ever there was a relationship that shouldn't have been immortalized in romantic fiction, it was theirs.

Cassie's eyes shone. "You seem really moved. I'm pleased."

Moved?

Panic rose inside her. The edges of her vision grew dark and the air felt trapped in her lungs. She was struggling to breathe when she felt Andrew's hand close over hers. His fingers tightened and she clung.

He knew. He understood. And he was telling her everything was going to be fine. She could already hear his voice in her head. *It's just a book. Fiction. No one will guess the story itself is based on your relationship with Rob.*

And he was right. She should relax.

"I don't know what to say."

Cassie smiled. "You don't have to say anything. I can see you're a little overwhelmed. I can't think of a better tribute to my parents. What you shared will be there in print forever. With luck, millions will read it."

Millions.

In print forever.

Nausea rose inside her. In her mind, she was back there on that awful night, Rob's body twisted and broken at the bottom of the stairs.

She'd sat there sobbing over his body, thinking, *This is the end. It's over.*

But now Cassie, in her innocence, had dredged it up again.

Just when she thought she'd put Rob Dunn behind her forever, he managed to worm his way back into her life.

What was she going to do?

She had no idea. But the first thing was to read the book and see just how much damage it was going to do.

18

Adeline

"Could you stop pacing?" Adeline loaded a beach bag with sunscreen, a towel, a bottle of iced water and her e-reader. "The constant movement is making me seasick."

Cassie stopped, pausing on her toes like a dancer. "Do you think she's read it yet?"

"Since you asked me five minutes ago? I doubt it. You only gave it to us last night and it was gone midnight when we finished dinner. She probably fell asleep right away and hasn't even read the first page yet. Relax."

"I can't relax." Cassie wrapped her arms around herself. "Do you know how stressful it is waiting for your own mother to give you feedback on your book? Particularly when your mother is a successful author."

"No. But I can imagine."

"It's terrible. I thought it was bad waiting to hear from an agent and awful waiting to hear from a publisher, but this is twice as bad. What if she hates it?"

Adeline suspected that if Catherine hated it, she would never say so. "Not that I know anything about publishing, but if a major agent and a major publisher want it, then it hardly matters what your family think."

"It does. It matters more than anything." Cassie paced across the bedroom again, vibrating with nerves. "Perhaps it's because this story is personal. I'm hoping I've got the details right."

"Why do details matter? I thought it was supposed to be fiction."

"It is, but it's closely inspired by all the stories Mum told me. I want to do justice to what they shared. Immortalize their story." Cassie stopped pacing. "It's my tribute to my father. My way of keeping a little piece of him alive."

"Yes, I see that." Adeline thought about how hard it must have been for Cassie, growing up with no father. And she thought about her own father, and how much she loved and admired him (even when he made questionable decisions).

"Did you see how emotional it made her?"

"Yes."

There was no doubt that Cassie's unexpected announcement had changed the tone of the evening. In some ways, it had helped because it shifted the focus away from the upcoming wedding. The undercurrent of tension had been replaced by a note of celebration.

And it was true that her mother had been emotional, but there had been something else too. A look of panic? Had her sister seen that?

Maybe their mother was upset about having a spotlight shone on that particular time of her life given that she was about to remarry her first husband. Her father had seemed

remarkably relaxed about the whole thing (which was typical of him), but the situation couldn't be entirely comfortable for him, could it? Or her mother. If they were getting
married again, then presumably they were trying to put that
part of her mother's life behind them.

Or maybe her mother was concerned that someone would
recognize the story and know it was about her. Apart from
the occasional glorious photo of Corfu shared on her social
media accounts, she was fiercely protective of her private life.
And Adeline was grateful for that. It was a relief to her that
most people had no idea that Dr. Adeline Swift was related
to Catherine Swift, the novelist. She preferred to live her life
below the radar.

Cassie looked at her. "Did you read it?"

"Cassie you only sent it to us eight hours ago! You need
to chill." She didn't add that she'd lain awake staring at her
laptop, willing herself to open the document. It was true
that she'd been eager to read it, right up to the point where
Cassie had said that it was inspired by her mother's relationship with Rob Dunn.

That relationship had blown Adeline's life apart. Did she
really want to read about it? In the end, she'd decided that
her emotions had been battered enough for one day and
she'd closed her laptop and promised herself she'd read it in
the morning when she'd hopefully be feeling stronger after a
good night's sleep. Instead, she'd reflected on the conversation
she'd had with her mother. After her boat trip and swim with
Stefanos, she'd felt calm enough to meet her mother. This
time she'd simply listened as her mother had said all the same
things her father had said. It still made no sense to Adeline,
but she hadn't tried to reason with her or change her mind.

She smiled at her sister. "I've transferred your book to my
e-reader and I'm going to read it on the beach. How much

of the story is factual?" She asked the question casually and Cassie gave a tiny shrug.

"I suppose you could say it's fictionalized fact."

"Is there a sex scene?"

"Yes. But I wasn't thinking of our mother at that point, obviously. No one wants to think about their parents having sex, even fictional sex." Cassie's face was scarlet. "Do you think she's worried about that? Now I feel like hiding under the bed."

"The floor is hard and there isn't a lot of room under the bed so I'd stay where you are." Adeline pushed aside her own unease and hugged her sister. "Relax. This is your big moment. You should be enjoying it. It's going to be fine."

"Are you sure?" Cassie clung to her, a ball of warmth and nerves and shimmering anxiety.

"I'm sure." Adeline released her and grabbed her bag.

"Are you really reading it today? I hope you don't hate it. I didn't dwell on the affair part. I focused on the love they had."

Adeline felt a twinge. "Cassie, it's fine." It wasn't fine, but she wanted to support her sister. It was just a book, that was all. How much pain could a book cause? "Are you sure you don't want to come with me to the beach?"

"No. I have a video conference with my agent and my new editor, and then I have to write a biography for myself. That will be short. *Cassie Swift was born, went to college and then wrote a book.* I need to embellish it. Make it sound more interesting."

"Cassie Swift?" Adeline reached for her sunglasses. "You're using Mum's name?"

"The publisher really wants me to. I told them I wasn't sure. For a start I'm not *Swift*. But they said it was no different from using a pen name. They say that Cassie Dunn doesn't have the right ring to it."

Or maybe they wanted to exploit the Swift name. Adeline slid her bag onto her shoulder. She needed to stop being a cynic. She knew nothing about publishing.

"Don't worry about that now. Enjoy the moment." She grabbed her hat and checked her reflection in the mirror.

Cassie studied her. "You look fantastic. That cover-up is gorgeous and your swimsuit looks pretty underneath. You look good in turquoise."

"You don't think it's too…naked?"

"I do not. You're at the beach, Adeline. What time are you meeting him?"

Adeline felt her cheeks warm. "Who?"

"Stefanos." Cassie waggled her eyebrows. "You're looking exceptionally hot, and you're wearing just a touch of lip gloss."

Was she that obvious? "It's lip sunscreen."

"Of course it is. This is romantic. You haven't seen each other for two decades and then *wham*, you see each other and that's it."

"You really do have a skill for fictionalizing reality."

Cassie gave a happy shrug. "Call it what you like, but the fact that you're seeing him again today, less than twenty-four hours since you last saw him, tells me something."

"It should tell you that I'm keeping myself occupied. You're going to be busy for most of the day, and our mother has a meeting with the wedding planner, although why you need a wedding planner when there are only going to be a handful of people at the wedding, I have no idea." She was trying hard to accept things the way they were, but still the idea of the wedding itself didn't thrill her. She hoped she'd be able to wear a suitably happy expression.

"You don't have to make excuses. There are numerous ways to occupy yourself on the island, and you've chosen to spend your day with Stefanos. But don't worry—" Cassie held up her hands "—I get it! You're probably afraid to give me details in case you appear in my next book, but I promise that basing a book on real events was a one-off. From now on, I'm fiction all the way. The book I'm writing now has an eighty-year-old main character who is doing outrageous things, and it is entirely the product of my imagination." She jumped as her phone pinged. "That's Oliver. I said I'd call him to catch up before my meeting."

Adeline headed to the door. "I'll see you tonight. Have fun planning your next bestseller." As she walked across the patio and down toward the path that led to the village she heard her sister's breathless voice.

"Olly? Can you believe it? It's actually happened!"

Adeline smiled and kept walking. Her sister's excitement was infectious and uplifting. It was a reminder that good things happened in life, and when they did, you had to savor every moment.

And she'd already decided that whatever the book was like, she would say she loved it.

She felt better about everything this morning. Maybe it was because she'd had a good night's sleep, or maybe it was because she'd woken to find a message from Stefanos waiting for her on her phone.

Join me for a boat trip and lunch?

Her instinct had been to refuse, but then she'd thought, *Why not?*

She'd go, if only to prove to herself that her father was wrong about her.

The beach was crowded, and she followed the path until she reached the end of the bay, where Kostas had his boat business. She felt a twinge of nostalgia, remembering him from her childhood.

Stefanos was standing on the beach, helping a family board one of the boats.

He saw her, waved and then gestured that he'd be five minutes.

She waited while he joined the family in the boat and gave them instructions and then he sprang from the boat into the water and waded back onto the beach.

"I wasn't sure you'd come." He leaned down and kissed her first on one cheek and then on the other. She felt the scrape of stubble against her cheek and breathed in the fresh scent of citrus and sea salt. She rested her fingers on his shoulders, a light touch against hard muscle.

She felt something uncurl inside her and stepped back, unsettled. "I wasn't sure I would either."

"What persuaded you? My looks, my dazzling conversation or my legendary cooking skills, inherited from my mother?"

"None of those things. I'm here for your boat."

He laughed. "Sounds good to me. And I'm not cooking. I'm taking you to lunch with a friend. When you've eaten the fish in his restaurant, you'll never want to eat anywhere else."

She glanced down at her casual cover-up. "I'm not dressed for elegant dining. I assumed we were having a simple picnic. Maybe a swim."

"There's nothing simple about my picnics, but plenty of time for you to discover that. And you look great." His gaze skimmed her briefly. "How was last night? Did you survive?"

"It was interesting. Better than expected." Thanks to Cassie's news, which had shifted the tone and the focus.

"I can't wait to hear all about it." He gestured to the boat bobbing close to the shore. "That one's mine. Do you mind getting wet? Do you have to be back by a certain time?"

"No to both questions."

There was far too much drama in her life for her liking and she was more than happy to escape again.

You see, Dad? I'm more than capable of being spontaneous when I want to be.

But she wondered if that was because of Stefanos. With him, she remembered the person she'd once been, before life events had taught her to be careful. It was like glancing across the street and spotting a familiar face but not being able to place it.

She hoisted her bag higher onto her shoulder, lifted her beach wrap high on her thighs and waded through the cool water.

"Here, I'll take that." He removed the bag from her shoulder so that she could use both hands on the ladder. She climbed onto the boat and then turned and took her bag from him.

He climbed up after her, pulled up the anchor and headed out into the bay. The boat bounced over the surface of the water and she tipped her head back, enjoying the feel of the sun on her face and the spray of seawater cooling her skin.

"Where are we going?"

"I'm going to show you my house."

She sat up, interested. "Is it far?"

"About ten minutes by road. The same by water."

She saw him smile and had a feeling she was missing something, but she had no idea what. It still surprised her that he'd bought a home here, rooted himself to a place he'd been so determined to leave. She was looking forward to seeing it, not because she was interested in the home itself, but because she was interested in him.

As he'd promised, it was around ten minutes before he

guided the boat round a headland and ducked into a hidden cove.

The land plunged steeply down to the water. A white pebbled beach was fringed by a backdrop of tall cypress trees and pine, and a wooden jetty stretched into the clear blue water. A few houses nestled in the trees, and she sat for a moment, drinking it in.

This was the authentic Corfu, far from the flashy resorts favored by tourists.

"You live here?" She felt envious. Waking up to this every day felt more like a dream than a lifestyle.

"Home sweet home." He guided the boat against the jetty and she felt a stirring of familiarity.

"I know this place."

He smiled and stepped off the boat onto the jetty. "Took you a while."

"We came here that day you stole your father's boat."

"I thought we agreed on 'borrowed,' but yes. This is the place." He secured the boat and held out his hand to her, but she shook her head.

"I want to swim."

"Now? I planned to give you the tour, make you a cup of my exceptional Greek coffee and then swim before lunch."

It was tempting, but not as tempting as the water.

She made the decision instantly.

"Right now." She shaded her eyes and gazed across the bay. The sea glistened.

She could feel him watching her.

"I thought you weren't spontaneous?"

"I'm not usually." She smoothed her hair back and secured it tightly with a band.

"Is this sudden transformation my fault?"

"Maybe." She smiled. "You're a corrupting influence."

"That's what your dad said that day I took you on the boat. He yelled at me, because you could have drowned."

"We scared him, but I don't know why. I've always been a strong swimmer."

"The waters are deep here," he said. "He was right to be upset with me, although I have no idea how he expected me to control you. You always did whatever you wanted to do."

"I still remember how the water felt that day." She turned her head to look at him. "You saved me. This place saved me. I can't believe you bought a house here."

"I've always thought it was special," he said. "Not so special in winter of course, when the wind is howling and the storms hit. I'm not romanticizing it."

"I've always enjoyed storms."

"Come back in December. You'd be welcome." His gaze connected with hers and for a moment she imagined it, returning here in winter. She imagined *him*, content in this place he'd made his home.

"I can't believe this is your life."

"Why? Because it seems like an odd choice?"

"No. It's a good choice. A brave choice." She remembered what he'd said about living life without ever questioning whether there might be something better out there. He'd taken a risk, with no guarantees that it would work out. "I suppose I'm a little envious."

It made her think about her own life, and her own choices. Would she have the courage to make a change like this?

The water was translucent and inviting. She felt an almost desperate urge to slide into its clear blue depths.

She tugged at the ties holding her cover up in place and tucked it into her bag.

"Nice swimsuit." His voice was roughened and she laughed.

"It's the same one I wore yesterday, but a different color."

"I thought it was a nice swimsuit then too." He held out his hand. "I'll take your bag while you swim to shore. If you're sure you want to do this."

"I'm sure." She handed him her bag and dived straight off the side of the boat. The cool water closed over her heated limbs, sound was muffled, and for a few blissful seconds, she stayed submerged. Then she rose to the surface, cleared the water from her face with her hand and saw Stefanos strolling toward the beach, her bag slung over his shoulder.

She closed her eyes and floated on her back for a moment, feeling the sun on her face and the water play with her hair. It was the most relaxed she had been since she'd stepped off his boat the day before. She could have stayed in the water, floating, but then she remembered that he'd booked a restaurant for lunch, and she rolled onto her front and swam slowly to the shore.

He was waiting for her as she emerged from the water. "Good?"

"Oh, yes." She squeezed water from her hair and wiped her face with her hand. "I've messed up your plan. Sorry."

"I didn't have much of a plan. Bring you here. Eat something." He shrugged as he handed her the bag. "You can swim for longer if you like."

"No. We can do that later." She pulled a towel out of her bag and dried her face. "I want to see your house."

There was one couple sunbathing at the far end of the beach, but other than that, they had the place to themselves.

She glanced around, drinking in the solitude and the endless blue.

"Why so few people?"

"The water shelves steeply so it's not great for children. Also there are no tavernas here and no stores. Nowhere to buy yourself a drink or a snack. Tourists usually choose to be a little closer to civilization." He gestured to a path that climbed steeply upward. "My house is that way. It's not far. Are you in a rush to get back?"

"No rush. My sister has a work meeting, and my parents are meeting the wedding planner." She slid her feet into flip-flops but decided to let her costume dry before she put on her wrap.

He waited for her. "Cassie has a job?"

"It turns out that my sister has written a novel. I'll tell you about it, but I might need caffeine for that." She shaded her eyes and glanced up the path. "I remember wondering where that led. I can't believe you live here. Did you have to do a lot of work on the house?"

"A bit. Working on this place kept me occupied during the winter. I stayed with my mother while I did it, so I was able to support her while she adjusted to living life with-out my father. The renovation was a welcome distraction. There's something about hard physical work that takes your mind off things."

"Losing a parent is hard." She'd been in the water only moments earlier but already her skin was dry and she felt the intensity of the sun beating down. "Sorry, that sounded glib and careless coming from someone who still has both hers."

"It didn't sound glib. It's true. And loss comes in different forms. You lost your mother too, in a way. You certainly lost your sense of security."

She was surprised that he could see it so clearly.

"That sounds like something Dr. Swift would say."

He smiled. "She's pretty smart, that Dr. Swift." He held out his hand and she took it, feeling the strength of his fin-gers as he helped her up the steep path.

"She's only smart with other people's problems," Adeline said. "She doesn't find her own easy to handle. I just wish my parents had told me what was happening, instead of springing it on me like this. I don't understand why they kept it a secret."

"I understand your frustration." He shortened his stride to match hers. "My parents kept things from me too."

"They did?"

"Yes. It turned out that my father had been ill for a while, but they didn't tell me. Nor did they tell me that the business was on the verge of failing."

She paused, breathless in the heat. "They kept all that from you? Why?"

"I don't know. Pride? My dad's stubborn determination to fix everything himself? Parental instinct not to worry offspring?" His shrug revealed his frustration. "Your guess is as good as mine. Every week I called home, and every week he told me everything was fine and handed the phone to my mother because small talk wasn't his thing. As if heart problems and business problems were small talk. Needless to say, once I found out the truth I felt like the worst son on the planet."

She could feel the pain and the guilt coming off him in waves and her insides ached with sympathy. "You're blaming yourself for not being a mind reader?"

"For not asking the right questions. For not coming home sooner. If I'd been here, maybe I would have sensed something was wrong. I might have seen what they weren't telling me. But I was living the busy life I'd created for myself and I saw nothing that they didn't show me."

She came across it all the time in her work. Regret.

"You couldn't possibly have known. And they made a choice, Stefanos. That was what they wanted. They probably thought they were protecting you." They started walking again, their pace slow but steady.

"Maybe, but if I'd known my father was struggling, I would have come home and helped and maybe things might have taken a different course," he said. "I was angry—frustrated—that they hadn't shared what was happening. It was a difficult time." They'd reached the top of the path and he led her up a set of stone steps that wound through the gardens to the house.

"Parent-child relationships can be complicated." *She knew that better than most.*

"I'm an adult."

How many times a day did she tell herself the same thing?

She thought about her own parents. "But you're still their child and that alters the way they see you, and behave toward you."

"I wish I'd had a straight conversation with them," he said. "It was only after my father died that I realized he was right about many things. I was chasing money and clawing my way up a ladder I assumed I wanted to climb. Whenever he pointed out that my life didn't include the one thing I'd loved more than anything—the water—I dismissed it. I thought I knew best. Turns out I didn't. I wish I'd paid more attention to his point of view. I wish I'd listened more."

She felt a twinge of guilt. She hadn't tried that hard to see her parents' point of view, had she? She'd just assumed they were making a mistake and tried to find a way to make them both see it.

Resolving to try harder, she followed him through the gardens. They were wilder than the gardens in her mother's villa, less structured, but no less attractive for it. Two large lemon trees pressed close to the path, heavy with fruit.

She was thinking that maybe she wasn't as physically fit as she'd thought when the path opened onto a pretty terrace and there was the house.

She stopped, enchanted. The walls of the house were a pale stone and the wooden shutters were painted a vibrant shade of blue. Geraniums tumbled joyfully from terracotta pots and a vine clambered over a wooden trellis, shading a seating area overlooking a pool and the beach beyond. She imagined sitting out here on a summer evening, watching the sun set over the ocean. "It's perfect."

"I think so. Come and see inside." He was still holding her hand and she didn't pull away as he led her into the house.

It was simply furnished, decorated mostly in white with touches of cobalt blue, which reflected the color of the sea and sky that stretched beyond the windows. She could imagine it cool in the summer, and cozy in winter.

The master bedroom had French windows overlooking the terrace and the beach far below, and there was a small second bedroom that he was using as a study.

She blinked. "You use three computer screens?"

"I used to work in tech. There are some things I can't give up. I still do some freelance work to boost the income from the boat business. I enjoy the variety." He led her back downstairs to the kitchen and opened doors that led directly onto the terrace. "Coffee?"

"Please."

He poured two cups, put two diamond-shaped pieces of honey-soaked baklava onto a plate and carried it out to the terrace on a tray.

Adeline slipped on her cover-up and stretched out on one of the comfy outdoor sofas. "This is bliss. The position is incredible."

"Yes. It's been interesting seeing it change through the seasons," he said. "You should see it in spring. The place is covered in wild orchids."

She assumed it was a random comment, and not an invitation but part of her almost wished it had been an invitation. *What was happening to her?*

She took a piece of baklava, tasting the flaky sweetness. "This is delicious. Your mother made it?"

"Of course." He picked up his coffee. "I could pretend I chose the house for its views, but the truth is I bought it because there are reliable onshore winds in the afternoon. The sailing is the best."

"I'm just pleased you found somewhere that works for you." She slid off her sandals and curled her legs under her, nursing her coffee in her lap. "The house must have been here when we came to this beach all those years ago."

"Yes. But I only discovered it later." He put his cup down. "What happened after you left all those years ago? Fill in the gaps for me."

Comfortable in the shade, she told him how she'd gone to live with her father in London, about how difficult it had been to be sent away with no warning. How witnessing her father's distress had affected her deeply. How her connection with her mother had been torn and never really mended.

And he listened closely, paying attention. "I couldn't believe you left so suddenly. I asked my mother about it at the time because I was upset that I'd lost my friend."

She felt a stirring of warmth inside her.

"And what did she say?"

"That your mother was doing the only thing she could possibly do in the circumstances." He rested his arm across the back of the sofa. "And then she refused to talk about it again. But she started bringing Cassie over to our house often. And when I asked her about it, she said that Catherine had to work. I could never figure out why her father didn't look after her. Not that I didn't love little Cass, but it seemed odd to me. Rob Dunn wasn't working. He used to hang out at the bar on the beach most days. I saw him whenever I went to help my dad."

Adeline thought back to that time.

"I remember so little about him. I don't remember spending any time with him when I lived here."

He gave her a long look. "I often wondered—" He stopped and she frowned.

"What?"

"Nothing. More coffee?"

"No thanks. What were you going to say?"

"It's not important."

"Stefanos—" she leaned forward "—we always told each other everything."

He pulled a face. "As you reminded me, that was a very long time ago."

"It feels like yesterday."

"Yes," he said. "It does." His gaze connected with hers, his eyes velvety dark.

She felt her heart alter its rhythm and with some effort she shifted the conversation back.

"I thought I had a clear recollection of that day my mother told me I was going to live with my father. Leaving the island, Cassie and y—" She almost said *you* and stopped herself in time. Revealing that she'd missed him was too much even for her new, more open self. "But when I talked to my sister, she made me question it."

"Your sister would have been two years old?"

"Yes. But my mother has talked about it with her. And what she said didn't make sense." She paused, embarrassed. "Sorry, this must be very boring for you. You've already endured more than enough of my family drama."

"And I've shared my family drama with you, so don't stop now. What didn't make sense?"

Adeline put her cup down and shifted in her seat. "Cassie told me that after one of my visits when I was older, my mother cried after I left. Sobbed. And when Cassie asked her what was wrong, she told her that life could sometimes be very complicated. She said she missed me." And Adeline hadn't been able to stop thinking about that. "If she missed me, why did she send me away? I don't know what that means."

"Have you asked her?"

"No." There were some questions that were better not asked. "It's all in the past, isn't it? I thought it was best to move on. It's not as if anything can be changed now."

"Maybe not, but sometimes understanding something can help."

"Maybe." She uncurled her legs and stood up, conscious that she'd been dominating the conversation. "You promised me lunch and swimming."

"I did."

The afternoon passed far too quickly. They had lunch at a little taverna up the coast in a cove that could only be reached from the water. The food was as good as he'd promised, and they sat and chatted for ages, and then returned to the beach below his house.

They swam for a while and then Adeline returned to the beach. She reached into her bag for her bottle of water, and saw her e-reader there. Cassie's book was waiting for her.

Her heart sank. She *had* to read it. She should start the book now, while she was with Stefanos and her mood was good.

She opened the book, started reading and lost track of time.

"Whatever you're reading, it must be good. I've been try-ing to attract your attention for the past five minutes." Stefanos draped a towel around his neck and sat down next to her. Droplets of water clung to his lashes and the shadow on his jaw.

"It's Cassie's book. It's a love story inspired by my mother's relationship with Rob."

His smile faded and his gaze searched hers. "And you're all right reading that?"

"I didn't think I would be, which was why I thought I'd start it now with you here. But it's good." She glanced at her phone, surprised by how much time had passed.

Stefanos was frowning. "The story is based on your mother's affair?"

"Yes, although obviously it's fiction and that part isn't the focus. It's really about their love story." And something about the writing had tugged at her. She'd felt their love and their urgency and desperation to be together. "This is going to sound weird, but for the first time ever, it gave me some insight into why two people might want to be together despite the obstacles."

He seemed amused. "Are you telling me you don't believe in love?"

"I do, but I don't have a traditionally romantic view of it. I think when you feel an instant connection with someone across a crowded room, that's physical attraction, not love. And I don't think there's such a thing as *the one*. How can there be? There are eight billion people on the planet. If there was only one person for us, we'd all be single."

He laughed. "That's true."

"But despite that, I'm still loving this story. I don't know what that says about me."

He leaned across and brushed sand from her leg. "It says you're turning into a big old romantic, Dr. Swift."

"Okay *that's* a scary thought." Laughing, she slid her

e-reader back into her bag. "I'm relieved, to be honest. I was dreading reading it, but it's a heartwarming story, although obviously I haven't reached the part where he dies."

"Death does have a tendency to interrupt things." Stefanos rubbed his hair dry with a towel. "Does your mother know about this book?"

"Yes, but she hasn't read it yet. Cassie only gave it to us late last night. She's probably reading it right now."

He draped the towel round his neck. "You don't think it will upset her, given that she's remarrying your dad?"

"I wondered about that. I think Cassie wondered too, although to be fair, our mother didn't share what was happening so there's no blame attached to Cassie. I was scared of reading it, but there are no triggers for me." There was nothing controversial in it. Nothing that seemed too personal. Just a straightforward love story that ended in tragedy. From what she'd read so far, she felt reassured. And also relieved, because part of her had been dreading that this might drive a wedge between her and her sister.

"So you think your mother will be okay with it?"

She smiled at him. "The one thing I *do* know about my mother is that she is an incurable romantic. I can say with complete confidence that she is going to love the book."

19

Catherine

Catherine leaned over the toilet and lost the contents of her stomach.

"Catherine?!" Andrew hammered on the bathroom door.

She sank down onto the floor and leaned her head against the cool tiles of the bathroom, trying to settle her insides.

Her life and her lies had caught up with her.

She crawled back to the toilet and retched again. Andrew rattled the door.

"Catherine? Are you okay?"

No, she wasn't okay.

The pages of Cassie's novel were strewn across the floor where she'd dropped them. Page 96 had slid to the opposite side of the bathroom and page 208 had somehow drifted inside the walk-in shower, the print gradually blurring as droplets of water from Andrew's earlier shower soaked through the paper. The other pages were an untidy jumble, mixed up, out of order. It didn't matter. She knew she was never going to read the words again.

People said you could leave the past behind and move on, but it wasn't true. You could pretend to move on, you could say to yourself *I'm doing great*, but that thing you were trying to forget was always there in the corner of the room, waiting to pounce.

"Damn it, Cathy." Andrew banged the door and she staggered to her feet and held onto the washbasin.

She stared at herself in the mirror. *This is your fault. You did this.*

That was what happened when you wrote romance for a living. It became harder to separate fact from fiction. You spent so much time in the land of happy endings that you forgot it was a job, and thought it was life. You started to think that anything was possible and maybe Prince Charming really would have searched his kingdom for the woman who was dumb enough to wear a glass slipper (glass? Seriously?).

She made it back to the toilet just in time and dimly heard a scraping sound and then the sound of the door opening.

"Cathy, sweetheart?" Andrew was on his knees next to her, holding her hair back, stroking her shoulders and telling her that everything was going to be fine, which she knew for a fact wasn't true because everything definitely wasn't fine and she couldn't see how it ever could be again.

She heard the sound of taps running and then felt the bliss of a cool flannel against her burning forehead.

"Was it something you ate? It couldn't have been lunch. We both had the lamb and I'm fine." He noticed the pages scattered across the floor. "Is that Cassie's book? Is this about the book?"

It wasn't about the book, exactly. It was about her life. Her choices. Her mistakes.

"Andrew…"

"It's the book that upset you?" He stooped and gingerly retrieved a couple of the discarded pages. "I'd made up my mind I wasn't going to read it."

"Don't. It's all fiction. What are you doing…?" she gasped as he scooped her up in his arms.

"I refuse to have a conversation this important on the floor of a bathroom, even if that floor is Italian marble." He carried her into their bedroom and lowered her gently to the bed. "Now tell me exactly what has upset you. Has she somehow found out the truth?"

"No, it's not that. She has told the story almost exactly the way I told it to her. And the writing is wonderful." If she weren't feeling so ill and traumatized, she would have been impressed. *Her baby had written a book!* "The characters leap off the page. She has real talent."

"But?"

"But I wish she hadn't used her talent on this particular story." Her eyes filled. "She thinks it's a way of immortalizing her father."

Andrew's smile was twisted. "And if ever there was a man who doesn't deserve to be immortalized, it is Rob Dunn."

"Exactly." Her voice was a whisper. "This book *celebrates* him, Andrew! He's a hero in this story. And I don't want to celebrate him. I want to forget him, but now I'm never going to be able to because he's right there in print. It's as if he's mocking me from beyond the grave."

"You're shaking." Andrew removed his shoes and lay down on the bed next to her. He pulled her into his arms. "Sweetheart, we're not celebrating him. We're celebrating Cassie's book. Which is fiction. The story can't possibly be close to the truth because you haven't told her the truth."

Yes, it was fiction. She knew it was fiction because she was basically the one who had written it. Ironic, really. Cassie had used the stories she'd told as inspiration, which meant that Catherine had inadvertently contributed to her daughter's book. If she'd had a better sense of humor she might have laughed.

"You don't understand."

"Then help me understand." He stroked her hair gently. "Tell me what you're thinking."

"I've tried to put it behind me. That's what you do with a mistake, isn't it? Forgive yourself and move on. That's what people say. I haven't forgiven myself, but I have tried to move on."

He held her tightly. "And you have."

"No. And now I never will. This book has made sure of that. If it's a success, and with the Mighty Madeleine pushing it and a publishing deal that big, they're going to support it with a massive campaign so it *will* be a success, everyone will be talking about it. People will ask *me* about it."

"Only if they know you're connected, and they don't need to know that."

"She's dedicated it to her parents." She couldn't bring herself to say the word *us*. "Us" implied a team, and she and Rob had never been a team. "Of course they're going to know." Occasionally, Andrew's optimism exasperated her, but at the same time she was grateful for it. She needed it. She'd lost her ability to trust, not just people but her own judgment. She envied people who genuinely believed everything would turn out fine. Once, she'd been like that. She'd believed good things happened to those who deserved it. That most people were good underneath. She'd thought she was living a romance, exactly like her books. It had taken a while for her to realize she was in a horror story and that trust was like virginity—once you lost it, you lost it. Gone. Andrew hadn't lost it. He still believed in the goodness of people and that life was very likely to turn out just fine, so she'd strapped her fragile, cynical self to him, hoping that his optimism was robust enough to carry the weight of both of them. There was nothing wrong with that, was there? It was like splinting a broken leg. You did what you had to do.

He hesitated. "All right. Let's say you're right about that and maybe you are, because no one knows more about publishing than you do, but Cassie's story isn't your story, is it? If it's inspired by everything you told her, then it doesn't begin to touch on the truth. She has the official version. The version you created for her. No one is going to know what really happened."

"I know what happened." Her teeth were chattering. She was back there, reliving every long dark day, but particularly that last day, which had been the longest and darkest. She felt as if she were falling back into the deep dark hole that had trapped her for years.

Andrew was still trying to understand. She could almost see the parts of his brain moving together, trying to make connections.

"So it's not your readers finding out that bothers you? It's not the idea of people catching a glimpse of the *real* Catherine Swift?"

The real Catherine Swift. Who was she? She'd come so far from the person she once was. She was like one of those upgrades that your phone forced you to install that then changed everything beyond recognition.

She consoled herself with the knowledge that everyone

changed over time. Life eroded you until you were a different shape.

There were days when she didn't even know herself. And then there were the parts she did know, but hid from the world. But she didn't feel guilty about that. Not sharing everything didn't make her fake; it made her just like everyone else. All those happy, blissful pictures on social media? All those *#blessed*, *#grateful*, *#lovemylife* hashtags either represented naivety (bad stuff hadn't happened yet) or a major cover-up (bad stuff had happened but they weren't sharing it). Everyone showed a selective side of themselves. It was how the world worked.

"I don't want readers asking questions about my private life. I don't want Cassie talking about my private life. I don't want the attention." Attention was never good when you were trying to hide something. But what really mattered wasn't what she was hiding from readers, or what she was trying to ignore herself. What really mattered was what she was hiding from her own children. "Don't you see? I spun that story not just to protect myself because I wanted to put it behind me, but to protect my children. I thought a lie was better than a truth."

"I know." He pulled her close. Kissed the top of her head. "You're a wonderful mother, Catherine."

She gave a choked laugh. "We both know that's not true. I can't imagine anyone who could have made more of a mess of parenting than I have and that's frustrating and distressing because I tried so hard. And for a moment today when I was talking to Adeline, I really thought that maybe I could fix things. That this was finally my chance to mend my relationship with her. Now, instead of having a fractured relationship with one daughter, I'm going to have a broken relationship with both of them."

Andrew sighed. "You're assuming this will damage your relationship with Cassie."

"How can it not? This is her dream, Andrew. And I'm going to take it away from her. I'm going to be the one who squashes it flat. Not an agent, not a publisher, not even the reading public. Me. Her own mother."

He rolled onto his back and stared up at the ceiling. "Maybe there's a way to fix this."

"The only way to do that is to ask Cassie to withdraw this book. She won't have signed a contract yet." The thought of it made her feel ill. "How can I do that to my daughter? This is her dream, and I remember how that feels. How can I kill that dream? But I'm going to have to. For everyone's sake, I can't have that book out there."

Andrew sat up. "There has to be another answer." He turned to look at her. "You don't want to celebrate Rob, but if you get rid of the dedication, then there is no hint of Rob. And who is Cassie Dunn to the reading public? You have to figure out what you want."

What she wanted was for Cassie never to have written the book.

She caught sight of the clock on her nightstand and groaned. "We have ten minutes before they arrive for dinner. And I don't know what to do." She forced herself off the bed and into the bathroom where she splashed cold water on her face.

Andrew scooped up all the scattered pages of Cassie's book and stuffed them into the bin roughly, as if he resented the pain those pages had caused her. That was Andrew, still good despite everything. He should have restored her faith in people, but he hadn't really. He'd just restored her faith in him.

She did her best with makeup, although it was a half-hearted attempt. She pulled on a dress that usually made her

feel good but not today. It was going to take more than a
dress to rescue the situation.

She walked onto the terrace and for the first time in her
life took no comfort from the froth of bright blooms that
bordered the path. The heat of the day had settled into the
evening, humid and oppressive. There was no breeze. Everything about the day seemed designed to make her sweat.

Adeline and Cassie arrived together, both of them laughing about something. They didn't seem bothered by the heat.

Catherine felt sick because she knew that soon they
wouldn't be laughing. Still, she'd wanted her daughters to
bond. That was one good thing at least. They had each other.
And hopefully, whatever happened, that would last. They
wouldn't be alone.

It was Maria's night off and the table was loaded with salads and delicious cold dishes that she'd prepared before leaving to visit a friend in the neighboring village.

Adeline pulled out a chair and flapped her hand in front
of her face. "It's hot this evening." She sat down, her hair
tumbling loose over her shoulders.

Catherine might have wondered at the change in her, but
she had other things to think about.

Adeline was watching her across the table. "Are you all
right?"

Catherine had done her best to hide the way she was feeling, but clearly hadn't done a good job. Adeline had seen
something in her face. Something Cassie hadn't noticed. Perhaps it was because Adeline was more attuned to the signs of
emotional trauma. She saw trauma all the time in her work,
particularly in the beginning when she'd seen patients face-
to-face. She'd told Catherine once that she preferred dealing with people's issues from a distance and Catherine had
understood.

She would have been happy never to look trauma in the face again. Unfortunately, she wasn't being given that option.

But that was how life worked, wasn't it? The bad invaded the good. It was like bindweed in the garden, wrapping itself around healthy happy plants, choking them. And no matter how hard you tried to get rid of it, tug it out at the roots and banish it, it always managed to grow back.

She swallowed. "I hope you both had fun today."

"We did. You look tired." Adeline didn't seem about to let the subject drop. "Have you been working?"

"Yes. I'm coming to the end of a book. I almost have a finished draft." She could have said that she hadn't even opened her laptop, but then they would have looked for another reason to explain the fact that she looked pale and drained. It was only a brief respite of course, but Catherine grabbed it greedily.

"I've been reading Cassie's book and it's fantastic." Adeline drizzled olive oil onto her salad and smiled across the table at her sister. "Still can't get over just how good it is."

Cassie was beaming too, delight and pride clinging to her like a suntan.

"I've been biting my nails all day. I was so scared you'd hate it."

"I'm loving it." There was fresh warm bread in the center of the table and Adeline leaned across and helped herself.

Catherine marveled that things could seem so normal on the surface while being so spectacularly wrong. She could feel Andrew's tension. His foot moved under the table, *tap, tap, tap,* something he only did when he was very stressed. He was waiting for her to say something. She was waiting too, although she wasn't sure exactly what she was waiting for. The right moment? What was *that* going to look like?

"I spoke to my agent this morning. We've accepted the deal." Cassie looked at her. "And I have a favor to ask."

Catherine had been waiting for the right moment and she had a feeling she was looking at it now.

She should speak, before Cassie had a chance to say anything else. But she wanted to stay in this moment where everything was still all right. She wanted to treasure those last precious minutes before she destroyed her daughter's illusions. Who knew what would be in her eyes then? Hurt. Blame. Pain.

"It feels a bit awkward asking," Cassie had obviously given up waiting for her mother to prompt her. "My agent, and the publisher, wondered if I could use your name. I'd be Cassie Swift. They think it has a nice ring. And you can absolutely say no, of course, but…"

"No." The word shot from her lips, cutting through the warm atmosphere.

Adeline sat up straighter, startled. "At least think about it."

"I don't need to. You can't use my name."

Some of the joy left Cassie's face. "Of course. That's no problem." Her smile was stiff and forced. "We can publish it under my real name. Or use a pseudonym or something."

"Wait…" Adeline leaned forward. "Why can't she use *Swift*? Maybe it's cashing in on your success, but as it's Cassie who is the ultimate beneficiary, does it matter?"

"It matters to me." Cassie frowned. "I'd rather do it by myself."

"I'm not only talking about the name," Catherine said. "You can't publish this book, Cassie." Watching her daughter's expression change caused a physical pain. Never had she hated herself more. "I'm sorry. I know how much it means to you. I know how exciting it all is. But you can't do it."

"Stop." Adeline stood up, the angry scrape of her chair

mirroring her visible outrage. "How can you say that? This isn't about you!"

"It's no use being upset with me, Adeline, and I'm afraid it is about me. That's the point." She'd come so close to fixing things with her eldest daughter, but now she was going to have to crush those vulnerable new shoots. "I can assure you that however upset you are with me, I'm even more upset with myself."

"You read it and you hated it." Cassie looked mortified. "You hated my book."

"No. I loved it. It's a wonderful, emotional story that somehow managed to break my heart and be uplifting at the same time. That takes real skill, Cassie. I can understand why publishers have been fighting for the right to publish the book."

Cassie exchanged bemused glances with her sister. "But if you loved it, then why are you telling me I can't publish it?"

"Because both the book and the publicity that will undoubtedly surround it risk throwing a spotlight onto my relationship with your father, and I can't handle that. I can't go through that again. I can't go back to that time." Her heart was pounding so hard she thought her ribs might crack.

Andrew moved his chair closer to hers and put his arm round her.

"I've upset you?" Cassie was horrified. "Now I feel terrible. I didn't realize it was still so raw. I know how much you loved him, and I thought this would be a way of celebrating that love."

"You don't understand. And that's my fault." Emotion gathered in her throat like a storm waiting to burst. "I don't want people talking about my relationship with your father. I don't want any sort of…celebration. I'd rather it was forgotten."

"You mean because of Andrew?" She shot a look of apology toward her soon to be stepfather. "I didn't know about Andrew when I wrote it."

And that was her fault too. Not sharing the fact that she and Andrew had rekindled their relationship was another mistake in a long list of mistakes.

"It's not because of Andrew, although I have no doubt he would prefer not to have that particular chapter in my life raked up again. That isn't the reason."

"Then why? If I've made any mistakes, then I can fix them," Cassie said. "It's a fictionalized version of reality, obviously. I based the story on everything you told me, so why can't I talk about that?"

There was a heavy pause. It was like standing on the edge of the cliff, waiting to dive.

"Because it's not true. None of it is true." Catherine's mouth felt so dry it was almost impossible to force the words out. "The man I described to you was the man I wanted him to be. The man I thought he was when I married him. The man you deserved to have as a father. But that wasn't who he was. Rob Dunn was controlling, manipulative and violent. Abusive. Your father was as far from a romantic hero as it is possible to be."

20

Cassie

Cassie felt lightheaded. Abusive? Her dad?

It was a moment before she could speak.

"You told me he was the most perfect man you'd ever met. You said that you knew right away that he was the right person. That what you shared was special."

"And at first that's how I felt. But people can deceive, and Rob was one of those. I was trusting. Naive, I suppose," her mother said. "I've thought of it often, and wondered why I didn't see it. Believe me, I have blamed myself for a long time."

Andrew frowned. "Cathy—"

"I know." She lifted a hand to stop him finishing his sentence. "You're going to say that it wasn't my fault, and I try to convince myself of that. I didn't see who he truly was because he didn't allow me to see it. He was cunning and clever. But still, it's hard not to blame myself."

Cassie felt every beat of her heart as it punched hard at her ribs.

"You're saying that everything you told me about my dad was a lie?"

Her mother flinched. "You have to understand I was trying to protect you. I didn't think you needed to know the truth. He was dead. What did it matter what he was really like? It was in the past and it was supposed to stay in the past."

She'd only ever seen her mother sure and confident before. Her mother was a winner. A superstar. There wasn't a problem in life that she couldn't handle. Or so she'd thought, but now she was seeing another side to her. She saw uncertainty and vulnerability. She saw regret and fear.

Fear.

Cassie watched as Andrew tightened his hold on her. Saw him soothe and support her mother through this trauma.

Her father. *Her dad.*

She couldn't make sense of it.

It was like reading a novel, expecting it to be romance and discovering that it was crime fiction.

"I don't understand." She started to shake. First her hands and then her legs. "You told me so many positive stories about my dad."

"And that's what they were. Stories."

The horror of it clung to her, covering her skin like a film of sweat.

"But I believed them." Maybe she was the one who was naive. "I believed what you told me."

"Why wouldn't you? It's what I do, isn't it? It's my talent. Probably my only talent," her mother said. "I write fiction.

And almost every single thing I told you about Rob Dunn was fiction. And I know I should feel guilty for not telling you the truth. But how could I? How do you tell a little girl the truth about her daddy, when the truth would keep her awake at night?" Her mother's voice broke and her eyes filled. "How do you?"

Cassie felt tears on her cheeks too. She brushed them away. Her dad.

She'd never known him, but she'd always *felt* as if she knew him. She'd conjured him from her imagination with the help of her mother's stories. She'd created someone who had been part of her life. He'd been a real person to her, and now she could feel him fading. She wanted to reach out and grab that image before it vanished forever.

"So you've told me the fiction." Her mouth was dry. Her lips were dry. "Could you tell me the facts? All of them. Unedited." Maybe she'd live to regret that request, but she knew that she needed the truth.

Cassie didn't even realize Adeline had moved until she heard the scrape of a chair and felt her sister's arm slide round her.

Later, she'd think about the fact that Adeline had moved to comfort her even though she must have been feeling plenty of emotions of her own, but for now she was just grateful for her support.

Her mother wiped her eyes and took a sip of water.

"I met Rob in a bar, exactly the way I told you. He was charming. Andrew and I had separated by this point." She put the glass down, her unsteady hand sloshing some of it over the edge. "I was at a very low point in my life. I was vulnerable, and Rob was caring, attentive and good company. He was exactly what I needed, or so I thought. He told me he ran his own tech business and could live and work where he liked, so he'd chosen Corfu. It wasn't true, but when someone tells you something, you don't automatically assume they're lying, do you? You don't fact-check everything you hear. Or maybe you do. Maybe it's different now, with social media, and dating apps, and everyone presenting a false front to the world. Who is to say what's real and what isn't? Maybe you always question what people tell you, but I didn't. I believed he was what he said he was. *Who* he said he was."

Andrew took her hand. "You don't have to relive this. I could tell them the rest."

"No. I need to do this." But the way she clung to his hand hinted at the scale of the ordeal. "I believed everything he told me because it didn't occur to me not to. I thought I was worldly and wise, but I was neither. Rob Dunn was a skilled con artist. A manipulator and a master of invention, better at playing a character than I ever was at writing one. Had the circumstances been different, I might have admired his creativity. He knew exactly what I needed, and he gave it to me. He'd read my books. Studied them. He knew how romantic heroes behaved, and he modeled himself on what he read. He reeled me in like a fish on a line. Nothing was too much trouble. He listened. Bought me thoughtful gifts. Made me laugh. He treated me like the most important person in the world."

Cassie sat without moving. She could sense the darkness that was coming. It hovered beneath the words her mother was speaking, an unseen menace. It was like witnessing an approaching storm and waiting for it to break.

She felt slightly removed from reality, as if she was watching this play out from a distance.

The food lay in front of them, forgotten.

"I became pregnant," her mother said. "We'd only been together for two months. I expected him to be horrified, but he was delighted. At the time, I thought it was another demonstration of his love. Of this wonderful romance we were enjoying."

"Control." Adeline spoke softly. "He saw it as another way to control you."

"Yes, although sadly I didn't have your perception. It took me a while to see it. I suppose I was besotted." The glance she sent Andrew was mortified and apologetic. "He was charming and attentive. And then Cassie was born and that was when everything changed."

"Because he had to share you," Adeline said, and Catherine gave a weary smile.

"If I'd known what you know, then maybe I never would have found myself in the situation I did. I saw it though, finally, in the weeks after Cassie was born."

"But that doesn't make sense." Cassie's head was swimming. "You already had Adeline. It was never just the two of you. He always had to share you."

"Adeline was older. And you were always a very quiet, thoughtful, self-contained child." Catherine glanced at Adeline, her smile tired. "You loved to read, and draw, and sometimes you'd just sit and think. I think Rob barely noticed you in those early days. But then Cassie was born, and everything changed. Babies are demanding of attention." She looked at Cassie. "You had terrible colic in those early months, and you cried a lot. That was when I saw him change. Or rather, that's when I saw who he really was."

Andrew shook his head, although this couldn't have been the first time he'd heard the story. "I wish you'd told me. Right at the beginning, when you first realized."

"How?" Catherine's voice was barely more than a whisper. "The ink wasn't dry on our divorce papers. You were angry with me because you'd hoped we might fix things, and maybe we would have done. Who knows?" She gave him an agonized look. "I couldn't tell you. I had too much pride. I'd made a huge mistake, but I believed I was stuck with it. I couldn't see how to unravel it. And I didn't know, at that point, how bad it would get."

"I wish I'd known too." Adeline looked pale and tired. "I would have helped."

"You did help. You were the reason we stumbled through those first couple of years. You adored your little sister and you spent almost all your free time with her, which meant that I could work and pander to Rob's need to be the center of attention. But sometimes it went wrong."

Adeline removed her arm from around Cassie. She sat up straighter, eyes wide. "That time you broke your arm…"

"He broke it," Catherine said. "My publisher had asked me to do a book tour to support my twentieth book, *Forgotten Wishes*. Rob didn't want me to go. *Make an excuse*, he said. *Tell her no.* I tried to explain that it was part of my job. He said that I wouldn't be able to sign books with a broken wrist."

Adeline was horrified. "Why didn't I guess?"

"Why would you? You were a child. And although the divorce had shaken your sense of security, you didn't have any reason to doubt what he told you. You hadn't encountered violence." She paused to breathe. "And I didn't want you to."

"He wouldn't let us into the room," Adeline was frowning as she thought back. "He told us you needed to rest. I thought he was being caring."

"Us?" Cassie turned to look at her sister.

"Yes. You were there too," Adeline said. "You were little. You wanted Mum. You were squirming, I remember that. You wanted to go to her, and I kept asking him if we could see our mother just for a minute. He told me to think about someone other than myself. That you needed rest." She swallowed. "He was keeping us away."

"He didn't want you to see me at my worst," Catherine said. "Perhaps he was afraid I might say something to you. I was relieved you stayed away. He frightened me."

Cassie felt those words deep in her stomach. Frightened? This was her father they were talking about. Not some stranger. Not one of those stories that you read in the media. *Her dad*.

Not a hero at all. Not the love of her mother's life. Not *the one*.

She heard an intake of breath from Adeline.

"The vase…"

"You remember that?" Catherine gripped the edge of the table, turning her knuckles white. "Yes, he threw it at me when I told him I was expected to fly to New York to meet my agent and publisher. He said if I did, he'd take both you and Cassie and I'd never see you again. Would he have done it? I don't know. And I was trying hard to protect you both from what was going on."

Cassie felt a humming in her ears. She couldn't connect what she was hearing with real life. She couldn't connect it with her father.

"At that point, I didn't know what to do," her mother said. "I knew it was just a matter of time before he seriously hurt me. I was afraid for you girls, and what he might do to you. About what might happen to you if I met with an accident. I swallowed my pride. I called Andrew and asked him to take Adeline. It was one less child to worry about." She reached for Andrew's hand and he murmured words that Cassie couldn't hear.

Maybe it was because her head was still buzzing with other words.

If I met with an accident?

Had her mother been afraid for her life?

"You sent me away to protect me?" Adeline's voice was barely audible. "Not to punish me. Not because you were tired of me, or because you didn't love me enough, but to protect me?"

"Yes. It was the hardest thing I have ever had to do, and I knew you'd hate me for it. You adored your sister and she adored you. But I couldn't see an alternative. And I couldn't tell you the truth, so I simply told you that your father and I had decided you were going to live with him."

Adeline's breathing was shallow. "I thought I was in the way. I thought I was disrupting your new life. I thought you didn't want me as part of your family."

"No." Catherine shook her head, emotion thickening her voice. "Sending you away almost killed me. But I couldn't see another choice. Sometimes love requires seemingly impossible sacrifice. It seemed like the right thing to do, although I've questioned it a million times since. We were very close, you and I, and I shook your faith in love. And in me. And I've never been able to fix that rift I caused between us. Apart from getting involved with Rob Dunn in the first place, it has been the biggest regret of my life."

Adeline looked strained. "I didn't know."

"And I couldn't tell you without revealing the truth to Cassie, and I couldn't do that. You had a close relationship with your father, but she had no father. Only a memory that I created." Catherine looked at Cassie. "As you grew older, I occasionally thought about telling you the truth, but I couldn't do it. You were happy and optimistic. You had such faith in people, and I didn't want to take that from you. And what was the point? Rob was gone."

Cassie sat without moving.

She'd always felt lucky that she had such a close relationship with her mother. Her friends had envied her. *Your mother
is so cool.* And when they'd moaned and bitched about how
their mothers nagged about everything from their hair to the
state of their bedrooms, and how they never listened, she'd
said nothing because her mother always listened. When she'd
been debating which colleges to apply for, her mother had
helped her think it through. And when she'd admitted that
she hadn't known what career path to follow (because she
hadn't wanted to mention her writing ambitions), her mother
hadn't tried to push her in a particular direction, she'd simply said *take your time.* Maybe she only had one parent, but
she had the best. Or so she'd thought.

It was hard to get her head around the fact that her mother
had been lying to her for her whole life. That her past was as
much a work of fiction as one of her mother's stories.

In her mind, she saw her life as a book with pages torn
out. Part of it was just *wrong.* It was like an editor saying *you
need to delete this chapter.*

It was true that she hadn't lost her ability to trust. She'd
never had a boyfriend cheat on her, and her friends were a
tight-knit group who might be occasionally annoying, but
were never toxic. Sure, some people were more complicated
than others but that was what made them interesting. She'd
had life easy up until this point. She knew it and had been
grateful for it. But that didn't mean she was naive. She knew
life could be tough. She'd assumed it would be tough for her
one day. That her turn would come. Ups and downs. That
was how it went. If you were lucky, you had more ups than
downs.

But never before had she considered that her life had been
easy because she'd been shielded from the bad stuff. And it
was true that by not knowing, she hadn't lost her faith in peo-

ple as Adeline had done, but how much worse was it to have lost faith in your own mother? What else had she lied about?

"You could have told me," she said. "You could have been honest. You could have told me the truth and I would have handled it." Was that true? She didn't know, but she hoped it was. Generally speaking, people coped with what came their way in life. Maybe, if asked beforehand, they would have said *there is no way I'd be able to cope with that*, but what was coping except getting out of bed every morning and getting on with things?

Did her mother not think she would have kept going?

"Maybe you could have handled it, or maybe I would have forever regretted telling you something you didn't have to know. Once you say something like that, you can't unsay it." Her mother sounded tired. "Or maybe part of me thought that with Rob gone I could delete the past. Maybe I was doing it for me too, so that you didn't ask questions I didn't want to be forced to answer. I wanted to put it behind me. I suppose I thought if I lied to you, and lied to myself, I could pretend it had never happened."

By writing her book, by using what she'd thought was her parents' blissful relationship as "inspiration" for her novel, she'd forced her mother back to that time.

"If it hadn't been for my book, would you ever have told me?"

It was a moment before her mother answered.

"Probably not."

And she would have gone through life not knowing the truth. And maybe that would have been better because certainly the truth was hard to handle.

"You said I wasn't like him. Was that a lie too?"

"It wasn't a lie. You are nothing like him, in appearance or personality."

Questions crowded her brain, queuing up to be asked. "What happened after Adeline left?"

"Things deteriorated. You missed her." Her mother was still looking at her. "You became clingy, and Rob became more and more impatient. I couldn't leave you alone with him, so I canceled all my engagements. Whenever I had to leave the villa for something, Maria took you."

"This isn't…" Adeline pressed her fingers to her head. "This just isn't the story I had in my head. It's as if you've changed my history."

Cassie's history had been changed too. How many times had she talked about her parents' love story? They embodied everything she believed about love and relationships. She'd wanted a love like theirs. She'd envied it. And now here was her mother telling her that none of it was real.

She felt numb.

"How often did he hit you?" Her lips were so stiff she could barely voice the question.

"Sometimes we'd go months without incident, and I'd think that maybe he really meant it when he said he would never do it again. And then something would set him off. It was my fault, he said. It was always my fault, and spun so cleverly that I believed him. And each time was a little worse. It felt as if it was escalating."

"Why didn't you leave him?"

There was a long tense pause.

"Because of you." Her mother's voice was barely audible. "He threatened to take you, and I was afraid he might hurt you."

Cassie felt a pressure building in her chest. Her mother's anguish was raw and naked.

"His death…" She was almost afraid to ask. "Did that happen the way you told it?"

"He fell down the stairs. We'd been out for the evening and he'd had too much to drink. I'd left my shoes at the top of the stairs and he tripped." Her mother looked directly at her. "Those are facts. They're in the police report."

What had she been expecting? Another confession? *Your father didn't die the way I told you.* The revelations had clearly made her jumpy. She was questioning things she shouldn't be questioning.

"You must have been relieved."

Catherine hesitated. "It was a terrible time but yes, part of me was relieved. Does that make me a bad person? Maybe it does. I don't know. I kept thinking that I'd been given a second chance, and that he could no longer hurt us." Her mother gave a watery smile. "But he's hurting us now, isn't he? Dead for almost two decades, but he still has the power to hurt. Perhaps I should have told you, but I didn't see why you ever needed to know. Your early life had been blighted, but you didn't remember it. I had a chance to wipe the bad away for you, and I desperately wanted to do that. I had the skills to tell a good story, so why not use them this way? Why should you suffer for my bad decision? I hadn't anticipated a time when I'd be forced to tell you." She slumped in her chair, drained. "Maybe it was a mistake. Maybe I should have told you the truth. I discovered that sometimes being a parent means making impossible decisions. You do what you think is best, but one person's best is another person's bad decision. I'm sure you're upset. I'm sure you're angry with me. And I don't blame you."

Upset, yes. Angry? Maybe, a little. Hurt, definitely.

Cassie rubbed her fingers over her forehead.

She couldn't think. She couldn't process it. All her life she'd been waiting for a relationship like the one her parents had. But that had never existed.

"I need some time on my own." She stumbled to her feet, knocking over her chair in the process and her mother half rose to her feet.

"Sweetheart..."

"I'm okay, really." She grabbed her phone from the table and knocked over her glass. She picked it up and threw a napkin on the puddle of champagne. "It's a lot to process. I'm fine. Don't follow me. I'm sure Adeline has questions too, so maybe you can talk a while longer." She flashed a smile, which she hoped would stop them following her, and sped from the terrace.

Her head throbbed. She felt weirdly detached. All these years she'd been telling everyone that her parents had the perfect relationship. And at first her mother had believed it *was* the perfect relationship. So how did you ever know? How did anyone know?

She'd been grieving the loss of her father, but the man she'd imagined never existed. He was a fictional character, and nothing more.

Now she had a different image in her head. An image where her father's handsome face was contorted with rage as he flung a vase at her mother. *Broke her wrist.*

She pressed her fingers to her head, trying to delete that horrible image.

She'd reached the cottage and kicked off her shoes. The tiles of the patio were still warm under her feet and the peace of the evening was broken only by the faint sound of the ocean and the rhythmic chirping of cicadas. She dropped onto one of the loungers, feeling the press of heat around her. Her notes were still there from her meeting with her agent and publisher and she pushed them onto the floor, unable to look at them. If she hadn't written the stupid book, she wouldn't be sitting here feeling as if her whole life was a lie, and her mother wouldn't right now be crying on the terrace.

How could such highs and lows happen all in the space of one day?

She felt muddled and confused and drenched in sadness. So she did what she always did when she felt bad and wanted to talk to someone.

She called Oliver.

He answered immediately.

"Hi, Cass. I got your message about the book deal. Congratulations. I hope you're talking to me with a glass of champagne in your hand."

Hearing his voice snipped the last threads of her control.

A scald of liquid seared her sunburned cheeks. Tears. Big fat tears. "Not really. Are you busy? You're not on a date, are you?" The thought of it made her stomach plummet. She imagined a day when she'd call and the phone would be answered by some laughing girl who would say, *Hi Cassie, Oliver will call you back when he has a moment.* She'd hear giggling in the background and know this wasn't going to be that moment and maybe he would eventually call back but it would be days because she was no longer the most important person in his life.

Why couldn't her best friend have been a woman? It would have made things so much easier.

"I'm here," he said. "At home. What's wrong? Is it your sister?"

"No. She's been great." Where should she start? "It's been a bit intense here. And I feel really…" Her emotions slid into her voice. She started to cry again.

"Cassie? Cass?" Oliver's voice came down the phone, urgent and concerned. "Tell me what's happened."

"It's all because of my stupid—b-book…" She stuttered out the words but couldn't finish her sentence.

"Your book? You said they loved it. Have they changed their minds? Are they allowed to do that?"

"They haven't changed their minds."

"Then what's wrong?"

She scrubbed her hand over her face and tried to pull herself together. "I told my mother all about it."

"Good. I've been urging you to tell her for ages. I bet she was proud. Did she love the dedication?"

Thinking about the dedication made her cry even harder. "No."

"Cassie—" Oliver's voice was deep and firm "—take a breath. Whatever has happened, we're going to figure it out together. Tell me slowly. And tell me all of it."

It was a jerky, sob-filled conversation and several times he had to interrupt her and ask her to repeat things but she stumbled through it, relaying what her mother had told her.

When she finished, Oliver was silent for a moment.

"I don't know what to say. That must have been tough to hear," he said. "How are you feeling? *What* are you feeling?"

"I don't know," she hiccupped. "I'm angry that she didn't tell me, but part of me wishes she hadn't told me because I had these lovely illusions—and I know now that they really were only illusions, but I was happy and I thought my life was great and now—"

"Your life is the same, Cass," Oliver said gently. "That hasn't changed. Whoever your father was, whatever he did, doesn't change who you are. You still have the same good people in your life who love you. Your mother still loves you. This must have been so tough for her too. I guess she was trying to protect you."

"Yes."

"I don't envy her. Telling you, or not telling you—that's not a decision I would have wanted to make."

"I know." And she realized that she hadn't given enough thought to how very hard it must have been for her mother and what an impossible position she must have found herself in. "I think at first she was focused on survival." She'd often pictured her parents together and those images had always been soft. Loving. Arms wrapped around each other in a hug. Gentle touches. Kind words. But those images had been replaced with something else. A blow that bruised. Words that wounded. And fear.

How would she have handled that?

She realized what a safe, protected life she'd led up until this point.

"I feel as if I've been living a lie, as if my whole life story has just been rewritten." She sniffed. "And I preferred the earlier version."

"I can imagine. How about your sister? I guess her life story has also changed. She must have feelings about the whole thing too. Have you talked to her?"

"Not yet. Not alone. I just—" She swallowed. "I wanted to talk to you. I needed…"

What exactly had she needed? She'd needed *him*, that was the truth.

"You wanted to think it through with someone who wasn't directly involved." His voice changed and she could tell he was shifting his position, making himself comfortable. She imagined him sprawled on the oversized sofa in the living room. He was probably wearing his favorite sweatshirt and his old comfy jeans that clung in all the right places. She loved the way he looked in those jeans. Hot, in a relaxed not-trying-too-hard kind of way.

She frowned. *Hot?* Okay that was weird, thinking that way

about him. Or maybe not. She knew when her girlfriends looked good, so why not Oliver?

His voice came down the phone again. "Do you want to know what I think?"

"Yes. That's why I'm calling. You're the calm, sensible one in this friendship. I'm the drama queen."

For once, he didn't laugh. "You're not a drama queen, Cass. You just don't hide your emotions, and I like that."

She sniffled. "You do?"

"Yes. It makes you easy to figure out. And what I think, is that you should give this time to sink in and not try and fix it right away. You've had a shock. You've got to let it simmer. You've all got some adjusting to do. It must have been distressing for your mother to have to tell you all this, and rake it all up. Talk to her. And talk to your sister."

It was good advice.

"I'm going to have to ditch my book." And she felt guilty even caring about that given the bigger issues, but she did care. She'd been so proud of the story and excited about the promise of what lay ahead.

She'd thought her mother would love it. Never in a million years had she thought it would hurt her.

"I don't think you should do anything at all right now," Oliver said. "I think you should pause for a few days. Let it all settle, Cass."

"Yes. You're right. And thank you. You're the best. I love you."

She slapped her hand over her mouth. Love you. *Love you?* Where had that come from? Had she really just said that? And did she even mean it?

She let her hand drop, stunned.

Yes, she did. She loved Oliver.

Not as a friend. As something so much more.

Her breathing felt shallow and unsteady. For years, she'd been waiting for a love like her parents' to come along and all the time love had been right under her nose and she hadn't recognized it. She'd been waiting for something different. Looking for something different. And she'd missed the real thing.

Oliver.

She thought about the way he made her laugh, and how he stayed up late listening to her if she was upset even if he had to get up early the next morning,

And then she thought about how her life might be if she found a small apartment of her own as her mother had suggested. No more long lazy evenings sprawled in the garden sharing a bottle of wine, surrounded by the sweet smell of grass and the hum of bees. No more waking in the morning to find a mug of tea by her bed where he'd left it before going to work. No more arguing about who was cooking dinner, and who was choosing what they were watching on TV.

A life without Oliver would be like a pizza with no cheese. A swimming pool with no water. It would always feel as if something important was missing.

She felt a tiny buzzing in her brain and a swelling in her chest and then an explosion of something that could have been panic.

She'd always thought it was friendship. But now she knew it was so much more than that. It was love.

She was so focused on her shocking discovery that it took her a minute to realize he was silent.

"I meant that I love you as a friend, obviously." She croaked out the words, tried to inject some laughter, hoping that she hadn't ruined everything, and was relieved when he responded.

"Sure." His voice sounded strange. "I know what you meant."

She'd freaked him out. And it wasn't surprising. She was freaked out too.

Oliver. All this time.

He cleared his throat. "Do you want me to come, Cass? I can fly out if you need me."

Her insides warmed. She needed him badly, and he was offering to come so why not?

She opened her mouth to say, *Yes, I need you*, and then she heard a sound in the background.

"Is someone there? Do you have company?"

There was a pause. "Suzy," he said. "Suzy came over."

Suzy. Suzy with the hair like silk and perfect teeth.

If her heart had felt bruised before, it was crushed now.

What was she going to do? What was going to happen when she was back home? She and Oliver shared a house. They ate meals together, went for drinks together. He'd be with Suzy and she'd have to smile when she bumped into Suzy in the bathroom in the mornings, and say good morning in a cheery voice, and not mind when she dried her skimpy underwear on the washing line in the garden.

"Hey, Cass?" Oliver's voice came down the phone. "You still there?"

"Yes." Her voice was a croak. "Still here."

"And sounding weird. Did you swallow a bee?"

"No."

"You've taken to smoking fifty a day?"

"Still no."

"Then why are you sounding as if you've just sung your-self hoarse at a stadium concert?"

All those things she'd thought she'd known about love, she'd never known it could ache like this. She almost said something because her feelings were stronger than her sense of dignity or self-control. But she didn't want to put him in a difficult position. She didn't want him to feel awkward, and have to find a gentle way to tell her that she was and would always be his dearest friend but he didn't think of her *that way*.

"Too much crying," she said. "Sorry. I'm glad Suzy is there with you."

There was a pause. "Are you?"

"Yes, of course." The idea of it was killing her, but she loved Oliver. She wanted him to be happy, and if that meant being nice to Suzy, then she'd be nice to Suzy. "I don't need you to come. It's great just to chat, although I didn't mean to interrupt your evening."

"You weren't interrupting anything. Will you let me know how are you? I want updates. Call me."

"Sure. I'll call." She imagined Suzy picking up his phone and seeing the caller display. *It's Cass*, she'd say, and they'd both roll their eyes and try to figure out how to gradually squeeze her out of Oliver's life.

She wouldn't be calling.

"Cass?" Oliver's tone was sharper and she wondered if he'd read her mind. "I'm here for you, you know that don't you?"

"I know. I feel better already from just having talked to you, and I'm going to do what you said and let it simmer. Bye."

She ended the call as quickly as if he were a stranger trying to sell her windows she didn't need or offering her a new phone plan.

Cassie dropped her phone onto the lounger.

She'd always thought love would look a certain way. She'd always thought she'd know it the moment she saw it. But now she realized love was as specific to the person as all the other things that made a human being individual and unique. One person's romantic disaster might be another person's happy-ever-after. Why hadn't she seen it before?

She was in love with Oliver, and the only reason she hadn't seen that was because she'd had this clear image of what love should be. But that image had been a mirage and it was gone now.

Love, for her at least, was what she felt for Oliver.

She slumped back on the lounger, feeling as if she'd aged a decade. Usually she felt nothing like an adult, but tonight she felt the full weight of being an adult.

She heard the sound of footsteps and then her name being called.

"Cass?" The urgency in Adeline's tone alarmed her.

"What?" She was already sitting up and reaching for her shoes when Adeline appeared, breathless.

"It's Mom. She's collapsed. Chest pains and struggling to breathe. They're taking her to the hospital now. My father is going in the ambulance with her."

"Ambulance?" Cassie stared at Adeline, her brain numb and working in slow motion.

"But that isn't possible. She's super healthy. She eats salad and seafood. She swims and does yoga." She was ignoring the fact that a person could do all those things and still get sick.

"Dad thinks maybe it was the stress of telling us, and thinking about Rob."

Cassie jammed her feet into her shoes, hurting her toe in the process.

This was all her fault. She was the one who had forced her mother to confront her past. She was the one who had insisted that her mother tell her everything, even though it was clearly a traumatic time in her life.

And now she being rushed to hospital. What if she died?

Cassie hadn't even had the chance to tell her she loved her.

That she understood and would probably have done the same thing in her mother's position. Instead, she'd been cold and more than a little judgmental. What if it was too late and she never got the chance to say those things?

Just when you thought life couldn't get worse, she thought, *it got worse.*

21

Adeline

Adeline clutched the seat of the car, wishing her sister would slow down. At this rate, they were going to arrive at the hospital as patients, not visitors.

But Cassie was panicking and, for the first time in as long as she could remember, Adeline was panicking too.

She couldn't stop thinking about what their mother had told them. Something fluttered inside her and for a moment she was a child again, before her heart had been bruised and her trust shaken, before she'd learned to keep a distance between her and her emotions.

A bump in the road almost sent them airborne and Adeline bit her tongue and banged her head.

"Cassie…" She ran her tongue over her lips, checking it was still attached. "I know you're worried, but slow down."

Cassie's fingers were white on the wheel, her gaze focused on the road ahead that swooped and curved in switchbacks.

"Sorry. I know it's not a great road, but it's the shortest route to the hospital. I've been driving here all my life, or so it feels. I could do it with my eyes shut."

"Open would be good." She decided not to point out that *all my life* wasn't very long when you were only twenty-two years old.

"The ambulance crew probably don't even know this way."

Or maybe they wanted to deliver their patient alive, Adeline thought.

It was the strangest feeling, weathering yet another crisis with a sister she'd had virtually no contact with since childhood. It was as if the universe was determined to throw them into the most intense situations possible. In many ways, her sister's personality was the same as she'd been as a toddler. Warm, impetuous and positive. Although there wasn't much sign of the positive side of her right now.

It was funny how differently people handled stress. Cassie rode it, every emotion right there on the surface. She'd be the type who screamed on roller coasters and sobbed at sad movies. Adeline had never sobbed over a movie and had never screamed on a roller coaster.

She'd never fallen in love.

"I didn't tell her I loved her," Cassie said. "What if we're too late? What if I don't ever get to tell her that again? What if the last thing she thinks about is me leaving the dinner table to be by myself? I should have hugged her and said how sorry I was that she'd been through that. How sorry I was that she'd ever found herself in a position of having to make that choice about what to tell her children." Cass pressed her foot to the floor and Adeline's head hit the neck rest. If they had to do an emergency stop, she'd have whiplash.

"Pull over, Cass, and calm down. You're not safe to drive."

"I'm safe. I just want to get there." Cassie brushed the back of her hand across her cheeks. "And I'm not a calm person in the way you are."

Adeline didn't feel calm at all. She felt lost and shaken. She opened her mouth to say something but then closed it again. She'd be fine. She'd learned how to manage alone, which was good because her sister wasn't in a state to absorb her stress along with her own. When they arrived at the hospital, she'd find somewhere quiet to gather herself and gain control. In the meantime, her focus was her sister.

"You're going to be able to tell her all these things, Cass. And she knows how much you love her. You two have always been close." She tried to put some distance between her and the problem. She imagined this situation was something someone had written to her about.

Dear Anxious, it's always worrying when we feel we may not have a chance to say the things we wish we'd said.

"How do you know she knows? Did she say something? What happened after I left?"

"Not much. She was wondering if she'd made all the wrong decisions, if she'd been a bad mother."

"I made her feel that way. I should never have forced her to talk about it. Relive it. I feel terrible."

"Cassie, this is not your fault. What you heard was shocking. Of course, you wanted to hear the truth. *Look where you're going!*" Adeline waved her hand at the road. "Concentrate. If you drive us into a ditch, that will definitely be your fault."

"I'm concentrating. And it affected you too, but you didn't put her under pressure the way I did. And I haven't even asked how you're feeling. And do *not* say *fine* because I'm going to know that's a lie, and it will make me feel even more crap about not being able to manage my own feelings as easily as you do."

"I'm not fine. And I never said it was easy."

Cassie slowed down and briefly put her hand on Adeline's knee.

She felt that touch and she felt the warmth and love behind the gesture. It made her question her urge to always handle problems alone.

"Actually, I'm feeling shaken, like you." The confession tumbled past the barriers she'd built. "I had a clear view of the past, and that has changed."

"Yes. That part is hard."

"Harder for you." Adeline stared into the darkness, watching as the headlamps illuminated the edges of the road. They were close to the town now and lights shimmered in the distance. Civilization. The hospital. Their mother. "How are you doing?"

"If you're asking me if I've got used to the idea that my father wasn't ever going to win a dad-of-the-year award, I'm not sure. I think it's going to take some getting used to. But even though that's true, I still wish I'd been more sympathetic about how she might be feeling. I wish I'd thought about *her* instead of making it all about me. I wish I'd told her that I understood. That I loved her. That I was sorry she'd been through all that. How could she have just collapsed? She's never been sick in her life." Cassie's voice cracked and Adeline reached across and squeezed her sister's hand briefly.

"Let's not panic until we have something to panic about. I feel bad too, for never once wondering if there was more to her story."

Regret, Adeline thought. One of the most common themes in the letters she was sent. They all started with the same words. *I wish...*

Things a person had said or hadn't said. Things they'd done or hadn't done. It was sad how many people held on to emotions and feelings and only released them when it was too late.

Was it too late for her? Because she was suffering from her own version of *I wish*. Regret tasted sharp in her mouth, like lemons.

It had never occurred to her that there might have been a hidden reason behind all her mother's actions. She'd looked at it superficially through the eyes of a child, and maybe that was excusable, but what about later when she was older? She'd allowed herself to stay as that injured child and never stepped out of that place and questioned it.

Now, with information laid out in front of her, it was clear.

The signs of abuse had been there, but to see something you had to be looking, and she hadn't been looking.

"Even if you'd asked," Cassie said, "she probably wouldn't have told you. She didn't want to talk about it. If it hadn't been for my stupid book and the fact that I was about to force the subject into the public domain, she never would have had to."

"Your book wasn't stupid. Your book was brilliant. You're a very talented writer."

Cassie sniffed. "Thank you. That's all history now. I don't even care anymore. The only thing I care about is that our mother is okay. As long as she is fine, I'm never going to complain about anything ever again. I'm so glad you're here."

Adeline reached across and gave her sister's leg a squeeze and Cassie glanced at her.

"There's something I need to tell you. I wrote to you. To Dr. Swift."

Adeline smiled. "I know."

"You *knew*? How?"

"I didn't know right away, but something about that letter

stayed with me." Adeline felt a tug of emotion. "I assumed you'd forgotten about me. You had a whole life that didn't have me in it. I assumed you didn't miss me."

Cassie swallowed. "That proves you're not as smart as you seem."

They arrived at the hospital, parked the car and rushed inside. Adeline was conscious of the echo of her heels on the floor and the soft tickle of her dress against her bare legs as it flipped and swirled with the movement. She doubted anyone had ever been more inappropriately dressed for a hospital visit but she didn't care, because there was her father, his hair standing on end where he'd raked his fingers through it repeatedly, his eyes tired, arms waving as he spoke slowly and loudly, trying to give information to a woman in a uniform.

Relief flashed across his face when he saw Adeline and Cassie. "They're examining her now. They wouldn't let me stay with her. They need her medical history but my Greek isn't up to it."

Cassie took over, speaking fluent Greek, giving the staff the information they needed and then there was more waiting, and more self-recrimination.

"I shouldn't have let her tell you," her father said. "I should have done it myself, to protect her from it."

Adeline put her hand on his arm. "Dad…"

"I know you don't understand. You see all the reasons I shouldn't be with her, but you don't see the reasons that I love her. You think the pair of us are making a mistake, and there have been mistakes, that's true—me letting her go in the first place, your mother marrying Rob and then that useless waster who only wanted her money, but the two of us? We're not a mistake. We've just found each other again, Addy." He slumped onto one of the chairs in the waiting area, childlike and helpless. "What if I lose her?"

Adeline sat down in the adjacent chair and put her arm around him. Her insides felt raw. Her throat stung with unshed tears. "Let's wait and hear what the doctor has to say." She tried to sound calm and rational even though she wasn't feeling calm or rational.

Her father stared at his hands. "Our wedding is only days away."

"I know, Dad."

The weight of his worry almost crushed her. Her father's pain was a living thing, agonizing to witness, and she knew then that even if she would never understand it, the love he felt for her mother was real. She had no right to question that.

She understood now that every relationship was a private world, a whole story where an outsider would only ever be given a glimpse.

He buried his head in his hands and she felt a wave of sympathy and also guilt. For better, for worse, he clearly adored her mother.

A large clock on the wall showed that fifteen minutes had passed. It felt like fifteen hours.

Was there any activity more soul-destroying than waiting for news of a loved one in a clinical, impersonal hospital corridor? People scurried past, all wearing different expressions. Worry, purpose, determination. Every time someone new appeared, her father would glance up, hopeful, and then slump again when the individual didn't even glance in his direction.

It felt incongruous sitting in a soulless corridor in the floaty summer dress Maya had picked out for her. Everyone who passed glanced at them and Adeline wished she'd paused long enough to grab a sweater or to change into jeans and a T-shirt. Something less celebratory. Because what was there to celebrate?

Stress formed a tight band around her ribs. It was difficult to breathe. She was a coper, and yet right now she wasn't coping.

She shifted on her seat and felt the heaviness of her phone in her pocket.

On impulse, she pulled it out and opened the message Stefanos had sent after their trip to his house the day before. He'd promised to cook her dinner the following evening. She glanced at the clock and realized that tomorrow was now today.

She hesitated, but the yearning to talk to him was stronger than the urge to handle this alone.

Unable to stop herself, her fingers moved on the keys.

My mother collapsed. I'm at the hospital.

She pressed Send and immediately regretted it. Why had she messaged him? What did she expect him to do? She should be handling this alone, the way she handled everything else.

She was about to message again and tell him to ignore her message when his response pinged on her phone.

On my way.

Just three words, but never had three words had such a calming effect.

He was on his way. Coming here, to the hospital.

The terrible tightness in her stomach eased. She could finally breathe again.

She could have told him not to come, that she was fine, but she wasn't fine and she could do with his particular brand of steady support.

She messaged back.

Thank you.

It felt like hours, but finally a doctor appeared and walked toward them.

Andrew shot to his feet so quickly he staggered, and Adeline grabbed him.

"Take a moment, Dad."

"Tell me. Is she…?"

"She is doing well. It was a panic attack." The doctor spoke excellent English and Andrew stared at him as the words slowly penetrated.

"Not her heart?"

"No, although the symptoms can be surprisingly similar. With a heart attack, pain is often experienced in other areas as well as the chest—jaw, arm, neck. During a panic attack, the pain is usually in the chest."

"But her heart was beating so fast."

"That can happen in response to emotional distress." The doctor paused. "I understand that she was upset about something immediately before experiencing the symptoms. She wouldn't talk about exactly what happened, but perhaps addressing that might help. I want to keep her in while I wait for some of the test results to come back, just to be safe, but after that you should be able to take her home."

"Home?" Her father let out a shaky sigh and turned to her. "She's not going to die, Addy?"

"No, Dad, she's not going to die."

Her relief was every bit as great as her father's.

They hugged, and then her father lifted his head and reached out an arm to Cassie who was standing alone and a little apart from them.

She hesitated, and then joined them in the hug.

"She's going to be okay." Andrew gave her an awkward pat. "She's going to be okay, sweetheart."

"Yes."

The doctor smiled. "You can see her. That might reassure you. Although just one of you at a time. If you come with me, I'll take you to her."

Andrew pulled away from Adeline. "Do you mind?"

"Of course, you should go first." She gave him a little push. "Give her our love. Cassie and I will wait here."

Watching her father hurry down the corridor, Adeline saw what she should have seen right away.

"He loves her," she murmured, and Cassie nodded.

"Yes."

"I don't understand it. But maybe love isn't something we can always understand."

"I definitely don't understand it." Cassie's voice was small and she wrapped her arms around herself. "I think I might be in love with Oliver. In fact, I know I'm in love with Oliver."

Adeline turned to look at her sister. "Your friend? The guy you share a house with?"

Cassie turned pink and gave an apologetic shake of her head. "I shouldn't even be mentioning it. It's not important. Sorry."

"Are you kidding? I'm grateful for the distraction. And any happy story is welcome right now."

"It's not a happy story." Cassie stared ahead, watching as Andrew disappeared into the room where her mother was.

"It isn't?"

"He's in love with Suzy."

Adeline sighed.

Love was so relentlessly complicated.

She thought about what Cassie had told her so far. "Are you sure about that?"

"Yes. And the most annoying thing is that I picked her out for him. We were going through his dating app after a glass of wine. Suzy has great teeth, and hair like silk so there's not much competing with that."

Adeline wondered if her sister had looked in the mirror lately.

"But you and Oliver are good friends."

"Best friends. I can talk to him about anything and he talks to me about anything and everything."

"Maybe you should tell him how you feel, so that there's no misunderstanding. I don't want you to be staying with me when you're ninety and be forever regretting the fact that you never told him how you felt. I don't want you feeling sad about the seventy years you could have had together."

Cassie laughed. "You do realize if I'm ninety, then that makes you a hundred."

Adeline rubbed her bare arms, wishing she'd brought a sweater with her. "I intend to age well, and part of aging well is to look back on a full life well-lived. We tend to regret the things we don't say every bit as much as we regret the things we do say. If you love him, tell him."

"You're sounding like the daughter of a romance novelist, rather than a sensible psychologist."

Adeline thought about her message to Stefanos. "I'm not sounding like myself, that's for sure. I've decided that love isn't one of my areas of expertise. From now on, I'll be shunting those questions to someone else. You seem to know a lot about love. Maybe you can handle them."

"I don't know anything about love either. I'm clueless," Cassie said. "But if I'm supposed to throw caution to the wind and tell Oliver I love him, then you should definitely have sex with Stefanos."

Adeline gasped and glanced around. "Do you have to share that thought with the whole of the hospital?"

"Just saying."

"If you could *just say* in a quieter voice, that would be good. Or maybe not at all." Adeline paused as her father emerged from the room and gestured that one of them could come in. She turned to her sister. "You go next."

"Are you sure? Thank you." Cassie kissed her on the cheek and all but sprinted up the corridor.

Adeline sat back down on the hard chair and her father joined her. His step was lighter, his frown lines less pronounced.

"How is she, Dad?"

"Better," he said. "Feeling a lot calmer."

"Stefanos is on his way." She said it casually. "In case we need anything."

"I'm sure I'm not the reason he's coming, although there is no doubt he's an excellent young man." Her father stirred. "How's it going between you and him?"

"I don't know what you mean."

"If that's true, then you've just made me sad." He put his hand on hers and gave it a squeeze. "Thank you for being here, Addy."

"Of course. I'm relieved she's going to be okay." She paused. There was so much she needed to say. "I'm sorry if I made things difficult for you, Dad. I love you so much and I feel as protective toward you as you do toward me. But I can see now that I handled it badly. I just want you to be happy, I hope you know that. Do you forgive me?"

"Nothing to forgive. You didn't understand, and frankly I don't blame you. Some things aren't easy to explain or comprehend. They just are."

"Maybe."

They sat side by side in the hospital corridor. She'd forgotten how good this could feel. How the presence of someone you loved was often enough to offer comfort.

"You look good in that dress, Addy."

"I look ridiculously out of place in this dress." She tugged at the hem, but it refused to sit anywhere but above her knees. "It's not exactly suitable for hospital visiting."

"I disagree. I think you should dress like that more often. It suits you. You look relaxed, instead of buttoned-up."

She sighed. "I sense another lecture coming on."

"Not a lecture. Advice."

"You always used to say that you wouldn't give me advice because you didn't know what you were doing."

He gave a soft laugh. "That was because I found being a father terrifying. I wanted you to make your own decisions so that I couldn't be held responsible."

She smiled. "You were a brilliant dad. You still are."

"I don't know about that, but I try. And it's because I'm trying to be a good dad that I'm giving you advice," he said. "After all, you gave me advice."

She turned to look at him. "You ignored my advice."

"And you're free to ignore mine, but I hope you won't." He squeezed her hand again. "Let him into your life, Addy. I know you're scared. I know you're protecting yourself, but when you shut out risk, you shut out happiness. If you walk away from this relationship, I'll never forgive myself."

It should have been unsettling that he knew her so well, and in a way, it was, but it was also comforting. That was love. Allowing someone to know the real you.

"Firstly, it's not a relationship. And secondly, since when have you been responsible for my love life?"

"I feel responsible," he said. "Maybe not for your love life but for the emotions that drive all your safe choices."

She tugged at the hem of her dress again. "Safe choices are underrated."

"No. They're driven by fear, and in your case, your mother and I are responsible for that fear. *I'm* responsible. You saw me brokenhearted and you decided you didn't ever want to let yourself be in that position. I should have done a better job at hiding my feelings when you were around. You were just a child, but you were always so mature and wise that I treated you like an adult. I'm not making excuses. I'm saying that I can see now that I was a terrible parent to you."

"Stop…" She put her hand on his arm. "You are a wonderful parent. You were always there for me. And I didn't expect you to sanitize life. This is how it looks. Messy. Imperfect. Complicated."

"But you saw the misery and the pain, but not the love. You never understood that part."

"I liked being treated as an adult. And you wouldn't have been able to hide your feelings from me. I would have known you were faking it, and I would have hated that. I like the fact that we've always been able to talk about everything. I like the fact that we're talking now."

"I like that too. Still, you're dating people like Mark because of me."

She stared down at her legs. She actually had a little color in them. They weren't exactly bronzed, but they weren't white either. "I'm not actually dating Mark. We had a disagreement before I came to Corfu. We broke up."

"You did?" He brightened. "That's the best news I've had in a long time."

"My broken relationship is good news?"

"I think it might be. Are you sad?"

She stared at the blank hospital corridor. "I—no. I'm not sad."

"And that doesn't tell you something?"

"Dad…"

"Of course it does." He patted her hand. "You're a smart girl. He was wrong for you. But Stefanos—"

"*Dad…*"

He ignored her warning tone. "Stefanos is the kind of man you need. He's not afraid of feelings. He's not afraid of life. He's perfect for you. Have a wild affair. Enjoy yourself."

She felt a rush of exasperation but also humor. This conversation was almost a relief, given the one that they could have been having if something had happened to her mother. "Are you really supposed to be saying that to your daughter?"

"If you want to be treated as an adult, yes."

"It's about boundaries, Dad. If I'm not allowed to meddle in your life, you're not allowed to meddle in mine."

"It's a parent's duty to meddle," he said. "And also to fix a mistake. I made a mistake with you."

She paused. "You mean that time you dropped me off at school when school was closed?"

His shoulders shook. "Did I do that?"

"You did. They'd allocated the day for teacher training. School started a day later."

"How was I supposed to know that?"

"I think they sent you a letter."

"Did it look official? I was never good at reading anything that looked official," he said. "I'm not sure that counts as a mistake."

"How about the time you tried to braid my hair and we had to go to the hair salon to have it untangled?"

"That probably was a mistake," he admitted. "But not as big as some of my others. It's a wonder you're not scarred, Addy. And maybe you are. If I don't see you happy and taking a risk with your heart, I'll assume you are. And I'll blame myself forever. It's only fair to warn you I might die of the guilt."

"Ouch, that's a bit strong." She smiled, as he'd intended. "So I'm supposed to take no end of romantic risks just so that you feel all right about yourself? That doesn't sound fair."

"Life isn't fair. But it can be good, if you'll make it so. There are going to be lows, whatever you do, so why not put some highs in there too? I love you, Addy. I hope you know that."

She felt a lump fill her throat. "I do know that."

"Good. And there is no love quite like the love a father has for his little girl."

There was no love to match the love a little girl felt for her daddy either, providing she had a daddy like hers. She thought about Cassie, and realized how lucky she was.

"Now you're getting soppy."

"I know, but sometimes these things need to be said." He gave her hand a squeeze. "Don't go back to London, honey. There. That's another thing that needs to be said."

Her heart beat a little faster. "My apartment is in London. My job is in London. My life is in London." But already she was thinking about how it would feel to go back to her carefully structured routine and predictable life. Even Mark had been predictable. That was why she'd been with him.

"I'm hearing excuses, not good reasons," her father said. "So often in life we find ourselves anchored by things that aren't important. Your apartment can be rented. Your job is mostly remote. Your life is where you choose it to be. Why not spend the rest of the summer in Corfu and see where it leads?"

She thought about the way it felt to swim in the ocean. She thought about Stefanos, and the way he listened and never criticized her choices. The way he'd come home to support his family.

She thought about his house above the bay, and the life he'd chosen.

"Spending the summer here would be reckless and irresponsible."

"Which is why I think it's *exactly* what you need."

"You just want me to have sex with Stefanos, and a father shouldn't be encouraging his daughter to have sex."

"I think we've established that when it comes to being a father, I don't hit all the top notes."

"Maybe I don't find Stefanos attractive. Did that thought occur to you?"

And then she glanced up and there he was, striding down the corridor toward them, and she felt a rush of relief and gratitude that he was here and something else. Something more powerful that left her heart racing and the breath trapped in her throat.

She stood up without even realizing she'd done so until she heard her father's quiet chuckle.

"Not attractive at all," he said. "Let him into your life, Addy. Go for it."

She hoped Stefanos hadn't heard that last remark, but didn't have much opportunity to worry about it because he swept her into a hug and it felt so good that she allowed herself to lean against him for a moment, anchoring herself against hard muscle and strong arms.

"You didn't have to come." She curled her fingers into the front of his shirt.

"I wanted to." He pulled her closer. "How is she? Is there any news?"

Cassie emerged at that moment, her eyes red-rimmed and watery.

"She wants to talk to you, Adeline."

Adeline eased away from Stefanos. She almost wished he'd come in with her, and the thought shook her. She was used to doing things by herself. She wasn't used to leaning on anyone. And this particular conversation had to be had alone.

She looked up at him. "Will you wait?"

He didn't miss a beat. "I'll be here."

22

Catherine

Catherine lay in the hard hospital bed, feeling foolish and relieved at the same time.

When the pain had exploded in her chest, her only thought had been how cruel it was that she was going to die before making peace with her daughters, and before she'd married Andrew for a second time.

For her, it had always been Andrew, even though she'd lost her way.

While the staff were busying themselves around her, drawing blood and monitoring her heart, she'd been making promises. She'd promised herself that if she got through this, she'd be a better person. She'd spend time rebuilding her relationship with Adeline. She'd answer all of Cassie's questions. She'd put real people in front of fictional ones.

She'd stop worrying about things that weren't important,

like whether she'd sold more books this time than she had last time. Who cared if she was number three? Three was good. Three was better than four.

If she recovered, she was going to send a bottle of champagne and a congratulatory note to Miranda.

When the medical team had told her that her heart was just fine, and that it was a panic attack, she almost hadn't believed them.

How was that possible?

But apparently it was, and the relief was enormous. It felt like a miracle.

She'd wanted a second chance, and now she had one.

And then Andrew had appeared, his face lined with worry. He'd understood what a strain the evening had been. While she'd been worrying about Cassie and Adeline, he'd been worrying about her.

People thought love was a straight line, but so often it was more like something a toddler would draw with a crayon, full of ups and downs and wiggles.

She was lucky to have someone who cared as much as he did.

Then Cassie had come into the room and hugged her, and told her how much she loved her, and that she understood how very hard it must have been and why she had chosen not to share the truth until this moment.

And now, finally, Adeline. In some ways, this was going to be the most difficult conversation of all.

She braced herself as her daughter pushed open the door.

"Hi, sweetheart." Her voice wasn't steady and then she realized that Adeline looked as nervous as she felt.

She settled herself in the chair next to Catherine's bed. "How are you feeling?"

"A little foolish to be honest. And angry with myself for

letting something that happened so many years ago get to me so badly. And for not trying to find a way to fix things with you sooner. Forgive me, Addy." She reached out a hand and was relieved when Adeline took it.

"I wish you'd told me," she said, "because it would have helped everything make sense, but I understand why you didn't."

"Do you?"

"Yes. Now you've explained. Now we've talked about it. I wish we'd done that sooner." Adeline held tightly to her mother's hand. "I'm surprised Dad didn't say anything. We talked about everything else."

"I made him promise not to. You were such a loving child. You would have insisted on coming home to be with me. You would have worried yourself to sleep every night."

"So instead you chose to make me angry with you."

"No. That was a side effect of the decision I made." The memory of it almost choked her. "When you're living through a crisis, particularly a situation where you're threatened both physically and emotionally, you're not always thinking straight. You're not thinking *how is this going to affect my daughter in the future*? You're thinking *how can I survive today*?"

"I can't imagine what I would have done in your position. I hope I never have to find out. But I'm glad you protected Cassie."

"And I'm glad you feel that way," Catherine said. "You were always so close when you were young."

"I think we're going to be close again. I'm happy about it."

"So am I." Catherine stroked Adeline's hair as she'd sometimes done when she was young. She had such beautiful hair, a rich dark brown. She looked so like Andrew, whereas Cassie looked like her. Not like Rob, thank goodness. There were no reminders there. "I wish I could change what happened."

"Best not to think like that. If you change something in the past, then everything that came after it changes too. Maybe you wouldn't have had Cassie. Maybe I wouldn't have been so close to Dad."

"That's a nice positive way of looking at it."

"I'm sorry you found yourself in that position," Adeline said, "but I'm glad you're happy now. And I'm glad that you and Dad are going to be together again."

The relief was huge. "Are you really?"

"Yes. Not that I'm expecting us to recreate the past. It will be different. There's Cassie to think of for a start."

"This has been a terrible shock for Cassie. I've ruined all her illusions about romance."

"Maybe." Adeline looked thoughtful. "But maybe it's not a bad thing to see more clearly. You might have done her a favor. Let's see."

Catherine had a feeling that Adeline knew something that she didn't, but she didn't press.

"Whatever happens, she'll have you to talk to, and that's good."

Adeline pulled her hand away and smiled. "I don't think I'm an expert on romance. I leave that to you and Cassie." She stood up. "You must be exhausted and I know Dad will want to see you again, so I'll let him come in now and we can talk again later." She hesitated and then leaned down and kissed her mother lightly on the cheek.

It was the first spontaneous gesture of affection she'd shown her in a long time and Catherine felt something bloom in her chest. *Hope.*

It was a start, and hopefully it would grow from here.

She reached up and hugged her daughter tightly. "I'm

proud of you. I hope you know that. And I know you don't need a mother," she said. "You're too old for that. But I'm hoping you have room in your life for a friend."

"I'll always need a mother." Adeline's voice was husky and for a moment they stayed like that, each of them adjusting to the shift in emotions. And then they both heard the door opening and there was Andrew standing there with Cassie.

"They say you'll be able to go home in a couple of hours," he said to Catherine, "so Cassie and I thought we'd go and grab a coffee, spend a bit of time together, and then come back and pick you up once you're ready."

Catherine felt a rush of love and gratitude. She didn't have to worry about him building a relationship with Cassie because she knew he'd take care of that. And she had an instinct that they'd get on well once that initial awkwardness passed. Cassie might yet find herself with that father figure that had always been missing from her life.

Andrew gave Adeline a meaningful look. "Stefanos is waiting to take you home, Addy."

Catherine saw her daughter's cheeks glow pink. Interesting.

"I thought I'd wait with you," Adeline said.

"No sense in us all waiting around here now that we know your mother will be fine." He waved a hand dismissively. "Cassie will drive us."

"If you're sure." Adeline walked to the door. "I'll have my phone on."

"We won't be calling. Relax. Have fun."

Adeline left and Catherine saw Cassie and Andrew exchange a grin, as if they were both in on a secret that no one else shared.

Catherine shifted position, trying to get comfortable. "Have you two been matchmaking?"

"Maybe," Cassie said. "A little. I'm afraid we were horribly obvious."

"*You* were obvious." Andrew said. "I was subtle."

"Subtle? You asked him if he could take Adeline home, and then suggested that his place might make a nice change of scene."

Catherine laughed, enjoying the exchange. "Did you really say that?"

"He really did." Cassie walked across the room and perched on the edge of the bed. "But Stefanos didn't seem at all flustered so hopefully we haven't blown it for her."

Hopefully not.

Stefanos and Adeline. Maria would be pleased if something happened between them.

But Catherine wasn't going to comment on it. She wasn't going to interfere.

She wasn't in a position to give anyone advice on their love life.

It had taken her this long and a lot of missteps along the way to finally know what she wanted, and now she had it.

Andrew. And her girls.

23

Adeline

The car journey back across the island was smoother than driving with Cassie had been. Her tension was every bit as acute, although this time for different reasons.

She sat still, barely breathing, achingly aware of Stefanos, right next to her.

She could feel the steady thud of her own heartbeat, the slow uncurling of warmth low in her body.

She wasn't used to feeling like this. All her interactions with Mark had been controlled. Rational. Mark had been safe. Her emotions and composure had never been even remotely threatened, her feelings a steady, predictable hum, never hitting extreme highs or lows.

It was different with Stefanos. It wasn't only his confidence or love of life that drew her to him, or even the fact that he had far too much sex appeal for one man. It went deeper than that. It was the way he teased out that side of her she'd hidden away, the way he *knew* her.

With him, there was no point in hiding because he saw who she was.

Since she'd reconnected with Stefanos, it was as if all her defenses had melted into a useless puddle.

Dear Dr. Swift, I've met this guy and he's making me question everything about the way I live my life. I have always been cautious and protected myself, but I have a feeling that if I pursue this relationship, I could put at risk everything I've built.

Sincerely,

Unsettled.

She wondered how she'd answer a letter like that.

"You're quiet. Are you all right?" Stefanos glanced at her briefly before returning his eyes to the road.

"I'm not sure. It's been the strangest few days." The events with her mother had left her feeling unsettled and vulnerable. She turned to look at him, focusing on the practical. "Thank you for coming to the hospital. You didn't have to do that, but I'm glad you did."

"So am I. And I'm pleased she is going to be fine. What happened?" His voice was deep and velvety smooth and she thought that she could listen to him all day and never grow tired of it.

And because it felt good to talk, she told him about Rob, and the details that her mother had shared with them, and he listened in silence until she'd finished.

"I suppose it explains a lot."

"Yes." She paused, thinking back to that time. "It's the reason she never left Cassie alone. The reason she often left her with Maria. You guessed, didn't you?"

"Not until I was older. And even then, I didn't know for

sure. My mother never talked about it. I just wondered occasionally whether Rob might not be all he seemed to be."

Adeline leaned her head back against the seat. "I'm glad I
finally know the truth. It has changed things."

"You had a good conversation?"

"Yes. It felt different somehow. *She* was different. It feels
as if I finally have my mother back."

He reached across and took her hand. "I'm glad."

She stared down at their hands, locked together. She felt
the warmth of his fingers pressing against hers.

"You can drop me at the end of the road by the villa if you
like. No need to take me all the way."

There was a long pulsing silence. "Is that what you want?"

She didn't know what she wanted.

Or maybe she did.

Stefanos waited. "You've had a stressful evening. You need
to unwind before you try and sleep. Why don't you come
back to my place? We could have a late swim and something
to drink on the terrace. I can drive you back later."

The invitation hovered in the air between them.

The alternative was to go back to her mother's villa, take
a shower and go to bed with a book. That would undoubtedly be the safe choice and a few days ago she would have
made that choice without thought. But now?

She took a breath. "That sounds blissful." Not the swimming part, although that sounded good, nor the drink, although that would be welcome after the hours she'd spent at
the hospital, but the spending time with him.

They drove the rest of the way in silence and she wondered
if he was as aware of her as she was of him. Heat washed over
her. Her heart thudded against her ribs. Anticipation hovered
in the air, thick and sweet.

Finally, the road narrowed and they drove down the bumpy

track that led to his house. Tiny lights illuminated the drive-
way and the gardens and the moon sent a shimmer of silver
across the ocean. She stepped out of the car and breathed in
scents of wild thyme and oregano.

"I could fall in love with this place." Maybe she already
had.

"That's how I felt the first time I saw it." He closed the car
door. "Go and sit on the terrace. Dip your feet in the pool.
I'll bring us something to drink." He headed into the house
and she followed the path to the terrace.

The air pulsed with heat and the pool gleamed invitingly
in the darkness, an illuminated splash of bright turquoise, the
surface so still it could have been made of glass.

She felt a sudden yearning to jump right in and wished
she'd brought a swimsuit, but who packed a swimsuit for a
hospital visit?

She slipped off her shoes and felt the warmth press against
the soles of her feet.

Her mind was spinning.

*Dear Unsettled, for every gain, there is a loss. What you've gained
by controlling your life, you've lost in opportunities for discovery and
adventure. Once in a while, it's good to be spontaneous and follow
your instincts. Let life happen. Sometimes the best things that happen in life are the things we don't plan.*

Follow your instincts? Let life happen?

Was that really the advice she was giving herself? She was
the sort of person who never got a parking ticket, who ate
food before its expiration date, who never left home without
carrying an umbrella and wearing a high-factor sunscreen.

She gazed at the pool for a long lingering moment and then
out across the sea, velvet dark in the moonlight. The lights
from a yacht twinkled in the bay and the sky was scattered
with stars. She imagined living somewhere like this and in

that brief moment she had a vision of what her life could be like. Slower. Less pressured. The things that took on such importance at home in London didn't seem to matter here. Priorities shifted.

She heard footsteps and then Stefanos appeared beside her.

"I never get tired of that view." He handed her a glass of wine and she took it, her fingers brushing against his. "I approve of the way you dress for a hospital visit, by the way."

She laughed and glanced down at herself. "I have never felt more self-conscious. It's not as if I was sure about the dress to begin with. It's not my usual style. A friend picked it out for me. I think she's trying to encourage me to find my wild side."

"And is it working?" He put his glass down on the table without drinking, his gaze fixed on her face. Something in his eyes made it impossible to look away and she lost the ability to concentrate sufficiently to figure out the answer to his question.

"I don't know. I'm not sure I have a wild side. Or maybe everyone has more than one version of themselves." She felt a rush of heat and took a mouthful of ice-cold wine, trying desperately to find some of her usual calm.

"And which version are you tonight? I guess there's an easy way to find out." He took her wine glass from her. "Fancy a swim?"

Her heart was pounding. "Now?"

"Why not? I'm encouraging you to be spontaneous."

Wasn't that the exact advice "Dr. Swift" had just given her?

"I didn't bring a swimsuit." She couldn't quite figure out how to let go of the person she'd become. How to make that shift from cautious to spontaneous.

"If it makes it easier, I'll go first." He stripped off his shirt and his shorts and she had a glimpse of bronzed flesh and hard muscle before he plunged into the water.

She stepped back, but not quickly enough and she was showered in droplets. She looked at the pool, and at Stefanos who cut through the water with strong rhythmic strokes. At the end of the pool, he caught the side and looked at her, beckoning her to join him.

She saw the droplets of water clinging to his broad shoulders and the smile that touched his lips and she finally she figured out why she was still holding back.

It wasn't that she was afraid to be spontaneous. It was because she knew instinctively that this was a man who could snap her heart in two. He had the power to hurt her in a way Mark never had.

But she also knew that if she didn't join him now, she'd always regret it, and how much worse would it be to spend her life living with regret?

Before she could change her mind, she stripped off her dress and slid into the pool after him. The water cooled her skin and she let herself slide under the surface until she was submerged. She swam down to the bottom of the pool. For a moment, she was weightless, sound muffled and time suspended. The last of the stress she'd felt at the hospital melted away.

When she finally rose to the surface, Stefanos was next to her. Droplets of water clung to his eyelashes and the top of his lip.

She was filled with intense awareness, and then he slid his arm round her waist and eased her gently against him.

They stayed like that for endless seconds, the atmosphere electric with anticipation, and then she lifted her mouth to his and at the same time felt his hands tighten as he pulled her closer. She felt the hardness of his body press against the softness of hers, and then he was kissing her and she was kissing him back. He cupped her face in his hands and his mouth shifted, seeking out the secrets of hers, and she pressed closer, and closer still, consumed by an almost dizzying heat.

Cool water lapped against the heated burn of her skin. His hands dropped to her hips and he lifted her out of the water in a smooth, easy movement. She sat on the edge, weak and disorientated, wondering how he'd done that with no apparent effort and then he levered himself out of the pool, lifted her up, and the next moment she was lying on her back on the outdoor sofa.

She curled her arms round him, pulling him closer, feeling the heavy weight of him pressing her into the soft cushions. He kissed his way down her body, his mouth warm against her neck, her shoulder, the soft curve of her breast. The silken stroke of his tongue sent a thrill of heat through her, and the skilled brush of his fingers sent her pulse into overdrive. Sensations were spun together, blending and building to a level she'd never experienced before. The intimacy, delicious and unfamiliar, stripped away the last of her reserve. She wanted things from him that she'd never wanted from anyone else. Never dared to want. Excitement escalated, fueled by the brush of mouths and the tangle of limbs until their entwined bodies found each other and she was lost in the erotic rhythm of it, the last of her barriers dissolving as pleasure engulfed them both.

Afterward, she lay in silence, staring up at the scatter of stars above her, stunned.

She thought she knew herself, but maybe she didn't. Or maybe she'd done such a thorough job of closing part of herself down, she no longer really knew who she was. The sex had been incredible of course, but it was more than the physical, she knew that. It was intimacy. Trust. Sharing on a level she'd never allowed herself to experience before.

It made her feel vulnerable, but oddly enough not afraid. She didn't feel a flicker of regret.

Conscious that she was still naked, she tried to move but his arm tightened around her.

"Don't leave."

"I should get back to the villa."

"I wasn't talking about tonight, although I don't want you to leave tonight either. I was talking about generally." He smoothed a strand of hair away from her face and kissed her gently on the mouth. "Spend the rest of the summer in Greece with me. I can convert the spare room into an office for you, or you can just bring your laptop out here onto the patio and sit in the shade. We can take early morning swims together, and eat dinner on the terrace, watching the sun set."

Temptation lay like a feast in front of her, but still she couldn't quite dive in.

"I have a life in London."

"You could have a better life here, with me." His voice was husky as he leaned forward to kiss her again.

She kissed him back, feeling a slow stir of excitement.

"You don't think this is all a bit sudden? Maybe we should take time to think it over."

He rolled onto his side so that he could look at her. "Why would we need time to think it over? We're both adults. Also, we've known each other for a long time."

"But not like this."

"That's just circumstances."

Was he right? If they'd met a few years ago, would they still have reached this point?

"If we'd met again a few years ago, I'm not sure I'd be lying here now. I'm not sure I would have been ready for it."

"You're talking about the other version of you. This version would have been ready."

He lowered his mouth to hers and kissed her, and she thought to herself that if there was more than one version of her, then this was the version she liked best.

And maybe that gave her the answer she needed.

24

Catherine

Breakfast on the beach in Greece was all dazzling light and crystal blue waters. The splash of swimmers, the clink of a mast from a sailboat bobbing in the bay.

Andrew had walked down to the village earlier and reserved a table by the sand and now the whole family was gathered together.

Third time lucky, Catherine thought as she watched Adeline and Cassie scroll through the photographs they'd taken since arriving. All their planned celebrations seemed to get disrupted so they'd opted for a spontaneous breakfast at her favorite taverna, but this time there was no sign of the tension that had been an unwelcome guest at their previous gatherings.

She'd chosen to wear her favorite floaty white dress, and a wide-brimmed hat that shaded her face from the sun and prevented recognition by any tourists who happened to be fans. She was happy to sign books whenever she was asked, but today wasn't about her job. It was about her family.

Andrew was by her side, his chair pulled a little closer than usual so that occasionally she felt his leg touch hers under the table, and his arm brush against hers.

"How are you feeling?" He was attentive and loving, and she thought again how lucky she was to have been given a second chance.

Across the table, Adeline was deep in conversation with her sister and Catherine smiled, deciding this wasn't the moment to mention that she'd seen Stefanos's car dropping Adeline at the gates of the villa just after dawn.

Everyone was allowed secrets. And it wasn't as if she didn't have a few of her own.

For now, she had other things that demanded her focus.

She waited for a pause in her daughters' conversation.

"Cassie, I owe you an apology."

Cassie put her spoon down. "For what?"

"For telling you that you couldn't publish your book. That was unforgivably selfish of me. Your book is special, you are a talented writer and of course you should share that talent with the world."

"Actually I have something to say about that." Cassie put her spoon down and sat up a little straighter. "When we got back from the hospital last night, I did some work on the manuscript. I've made some changes. Just small ones, but enough to make sure that no one can connect the story with you or with Corfu. It's now set in Sicily. Oliver and I spent a week there last summer and I made loads of notes, so it was easy to make that change. And the dedication is different."

Remembering the last dedication, Catherine felt a flicker of trepidation. "What is the dedication?"

Cassie gave a soft smile. "It says *for my mother, the strongest and bravest person I know.*"

Emotion lodged in her throat. "Cassie—"

"It's true. I don't know how you survived that. How you came out of those years still able to love and trust."

"Well I made another mistake with Gordon Pelling, so I think maybe I'm not a good judge of character. But then I look at Andrew—" she slid her hand over his "—and know that I do occasionally get things right."

And that was what mattered, wasn't it? Not the route you'd taken, but where you ended up.

And she wasn't going to punish herself any longer. She could wish for the past to be different or she could accept what had happened and move on into this next chapter and enjoy it fully, unencumbered by guilt or regret.

If she'd been writing this story, that was what her main character would have done.

She would have shown resilience.

It was time she modeled herself on one of her own heroines.

Adeline put her coffee cup down. "I don't know how you managed to carry on writing romance. How did you keep on believing in it in those very dark years after Rob?"

It was typical of her daughter to ask such an insightful question.

"I'm a novelist. I'm writing a story. It's fiction, it doesn't mean that I have to share the views of my characters. Everyone's life experience is different, and it's no different for the people I write about." She paused, wondering if this was a good time to tell them. "But since you asked, I will tell you honestly that I have been struggling for the past couple of years. Maybe it's because my heart isn't in romance. Maybe I've done the same thing for too long. But I have some news on that front. I've written something else. I sent it to Daphne a few days ago. She loves it."

"That's fantastic." Cassie clapped her hands together. "But why wouldn't she? You've worked with her for decades and you already know she loves your work."

"This isn't my usual style. Or genre. It's a thriller. Or maybe a crime novel. I'm not sure how one would categorize it."

"Crime?" Adeline was intrigued. "But you've always said you want a book to have an optimistic ending."

"This has an optimistic ending. Unless you're one of the victims of course, in which case not so optimistic." In her years as a writer, she'd weathered all the highs and lows. She'd known writing could be hard, easy, exciting and frustrating, but never before had it been cathartic. Until now. It was like being back at the beginning of her career, when the excitement of creating had carried her along like the tide. When the writing itself had been enough. "Don't feel sorry for them. Each of those men deserved what was coming to them."

Cassie gave a curious smile. "Men?"

"I'm tired of books where women are the victims. Have you ever noticed that? The number of books that show a woman running away on the cover? Men so often hold the power, but not this time. Not in the book I've written. The power is stripped from them, layer by layer. It was rather exciting if I'm honest." She looked at her daughters, wondering if she needed to spell it out, but Adeline held her gaze and nodded. She understood, as Catherine had hoped she would, that although in real life it wasn't always easy or possible to get justice, between the pages of a book she'd managed to deliver justice and also find a certain level of peace.

Adeline smiled. "I'm looking forward to reading it."

"Me too," Cassie said, and Andrew grunted as he spread honey thickly onto bread still warm from the oven.

"My advice?" he said. "Read it with the lights on. Or better still, read it during the day in bright sunlight." He took a bite and honey dripped onto his fingers.

Cassie grinned. "What did Daphne say?"

"She is talking to my publisher right now, because although she adores the book, it most definitely isn't a Catherine Swift. Loyal readers have certain expectations as you know, and I think I've rather crushed those expectations. Or maybe I've stabbed them…" She leaned forward. "Either way, I think there may be a vacancy in the romance genre for a new Swift."

Cassie flushed. "I've decided I don't want to be Swift. That feels wrong to me. It always did. I'm going to pick a different name. Adeline is helping me."

"So far we've covered two pages of my notebook," Adeline muttered, "so don't expect this to be a quick process."

Motherhood was often a challenge, Catherine thought, but sometimes things came together and produced a perfect moment. Like now, with her family gathered round the table and Adeline and Cassie with their heads together, dark and light, laughing.

They finished breakfast and took a walk along the beach before heading back to the villa.

While Adeline strolled ahead with her father, Cassie fell into step beside her mother.

"Can I ask you something?"

Catherine felt a ripple of tension. "Of course. Anything."

"The night my father died…" Cassie stopped walking. "You said he fell downstairs. Is that what really happened?"

"Yes. As I told you, he'd had a drink and he tripped over a shoe."

Cassie looked at her steadily. "Did he hurt you that night? Before he fell?"

She should have been prepared for this question. She should have known it was coming and planned the perfect response.

"No, but he tried to." She saw no reason not to be honest about that. "He would have done."

Cassie slid her hand into hers. "I thought so. You don't have to hide the truth. I've already figured it out."

Catherine felt a tight band form around her chest. "You have?"

"Yes. You always said that you'd taken off your shoes at the top of the stairs because your feet were hurting after a long evening dancing. But I've been thinking about it," she said softly, "and I'm guessing that you lost your shoes when you were running away from him."

Catherine's heart was beating so hard she thought it might burst from her chest.

She'd promised herself that she was going to be honest about everything, but she hadn't anticipated this particular question.

"Yes." She croaked out the word. "That's what happened. But I'd rather not talk about it, if that's all right."

"We won't ever mention it again. Ever. But I wanted to know, that's all. No more secrets." Cassie gave her a hug and Catherine felt the warmth and love flow through her.

"You're not upset?"

"That he fell over your shoe? No. Well, the whole thing is upsetting of course, and I wish the whole story was totally different, but I'm relieved that it ended for you. Not a happy ending, I guess, but the best ending in a bad situation."

"Yes."

"I love you, Mom." Cassie squeezed her hand and then

gasped. "Is that—wait, it can't be." She shaded her eyes, gazed ahead and Catherine saw a man approaching.

He had his phone in one hand and an overnight bag in the other. The way he was looking around him suggested he had no idea where he was going.

"Oliver?" Cassie stood for a moment, bemused, and then rushed to greet him, her long floaty skirt flying around her legs as she ran.

Catherine watched as she flung herself at him and saw him lift Cassie and swing her round.

"I was about to phone you to ask for specific directions because you know how lousy I am at finding places." He hugged her tightly and Catherine thought that if her daughter stopped hugging him back and looked at him for a moment she'd see the expression on his face. Or maybe she was imagining it. What did she know about love anyway?

She glanced at Adeline and saw that her other daughter was smiling. So maybe she hadn't imagined it, after all.

Cassie finally let go of Oliver and stepped back. "But what are you *doing* here?"

"You sounded strange on the phone."

"You flew here because I sounded strange on the phone?"

"Yes. You didn't tell me what was wrong and you always tell me when something is wrong."

Cassie was laughing. "But you could have called."

"And then you would have been evasive again. I wanted to see you in person. I can stay in a hotel. Or get a flight home tomorrow or something."

"Did you bring Suzy?"

Who, Catherine wondered, *was Suzy?*

"No, of course I didn't bring Suzy." Oliver was frowning. "Why would I bring Suzy?"

"Because you're back together again."

"We're not. Why would you think that?"

"She was there when I called you last night."

"Because I was feeling down, and she came over to listen to me and give moral support. Not because we're back together." He stopped. "Wait—is that why you were funny with me? Because you thought we were together?"

"Why were you feeling down? And why didn't you tell me you were feeling down instead of letting me go on and on about my problems."

This is like a bad rom-com, Catherine thought, *where you just want to shake some sense into both characters.*

They were gazing at each other, oblivious to the rest of Cassie's family, the tourists, the sparkling ocean and the cloudless sky.

"If I was writing this," Catherine said to no one in particular, "this would be the moment when he kisses her."

And just as she thought that, Cassie wrapped her arms around Oliver's neck and pulled his head down to hers, kissing him passionately. His arms came round her and he kissed her back, his mouth hungry on hers. There was a desperation in the way they clung to each other.

Adeline cleared her throat and glanced at her mother. "Well, there you go," she said. "Seems as if you haven't entirely lost your touch when it comes to romance. Although technically she kissed him first."

They stood together, side by side, watching shamelessly as Oliver and Cassie murmured things that no one else could hear.

"Speak up." Adeline was grinning as she raised her voice. "We want to hear the dialogue."

Cassie turned, her cheeks pink and her eyes shining. "He loves me." She glanced back at Oliver, suddenly doubtful.

"You're *sure* you love me? You're absolutely sure? Even the really annoying things about me?"

"Cass, I've loved you for years."

"But why didn't you *say* something?"

"Because you kept saying that when you fell in love, you'd know it right away. Which I assumed was your way of saying you weren't in love with me."

"Oh, what a tangled mess," Catherine said. "It could be Shakespeare."

"You think?" Adeline glanced at her. "Comedy, I hope, not tragedy."

"Let's hope so. We'll know more in a minute, I'm sure. We have good seats. Did you bring popcorn?"

"I try not to eat between meals."

"I didn't know I was in love with you," Cassie was saying, "because I didn't know what I was looking for. I thought love would be like an elephant. I thought I'd know it if I saw it. But it turns out it wasn't like that at all."

"Love can be like an elephant," Catherine said, "when it crushes you."

"Keep your voice down," Adeline said. "If this was a book, it would end right here. Before the tough stuff comes."

Catherine watched as Oliver and Cassie kissed again, murmuring words against each other's lips, catching up on all the things they hadn't said and should have done. "They'll weather it," she said. "Whatever comes their way, they'll weather it. Look at them."

"I'm looking." Adeline shifted slightly. "I'm also burning. The sun is too hot to be standing here like this. We should go back to the villa before the audience gets sunstroke."

In the end, it was Andrew who took charge of the situation. He stepped forward, introduced himself to Oliver and suggested he join them up at the villa where they had ample room for another guest. Adeline joined them, kissing Oliver on the cheek and hugging her sister.

Catherine followed a little way behind, watching her family laughing and enjoying the moment.

She'd hoped that everything might turn out well, but she hadn't anticipated quite such a good outcome.

And finally, after all these years, the truth was out in the open. The important parts anyway.

Even if she'd wanted to tell the whole truth, she couldn't. It wouldn't have been fair because the story didn't just involve her, and who knew how Cassie might have reacted had she known the detail of what really happened.

Catherine hadn't lost her shoes running away from Rob. It was Maria who had put the shoes there. Afterward, obviously. She was the housekeeper. She wasn't in the habit of walking round the house, littering it with shoes. She'd thought it wouldn't hurt to give the police something to focus on. Catherine hadn't been thinking at all. She hadn't been capable of it. She'd sat, numb, at the top of the stairs, still clinging to the rail that had stopped her from plunging down the stairs with him.

That was where Maria had found her. How long had she been sitting there? Had Rob been breathing when he'd hit the bottom? She didn't know that either.

The whole thing had been a blur of horror and she couldn't even say for certain what had happened. She'd pushed him, she knew that, but she hadn't intended him to fall. She certainly hadn't intended to hurt him, even though he hurt her constantly. She'd been defending herself, that was all. Trying to stop him throwing her down the stairs. She'd been thinking of little Cassie, waking to find her mother dead. Cassie, with Rob as her only parent.

The idea of it had given her superhuman strength and resolve. Somehow she'd managed to hook her leg around the bannister and at the same time give him a hard shove. He must have been drunker than she'd thought because he was a big man and a single push from a woman her size, even a woman fighting for her life, wouldn't normally have caused him to shift balance, let alone lose it altogether. Whatever it was, that shove and the drink were finally the end of Robert Elliot Dunn.

He'd fallen heavily, smacking into the wall, cracking bones on the hard tile stairs as he bounced and rolled to the bottom where he finally smashed into her Italian tiles.

She didn't know how long she'd been sitting like that when Maria found her. Fortunately, her friend had made a habit of checking on Catherine after one of Rob's drinking sessions.

It was Maria who had peeled her cold, numb fingers away from the rail. Maria who had crouched over Rob's broken body, checking for a pulse. Maria who had dealt with the local police. Not that there had been much of an investigation. People had seen Rob drinking heavily that night. It was quite obvious what had happened. An unfortunate accident.

Catherine hadn't told them anything different. For two days, she hadn't been able to talk at all. Shock, they'd said in the hospital. Understandable. Such a lovely couple. Such a happy couple. The poor child. Now without a father.

It turned Catherine cold to think what could have happened. If she hadn't grabbed the railing, if he hadn't been quite as drunk, *she* would have been the one lying at the bottom of the stairs, and then what would have happened to Cassie?

She didn't feel guilty about not giving Cassie all the details. How would that help?

This particular secret would stay between her and Maria, held safe by their deep unwavering friendship.

And Catherine realized right then that wanting to change the past was a waste of energy. It didn't really matter what had happened before. What mattered was where they were now.

There was Cassie with her whole life ahead of her, poised on the cusp of something exciting, and Adeline who would hopefully find the courage to take some risks with her heart. And Andrew, kind and dependable, always there for her as she would be for him. She could regret the years they'd wasted, or she could celebrate the years that were still to come.

Andrew turned and held out his hand and she walked toward him, and her waiting family.

If she were writing this, she'd type *The End* right now (her two favorite words), but it wasn't really the end of course.

It was the beginning.

Epilogue

It was the perfect day for a wedding. Endless blue skies and the cooling waft of breeze to soften the heat. The gardens, bright with color, sloped down to meet the sparkling sea.

Catherine stood at the edge of the terrace with Maria.

Her family were all waiting for her, gathered around the floral archway that the wedding planner had arranged. Oliver, sweating in the heat, hand in hand with Cassie who couldn't stop smiling at him.

He'd been staying in the guest cottage, which had given Adeline an excuse to quietly pack her things and move along the coast to be with Stefanos. She'd said that she wanted to give her sister privacy but given that there were four perfectly good spare bedrooms in the main villa, no one was fooled by that.

And now Adeline stood close to Stefanos, and Catherine

saw his fingers brush briefly against hers and saw her glance up at him and smile.

And there was Daphne, her agent and friend who had flown in from New York to share this special moment with her favorite author.

She'd already sold Catherine's new book to a publisher in a whirl of excitement and multiple phone calls. They all agreed it wasn't a Catherine Swift, and that she should write under a new name for this new chapter in her career.

That suited Catherine. A fresh start. Another step forward into a new life.

She was willing to leave the old Catherine Swift behind and embrace the new version of herself.

She'd already decided on the dedication for her new book. *To Miss Bennett, who started it all.*

Would she have had such a successful career if she hadn't constantly been trying to prove herself? Possibly not.

Gazing at them all gathered there, she knew she had all that she needed.

In the end, life was enriched not by material things or even by personal attainment, but by people. It had taken her a while to understand that. Too long, but she understood it now, which made it all the sweeter that she had the people who mattered most to her, right here.

She turned to Maria and hugged her and Maria hugged her right back.

Neither of them said anything. They didn't need to. It was all there in the tightness of that hug. Some friendships came and went, but some deepened and lasted for a lifetime. She knew that while they were both breathing, she and Maria would always be there for each other.

When Maria eventually pulled away, there was a tear in

Acknowledgments

This is the hardest part of the book to write because the book you're reading is the result of a great deal of hard work by a number of people, who all deserve to be thanked.

I'm enormously grateful to Susan Swinwood for her insight, wisdom and patience in editing this book.

Thank you to my brilliant publishing teams in the US, Canada and the UK. I'm grateful for the talent and commitment of everyone involved in the publishing process. In particular Loriana Sacilotto, Margaret Marbury, Susan Swinwood for your continued faith in me. Lisa Milton, Manpreet Grewal and the brilliant publishing team at HQ Stories in the UK for working so creatively (and hard!) to get my books into the hands of readers. Your enthusiasm and commitment is incredible. You're simply the best and I know how lucky I am.

I'm fortunate to have readers around the globe, and for that I'm thankful to the dedicated teams who publish my books worldwide. It's exciting to see my books everywhere, from Iceland to Brazil!

Thank you to my brilliant agent Susan Ginsburg for her tireless support and encouragement. Also to the wonderful Catherine Bradshaw and the rest of the team at Writers House who manage everything so efficiently.

My friends are a constant source of support, as are my family who endure the strange habits of a writer with admirable patience.

Thank you to all the booksellers, librarians, bloggers and reviewers who do so much to promote reading, and to all my readers who keep buying my books and encourage me to write more.

the corner of her eye. She thrust the posy she'd been holding into Catherine's hand.

"Go."

She stepped forward onto the terrace, and there was Andrew, looking smart in a linen suit, not so very different from the man she'd met in the café all those years before.

She felt a flicker of excitement and a rush of anticipation.

People said that you couldn't go back, but who wanted to go back when you could move forward? When the future promised to be a better place than the past?

She walked toward him, past the smiles, greetings, compliments and the flurry of rose petals until she stood in front of him.

Andrew held out his hand. "Ready?"

She smiled and took his hand.

★ ★ ★ ★ ★